Illegal Contact

A Sports Workplace Romance

Ella Haines

LIBRA LIBROS LLC

First edition May 2023

Cover designed by Get Covers

Edited by Karen Washo from Utterly Unashamed

Proofread by Lily Luchesi

ISBN 978-1-956865-29-5 (paperback)

ISBN 978-1-956865-28-8 (eBook)

Published by Libra Libros LLC

Contents

Author's Note About Content Warnings

See list of content/trigger warnings here on my site at www.EllaHaines.com/Triggers

The list is also found at the end of the book through the table of contents

WARNING: will possibly contain plot spoilers by nature of disclosing – proceed as you are comfortable

C H A P T E R O N E

August 7, Saturday
Jen

"Excuse me, but I think you're in my chair," a low, gravelly voice rumbled from behind Jen, and tingles broke out on her skin. She rushed to stand and vacate her apparently stolen chair at the bar but, as she turned to apologize, she found herself staring into a pair of gorgeous hazel eyes that had her pausing to catch her breath.

Oh, God.

John Costner.

The veteran quarterback and long-time captain of the hometown Springfield Spartans stood in front of her. His solid frame filled out his expensive suit and his normally clean-shaven face had the beginnings of a dark five o'clock shadow.

Jen curled the fingers of her free hand tight so she wouldn't give into temptation and reach out to see if the bristles felt as stiff and scratchy as they seemed.

He raised a dark eyebrow at her frozen stupor and she rushed to transfer her drink to her left hand and extend her right, all too aware of how wet it was from holding her iced glass.

"Sorry...um, yeah. It's a nice chair. Good. Comfortable. Well-placed."

God, she was an *idiot*.

She smiled weakly into the face of her favorite player and tried not to wince at her absurd rambling.

A smile that bordered on cocky crossed his lips, and Jen once again found herself fighting for breath. Good lord, this man was stunning.

And an incredibly intelligent athlete.

John had been in the National Football League for fifteen years and was the starting quarterback for the Spartans for each of those years. He was an all-pro, future Hall of Famer who almost single-handedly brought the Spartans to their handful of Super Bowl appearances.

He shook her hand and his warm grip had Jen's heart racing. When she caught his eyes lazily traveling down her gala dress to her high heels, her heart paused and stuttered clumsily in her chest.

My God. Was this really happening?

"John," he said. That deep, smoky voice again sent shivers down her spine.

Take me, I'm yours.

She berated herself for staring at him like a lovestruck fool but couldn't seem to force herself to say anything else.

John didn't seem to mind though. Instead, he stood there patiently, holding her hand gently. His eyes danced as he examined her. His thick brows climbed again as he nodded toward the bar and chairs.

"Join me?"

Uh, yes.

Jen took in a heaving breath to try to anchor herself but lost all sense of control when she saw his eyes dip briefly towards her chest. When his nostrils flared and his eyes darkened, she gently tugged her hand free and approached the neighboring chair.

"I'd love to," Jen said.

John gave her a swaggering smile that had her stomach clenching and her inner fangirl squealing.

Was this really happening?

John pulled the bar stool out slightly for her and tucked it back under her as she gingerly lowered her body into it. Her Latina booty and thicker, athletic thighs were not exactly what the designer had in mind when they made this dress. However, Jen's best friend,

Lexie, declared this was 'the dress' for her and would accept no compromises.

Actually, Lexie probably never compromised a day in her life, so maybe she didn't know the meaning of the word.

The little tyrant.

Lexie was the daughter of William Galloway, owner of the Springfield Spartans, therefore she was always invited to attend charity events like the one tonight. Jen, however, usually managed to avoid being her wingman during their decade-plus of friendship, but tonight Jen gave in.

And now, here she was. Sitting with her athlete celebrity crush.

Maybe it was fate.

"You clearly know who I am, but I don't know a thing about you." John paused and gave her a small smile. "Except for the fact you're a chair thief."

Jen felt the start of a small blush. She raised her hand to tuck an errant strand of hair behind her ear before answering, searching for anything she could say that would sound alluring and sexy. His eyes followed the movement, the look tangible on her skin, and she almost sighed.

"I'm a massage therapist. I specialize in sports medicine and preventative rehabilitation." Jen laughed at his look of surprise. "Yeah, I don't really belong here. I'm actually feeling a bit like a fish out of water at the moment." She looked around the extravagant room and waved a hand. "But one of my friends dragged me out tonight, so here I am."

He gave her an assessing look and then looked around the formal banquet hall. "I think you probably fit in more than most." The approving look he gave her had her suppressing a shiver of attraction. "So, this friend... Female? Male? Other?"

"Female." She said nothing else, trying to be seductive and mysterious but almost ruined it when she couldn't stop her cheeky smile. She rushed to hide it by taking a sip of her drink. Seductress wasn't really her normal play for a man, but it was worth a go.

"So that means you're available to be having this drink with me?" He took a sip of his own drink.

She nodded.

He grinned and tipped his head at her. "So, Ms. Massage Therapist, you do pre-hab work?"

Gah! She never actually gave him her name.

"Jen."

His eyes sparkled. "Ok, Ms. Jen, you do pre-hab work?"

Jen smiled up at him, more than happy to discuss her field of expertise. What else was she going to talk about with John "The Saint" Costner?

"I do. I played soccer in college and majored in physical therapy. My dreams changed after a few years, and I fine-tuned my goals. Now I'm working to open my own therapy clinic. I have an orthopedic specialization and absolutely love working with athletes and fitness freaks like me."

His almost-green eyes danced over her features, drinking her in. He looked so intense that, once again, she felt overwhelmed with her *awareness* of him.

Out of all the women in the room, he singled her out? Was she dreaming?

"I already know what you do." Jen tilted her head, trying to fill the silence. "Tell me something I don't know."

His forehead wrinkled as he looked up in thought, as if he was trying to think of something unique. He'd have to try hard to surprise her; she was a huge fan, though she was doing her best not to show it.

"One thing about me...huh...well, I sold my house when the market was great, and moved into a broken-down mixed-use property over in West Springfield. In my free time, I'm working on renovating the abandoned space."

Well, success. She didn't know that.

She tipped her glass in his direction. "Point to you."

His grin cut deep creases into the side of his cheeks as he looked at the mirrored wall behind the bar. "This friend that brought you here..." He made a show of looking around. "Is she coming back anytime soon? Or did she leave you to fend for yourself against the wolves of the Springfield elite?"

Jen chuckled. Lexie was her oldest friend and would, without a doubt, bail her out of jail without any questions asked. Actually, in Lexi's case, she'd be sitting beside Jen, having been the reason they got arrested in the first place. Lexie was not known for being reliable...or predictable. Jen gave a quick glance around the room in search of her friend.

"At the current moment, her status is unknown. She could come back in ten seconds and hand us a hotel key. She could tell you to get lost. She could tell me she's leaving early because she met a fantastic guy. Or she could come back and tell me *we* need to leave early because she decrees the party is dead." Jen shook her head. "Really, it's a roll of the dice with her."

John's eyes sparkled. "But she'd approve of me sitting with you?"

Jen laughed before she could help herself. "If you were some no-name athlete or a rookie on the team, I'd actually be wondering if she put you up to this to give me some company." She leaned over and nudged his shoulder with her own. "As you are neither, I feel fairly confident she didn't put you up to this. Unless...did she ask you to come over here and introduce yourself to me?" She gave him an assessing look, not really believing that Lexie did that. Lexie had known John for years, even though John didn't know that Lexie was the friend Jen was talking about.

John shook his head, his eyes sparkling.

That shiver of awareness struck again.

He challenged her back. "Maybe I'm the victim here and you're a stone-cold fox out on the prowl. Maybe you're experienced at tricking men into thinking they're in the power seat but, really, you're pulling all the strings. For all I know, I'm the target." He lowered his eyes at her dramatically. "Did you purposely steal my chair when I stepped away for a minute? The guys on the team are as equally nefarious and meddlesome as your invisible friend."

They paused at that moment, leaning in and grinning at each other, both confident in the serendipity of their meeting.

Look at those lashes. Hell, she could basically see each one individually. They were dark, short, and spiky. And goodness, there were a lot of them. How had she never noticed before? Hell, she had a freaking blown-up poster of his face on her wall in college.

Jen leaned back and gave him a secretive smile. "Maybe someone did, maybe they didn't. I can't talk about it, and I can't talk about why."

John's smile started slow but grew bigger at her obscure movie quote. Jen felt the warmth spread down to her toes.

That was the look of a man who didn't know the meaning of the word defeat and found the perfect competitor. As he sat there assessing Jen, she wondered if she made it too easy for him but knew she didn't much care. She was basking in the attention of a handsome, intelligent, and entertaining man.

Jen then eyed John critically, trying to keep the humor off her face. "I'm starting to think I didn't steal your chair at all. Have you spoken to a therapist about this unfounded idea that all chairs belong to you?" His roar of laughter had her stomach tightening in pleasure.

If it was nothing more than small talk at a bar? Okay, then. It was still fun and thrilling. If it became something more...

She felt like Cinderella and she was sure as hell going to enjoy the attention while it lasted.

After thirty minutes of happily bantering over everything under the sun, including the future success of up-and-coming athletes, the best college sports teams, whether or not she could disarm him in five seconds or less with her decade-plus of Krav Maga classes, and whether he could beat her in a game of chess, John signaled the bartender and asked for a refill.

Jen smiled up at him, more than happy to continue their current discussion on massage, pre-hab, and its benefits to athletes. It was her life's passion, after all. But her heart fell when he looked over her shoulder and did a double take with a small frown tugging at his lips.

"Actually, I need to step away for a few minutes, my agent is summoning me to the dog and pony show." He gave her a small smile that belied just how much he didn't want to step away. "Feel like waiting for me here and I'll be back when I'm done?"

She stared up into his gorgeous eyes and thought, *why not,* and took a chance at suggesting an alternative.

"Or we could get out of here?" she proposed.

He blinked, and another sexy, slow smile revealed his perfect teeth.

The look was absolutely carnal, and it had her toes curling in her painful heels.

In a low, smoky voice that had her body tightening, he said, "I like your idea better."

She smiled back at him and did a sideways nod toward where he looked before. "Go. Bless the people with your presence. Kiss hands and shake babies. I'll be here when you get back."

He barked out a deep chuckle that danced along her skin. Somehow, making this rather quiet man laugh felt like the sweetest victory, and she couldn't wait to see what other noises she could elicit from him later.

John leaned in close, his bristles scraping her cheek and neck. He gave her a soft nuzzle and a light kiss on her neck. In a soft voice, he said, "I'll be back as soon as I can."

It was full of promise.

Yes, please.

He paused, their faces close, and she gave him an affirming nod.

There was no way she was leaving this seat. Lexie would have to deal.

After her nod, he nuzzled toward her ear, dragging his lips along her skin. It made it a million times harder to sit still and not reach for him.

She inhaled deeply and caught a hint of woodsmoke and cedar. Heaven.

In a barely-there whisper he said, "Don't move an inch, my little thief." John gave a hint of kiss to the area under her ear, causing goosebumps to erupt *everywhere,* and then, he was gone.

Jen's eyes nearly rolled back into her head at the sensations firing around her body.

She couldn't even count the number of things she'd love to steal from him. An orgasm, or seven, would be a good start.

Dear lord.

That man was sex on legs and she couldn't wait for him to get back.

Chapter Two

August 7, Saturday
Jen

Jen left her seat.

And she hated that she had to.

About ten minutes after John left, Lexie found Jen and stole John's abandoned drink.

"I've been here the *whole* time," Lexie said breathlessly as she adjusted her ridiculous jean skirt and purple corset top. Lexie was the perfect mix of gothic, steampunk, and rock chick. It was a weird mix and Jen never knew what style Lexie was going to rock on any given day. Neither did Lexie's mega-rich, mega-intelligent, mega-reserved father. Luckily, even with her outrageous antics, headstrong attitude, and her radical wardrobe, her father still adored her.

But seriously? What was Lexie asking her to cover for now?

Jen didn't even bother asking.

Which was good, because Lexie wouldn't have had time to get an answer before Lexie's dad graced them with his presence.

"Girls. You look wonderful." He gave Jen a passing one-arm hug and went to his daughter. "You look memorable as ever, Lexie-Lou." He squeezed her tight.

The guy didn't even wince as he lied through his teeth about her horribly out of place outfit. Seriously...Father-of-the-Year.

"You like? I got some of these pieces for Comic-Con last year." Lexie waved down at her outfit and did a little hop on her platform, knee-high boots.

Lexie's dad was a saint. In more ways than one. Hell, the number of times he'd shown up as a father figure for Jen over the years was incredible. That wasn't even counting him paying for her schooling, degrees, and certifications. Jen fought with him for years over those offers of financial support, finally caving when he said they could structure them as loans. William knew her dad's issues, so even with William's busy schedule, he made damn sure Jen didn't miss out on having a dad to stand with during picture time for her college senior game and many other countless times over the years. This man was the reason that she was able to be where she was today.

"I can always count on your sense of flair to liven the place up."

Lexie fluffed her hair dramatically at the compliment and looked at Jen.

"Jen thought I wasn't dressed up enough."

Jen gestured towards Lexie's outfit and then across the room toward all of the other guests dressed to the nines in classic black tie and cocktail dresses. "Well...I wasn't wrong." She raised her eyebrows at Lexie.

Any doubts Jen had about her own, much more conservative, classic A-line dress quickly vanished in the presence of Lexie's irreverent jean miniskirt that had plaid patches sewed onto it, a flowy fuchsia peasant top with billowy sleeves capped with a dark purple corset, and Lexie's signature jet black hair tied into ridiculous pigtails with ribbons.

Lexie snorted, rolled her eyes, and waved her hand insolently at the other guests.

"It's my dad's nonprofit fundraiser. They're hardly going to kick me out."

William was an environmental engineer that pioneered the multi-billion-dollar company, Ernurbar. Years ago, the man fell for a football fanatic and, in an act of love, and possibly boredom, William relocated a professional football team to Springfield, Massachusetts. Everyone thought he was crazy for stationing a team so close to Foxboro, but the team thrived in Springfield. The city and surrounding towns embraced the new team, and in turn, the team brought tons of life and prosperity to the area.

"Well, Lou, that's not really the attitude to—" William started.

"Oh my god! I've been looking everywhere for you. Did you see Ryan Cole is here?" Jen and Lexie's friend, Megan Lowell, hustled over, grabbed Jen's arm, and shook it in excitement. "And he's so much more handsome in person!"

"Lady, you are not wrong," Lexie agreed.

"Lexie already waxed poetic about his perfect baby blues." Jen smiled at Lexie's out-of-character blush.

Megan winked at William. "Get ready, William. Lexie will have you paying for a wedding in no time."

William's face lost all color and his head whipped to his only daughter.

"Psh." Lexie dismissed the concerns. "I'm not the settling down type, Daddy-oh. Don't lose sleep over me." Lexie's head bobbed as she searched the surrounding crowd. "But I did just see Danny Parker. So that might change things."

Megan's head whipped around, and she lifted onto her tiptoes to scan the crowd as well. Megan put her hand on Jen's arm and used her as a prop, pushing up on her own toes. At five foot two, Jen wasn't exactly able to see over anyone's head.

"I haven't met him yet." Megan's green eyes raked over the crowd. Lexie's eyes were so light, they were almost ice-blue, while Jen's were tawny like her deadbeat father's. As a trio, they were certainly a varied bunch.

"Ladies—" William started.

"He had a great season last year, even though I heard he played with an injury," Lexie said, ignoring her father's attempt to get their attention. Her head twisted as she looked for a hint of the sexy Springfield Spartan.

"He wasn't the only one playing through injuries last year. Did you watch the second half of the Spartans' season? John Costner looked like his arm was going to fall off during most of the fourth quarters last year, and the poor guy was limping to the barn," Megan chimed in absently, her head still on a swivel for more glimpses of the local hotties.

The Springfield athlete pool was deep and delicious.

Jen looked around for her particular athlete from earlier, keeping mum on the subject of his last season's performance as the girls chattered on. Jen remembered watching his slow recovery time after taking hit on top of hit. Commentators always made a big deal about his ribs, fingers, or ankle. But to Jen's eye, she could see him favoring other areas as he ambled across the field. She thought she detected a neck issue at one point though the media never made a peep about it.

"Hey, we made it to the Super Bowl." William's chin tucked in and his brows furrowed at the girls and their comments.

No dice on finding John—apparently, he wasn't freed from his obligation yet.

"Dude." Jen turned back to William. "Megan's right. Go rewatch his game against New York last January. His arm looked shot. Hands down a great quarterback. One of 'The Greats' even. But he's been in the league for fifteen years. He's allowed to feel those aches and pains of an older veteran. I'm surprised he's played this long, actually. Especially with so many of his offensive line retiring and being traded this past year."

"I'm being told it's a rebuilding year." William frowned. His lack of knowledge of anything football was starting to show.

Jen grew up with the sport. Heck, love of the Spartans was the one thing she and her dad had in common.

"They're not wrong. It will be a rebuilding year." She cut him a look. "You should really take more of an interest in your team, William. It's a great sport, you might find you enjoy it. And you should definitely make an effort while The Saint is still able to play. He raises the standard of play for all quarterbacks in the league.

Though, I'm not sure how much longer that will continue. He's approaching the end."

"He's still hunky, even knocking on retirement's door," Megan chimed in.

Retirement for a football quarterback was like late thirties—hardly ancient.

Lexie made a gagging sound. "He's like my uncle. Quit it."

Jen remembered John's smokey hazel eyes, the rough scratch of his beard, his slow smiles, and the small hand touches at the bar. Thank God he wasn't her uncle.

She suppressed a shiver. Jen looked around one more time, hoping she'd see him prowling her way, more than ready to take her someplace and thoroughly ravage her.

No luck.

Did he leave without her?

Jen tried to join in the conversation but couldn't stop thinking about John. Was he even coming back or was he just playing with her? He certainly seemed like he wanted to come back.

"Excuse me. Jen?" William's soft voice cut into her reverie.

She turned to William, whom she adored with every fiber of her being. "Yes, boss man?"

He huffed out an awkward laugh, which wasn't anything unusual. The man was a billionaire, but his people skills never evolved to that of a billionaire. Suave was not in his nature.

William waved her to the side. "A moment?"

Jen followed him away from Megan and Lexie, worried at his nervous expression.

"I, uh, have a question for you."

Well, he certainly wasn't wasting any time on pleasantries. Jen had to smile at his direct manner.

"What's up?"

His eyes had a tough time maintaining contact for any period of time, but that wasn't unusual. Instead, he watched the mingling people and wrung his hands together. "I, uh, we're having some problems with staffing for the Spartans. Lenny, our manager of the massage therapist team and a buddy of mine, has been stressed lately about his department. Turns out the last couple therapists he's hired have been...predators."

Huh?

William saw her expression and clarified. "Towards the guys on the team. He said they were more interested in rubbing elbows, or other body parts, with the members of the team and weren't doing their jobs. Then, they did find one good one at the end of last year, but he just gave his notice. So, Lenny is a little nervous about this upcoming season."

"Okay?"

Where was he going with this? Was he looking for her to spread the word to her contacts in the field?

"Lenny thinks that, given enough time, he could properly vet future hires and find one to stick, but with the days slipping away, he's worried that he won't be able to fill the needs of the team in the meantime. The guy giving his notice last week really put some gray in Lenny's beard." William shifted uncomfortably and looked at her. "I hate to do this to you, but would you be interested in coming aboard for a little bit and helping us out?" He was blushing and looking everywhere but at her.

Woah. What?

She was finally starting to turn a profit in her business.

"I know you've been working on this new business for a while now and it would be on hold while you worked for us, but Lenny is really stressing out. I've never seen him so anxious and he's not looking so great. Not that I'll tell him that. I just...I want to help my friend and the team. I don't really involve myself with the team, but when Lenny freaked out about it yesterday, I kept thinking of you. There's no one else I'd trust around the players and coaches. You wouldn't divulge any secrets or gossip to the media or other teams. You'd be completely professional and more than competent at the job. And of course, you could spread the word about your business. Lenny needs some help and I can think of no one better than you." His hands rubbed together quickly as he made his request. "Only until we find a suitable replacement, that is. Lenny's got some feelers out."

William had never once asked her for anything. Ever.

But wow. This was a big ask. He was asking her to press pause on her fledgling business, essentially resetting herself back to zero, to work with the Spartans. It'd be cool as hell to meet the players and see the inner workings of the beast. But...he was asking her to put her entire business on the backburner.

As she looked into Williams's nervous eyes though, it didn't matter.

Jen thought of him as her surrogate father. He'd do anything for her.

So, yeah, she could do this for him. After all, without him, she'd be nothing. She owed him so much, and unlike her father, she wouldn't let her debts go unpaid.

"Yes, of course. You know how much I love the Spartans."

The guy literally shrunk an inch as his shoulders lowered in relief.

"You have no idea how much I appreciate this, Jen."

She reached out and placed a hand on his arm, squeezing in affection. "You know I'd do anything for you and Lexie. Working for a team I love and doing what I love to do? Where's the sacrifice in that?"

He shifted. "Yeah, I know, but still. I'm asking you to put your growing business on hold."

She waved him away and rolled her eyes. "Nonsense, things aren't going that well," she lied. "It's not a problem at all. And you're totally right. It will be a fantastic networking opportunity."

William rushed in and gave her a tight squeeze. Hugging him gave her the same sensation as sitting in front of a warm fire at Christmas. He felt like...home. Like trust and family. God, she adored this man.

"Thank you, Jen," he said in a low, relieved voice.

"No problem, Pops. You know I'd do anything for you and that demon daughter of yours."

Jen felt her purse vibrate. She held her finger up to William and pulled out her phone. As she ducked away to check the caller ID, she paused at the unknown number. The area code was local, so maybe it wasn't spam, but a late-night call on a Saturday? It probably wasn't good.

Shit.

She hustled to a quieter spot and placed the phone to her ear. "Hello?"

"Jenny, it's me, Dad. You need to come stat or I'm a fucking dead man."

Jen's heart stuttered as it did every time she heard those words. She learned from experience that he wasn't being dramatic.

She looked around for Lexie to tell her she needed to go ASAP but she had lost sight of her small group, and John still wasn't back at the bar.

"How much?" she asked, her heart in her throat.

Some mumbling and a loud crash had her pulling her phone from her ear.

"Bring a couple grand."

Fuck. When was he going to *freaking* learn? Never, was the current bet.

She rolled her lips and closed her eyes, bracing herself.

Time to go pay another debt. Except this one was not temporary—it was lifelong. As much as she wanted to rendezvous with John, her family had to come first. And even though her entire being revolted at the idea of running out on John, loan sharks weren't the patient type.

She opened her eyes and wound her way toward the exit, swallowing down the tears that threatened to fall. So much for being brave and taking a chance with John at the bar. When would she ever have a chance to live for herself?

Chapter Three

August 14, Saturday
John

A week later, John approached his agent, Richie Mayne, at their table for two on the rooftop terrace of Versailles.

The view went for miles and the city lights twinkled brighter than the near-nonexistent stars. The glass dome across the top of the building protected patrons from the harsh New England elements and the climate-controlled space felt comfortable yet elegant. The lighting and ambiance represented luxury...and money. You didn't come to Versailles if you were worried about the bill at the end of the night.

"My number one client," Richie boomed.

"Mr. Mayne," John greeted with mock seriousness. They clasped hands and thumped each other on the back. "I bet you say that to all the guys." John winked.

"Now, now. Don't go saying things like that too loud or people might get the wrong impression." Completely unflappable, Richie motioned towards the chair across from him and urged John to sit.

Richie had been John's agent since he was first drafted fifteen years ago. The years had been good to John, and Richie always worked hard to get him the best contracts, both on the field and off. Few players nowadays were still playing for the teams that drafted them—John was one of the few. He learned from the best. He watched the all-time greats restructure their contracts year after year to allow for more cap space and create a stronger team. John could have left ten times over for an organization that would pay him more, but what good was that when it left the team with no money to pay for supporting players. A quarterback was only as good as his offensive line. Without their protection, he would take quite the beating on a weekly basis. By making sure his team could pay for those clutch, and often unsung players, he was ensuring his own health and success. It was a no-brainer.

As John lowered himself into the chair, he made eye contact and gave nods of hello to various familiar faces around the terrace. No one gawked. No one took pictures. No one asked for autographs.

A nice respite from everyday life.

Richie flagged a staff member down and they ordered drinks from the young gentleman in Versailles' sharp, black signature suit. Male, female, other—the staff all wore the same uniform with matching beret, embroidered with a stylish V in silver stitching. The place was pure class.

Richie dove into the latest gossip while they waited for their drinks.

John gave a small nod to a team member at the bar and a wink to the man's wife before focusing on Richie, dishing out the latest gossip on the young quarterback gunning for Costner's job.

"I told him he can't just ask for that kind of money without talking to me first," Richie tittered in delight. "There's a magic to negotiating. A rhythm. You have to really build up to that kind of ask." His hand reached out to take his drink from the server's tray.

John took his with a grunt of thanks and looked back to Richie.

"But, of course, you know me. I thrive on challenges. So, I said, let me talk to him. Five minutes. That's all I need." He started laughing. "I had it in three. I spent the other two minutes booking a tee time for this weekend." He slapped the table and took a celebratory drink. He grinned at John with a devilish light in his eye. "But it made me look really good to the kid. Going forward, he'll know to come to me first. Don't worry, old friend, it'll be a bit before that young buck replaces you as QB1."

John internally winced at the title 'old friend.'

He was hardly old, damnit.

He wished everyone would stop saying that. Fucking media. Even his dad gave him shit about being old now.

"You have it down to a science," John agreed, swallowing another small sip of his drink.

The waiter came back, asked for their order, and left again.

"Okay, now let's get down to the good stuff." Richie leaned forward and opened his mouth to start but then stopped and stiffened. The movement was small but the careful expression on Richie's face had John bracing in response.

John turned his head to see what caught Richie's attention.

Fuck, ice-bitch.

Great.

At the bar, with her newest beau, was John's ex-fiancé, Vicki. He was with her for four years before it ended with drama and heartbreak. They met when John was thirty and were engaged by his thirty-third birthday. She lived wild and loved the spotlight. Attention was her life's blood. Even though John stayed in the shadows of the media, he loved her for her energy and spirit. He wanted someone to provide for and she loved to be provided for. It was a match made in heaven.

Until it wasn't.

He caught her in bed with another man. As the man rushed from the apartment, John and Vicki traded verbal blows. She accused him of not giving her enough attention and putting his career first. He demanded to know why he had to be involved in every single wedding decision and didn't know why it mattered what fucking monogram style they used on the wedding napkins. That sent her into a rage.

He lost his six favorite whiskey tumblers that night.

She faulted him for working too much and not attending enough family events with her. He defended himself by explaining that his career put her in diamonds and private jets to visit said family. She said she wanted to start their own family and not hold off until the wedding. She was concerned he was getting older and wouldn't be able to enjoy her or their kids. He said he wanted to wait until he finished playing so he could be around more. She wanted to bump up his retirement date. He was inflexible on that front. He offered her almost everything, even after the affairs—he found out it was plural during their fight. No matter what he offered, it wasn't enough. She wanted to be the center of his world, and that was the one thing he couldn't offer.

Since their breakup, she had been making waves and gaining millions of social media followers. Many adored her, but no one in Springfield forgot the way that she did Saint John wrong. She might be the darling of the elite in L.A and New York. But in Springfield, she wasn't welcome.

In Springfield, she was Vile Vicki.

John felt a headache come on and his eye started to twitch.

Why was she here?

"Uh, well, this is new," Richie said across from him.

John turned to look at Richie, only to see Richie's eyes directed across the room. One of the newest area athletes slithered up to Vicki's side and was nuzzling her neck, his eyes closed. Vicki's eyes were open.

And on John.

"Jesus," John said, disgust rifling through him.

He rolled his eyes at Richie. "She must want something. That's the only reason she ever does anything." John refused to turn back and look at them again. He had met many women, and some men, over the years that took advantage of a professional athlete's clout and money. In the beginning, he never expected the worst from them, despite team veterans always warning him. But Vicki fixed that blind spot. He was no longer distracted by pretty eyes and a nice smile or someone too agreeable, too likable. He may have learned the hard way, but holy hell, did he learn.

Except for his mystery massage therapist at the gala last week. She seemed...different. He stepped away for longer than he wanted to and when he went back to woo her away with a promise of a nice dinner and a nicer evening, she was gone.

Coconut and lime-scented dust in the wind.

"So, let's talk contracts for next season." Richie clasped his hands together on the table in front of them. "I spoke with management and they're a little concerned about this current season. Not with you, obviously, but it's a rebuilding year for the Spartans. The GM feels great about the new draft picks. But when I spoke with Coach Mitchell, he expressed his concern about the lack of veterans on the team. Coach didn't think Brian put enough thought into the draft picks and left you a little exposed on the line. They also don't know how the new offensive coordinator will mesh with the team as the season progresses," Richie added in a quiet voice. "He was a surprise hire, and I can't really seem to figure out how he got the job." He resumed his normal speaking voice. "If you take any more of a pay cut, you'll be paying them to play, and naturally, that isn't going to fly. I know you tend to want to restructure your contract so they can afford other talent, but I think the other talent they're looking at is overvaluing themselves, so I think that's a no-fly zone this year."

Even though John felt antsy after seeing Vicki and her newest victim, he tried to focus on Richie and listen to his preamble. When he heard her fluttery, high-pitched laugh echo across the room, John forced himself to smooth the scowl from his face.

God. How could he have ever fallen for such an act?

Richie knew him well, so despite the tension that bracketed John's shoulders and mouth, he soldiered on. Richie could read a room and knew how to handle his various clients'...issues. He was also a workhorse and would get around to the nitty-gritty in a minute, which would fully distract John from the fact that his cold-hearted ex was in the room. Richie liked to remind his clients of everything at play before dropping the bombs.

"Now, don't get me wrong. I think we have some flexibility. Player benefits that you don't take advantage of that we can leverage. The Spartans have only been around for fifteen years; a baby compared to the other teams in the league. I think there's an opportunity for them to woo over other New England fans if they have the right players with the right look and the right attitude." He made eye contact again with a small smirk dancing on his lips. "This is where you come in."

John felt his upper body stiffen. He didn't know what Richie had signed him up for, but he already knew his answer. "No."

"Just listen."

"No."

"I've been a good agent, haven't I?"

"No."

"Ass," Richie laughed out. He soldiered on, unperturbed. "Come on. You're thirty-eight, man. I know we usually avoid the age discussion, but we need to have it. Especially with Brian taking Ryan Cole in the draft. I don't know what their plans are for you, or him, but we need to be smart and think ahead. Have you given any more thought to my suggestion about coaching?" He gestured at John's face. "The fans would love it." He paused meaningfully. "Managementwould love it."

He was only thirty-eight. Not eighty, damnit. The Spartans should be tripping over themselves trying to get him to sign a multi-year deal at the end of the current season. Sure, it was just the beginning of the season, but still, it never hurt to look ahead, and John planned to be around for many more years.

"I have it on good authority that William, in particular, would love it if you coached."

Shit.

John felt the blood rush to his face and the restaurant volume increase in his ears. He brought his eyes back to Richie's uncomfortable looking ones. John sighed. No one went against the team owner.

William was the youngest owner in league history. He made his money in renewable energy and even after donating fortunes to charity, he still had more money than he knew what to do with. A Springfield native, he decided to start a second New England football team. In Massachusetts, no less. Everyone thought he was nuts but with his money and connections, William got the green light. And here they were, fifteen years later, five-time division champions, and one Super Bowl win. Not bad considering over thirty percent of the league had yet to win a Super Bowl and had been around much longer than the Springfield Spartans.

Hopefully, this upcoming year, John would be adding another diamond-studded ring to his collection.

But that could only happen by outperforming the opponents and staying healthy.

"I'm not ready to be put out to pasture. I want to be head quarterback until I'm forty. It's not like I'm asking to still be on the roster when I'm collecting social security," he bit out, acid on his tongue. "They explicitly said they don't want to do a multi-year extension for me?" Tension had his voice getting louder and people started looking their way.

"That's not what I'm saying. Get a lid on it, John, Jesus," Richie hissed, running his hand through his blonde hair. "You need to see a therapist about this age complex. Christ." He took a gulp of his drink.

John heard nothing but roaring in his ears. He set down his drink before he broke the glass in his grip. Instead, he reached for his unused napkin and balled it tightly in his fist.

"I want a multi-year deal at the end of this season."

"Brother. Probably, not in the cards. They'll do one and revisit year to year."

"I want at least two."

"Not going to happen, champ."

"Make it happen, Richie."

"John."

"*Richie.*"

He had been playing professional football for fifteen years and led the Spartans that whole time. They owed him this. Whatever contract clause needed to happen, he'd make it work. He wanted the chance, his one fucking life goal, to lead the charge until he was forty.

Sure, it all started with a vindictive promise made to his relatively pessimistic father, but still. A vow was a vow.

And really, *two* more seasons. The Spartans could give him that.

After what John did for the team, *William* should give him that.

He'd take all the talk of being too old and make everyone who brought it up eat those words.

Too old to still dominate? Bullshit.

The staff came with their meals and lowered them to their placemats in front of them. The candles flickered in the slight breeze generated by their moving arms.

The warm spices and seasonings wafted up to him and he shifted when he heard his stomach rumble.

He grunted to Richie as he started cutting into his steak, mind working as he chewed.

"All right," he barked at Richie. "What about this? If I bring us to the Super Bowl, they need to agree to lock me in until I'm at least forty." John speared a piece of steak and stuffed it into his mouth, eyes darting up to Richie's.

Richie blinked in surprise. Trepidation etched into his features as he stared across the table. The bright lights of the surrounding buildings cast a slight haze beyond the windows to their sides. Richie didn't break eye contact as he reached for his drink, sipping while taking in John's expression. "Okay."

John cut a look around the restaurant and out over the city that he loved with his whole heart. He loved playing but he was fucking sick of listening to people lament about his age. He was in better shape than most Americans. So what if soreness ravaged him all the fucking time? Anyone would be hurting with the beating he took during the season. He needed glasses and forgot the names of words every now and then, it was all part of getting older, not dementia. It happened to everyone nearing forty.

It's not like he needed a nursing home, damnit.

He vowed to his parents that he'd make something of himself, and that football wasn't just a kid's dream to escape the life of a rancher. He'd already proven that to his mom, but his dad was a harder sell. Always had been. Fuck, he felt like a child for even caring about winning his dad's approval at this point in his life. But something in him wouldn't let it go. He made that promise, and he would fulfill it. He needed to buckle down this next year and shut up the haters. Laser-focus. He would demand nothing less from himself...and his teammates. After that, he could slow down.

Maybe track down his Cinderella who disappeared on him from the gala last week.

But first things first.

He needed to finish on top.

CHAPTER FOUR

August 15, Sunday
Jen

Lexie laughed as she sipped her mocha chai latte, pinky up in an exaggerated fashion. She looked out of place in her motorcycle boots, ripped black tights, another jean mini skirt that had safety pins threaded throughout, and a top that boasted fake tat sleeves. Heavy, black eyeliner framed her ice-blue eyes. Dressed in all black, the girl's only pop of color was some bright red streaks layered in her fine black hair. She even had a black diamond dimple piercing that only she could make actually quite darling.

The chick rocked the intrepid goth pixie look.

"I really thought the author was making up that part of her memoir," Lexie continued to gush.

They were sharing a meal at a local diner and discussing their most recent book. Sometimes, Jen still couldn't believe some of the turns her life had taken since high school. Who would have guessed she'd ever start a book club? She was never much of a reader or all that social really. She was always friendly, down-to-earth, and slightly introverted, and she never really got into the party scene. Yet here she was, leading a book club, attending charity events, and best friends with an heiress who wore brand names like they were from the donation bin.

Jen rushed to lean forward and agreed. "Yes! Me too. I couldn't believe that part was true. You hear stories about infertility centers mixing up embryos, but you don't ever hear about them giving out incorrect results." She sat back after grabbing some French fries smothered in ketchup and pulled her legs up onto the bench seat to sit crisscrossed.

This month's read was an infertility memoir their friend, Rose, requested. She was going through her own infertility struggles and thought the book would ease her sense of isolation during the process. The other girls were surprised at how much they loved the book. It gave them a little extra insight into Rose's life.

"Can you imagine how crazy it would be to be told that you weren't pregnant, only to hear later that they gave you the wrong test results?" Rose laughed weakly but her blue eyes weren't in it. Her bright orange hair, pulled back in a messy pony, showed how tired she was. If the lack of her normally very-styled hair wasn't a dead giveaway, the dark circles under her eyes throwing her smattering of freckles into dark contrast certainly were.

Rose's best friend, Chloe, winced and looked away. Chloe and Rose grew up together and were usually thick as thieves, but things had been tense the last few months. Chloe announced her pregnancy earlier that summer but didn't share the name of the father. To watch her best friend have an unplanned pregnancy...that had to kill Rose after *years* of infertility treatments.

Megan set her hand over Rose's. "I can't imagine how I would handle something like that. Especially after undergoing the emotional trauma of infertility as a whole." Megan was a local Certified Public Accountant with a heart of gold and a knack for being quick-witted and brilliant. She had her own tired eyes as she nibbled at some fries. She had a young daughter at home and a pregnant roommate who was not making the *best* life choices at the moment. It was draining for Megan though she hid it well.

But as broken as they all were, they fit.

Lexie continued, "Thank you for recommending this book. It was a good find." She looked around the small table and commented in a lower voice, "However, I fully expect there to be a substantial number of spicy romances in our future reads. This book was great and all, but Lexie-girl likes her smut." She gave them big eyes and finished with a grin.

They chuckled before diving in for more snacks.

As they were eating, Chloe looked at Jen. "When do you start for the Spartans?"

They all turned to Jen. She uncurled one leg and placed it on the ground, bouncing it slightly. "This week, actually." Jen cast a sheepish look toward Lexie. "How do you feel basically being my boss?"

Jen had bought an "I love my boss" T-shirt she was going to wear at their Krav Maga class later. She bought Lexie a matching one saying, "I love my employee."

Lexie squealed. "This week...already!" The future owner of the team started bouncing up and down in her seat. "Why didn't you remind me?"

Chloe widened her eyes at Jen from across the table and focused her attention back on the food in front of her, more than willing to let Jen manage Lexie's forgetfulness on her own.

"You literally just landed back in the States like two days ago."

Lexie gave her a droll look. "My phone works on the flight and overseas. No excuse. We could have gone shopping for sexy outfits for your first week."

"Lexie, she's not supposed to be sexing up the men. That literally got the other therapists fired." Megan gave her an exhausted look.

Lexie waved her away. "But what if she finds The One? Sexing up a player is always acceptable if he's The One. Love knows no line. Love knows no workplace boundary." She paused. "God, that would be freaking hot. Can we have a forbidden workplace romance for our next read?"

That actually sounded appealing. And a good distraction so Jen could stop thinking about how she would now be coworkers with one, very sexy, John Costner. She may even get to rub him. Holy hell.

"Jen, you didn't tell us, how'd the thing work out with your dad last week?"

Before she could answer, their reprimands started.

"Dude. Not cool. You can't just text us some vague message of 'if you don't hear from me in thirty minutes, call the police'. You've *got* to stop that shit," Megan bit out.

"The first time was freaky as all hell. Now? Now it's just terrifying and frustrating. Stop enabling the guy," Lexie commanded.

Even Chloe and Rose joined in to berate her.

Jen bit her lip and let them voice their concerns. They didn't understand having a dad with an addiction. Her dad had been a gambling addict for as long as she could remember. She had thirty-two years of evidence proving she couldn't change him, so she had to take the good with the bad. But lately...there hadn't been much good. But it's not like he was dead. He still had time to change.

As they continued to lecture her about enabling an addict and going to sketchy places to pay off his loan sharks before they could break his legs, fingers, or whatever else, she let her mind wander.

She knew all of their concerns. She had them herself. But her dad was all she had left of her family. If she didn't cover his debts, who would? What would happen to him? A couple of grand here or there kept her dad safe. Sure, she gave up substantial chunks of money, but it could be worse. Having to let her deadbeat dad move in with her because someone broke his fucking legs over a bad bet? No thank you.

Jen also let her mind drift back to more pleasant thoughts of John Costner.

Did he ever even come back for her last Saturday?

He probably didn't.

Or maybe he did?

She sighed as she thought of his soft shoulder nudges and finger grazes at the bar. She had never been big on body hair, but damn, even his forearm hair was sexy. The way his crisp white shirt had shifted up his arms as he moved his hands while speaking. Holy hell. The man was perfection. He even smelled good.

And she blew him off for her freaking deadbeat father.

Or maybe he blew her off and she didn't know it?

Regardless, they were now co-workers. Or...they would be once she checked into Human Resources in the morning. Nothing could happen between them now. *That* was an ethical line she couldn't cross. Having sex with a co-worker was as bad as having sex with a client. She'd never get another job again if word got out she was *that* type of massage therapist. Or, maybe she would get lots of potential clients, just not the kind she wanted. Her five-year business plan didn't include happy endings.

Even for the likes of John "Saint" Costner.

But she wouldn't be working for the Spartans long-term. Just until they found a steady employee. So maybe...maybe after, if she played her cards right.

She snapped back to the present when all the girls turned their heads as they heard a thunderous approach. She could feel the floor move and see their waters wiggle with each step.

Victor, the diner owner, grunted as he approached their table. He tossed his handwritten bill on the table in front of them. It only had the amounts for the French fries and an iced tea. They had each ordered full meals and shakes. "If I hear you talking about any X-rated romance books in my diner, you're all out on your rumps."

"Hey, be nice. We're not that loud," Jen whined at him while giving him a cheeky smile. He liked to act like a gruff old man, but he hid a heart of gold. Jen adored him and viewed him as the grandfather she never had. She liked to think he viewed her as a granddaughter that he may, or may not, have as well.

"Get yourself a good man and you won't need any of those smutty books." He clomped away.

"That's not true. I will always need these smutty books. And I don't need a man. I just need to win the lottery. Is that too much to ask?" she called after his retreating back. Jen smiled as he stormed through the flap leading to the kitchen, where they immediately heard him start to swear and bark out orders to the other cook.

"Always a charmer," Rose muttered under her breath while digging in her purse.

Chloe hummed in agreement while tying back her glossy black hair in a low ponytail, but Jen's mind was already back on John.

Jen remembered his gravelly voice and the way his nose rubbed against her neck before he left their little bubble at the bar. What if she had to massage him? No way could she hide that kind of heat. She'd be panting as she worked on him. She'd have to get exceptionally good at acting, quickly.

Because she'd be seeing him tomorrow.

CHAPTER FIVE

August 16, Monday
Jen

"Are you sure this is the right way?" Jen asked for the thousandth time as she dug her nails into Kenny's bicep.

"Yes, you drama queen, calm down. I know where I'm going," Kenny muttered.

"You said that five hallways and two flights of stairs ago."

"Stop talking, you're distracting me."

Jen dug her nails in a little extra, which caused him to look down and grin.

She gave him another painful squeeze and he chuckled. Kenny was a tight end on the team who had a friends-with-benefits fling going with pregnant Chloe right now. The adorable pair thought no one knew about their romance. Rose and her husband Brandon had no clue, which was probably good, because even if she and Chloe had issues at the moment, Rose would still kill Kenny for crossing that line with her friend. Chloe invited Jen and some friends over for a game night of Bullshit a couple of weeks ago and she and Kenny were clearly an item despite their efforts to hide it. There was no way Kenny was Chloe's baby bump daddy, but he sure as hell was playing the part to a tee. The man worshipped Chloe. It was a shame he couldn't see it beyond just being a temporary fling.

Jen looked around in awe as Kenny led her to the employee entrance. She had been to Baystate Stadium countless times over the years but had obviously never been in the underbelly of the beast. As Kenny steered her through the winding halls, she stared at the many accolades and pictures adorning the wide-set halls. Team colors decorated the walls and floor. The carpeted halls boasted an attractive dark navy, while the walls were a deep maroon. The color combination gave off an air of elegance and masculinity.

The only thing missing was the scent of woodsmoke and cedar.

Pictures lined the walls, showing coaches, players, the owner, and their families participating in numerous charity endeavors, celebrating victories, or relaxing together. They also displayed pictures taken after some of their championship losses. Jen thought it was a nice touch. Show the family mentality they promoted, in good times and bad, that they stayed together no matter what.

Kenny brought her into the HR offices and up to a pretty girl that couldn't be older than twenty-two with a decorated "Abby" nameplate on her desk. She blushed so furiously as Kenny approached that Jen started wondering if they had history.

Kenny gave a quiet "see you later" and ambled back down the hall.

"Give Chloe and the babies a kiss for me," Abby called to his retreating back.

A single-finger salute rose high in the air as he refused to turn around and engage with her.

After signing all the necessary paperwork and being given confusing instructions on where to go next, Jen focused on not getting lost and avoiding the sexy team captain.

Who quite possibly believed she blew him off.

She needed to be patient. Soon enough. She just had to do this favor for William for a few weeks and then it'd be game on.

• • • • • • • • • • •

"Most professional football teams contract out massage therapists and have them come in a couple of days a week. We're one of the few organizations that have actual therapists on staff. It's been pivotal in the success of the organization and its athletes. As you know, massage therapy is a necessary part of recovery and injury prevention and having massage staff easily accessible has made a huge improvement for the players and other staff too." Lenny Tudesci lectured Jen while marching down the abandoned halls. William was right, the man seemed stressed to the max.

As the lead therapist and department director, Lenny instructed Jen on her daily duties and responsibilities. The tour was fast, his speech was faster, and she was sure she'd get lost a time or two in the upcoming weeks. Even so, she focused on soaking in his words the best she could. Lenny had worked for the organization since its inception fifteen years prior and championed the initiative to have in-house therapists. His argument so compelling that lore had it that management hired him on the spot. His approach and success revolutionized the league's attitude toward massage therapy and its benefits. Hopefully, more and more teams would migrate toward the in-house massage model the Spartans pioneered.

She was in the presence of a massage legend.

"I believe one hundred percent that this is the best organization to work for. If I didn't believe that, I wouldn't still be here. Management and the players, appreciate all that my massage team does for them. We see some of the fastest recoveries in the league and fewer injuries in general." He cut her a severe look, his eyebrows forming a V over his nose. "Now let me be crystal clear." He enunciated each word. "There will be no fraternization with the players. None. If I catch even a hint of you forming an unprofessional relationship with any of these players, you're gone. No questions asked. Over. And no referral or recommendation for any future jobs. This is my department. What I say goes. This job, this department, this organization, is the culmination of my life's work. They accepted my pitch when no one else would. And I will not," he stressed, "have anyone on my staff jeopardizing that. Not even a pretty little thing like you. We had a girl do that a couple of therapists ago and she's no longer here. I mean what I say." He stopped walking and turned to face her. "So, if you're here looking to rub elbows with any famous, rich, vulnerable athletes, think again. That won't fly. I don't care who you are to William. No funny business on my ship."

He called her a pretty little thing. The feminist in her cringed at such a comment. But the woman in her felt flattered. She knew she was pretty but she wasn't what anyone would describe as long and lean. Jen played college soccer and kept the muscle tone in the years since. She was strong and fiery. She may be short, but she wasn't exactly little. More like...strong and fit. But to a man that stood over six feet, maybe it made sense Lenny would consider her little.

"No, of course not," she assured him. "If I had staff reporting to me, I would have the same policy. There's no room for pleasure in business. You'll see nothing but professionalism from me. Promise." She used her right pointer finger to make a criss cross over her heart and gave him the most innocent smile she could manage.

See? Pure innocence.

Lenny let out a snort and continued with his tour. He spoke about the history of the organization, his philosophy on treatment, and the massage preferences for each of the players. He promised her a cheat sheet later that she could study that outlined which players preferred which types of treatment. "To ease your growing pains," he said. She found it interesting, though understandable, that certain positions tended to prefer similar treatment types and locations.

Lenny continued, "For example, the quarterbacks on the team, whether first string or third, usually prefer a lot of neck, shoulder, and back-focused massages. A lot of the linemen prefer their therapist to focus on their legs and glutes. And so on and so forth for the various other positions on the team." His lips tipped down and his ever-present scowl deepened. "Do you even know what I'm talking about? Do you know the positions in football?"

Jen inwardly rolled her eyes. Only if you count memorizing stats, positions, plays, and watching every Spartan game for the entirety of their existence so she could have something to bond with her father over.

She couldn't even walk or talk when her dad brought her to her first football game in Foxborough. It wasn't the Spartans that she grew up watching but that was only because they didn't exist yet. As soon as the Spartans came to Springfield, the team and its management quickly ingrained themselves in the hearts of the surrounding communities. Even lifelong fans of other teams, like her father, were wooed away from their die-hard local loyalties with the skills, wits, and professionalism of the Spartan Nation.

Jen grew up scheduling life around football so she could spend time with her father. Then again, the man had a gambling addiction, and an obsessive belief that if he attended the games, he could influence the outcome.

"Of course." She patted herself on the chest. "Big football fan. Huge." She stopped and changed tactics. "But not too big. You know? I like the sport. But I'm not going to fangirl or anything...unless I meet Michael Dillion or Kyle Justice or someone." He stopped walking and placed his hands on his hips. "Just kidding," she blurted. "Obviously, I'm not going to fangirl or anything. I mean, they're great. Everyone on the team is great. It's a world-class team this year. Not that John Costner couldn't lead a blind cow to the Super Bowl." She dug this hole and despite her inner voice telling her to shut up already, she kept going to talk her way out of it. "I mean, he's been in the league for so long. He's a legend for staying on this team taking pay cut after pay cut for more cap space. And then there's the fact that there's never a bad word said about him." Lenny raised an eyebrow, now looking more entertained by her word vomit than disgusted. She was making headway. Charm them with awkwardness, her mother always said. "And obviously he's handsome." Lenny's other eyebrow shot up. "Not that *that's* a big deal. I mean, all the players are handsome. Um, yeah. Sorry. This is a disaster." She attempted to smile, though it was definitely more of a grimace. She used her hand to fan her face. "I'm a fan of football. I understand the positions. So, I get what you're saying." She took in a heaving breath. "And I won't be star-struck. A consummate professional—that's me." She thumped herself on her chest and hoped she didn't botch this before it even began.

Lenny chuffed out a disbelieving laugh and continued toward the water stations.

"Now, I'm not recommending the use of drugs to get through your day, but I do recommend a bottle of ibuprofen or acetaminophen to get through your first week of work. These boys have muscle. If you do your job right, your body will be sore at the end of the day after working on them." Only a veteran in his sixties would describe ibuprofen and acetaminophen as drugs. "You'll be on your feet and running around all day long. So, if you're not used to that, you're going to feel it. And if you haven't been working lately, you'll need to retrain for that level of activity." He cast her a look. "You look like you're used to being active, but that's nothing compared to what you're going to be exposed to here." He winced. "Exposed is the wrong word. If you're exposed to anything here, report it immediately. We don't tolerate that type of behavior." He grumbled something to himself that sounded an awful lot like, "Despite what some might say."

Her head whipped to the right to look at him.

What did that comment mean?

"It's not just the players you're taking care of. During times when there are no players getting worked on, coaching and office staff also utilize our services. It's a unique organization. You might have someone from accounting come visit you. Or someone from HR. Sometimes even William himself. The organization has always been incredibly supportive of all the staff, not just the players. It's a mentality that we grow, foster, and promote. If you have a problem with that, walk now." His eyes challenged her over his small glasses and she shook her head.

She gave him what she hoped was an earnest expression, and he continued.

"Keep track of who is getting what work done. Some of the boys don't understand that they can't get certain massages every day. Their bodies need time to detox and flush the released toxins, lactic acid, and metabolic byproducts from their bodies. Some guys love their massages though and don't want to listen to reason. Be their reason. Don't let them bully you."

She made a mental note to have a notebook with her to keep track of the players, their injuries, and the work they had done.

He finished up his tour with the massage therapy rooms. Jen asked a couple of questions about techniques and acceptable treatment styles that had him raising his brows at her. He jumped into discussing strategies with her and, by the time he finished, he sounded winded and rubbed at his chest absently.

The man loved talking shop.

Good to know.

Players flitted in and out as they chatted. Hopping up on tables for massages or jumping in ice baths. Some used the various tools around the room to do some self-stretching before snagging a nearby therapist to help. It was all good-natured ribbing and teasing between the players and Lenny. Several of the players gave her short nods when making eye contact as they walked by and Lenny introduced her to many of them.

Thankfully, the massage room wasn't set up as 'men naked under blankets.' They were all dressed...somewhat. It was one large room outfitted with a couple of massage tables, chairs, tables, and rubber flooring for floor work. It was set up for athletic and sports therapy-type massages rather than quiet, private, spa massages. Most just wanted a rub for twenty minutes on a pain point in between sessions. Some players jabbered the entire time, and some sat, or lay, in silence.

It varied.

But what it wasn't, was private.

Every hour she found herself being introduced to a new sports hero. It was totally cool talking to the players she had followed for years.

This wasn't going to be the same as what she was doing before but maybe the change of pace would be good for her so she didn't burn out. Being self-employed usually resulted in her working long hours for less pay; taxes were a bitch. It would only be for a short while. A couple of months at most. It'd be a little break and she could use the time to network and practice her pre-hab techniques as well. It sucked to lose her clients while her business was on hiatus, but maybe she'd meet some players that would like to have her treat them in a pre-hab capacity. And if she finally paid back William for even an ounce of his kindness it would be worth every single second.

She spent the rest of the day shadowing Lenny and the other therapists as they worked down the list of names on the whiteboard at the front of the room.

No sign of John Costner, thank God.

Jen wasn't quite sure what she was going to say when she saw him again.

Surprise? Sorry for bailing?

She *did* tell him her dad tended to drag her into his gambling trouble. John's face had turned scary at that admission and Jen changed the topic as fast as she could. She thought maybe that wasn't the path she wanted to take. Regardless, Jen hoped for at least a couple of days to figure that part out, but the following morning, Jen's barely-existent luck ran out.

Chapter Six

August 17, Tuesday
John

She was here. His Cinderella was here.

As a massage therapist.

So she didn't own her own pre-hab and massage clinic at all. She was the fucking new massage therapist for the Spartans.

He shouldn't be surprised.

Another liar.

He'd been so convinced by her bright eyes and intelligent banter. Her gorgeous face and perfect body hadn't played a part in his willingness to believe her at all. Right?

When he saw her here, talking to Lenny in the quiet hallway by the massage room, he thought he was hallucinating.

When John went to Lenny's house for dinner last week, Lenny had mentioned William found him a new therapist for his massage team. John commented about what a small world it was that he had just met an alluring one at a fundraiser.

Now, as Lenny stood there and introduced them, the thought was hammered home.

Small world indeed.

Sitting next to her at the bar, he hadn't realized how little she was. But standing across from her in the stark hallway, he was all too aware of the solid foot of height difference.

"Hi," she squeaked out. Her right hand shot out and she winced before pulling it back and offering a small wave instead. Jen looked at Lenny sheepishly. "We've actually met before."

Lenny's caterpillar eyebrows climbed high as he looked back and forth between them. He then shot John a disapproving look and said, "Jesus fuck, John," before turning back to Jen. "You didn't feel like mentioning to me that you had a relationship with one of my players when I talked to you about player relationships?"

Jen's pretty face went white at his stern tone and John felt himself bristle, wanting to jump to her defense. He bit his tongue; it wasn't his place.

"No, we didn't have a thing. We almost...well...we just...no...we met two weeks ago at the fundraiser. Nothing happened." Her amber eyes were wide and nervous, and her hands flapped while she tried to explain.

Gone was the blood-red nail polish from the gala that had John itching to see what it looked like wrapped around him. Just like in the fairy tale, all traces of the princess disappeared.

She was still gorgeous as sin though.

"Relax, man. Nothing happened," John chimed in. Finally letting his impulse to protect her rise to the surface.

Lenny looked between the two of them. Without saying a word, they presented a united front by refusing to look at each other and, instead, they focused solely on Lenny.

The massage manager gave them an exhausted look and sighed, his entire body drooping with the motion. He rubbed his face roughly before tugging at his maroon shirt collar and lowering his hands.

"I ask again." Another big sigh. "Is this going to be a problem?"

As if pulled by an invisible string, John and Jen turned and inspected each other. John felt his heart skip a beat and his stomach clench at the memory of her soft skin and funny stories. He remembered her tropical coconut and lime smell, how her long brown and blonde highlighted hair had curled in large waves, her teasing neckline, and her dress that dipped down to the middle of her back. Now, that tempting hair was pulled back in a severe bun. A far cry from the luscious waves that had danced when she laughed with him at the bar. And though she had half a pound of makeup on at the fundraiser, she looked even sexier now without it. Work sexy. Meet you in the supply room sexy. His kind of sexy. Fucking hell.

How could a woman in tan work pants and a maroon athletic polo look so...edible?

Lenny muttered, "*Fuck*, it's going to be a problem."

John jerked out of his moment of admiration and turned to Lenny, but not before he saw Jen's equally guilty look.

"It's not a problem," John reassured his friend. Lenny furiously rubbed his eyes.

"Lenny, seriously, it won't be. William trusted me for this. I wouldn't jeopardize that." Jen stepped towards Lenny as she pleaded with him.

William got her this job? At the fundraiser, she made it sound like she had a successful business and plenty of experience in her field. What happened in two weeks that she needed a new job? And how did she know William?

He caught himself. That was assuming anything she told him at the bar was true.

The evidence suggested that was not the case.

Lenny grunted and stalked away back down the hallway towards the massage rooms, leaving them to sort it out. John turned to his little enchantress and inspected her. Jen turned to him as if every millimeter she moved was painful.

"Well, hello again," John said in a deep voice.

Her eyes got adorably large, and she rolled her lips together. "Yeah, um, hi."

At her obvious discomfort, he crossed his arms over his chest and waited her out. From their brief time together, he learned she tended to ramble.

Was it weird to be excited to hear what lies her pretty lips would spill?

"I, uh, waited." Her hands rushed up to pat at her hair and then down again, where they started to twist together.

He raised a brow, not saying a word.

She nodded and shifted slightly. "I didn't know if you would come back." She trailed off as she peered up at him. "Did you?" She had the hint of a wince on her face as if she was afraid to hear his answer. "Come back?"

"Yeah, I came back."

Her face fell. "Oh."

Well, at least it seemed like she wanted their hookup as much as he did at the time.

"Yeah."

Her eyes darted around the small hallway while she looked for something to say. "I, uh, had to leave. There was an emergency."

Thereit was.

"I'm sure."

"No, there was. My...father had a thing. I had to leave."

Sure.

"Jen, I'm not that hard up for women. You didn't break my heart. I'm fine. Just surprised you bailed and that you're working here. We're good."

"No, I'm serious. I had to help my dad with something." Her voice rose a bit as she spoke.

John paused. She sounded serious and her face was earnest.

He cocked his head, inviting her to say more.

She shook her head. "I swear. My dad found himself in a situation that was...problematic. Like I told you over drinks, it happens sometimes." She waved a hand at their surroundings. "Hence why I had to leave."

Ah, fuck.

"What kind of situation?" He'd gotten enough details about her dad during drinks that John knew he wasn't exactly Father of The Year.

She better not be putting herself in danger. The thought came unbidden, but it felt right.

She waffled, clearly uncomfortable spilling details.

Well, hell if that didn't make his gut clench even more. Okay, so he'd get to the bottom of that soon enough.

His obvious attention and desire to pursue this line of questioning caused her to lose her embarrassment and her hot, little temper rose to the surface.

He got a taste of that at the gala when their discussion evolved from the most effective pre-hab therapies to the best college teams and their performances.

Pure fire.

He loved it. It had been a long time since a woman had challenged him.

He watched as she put a hand on her delicious hip and jutted a leg out in a stance that screamed *here comes a tongue-lashing*. He found himself leaning forward eagerly, ready for the battle.

"I'm not getting into it. I handled it. It's fine now," she bit out. "Believe me or don't, I don't care. But I did have to leave. And yes, I did have my own business, but William needed reliable help for the time being, and Lexie is my soul sister. So, that's why I'm here. I didn't lie about anything."

Her expression caused a hint of guilt to unfurl in his stomach and he shifted slightly. He rubbed the back of his neck while looking down at her and had to hold in a smirk when her eyes fixed on his flexing arm muscles. Good to know she wasn't too insulted by his doubt.

"Sorry you're upset." Her eyes narrowed at his phrasing, but he continued. "I've met a lot of people over the years that see me and other players as targets. I believed you when we were at the bar. But seeing you here, at my place of work, after telling me about all the work you did in your studio..." He let that hang there and she winced.

"I can see why you'd think I'd lie. But if you really were a target, wouldn't I have stuck around to see the deal through?" The fire fell from her face and was replaced by an earnest expression of regret.

Damn, she was pretty.

John shrugged. "I don't know. I just know how it looked to me and I'm explaining that."

She cast a quick peek at the massage room doors and then back to him. "I'm sorry I had to leave." Jen's voice was whisper-quiet, and it gave him visions of silk sheets and hot wax.

"Me too."

As they stared at each other, he felt a stirring that had him once again shifting on his feet and reminding himself that he was at work.

"So...you work here now."

Jen's wistful expression turned more professional as she looked away briefly. "Yup. For now."

"You'll be working on the whole team?"

She wet her lips before pinching them together. "I guess I work on whoever comes to my table."

John stared at her silently for a heartbeat. Then another. He couldn't look away from her pretty eyes and smooth skin. The longer they held each other's eyes, the hotter John started to feel in the sparse hallway. His skin started to prickle, and little shocks went through his fingers with the need to touch her soft skin again. When Jen took a large breath that had her chest expanding with the air, John couldn't stop his eyes from traveling down and watching the intake. Sure enough, evidence of her own arousal looked back at him.

He swallowed and tore his eyes away.

"Maybe I'll make sure I go to other therapists."

Jen crossed her right hand over her chest and held onto her left bicep, self-conscious.

John wanted to throw her over his shoulder and carry her to the nearest closet so she never felt the need to be self-conscious again, but he resisted the impulse. Barely.

What the hell was wrong with him?

Where did these caveman instincts come from?

She wasn't his to protect. She didn't look like she needed anyone to protect her. Hell, at the gala she spoke about how she had a green belt in Krav Maga and how she started when she was sixteen. The woman was a powerhouse.

"Yeah, probably a good idea. For now, at least," she said in a soft voice. There was a wistfulness in her expression that he felt right down to his gut. Hell, how could one conversation create such a longing and throbbing in a person?

She wet her lips again and swallowed hard. "I, uh, probably shouldn't say this, but this is only a short-term gig."

John found himself once again fixated on her pink, dewy mouth and barely heard her words. But when his brain finally processed what she said, he stilled, and his heart pounded a little harder.

"How short-term?"

She gave him a small smile.

Yeah, he processed her insinuation correctly. Her cute little teeth poked out and started chewing on that delectable pink lip and he felt himself losing focus again. Even with the interesting possibility of what her words might mean.

"*Very* short term. Maybe a month or two. Just until they hire a replacement." She looked up at him with a hint of mischief in her eyes, their tawny coloring spelling nothing but trouble and promise.

A month or two...that'd be the longest foreplay ever, but as he watched her eyes darken and those long lashes flutter, he decided it would be worth it. He could behave around her for that long. Heck, it might even be fun rather than torturous. As long as she didn't touch him and make it harder than it had to be.

He nodded and gave her a slow, hungry smile. "A month or two it is."

The barest hint of pink blossomed on the apples of her cheeks, and he felt his stomach tighten. Women didn't blush around him anymore. That she would blush even after flirting and promising a chance of another date? His skin prickled with excitement.

Male laughter rioted down the quiet halls and both of them startled. "I, uh, have to go back in there," she said.

John rolled his lips together and nodded, trying hard not to reach out and touch her.

As she walked back to the therapy rooms, John tried to be a gentleman and not ogle her.

But he was only human.

And her ass was divine.

Holy hell, how was he going to keep his hands to himself day in, and day out?

And worse, how in the world was he going to focus on football when he had that bombshell working with and, possibly, massaging him?

Just a month, just a month, just a month, he chanted silently. He chose to be optimistic and think of it as *very* short-term.

Then they could pick up where they left off.

A fiery roll in the hay, or seven, felt fantastic and all, but at the end of the day, what mattered most was the Super Bowl. And he needed to remember that.

Chapter Seven
August 19, Thursday
Jen

Jen sat at her ratty kitchen table, staring blankly at her phone screen. Her mind was in a fog, and she couldn't seem to focus on anything. She just finished a long day of work and couldn't wait to unwind with a rom-com and a glass of boxed wine.

Her phone buzzed with a text from her dad, asking if he could stop by her place tonight at seven.

Jen sighed heavily.

She knew what that meant. Miguel Medina was a gambling addict, and he had been for years. For as long as Jen could remember really. The last few years, it seemed like he made an effort to abstain, but he struggled. The night of the charity gala was a perfect example of him getting sucked back in. He had lost everything he owned, including his house and car, and even his wife. Or wives actually. He turned to Jen for help more times than she could count. She couldn't ever seem to say no. What kind of daughter would that make her? An ungrateful one. She couldn't stomach the idea of letting someone down the same way that her dad frequently let her down.

Even when he caused several of her more...explosive...breakups, she still couldn't cut the cord. It proved the guys couldn't hack it. They either loved her and could deal with her baggage, or they couldn't. It just sucked that they couldn't.

She hadn't seen or spoken to her dad much since the gala. She was tired of his constant requests for money, and she couldn't bear to watch him throw away his life. Not to mention, she didn't love getting dragged into his shady-ass situations. Maybe one day he'd realize he could lose her and it would be enough for him to turn things around.

Jen took a deep breath and watched the time change on her digital clock.

At exactly seven o'clock, someone knocked at her door. Jen took a deep breath and opened it. Her dad stood there with a worn-out expression. He looked older and tired, with dark circles under his eyes and slumped posture.

"Hi, Dad," she said, trying to sound welcoming.

"Jenny," he boomed, his eyes on the apartment behind her. "Missed ya, kid." He pulled her in for a big hug and then wound around her and into the apartment.

"Come on in," she mumbled, stepping aside slightly and closing the door behind them.

Miguel walked in and sat down on the recliner, making himself at home. Jen perched on the edge of a kitchen chair, her anxiety increasing with every passing moment.

"So, what's up, Dad?" she asked, trying to sound casual.

Miguel took a deep breath and looked up at her.

"Hadn't seen you in a while and wanted to see how you were."

Her bullshit meter started wiggling.

"I'm good. Busy." Jen watched him as his eyes moved around the apartment. When was the last time he was here? Had to have been months. It couldn't have changed that much, had it?

She looked around at the same worn curtains, same worn furniture, same rough-looking appliances and cabinets. She saw him looking at the art behind the couch and her eyes went there. Her only real items of value in this place. Custom paintings of Springfield, created by one of her friends, one of the few that wasn't in book club. Though not for lack of trying.

"Heard you got a new job."

Jen blinked and looked back to her father.

"Huh?"

"A new job, with the Spartans; Big Bill hooked you up."

She ground her teeth. Her dad knew good and well that he went only by William.

"I'm just helping him out while they vet some other candidates."

"Sure, sure." He waved an indolent hand. "I'm sure Billy has it all figured out so you get a nice payday."

"His name is William," she gritted out. "And I'm not getting any special treatment or pay. I'm getting the same pay as anyone in the position with my experience."

"Okay," he said. His golden cheeks looked sallow under his black facial hair.

Was he taking care of himself? He didn't look this rough the last time she saw him, and that wasn't during the best circumstances. He should look better now than he did then. Right?

Her dad's eyes clearly said that he didn't believe her. "So, what are the chances you can get your old man some tickets to a game?"

Of course.

"Very slim, Dad. I'm a massage therapist. The family box seats are for the players' families."

"What? Big Bill doesn't want the plebians mixing with the rich bitches?"

Jen rolled her lips between her teeth and looked out the window, using every ounce of willpower not to engage in a fight. Her dad was her dad. She needed to love him as he came. Warts and all.

"Just a game or two, Jenny-girl. You know they play better when I'm there."

God, she hated it when he called her Jenny. It was always when he was trying to manipulate her in some way.

"Dad, I'm sorry, I don't have the ability to get you tickets. Order some online or scalp them, but I can't help you."

Her dad's face turned blotchy, his sharp cheekbones more defined, as he clenched his teeth tight.

"You seriously can't even get me one ticket?" His deep brown eyes were dilated to the max and his nostrils flared as he stared at her in shock.

Jen shifted in her seat.

Jeesh, an enema while not sedated would be better than this.

"I don't get tickets allotted to me, Dad."

The way he refused to look away made her stomach curl and her skin itch.

"Maybe...maybe I could ask around. See if anyone has an extra ticket I could get for you."

His posture loosened but his face stayed assessing. "I don't want to put you out, Jenny. I don't want to make things hard for you at work."

He probably meant that to an extent...maybe.

Jen shrugged. "It's fine. I'll ask around and see what I can figure out," she said to get him off her back, knowing full well she would never ask anyone for tickets.

He hopped up and went to her, pulling her in for a big hug. His signature musky, smoky smell wasn't comforting like when she was a kid. Now it made her feel a lot of things.

Safe was not one of them.

"Thanks, Jenny bean," he said softly into her hair. "It means a lot that you'd do that for your old man."

Jen closed her eyes but didn't burrow in. It had been a long time since a hug from her dad made everything all right.

She almost missed those days.

Chapter Eight

August 26, Thursday
John

John's legs wobbled as he took the ball from his center and backpedaled. He scanned for the intended receiver and...

He wasn't where he needed to be.

Again.

It was a full-contact practice and the day had been long. He dreamed of the short whistle bursts that would signify the end of practice so he could head inside and have Lenny work on him.

They had to get this fucking play right.

And the guys weren't getting it.

John's focus the last few weeks amped up to level ten. He was throwing straight fire, hitting his receivers at the exact second they needed the ball. Plays developed and unfolded on the field before the players themselves saw them coming. Time slowed down for him. In slow motion his mind played out every scenario and how each player in front of him would respond and react. By anticipating those movements, the ball seemingly teleported into his receivers' hands. It was magic and he was a man possessed. John and the new offensive coordinator, Butch, absolutely gelled and spent many late nights drawing up plays on the classroom whiteboards. Some of the more veteran staff dropped in now and then, but the young recruits attended most often. A couple of the young kids soaked up whatever time they could with the brilliant minds of their veteran players and mastermind coaching staff.

His kind of men.

Who was *not* his kind of man was the punk of a quarterback they drafted in the first round.

Ryan Cole was a sorry excuse for a professional athlete. The kid took nothing seriously. Constantly gossiping at practice and lazily going through the motions.

But the asshole had a golden arm, John would give him that.

Natural talent would only get him so far though. The guy needed to buck up and take things seriously.

Maybe it was good that Ryan didn't challenge himself—gave John some extra job security.

John frowned.

He'd rather win.

Scratch that.

He'd rather be the one leading the charge for the win.

But a win was a win, even without him at the helm.

Luckily, with his drive this season, he'd be at the helm. No question. No other option.

What would he even do if he didn't have football?

He needed his fucking body to stop hurting. Every day felt like mild torture, even with Lenny's frequent therapy and massage work.

Even the surprise distraction of the team's delectable massage therapist, whom John tried to avoid like the plague, wouldn't stop him from leading the team to another Super Bowl ring.

He refused to acknowledge that every time they saw each other, the air felt too heavy and the lights too bright.

John needed her stint as their massage therapist to end stat so they could fuck. This long-haul tease was unusual for him and he didn't much care for it.

He was an immediate gratification kind of guy.

John had been around the block enough times to know what he wanted and got it *when* he wanted it. He respected her desire to keep things professional for the sake of William, but Jesus, a person could only take so much.

• • • • •**•**•**•** • • •

An hour later and John's head, neck, and shoulders ached. His quads and hamstrings weren't feeling great either. His guys needed to get their heads out of their asses, or they'd be here all night. Butch didn't suffer fools, and the offensive coordinator was on a rampage with their inability to run the sequence of plays as instructed. No excuses accepted. The man had an unhealthy obsession with sports bars, casinos, and the horse racetracks in New York, but he was nothing but football-focused when on Spartan turf, so John didn't hold his outside hobbies against him. John didn't care for the details as long as Butch strengthened the team and helped John get that second diamond-studded ring.

"If you bitches are going to stand a chance against Dallas in the season opener, you need to get this fucking right!" Butch bellowed. A lineman standing near him shuffled away a bit to protect his ears. Butch stomped over to a small gathering of players and started in on them.

"Yo, what are the chances Butch whips out a knife and cuts Gabe Garcia if he drops another fucking pass?" a wide receiver said to a teammate next to him.

Luckily, Butch didn't hear their comments and kept shouting insults and critiques at the players.

John watched with a wince as Butch grabbed Gabe by the facemask and lit into him, spit flying.

The kid wasn't deaf...but he would be after this was over.

"Dude. I'll cut him myself if he can't get this down," an offensive lineman panted out while glaring at the rookie getting blasted by Butch.

John started to feel too hot in his helmet and his sinuses started to burn. His nostrils flared as he heard the next player join in.

"Fuck, man. We can all get together after practice and run him over in the parking lot," a running back lobbed out. "Didn't see him there, officer. Whoopsie." He shrugged before popping his mouthguard back in and chewing on the corner.

"Maybe one of Butch's lackeys will rough him up."

Butch did have some rough-looking friends. John heard a couple of players refer to them as his 'enforcers' and his 'thugs' but he hadn't seen them do anything other than keep Butch company at events and parties.

"Support your fucking teammate," growled veteran lineman, Brandon Catcher.

"Dude. You're just saying that because you're not stuck running these crazy routes. I'm toast. Be honest, man, if you were stuck running every single play because Garcia had stones for hands, you'd be pissed too," a wide receiver whined.

"The kid couldn't catch the clap in Vegas," Brown chimed in.

Enough was enough.

John grabbed a couple of face masks of the offending players and whipped them around to stand in front of him. His angry look wiped the smiles from their faces, and they pressed their lips together. As John turned to deliver his message about focus and support, Gabe jogged over to their waiting group, his face red under his helmet, and his shoulders tight. He didn't say a word but stood next to Catcher, his eyes towards his toes.

Jesus, what did Butch say to the kid?

John could yell with the best of them, but he learned years ago that everyone had a line.

The kid looked past his.

He made a mental note to circle back with Gabe after practice and fix the shit rumbling around in his head. His thoughts were interrupted by more screaming and swearing.

Maybe he'd add a talk with Butch to the to-do list as well.

· · · · ● · ● · · · ·

This massage was garbage.

Lenny was rubbing a spot on John's back while asking him about practice. They usually conversed during his massages. John used it as a time to unwind and connect with someone that wasn't aggressively competitive. His friends and teammates were so intense, those conversations tended to go in circles. Rehashing the same shit, over and over. Sometimes, Lenny offered an outsider's insight that John or the guys might not consider.

But right now? Lenny kept missing the tender spot by an inch at least. John let the conversation trail off so Lenny could focus.

"Jennifer! My love! My darling! My soulmate! My body needs your magical hands!" Ryan, the young quarterback, stumbled his way into the massage room, one hand grabbing at his chest, the other reaching out in desperation towards the massage tables.

John stiffened at Ryan's entrance. Now he'd have to deal with his fucking flirting again. The tensing of his muscles had his neck spasming.

Shit.

"Really, Ryan? Do you have to make a scene every time?" Jen shot back from where she sat at her desk, making notes in her daily journal. She didn't even look up.

Good, the kid needed to be brought down a few pegs.

"Miss Medina, I need you. I'll give you anything. Even my name. Promise me you'll be mine forever and I'll whisk you away from this darkened hovel and shower you with riches you have never seen. You'll make wives of foreign sheiks jealous with your entourage. You'll make New York beg for your patronage. You'll make Hollywood beg for your face in movies. You'll bring the world to its knees with your stunning looks, and even better massage talents." He gasped and fell into the open massage table in front of her. His arms dragged down its side as his body collapsed on the floor next to it. His weight inched the table across the floor. The squeal of rubber on rubber grated to John's ears...and patience.

Here comes the headache.

Ryan flopped like a fish on the ground, his arm extended towards Jen's approaching figure.

"Get up, you big oaf." Jen lightly kicked at him. "And don't do that again, you need to injure yourself as much as I need to be the one to injure you." She nudged him, this time with a little more force. "Meaning. *Not. At. All.*" She kicked him with each word.

"Fine, fine, my love. Spurn my advances. But let the record show I tried," Ryan grumbled as he pushed to his feet and hopped onto the table. He shed his shirt with lightning speed and sat there grinning at Jen. "So," he drawled out, "do you come here often? And how do you want me?" He licked his lips and gave Jen a suggestive waggle of his brows.

How did he still have so much energy?

Or...better yet...did Jen *like* him?

"Oof." John let out a soft breath when Lenny pushed on a spot that was directly linked to a nerve.

"Sorry 'bout that," he heard Lenny mumble above him. John felt Lenny's fingers shift off his spine.

As people entered and exited the room, the volume increased. Someone went over to the radio and turned up the song. John tried to close his eyes and focus on his box breathing to drone out the sound of Jen and Ryan laughing. Ryan said something to Jen that had Lenny chuckling above him, further shifting his focus from John's screaming back and shoulder.

John curled his fingers tight. He wanted to choke Ryan and be the one to make Jen laugh instead.

John counted to one hundred before lifting his head up and interrupting their banter. "Actually, Len, can you shift over to my neck for a minute? I felt a couple of pangs today and want to see if you feel anything."

"Por supuesto, big man." Lenny's hands worked their way up to his back and neck.

Across the room, Ryan started moaning dramatically, eliciting chuckles from Jen. She must have retaliated in some form because Lenny's hands stopped rubbing as he paused to chortle as well.

Come on, man, pay attention here.

"Oh, wow. You have something tight right here," Jen's soft voice said as she did something that had Ryan groaning, for real this time.

"Yup," Ryan groaned out. "That's the spot."

John bet it was a 'spot' for him. John ground his teeth, fighting the jealousy and desire to wring the junior quarterback's neck.

"All right, let me grab something quick. Lay face down on the table. Be right back."

More rattling noises, talking, music, and a door slamming assaulted his ears. His eyes popped open, and he glared at the floor through his face cradle.

How hard was it to get a massage in a quiet room, damnit?

When he heard someone say his name, he pulled his head up and looked over to the door.

The coaches, Butch, and Mitchell stood there, surveying the room.

"Ah, my two favorite quarterbacks." Butch moseyed over to the board and added his name to Jen's column. "Tough day today, but I'm glad we finally got it." He paused in fake concern. "Your bodies must be killing you." He passed John and patted his sore shoulder with a rough thump. "I'm surprised you're even in here, John. Showing your aches and pains to the enemy and all that." He jerked his head over to Ryan, his head turned to face them. Butch snickered at his joke but Ryan's eyebrows shot together, and his lips turned down. Even Jen frowned and looked over at Butch with a small V wrinkling her forehead.

Lenny harrumphed from above John and kept rubbing. This time with a little more focus.

"I hardly think they're enemies," Jen scoffed as she walked back to Ryan, a warm compress in her hands. She had clearly grown comfortable enough in the organization over the past month and a half to feel safe in contradicting the offensive coordinator. "Plus, he's thirty-eight. He's allowed to be feeling it a little more than a twenty-four-year-old." She raised her eyebrow at Butch basically begging him to argue.

Uh...what now?

Did she just call him old?

Did she think he was old?

Lenny's hands tightened on his shoulders and tried to push him down, but John forced through the pressure and sat up.

"Thanks for the massage, Len. But this dinosaur is all set. Just needed a quick kink worked out. I'm good now." He puffed up his chest as he stared down Jen and Ryan a few feet away.

Jen's bun showed the wear of the day, and some loose strands of her hair wrapped into her chin-length, golden hoop earrings. Memories of the many times he took Vicki jewelry shopping assaulted him even though the women couldn't be more different. From what he had seen, Jen was a workhorse despite the fact that she was doing a job that wasn't her dream career. Vicki? Vicki wouldn't know a hard day's work if it bit her in her ass.

At his dinosaur comment, Jen's cheeks pinkened and her eyes darted back down to Ryan's exposed back. Without further comment, she continued to knead the muscles there.

Did she ever wish she was rubbing John's back?

He shook the thought off and stood up so the coaches wouldn't think something was wrong.

That idea went to shit when he wobbled slightly. His damn legs felt like jelly.

Lenny hadn't gotten to his legs yet.

Guess he'd be missing that piece of recovery tonight.

"Yeah, Butch. Don't make fun of the veteran for being tender. You ran him ragged today. He's had fifteen years of the grind. You should expect his body to need some TLC after a practice like that," Ryan said.

Ryan's voice and face were sincere, and it seemed like he was coming from a good place, but John wasn't a charity case. He didn't need the rookie defending him.

And at the end of the day, Ryan was his replacement.

And it felt like the kid was baiting him.

"Like I said. I'm fine," John muttered.

Lenny took a step in front of him. "I don't think you should go quite yet." John couldn't quite hear him over the other conversations in the room. Plus, his attention was focused on Jen and Ryan, and wondering what he said that had her giggling.

Fucking kid.

"You have a lot of demons in your neck and back. I think you could use some more time on the table. We didn't even do your legs yet. If it's too painful, we can go over to the mat and do some alternate stretching, or you can jump in the hot tub to recuperate. I can give the wife a call and ask her to make a house call to you tonight and do some acupuncture. Dottie said that seemed to help last time." Lenny's hopeful and earnest expression did little to settle the insult still simmering from the others' comments.

John wasn't old. It was just a grueling practice. He ground his teeth together.

John's eyes darted back to the board and saw Lenny's column was remarkably light while Jen's column was full almost to the bottom of the board.

He had been a loyal visitor to Lenny's table for fifteen years. But lately...lately his friend had been missing his normal magical touch. John looked over at the other two massage therapists that they had on staff. Both were part-time and not always around when he needed them. He looked back to the board and thought of his teammates that had been waxing poetic about Jen's healing powers. Some swore they had never felt better. A couple even claimed she unknowingly gave Reiki energy cleansings. John didn't know about any of that, but he needed a good massage stat if his body was going to last the season, and short of finding a massage therapist outside of the Spartan organization, his only option was Miss Medina.

He felt heat on his neck and turned his head slightly, catching the lady in question staring at him. Her face flushed before she tucked it back down again, working intently on Ryan's exposed back and shoulders.

Damn, nothing about this was going to be good.

But for the sake of his career, he needed her hands on him.

Everyone would buy that excuse...right?

Lenny clearly needed a push to accelerate the hiring process because shitting where he ate wasn't his MO, but hell if he didn't want to spank her ass for the old age comment. And then spend all night showing her how *not old* he was.

And once again, he found himself thinking of her and not his goddamn career and upcoming game.

Fuck.

CHAPTER NINE

August 30, Monday
Jen

"She misses you," Jen said softly to Kenny as she massaged the tender arch in his foot.

He grunted but otherwise didn't comment.

"Dude. What gives? Why'd you bail? You know she thinks you hung the moon."

Kenny ground his teeth together and looked around the empty room.

"Kenny," Jen pushed.

"Enough, Jen. There's shit you don't know. Okay? Just leave it alone."

She ground her teeth and fought the urge to push Kenny further. Unlike her father, Jen liked to think she learned how to hedge her bets. Because she was getting nowhere with Mr. McCarthy with the current plan of attack, it was time to fold 'em and move on.

Jen finished up his massage work in silence, trying to convince herself that she was doing the right thing by staying quiet.

Something happened between Chloe and Kenny and none of the girls knew what. One day they were tight, and the next they weren't. Rose was still totally in the dark about their affair though, so that was a blessing. The fact that Rose had her own pregnancy and its complications to worry about probably had *a bit* to do with her distraction.

The door to the massage room swung open and the scent of woodsmoke and cedar immediately hit Jen.

She closed her eyes tight. God, she loved that smell.

She didn't even have to look.

"Kenny," John greeted brusquely.

"Cap," Kenny grunted back.

Then they clasped each other's hands and did some testosterone-infused handshake that was utterly ridiculous. Men.

"Jen."

"John," she returned without looking at him.

Why was she breathing so loud? When was the last time she had some fresh gum? Did her breath smell all right?

"Any news on when Lenny will be in?"

"Dude. Don't even bother. Let Jen have a shot at you. She makes Lenny look like an amateur."

Well, that was a nice compliment given that she pissed Kenny off a few minutes ago.

John shifted but otherwise didn't commit.

"He's out today. He said he didn't feel well. The other guys are out today too. It's just me."

John looked around and his face took on a pained expression at the idea of her rubbing him.

"Your neck bothering you again?" Kenny asked in a deep voice.

She knew he had a neck thing he was keeping quiet!

John stiffened. "No. It's fine." The way he clenched his teeth together implied differently.

Not that she was going to say that to him though.

"The hamstring? I saw you rubbing it yesterday after practice. Give Jen a go at it, you'll feel like a new man."

"The hamstring's fine, Kenny."

Kenny's expression turned concerned, or more concerned. "How's your head feeling? You got rocked pretty good last week, and they didn't demand a concussion protocol on you."

"Jesus Christ, Kenny. I said I was fine."

Jen and Kenny stilled at the roar.

Jen peeked up at John, totally surprised at his explosion.

Note to self: never ask John about his suspected injuries.

Kenny inspected him calmly, apparently not overly bothered by the outburst. Then he gently tugged his foot out of Jen's lax grip and swung his legs over and off the table. He landed nimbly on his feet and slipped them into his slides.

"Yeah, fine. You're doing great. Not an injury to be seen. Got it. When you're drooling into your oatmeal, we'll talk," Kenny sniped out. Maybe he was more ticked off than he let on. He gave Jen a quick peck on the cheek and left, letting the door crash loudly behind him.

John's nostrils were wide, and his pupils were dilated as he stood there fuming.

Concern took over. "John?"

Jen moved to take a step toward him, and he retreated a matching step.

John waved her away. "Yeah, sorry about that. I'm fine."

She highly doubted that. Pain made people cranky.

"Want to sit down for a bit and I'll work on something? I have an opening."

John closed his eyes and took a deep breath. He held it for a count of five before releasing it loudly. He looked at her with tired eyes. "I don't think that's a good idea."

Deep breaths Jen, you can handle this.

"John, seriously, I can do my job without jumping you." Frankly, it was a little insulting he thought so little of her self-control.

John sighed again and Jen's fingers itched as she saw the way his right shoulder rose so much higher than the left. The muscles there had to be screaming. Her hands ached to get him under them. After a series of visits, that tension would be so much more manageable.

"Yeah, I don't doubt that. But I don't want to tempt it."

Jen put her hands on her hips. "Excuse me?"

John's eyes darted down to her chest where her low-cut tank exposed a good chunk of cleavage.

She crossed her arms and scowled. "I spilled my shake on my work polo, this was the only thing I had in a pinch. I haven't had time to go raid the extra clothing in the closet."

John's eyes were now on the ceiling and a pained look was on his face. "Yeah, sure, okay. But that doesn't mean this image isn't going to be burned into my retinas forever."

Forever, huh? Well, that was a tingly thought. The man saw his share of cleavage. That he liked hers...well, that was nice.

Jen couldn't stop the small smile.

"Don't," he growled out.

"Don't what?"

"Look so pleased with yourself," he grumbled.

"I'm not," she partially whined. She totally was. Pleased with herself, that was.

Lenny really needed to get on the hiring ball.

John leveled a tired but bemused look on her and she preened. He rolled his eyes back to the ceiling and took another breath. This time through his nose like he was smelling something deeply.

Maybe her? Shivers danced along her skin.

God, she hoped she put on enough deodorant this morning. She couldn't smell herself but who knew if he could.

"Jen?"

"Yeah, John?"

"If you find any extra shirts with numbers on them, do me a favor. Pick a linemen's number."

She threw out a hip in insult. "What? You don't want me to wear your number?"

John's eyes darted down to hers and he held them for a heavy beat.

Whew. She wanted to fan herself. Butterflies erupted *everywhere.*

Her toes curled in her sneakers.

"Miss Medina, if I saw you wearing my number...I don't think there are enough cold showers in the world that could rid me of that vision. Because all I'd be thinking about is you wearing my jersey...and nothing else."

Alarm bells rang. The desire to do something risky and reckless coming back in full force.

"How's your imagination?" she whispered, her breathing labored as she stared up at him.

"Very good," he growled back. "Why?"

She shouldn't be doing this. She shouldn't be doing this.

Alarm bells echoed louder.

Don't do it. Don't do it.

"Because I have your jersey at home. And I've done that exact thing that you're imagining. The rough jersey fabric feels...spectacular."

Oh, God. She was stupid and reckless. She should not have gone there. She only needed to wait a couple more weeks before poking the bear. She knew John was not the type of guy to tease like that.

What was she thinking?

The thrill of doing something risky, something...taboo...was powerful. No wonder her dad was addicted to the sensation.

His chest moved in deep pants as he stared at her with dilated and heavy eyes. She fought the blush and a desire to look away. As if in remembrance of the stiff fabric rubbing against her breasts, her nipples tingled, and Jen fought back another fresh surge of arousal.

God, she wanted nothing more than to wear her ratty jersey for John and have him see just how good it was. Why did he have such a hold on her thoughts? She barely even knew him, for Christ's sake.

Yet...everything she did know, she loved.

Focus on William. Focus on your debt. Focus on everything William has done for you.

John's face darkened further as his eyes dipped to where her very visible arousal was poking out under her tank. His neck moved hard as he swallowed. Absently, he wet his lips and his body moved as if he wanted to approach her. Then a pained expression took hold and he paused.

Before she could ask what was wrong, he was gone, marching from the room without another glance.

Then the massage room door slammed shut for a second time that afternoon.

She couldn't decide if it was for the best that he was trying to respect her wishes about professionalism in the workplace. But really, how much more could she take?

One little fling never hurt anyone, right?

CHAPTER TEN

September 2, Thursday
Jen

It had been a stressful few days since Jen made the stupid decision to flirt with John at work.

Now, whenever they were in the same room, the quarterback escaped so quickly, he left burn marks on the floor.

Not only had she been highly unprofessional, but she directly violated William's trust. He trusted her to let the players focus on the game and not get muddled down in drama. Could anything be more dramatic than a forbidden workplace romance?

It was impatient, stupid, and a shit way to repay the man to whom she owed everything. She needed to do better.

She needed to act like a *fucking* professional. Not like her *fucking* reckless adrenaline junkie father.

God, she was so stupid.

Especially now that John looked sore. Daily. And not just a little sore, but all-over sore. The type of sore that hurts just to breathe.

Some of the players had been whispering about Lenny's performance of late and Jen herself started to notice a vacant look on his face when he was giving massages. With the other massage therapists only working part-time and John's commitment to not sit at her table…it left the man with no great recovery options.

The guy needed a thorough rubbing.

And she knew she could do it and do a damn excellent job of it too.

So what if they were ridiculously attracted to each other?

That didn't matter right now.

His health mattered.

They were coworkers. Surely they could trust themselves enough not to act on any urges or cross any lines.

Well, no more lines. That first one was on her. She'd own that. No more funny business.

They'd keep their hands to themselves. For now.

Metaphorically, that is.

Her hands? Her hands had to be all over him.

Jen suppressed a shiver.

It would be glorious. It would also be torturous. She had never lusted over a client. But the thought of rubbing his thick muscles had her damn near salivating.

Something about the man was just...yum.

Plus, he would surely benefit from any work she did. She hated seeing him in pain. It wasn't affecting the team yet, but he was courting injury. As a professional massage therapist, a Spartans fan, and his co-worker, she couldn't stand back and watch the impending train wreck.

So, she had to find the perfect time to win him over and convince him to give her a chance.

As soon as she found the courage to implement said plan.

He developed one impressive glower whenever she was around. Well, correction, it came out whenever she and Ryan Cole were around together. She didn't get his issue with the guy. Ryan was adorable, young, and impressionable. A bit like a lost puppy. He wasn't quite welcomed by the guys on the team out of their loyalty to Saint John, but he should have been. He was a sweetheart. Obviously, John didn't think so.

John's zingers and one-liners to Ryan and the other more immature players had the rookies mostly falling in line. John's wit was legendary, and Jen secretly admired the delivery and intelligence behind his words. It was a pleasant change from the dopier and more juvenile shit that some of the other players tossed around.

She always felt a thrill zip through her when she caught herself and John engaging in banter as well. There was a certain excitement of needing to be on her toes around him.

The only time John reeled in his heated banter with her was when the coaches or other members of management were in the room. Jen worked on the head coach, Mitchell Underwood, several times now. She also had a standing appointment every few days with the new offensive coordinator, Butch Martinez. Both men were incredibly intense people and confident the team had what it took to be champions, despite it being somewhat of a rebuilding year.

Mitchell reminded her of Creasy, the bodyguard, in *Man on Fire*. He had this presence and severity about him that made her understand why his players went through such pains to impress him. He was the epitome of a disapproving father figure and everyone wanted to prove their worth.

Butch was a harder read. He seemed familiar somehow—like she had seen him before. But he gave no indication of knowing her at all. Though clearly intelligent and polite, he didn't seem to think much of the men and their abilities. He had his favorites and spoke highly of them, but the Eric Roberts-look-alike was an extremely critical person with incredibly elevated expectations for the men. He had an edge about him, a wildness that was hard to contain. He reminded her of her risk-hungry father.

Who had been suspiciously radio silent as of late.

From under a pop-up tent on the training field's sidelines, she watched the men practice. The offensive line stumbled and groaned in the direct sun. They'd been out here for hours, and their legs looked ready to collapse underneath them. John started to have increasingly sloppy throws, while Ryan only looked better and better as the day dragged on.

What was Butch thinking pushing them this hard?

He was risking some serious injuries out there. In the middle of the preseason, no less. The September heat was stifling.

Lenny grumbled under his breath every time he saw something that irritated him. He jotted down memos on his notepad about the various players and what they'd need to focus on later. After a particularly brutal hit on one of the receivers, Lenny ripped his cap off and crumpled it in his hand. He spun towards the athletic trainer tent and stomped over, cursing under his breath the entire way.

Jen could feel the frustration pouring off him.

She took over jotting notes with the two other therapists as they watched the next few series of plays. The players kept looking over at the head coach, hoping and praying for that sharp whistle signifying the end of practice. But Mitchell stayed focused on drills on the other end of the field leaving Butch to his own devices with the current group of victims.

When a player's body was prone a little too long after a particularly nasty hit, Jen started to fret. Enough was enough. She didn't know Butch's motivation but courting potential injuries of his players was not good business. Her head whipped around, looking for Lenny in the hopes that he could stop this madness. She saw him sitting on a bench by the water and misting station, pale as a ghost. She couldn't tell if it was the mist gathering on his face or sweat from the heat. She jogged over.

"Hey, old timer, what's going on?"

His eyes remained unfocused, and his hand was clutching the Spartan emblem emblazoned on his polo. The "Lenny" stitching wrinkled and unreadable with the tightness of his fist.

Jen squatted down in front of him while subtly pulling out her cell phone. They had medical professionals on staff, but a 911 call never hurt anything. It wouldn't hurt any more than a suspected heart attack. She ran through her first aid training while chatting to Lenny, trying to maintain composure as she spoke with him. Jen then pushed to her feet, waved over the nearest person, gave him quiet instructions, and started administering what little first aid she could. Luckily, Lenny was cooperative and agreed something wasn't right.

Which, Jen learned from watching the men on the team, was a miracle in itself. An alpha letting someone help him and agreeing to go to the hospital without putting up a fight?

A true marvel.

The practice came to a screeching halt as word spread.

Probably not the break that the players were hoping for.

At the head of the charge was John, pushing his way through the qualified medical professionals who were trying to monitor Lenny.

As they wheeled Lenny away, the players and coaches mingled and worried. Lenny wasn't looking great and even though they got him on his way to the hospital quickly...time was always precious in these moments. Every second felt like an hour and Jen chastised herself for not shaving off seconds here and there.

Could she have gotten help sooner?

Should she have realized something was bothering him earlier today when he was quieter than usual and kept rubbing at his chest?

His temper was as short as ever, but the light sheen of sweat even when they were inside was unusual. Should she have asked him about it then?

The what-ifs tormented her for the next couple of hours. The players came to the massage room subdued and silent, pointing to their problem areas, getting the work done, and then leaving. Even Ryan didn't do his usual teasing.

John walked in at one point and when he stalled in the door, Jen looked back up to find him looking confused, like he didn't know where he was or how he got here. Deep lines etched in his tired face.

Guess that made sense. Lenny had been working with him for fifteen years. They were more like brothers than co-workers, however distant in age.

Time to hit him when his guard was down.

"Hey, uh...John?" *Oh god, she loved saying his name.* "If you want to wait over on the mats, I can get to you when I'm done with Brandon."

There. An olive branch.

And...shot down.

"Nope. I'm fine. Just checking on everyone." John had dark circles under his eyes and was holding his shoulder at a weird angle.

She wasn't buying it. God, her heart hurt just looking at him.

She met his eyes and held them, swallowing the urge to go up and hug him. She didn't know him well enough for that, no matter how much her heart demanded it.

"If you don't want me to work on you, that's fine. But you really need to get someone to work on you." She took a bracing breath and threw her next challenge out. "You're a leader on this team and you had a physical practice today. Lenny himself made a note in his workbook earlier that he needed to do some deep tissue and myofascial release on you this evening."

John's head jerked.

"And you not doing that is punishing your body all because...well, you know." She trailed off, careful not to say anything more that would cause gossip. Not that the group in the room currently would say anything.

"I'm sorry. Do I look like I'm injured? Am I playing like I'm injured?" His voice lowered at the interpreted insult.

God, he was sensitive about his age and performance.

Big baby. She couldn't help her inner smile at his defensiveness, but she kept it off her face.

At over six feet tall and sporting the longer, leaner muscles of a quarterback and not a lineman, it was no wonder he was so captivating to fans. And she was no exception. She just wanted to snuggle up and burrow into his chest. Something about John felt so...potent. Yet, even as tempting as he was, he still had to be responsible and lead the team, and that meant taking care of his body.

Therefore, he needed to buck up and take her advice even if that meant being uncomfortable for ten minutes.

Almost as if he could tell that she found him endearing despite her frustration with his denial, his cheek muscle twitched under his closely cropped near-black facial hair. The longer scruff was a new look for him. A *good* look. His brown eyes sparked. His temper flared in response to the combination of her perceived insult about his performance and already being on a tightrope, worried about his friend.

Jen swallowed as she saw him prepare for battle. Maybe calling him out right here wasn't her best idea...but even in the face of his temper, the damn thrill of bantering with him had her doubling down just to get her blood pumping. And from the light in his eyes at her challenge, maybe his own blood was readying for their sparring as well. Hell, if he needed the distraction from worrying about his friend, who was currently having open heart surgery, she could help.

"Your players look to you to guide them. If you don't take care of your body when you clearly need to, then you aren't leading by example."

John crossed his arms.

"Don't go worrying about my body, darling." He put a heavy southern drawl on the word *darling*. "I can still perform. I don't need you thinking about my body. I'm a grown man, as I believe you've pointed out before." A flare of hurt showed in his eyes but even so, there was a glint there, an excitement at razzing with her.

His damn age thing again. *Really?*

He continued to glower. "I've been taking care of myself for a while now and will continue to do so for many more years. I don't need you mothering me. Lenny's a good friend. I'm worried about him. He does excellent work. But that doesn't mean I can't do my job without him here." He surveyed everyone else in the room and his eyes shot back to her. John looked like he wanted to say more but hesitated as his eyes flitted back again to the others in the room.

She lowered her voice and took another step closer. "One shot. Just give me a chance to do my job. If it's too uncomfortable, we'll stop, and I'll never push again. But, John, look at yourself. You can't even hide that you're aching as you stand here."

At her comment, he pulled his right shoulder a little straighter and shifted his weight on his legs.

Too late, handsome. I caught you.

Jen jutted out her hip with enough sass to choke an elephant.

"If you let me do my job, I can help." Again, she kept her voice low.

His eyes held no compromise, but she knew she had to try. At the end of the day, this was her job.

"I thought you wanted another ring?" she asked quietly, looking up into his face. Again, she noticed his ridiculously sexy lashes.

He took a breath big enough to expand his whole chest. Hopefully, the result wouldn't be him roaring at her for pushing too hard and questioning his judgment. She decided to interrupt before he could say...or shout...anything.

"Just let me do my job, ok? Give me a chance?" Holding his eyes with her own, she felt flurries form in her stomach. They only started to flutter harder when she saw his own hands clench in awareness.

His eyebrows twitched in doubt, and he looked once more around the room. "I'll think about it."

And without further ado, John turned and left.

CHAPTER ELEVEN

September 2, Thursday
Jen

Jen stayed until the last therapist finished that night. She worked on her last player over an hour ago, but she'd been staying late every night with Lenny anyway. As she walked through the dark and eerie parking lot, she tried to brainstorm ways to win over John. As a therapist, she knew his performance would improve after she got her hands on him.

She was *that* good.

And getting her hands on him would be pretty...exhilarating. All those long, thick, experienced muscles...

The ringing of her phone echoed in the silence of the parking lot. She didn't want to take the call, preferring to strategize her next move with John, but it could be her dad with an emergency.

Even more reason not to take it.

Instead, Jen put it on speaker, loaded her things into the old car, and willed it to start by sheer faith. She wasn't even able to say hello before Lexie's haughty voice whipped through the phone speakers.

"I just read there was another robbery in your apartment building."

"God, Lex. Who let you onto the neighborhood watch boards?" Jen flipped her blinker and turned out of the parking lot and onto a quiet Springfield back street.

Lexie sniffed. "Well, Janine said–"

"Who the hell is Janine?"

"Will you just listen?" After a pause. "As I was saying…Janine said she heard them this time. They were in the apartment right next to her. She heard them speaking Spanish."

"Everyone speaks Spanish here. Again, who is Janine?"

"From 4B. You know Janine. Her husband, Marty, just retired from Hatfield Handlers."

"No, Lex. I do not know Janine."

"They had the parakeet that died last year."

"Still don't know them, Lex."

"Of course you do."

"Oh, the parakeet lady?" At Lexie's excited intake of breath, Jen sighed. "No, Lexie Lou, I don't know them. I don't know most of my neighbors." Mickey and Benji down the hall were pretty much the exception.

She heard her friend sniff again. "Well…you should. Maybe you'll meet a handsome architect who will sweep you off your feet and give me nieces and nephews before I'm gray."

Jen rolled her eyes. "One, you've seen my apartment building, architects don't live there." Jen heard Lexie's dismissive grunt. "And two, don't joke about my biological clock."

Lexie repeated her words back to her. "One, I've asked you multiple times to move in with me where it's safe. And two, my building does have architects."

"Architects-smarchitects."

Who needed an architect when she had a hunky quarterback with hypnotic eyes, thick hair, sexy beard, sexier muscles, and cutting wit?

Jen let Lexie rant about her latest drama and Jen parked her car in a dark spot fifty feet away from her building.

Not a bad walk, though she wished it was better lit.

Lexie's voice still rambled in the background as Jen took a minute to survey the building. It was in a good area, but the building itself, and its management, just weren't so great.

It used to be pretty, once upon a time, but New England winters and lack of upkeep had been hard on it. The classic brick needed some TLC and some of the windows, boarded up with plywood, had been generously spray painted by the more artfully inclined.

Jen heard a pause hit the air and jumped in, not knowing when Lexie's next breath would be. "Got to go, Lex. I'll call you tomorrow?" They said their goodbyes and disconnected.

As she dragged her sore feet up the sidewalk to her apartment building, she heaved open the sticky front door. Jen held her keys protectively, sticking out from between her knuckles with her phone clutched in her other hand. Jen wasn't usually this paranoid about entering her building at night, but it was later than usual and a lot of unknown cars dotted the road. Add to that the loud music and the scattering of alcohol cans and bottles on the front walk, Jen decided to be a little more cautious than usual.

As she walked between the clusters of people lounging in the hall, she gave no-nonsense nods of hello but made sure not to make eye contact and not to slow down. She prided herself on being a tough cookie, as her dad always said, but she lived alone, and she had common sense.

Even if it didn't come out around a certain football player.

A couple of men tried to stop her progress with various comments, but she kept winding through the halls and up the stairs.

Don't slow the pace.

Appear on a mission.

Fake a phone call.

She also had her Krav Maga training to fall back on in case someone got physical, but it wasn't like she was bullet or knife proof. She ground her teeth as the comments got louder and more colorful. More and more male laughter joined in. A small bead of sweat trickled down her temple. Just as she was about to get to her door, she had a change of heart and continued two more doors down.

She thumped on the door and called out, "Honey, I'm home. Let me in, I forgot my keys." She kept kicking the door on the kickplate in a bored manner. She looked back at the men who had followed her down the hall and rolled her eyes as if inviting them to join in on the joke.

A giant bald, Black man ripped open the door and one of her admirers let out a low whistle. The hulking figure loomed in the doorway, scowling down at the group behind her as they dispersed.

His nose scrunched and he stared at her. Menace oozed off him as he eyeballed the remaining men in the hall.

"Hi," she chirped at him and squeezed past him into his apartment. She heard the door snap shut behind her.

"Honey, you look wrecked. Come over here and join me. Boo Boo was just doing my nails." A flamboyantly gay white man sat on the purple velour couch in the living room. He had a white mud mask coating his face, his pink terry robe tied tight in the middle, and his feet propped up on a deep purple ottoman. His hair tonight was bright bleach yellow which reminded Jen of a dandelion. "Boo Boo, can you get Jen a mask as well? She looks terrible."

"Hey!" Jen defended herself.

She didn't look *that* bad.

"I'm here for the hard truths, sweetie. Trust in the love." Mickey took a delicate sip of his martini and smacked his lips before flashing his blue eyes over to her. "What happened, love bug? You look beat."

A martini appeared in front of her. As well as a plate of cheese and crackers. She mumbled a quiet thanks to Benji as he lumbered back into the kitchen, a dish rag thrown over his impressive shoulders.

She sighed wistfully at his attractive figure.

If only he was straight.

Jen shook her head as she reminded herself that she didn't need a man adding to the chaos of her life. They just let you down when you needed them most.

Jen explained her day and the shitshow that work had become. First with John, then with Lenny. Then she wallowed about her age—finally letting John's ageism fears start to affect her as well. She was thirty-two and the years were slipping by. Not only for creating a career that she loved but also on the biological side.

She was fine with not having a man, but as Lexie so lovingly pointed out earlier that night, Jen wasn't getting any younger. And it's not like she could meet any guys at work. The whole co-worker thing was a no-no on so many levels. Otherwise, she would have cornered John long before now.

To top it off, now here she was, hiding out, after having her second close call this week with her less-than-reputable neighbors.

She needed to find a new place before a close call became...not close.

She sighed and sank deeper into the deluxe couch. If she could have sunk through the floor, she would have. That's how much weight sat on her shoulders.

"Ahh, honey, put your feet up. Boo Boo will give you a pedicure while you relax. And while you relax, you can regale me with all the tasty morsels of gossip you pick up on a daily basis from those beefcakes you get to stroke all day long." Mickey sighed, his hand draped over his forehead, not quite touching it, or it would ruin the mask.

"I'm right here," Benji reminded him as he came back over and knelt at her feet.

"Big man, I couldn't not see you if I tried." Benji winked with a savage lustiness that had Jen choking on her sip.

"Jeeze, you need me to leave?" she choked out between coughs.

"No, honey bunches, we got all night after Boo Boo walks you back through those degenerates to your apartment." He picked his head off the back of the couch and looked at her crossly. "Speaking of which, you friggin' call us when you get home, and the building looks sketchy. We've talked about this, missy."

"Don't get your panties in a bunch. I know," she dragged out. "I forgot and had a lot on my mind."

"Like I'm wearing panties." He stuck his nose back in the air, rested his head back, and closed his eyes. Jen's eyes darted to his ridiculously short robe which had ridden up on his perfectly tanned, toned, and smooth thighs. She darted her eyes away as soon as she realized what she was doing.

She caught Benji's gaze and felt her cheeks approach sun-levels of heat. She took a healthy gulp of her drink and looked away as his broad cheeks widened into a blinding smile.

After a few minutes of chitchat and Mickey's ridiculousness, blue lights started to flash through the windows and dance across the back walls of the apartment. As Benji massaged her feet and she shared stories about the drama at work, they heard the noise and thump of the music die down. The raucous laughter faded away and they heard the breaking of glass through the cracks in the open windows. Among the night sounds of the city were the signature horns honking, dogs barking, people yelling, and occasional bouts of shouted expletives.

Ah, the city.

Jen loved it.

Just not this part of it.

She wanted to be on the outskirts. Maybe have a house with a yard. Room for kids and a dog. A patio for her husband to grill hotdogs on the Fourth of July.

Was that too much to ask?

She was thirty-two and it was about time to start living her dream before she was too old to really enjoy it.

Gah! She sounded like the media talking about John.

Maybe he was on to something...

No.

John was totally being overly sensitive about discussions concerning his age. She didn't need to fall prey to his complex as well.

Technology and healthcare had come a long way. She didn't need to focus on the biological clock ticking in her ear.

Or her paused business.

Or how everyone she went to high school with seemed settled in their lives...yet here she was, doing a job that was...fine but not furthering her dream at all.

She felt every bit of her single status.

Ugh!

As she regaled her friends with the drama of her life and the frustrations that a certain quarterback caused her, they hummed and gasped at the appropriate spots and let her rant. When she stopped talking, she not only had freshly painted toes, but her nails matched, and her face was basking in a homemade mask. Benji massaged her scalp and let her wild mane of hair free from its stern bun she wore every day.

"I swear, how you don't have a migraine every second of every day baffles me," Benji murmured as he wove his fingers into her hair, being cautious of the parts that were stiff with hair spray.

"Years of practice." She sighed and closed her eyes. "I learned if I don't control it in the morning, it only gets wilder. At this point, I should be sponsored by hair spray companies."

"Girl, if I had hair like yours, I'd be letting it flow free all day. With your coloring and those blonde highlights, add some sparkle, sequins, and some stilettos and I'd be working the stage every damn night. Gosh, what I wouldn't give to have you with me on burlesque night when I sing 'Proud Mary'. We'd make thousands. Those toned thighs could crack walnuts." Mickey reached over and slapped her muscular thighs with a firm hand.

She chuckled and relaxed deeper into the head massage.

"I think I know the problem," Mickey declared after the small lull in the conversation. Like Lexie, Mickey wasn't comfortable with silence.

"Sock it to me, big boy," Jen encouraged but otherwise didn't move a muscle. She was too busy basking in the pampering.

She needed to find a man who would pamper her like Benji.

"You need to fuck Saint John," Mickey said, going for broke.

She shot up so fast that Benji's hands ripped out several significant chunks of hair. She whipped around to face Mickey.

"Say what now?"

Her hands moved up to massage her wounded scalp, feeling for bald patches.

"You. Need. To. Do. Him." He clipped each word with a hand flail. Like what he said wasn't a complete ethical violation not only to the Spartans, William, and her career if it ever got out. "Ride him. Take him to the pony show. Give him a tease and tickle. Light his fire. Rev his engine." He peered down his nose at her. "Do I need to go on?"

She gritted her teeth and thought of how sad Benji would be if she killed Mickey.

"How," she ground out, "would that be repaying William for all his kindness over the years?"

God, what was Mickey thinking?

She would be risking her job, her reputation, and her relationship with William. Her entire future. What was wrong with her that she couldn't just be patient and wait till the end of her time with the Spartans? Was she really so like her father that she couldn't handle the slightest delayed gratification for the sake of repaying a debt?

She looked to Benji for backup.

"Sorry, love. I think he's right. You guys have too much tension. Too much passion. Got to take the edge off if you want to be able to focus going forward," Benji said.

Her jaw dropped.

"How can you say that? You know everything that would be at stake if word got out," she shrieked again. She looked around for the martini glasses and tallied the empty drinks. They hadn't drank *that* much.

"I'm being serious. Give him a special happy ending massage. Help him with all his tension and raw, masculine sexuality," Mickey purred and winked salaciously. "Remind him to leave a tip."

"Dios mío. You've gotto be joking." She stood up and stalked towards the windows and back again. "One, that's a huge violation of the code of conduct. Not only one that I imposed on myself when I became licensed, but a breach of my duty as a Spartan employee as well. It's highly unprofessional. If it got out, I'd never work again. Can you imagine how upset William would be with me?"

"If William didn't disown Lexie after her time in Panama, then I hardly think he'd freeze you out for having a consensual adult relationship with one of the players. Plus, the guy loves love, he'd hardly crucify you."

"Love is one thing. Going at it like rabbits with one night left to live is an entirely different beast!"

"Notice how she didn't say she wouldn't ride him like Seabiscuit if given the chance though," Benji mumbled to Mickey while taking her spot on the couch.

Her jaw, once again, dropped. "Duh, he's a freaking god. I'd be all over that in another life. But if we were ever discovered, I'd be ruined." Mickey and Benji shared a knowing look and looked back at her with raised brows. She waved them away. "The risks would be too great." She took a deep breath and let it out. "Plus, it's not like he's a forever kind of guy that would make it worth the risk."

"But would the risk be worth the orgasms?" The guys giggled and exchanged a quick kiss.

"Guys. Come on."

"Doll, I'm being serious. Figure out a way to work off the tension between you two and make it work. And obviously, my vote is sex. It's incredibly powerful." Mickey shot forward and whipped around to face Benji. "Oh my god! What if she got pregnant and had John's love child?" He squealed and clapped his hands. "I call godfather! My lord, that child would be gorgeous. It'd be like if J-LO and John Krasinski had a baby." He stared off into the distance, his eyes big and excited. "Boo, can you see it?"

Benji rubbed Mickey's back and hummed in agreement, also staring at the opposite wall, lost in thought.

"Guys!" Jen stomped her foot.

They both looked back at her and gave her the same beleaguered expression.

"Fine. Don't. It was just a suggestion." Mickey shrugged his shoulders without a care in the world and sat back into the curve of Benji's ridiculously muscled and shirtless chest. His tattoos were hard to see with his dark skin, but if you knew where to look, you could see the various nods to his favorite things in life. Over his heart was Mickey's name. On one arm was 'Mom and Dad,' and on his other arm was a tribal tat that wound its way up to his shoulder. Up his torso was his last name. Benji also had a wilder side in college and spent a lot of time in the clubs. So, he also had some UV tattoos hidden all over as well.

He made sure to avoid black lights at all costs now.

Jen would kill to see him lit up in a club.

But she wasn't holding her breath.

As a schoolteacher and happily married man, Benji wasn't trolling the clubs anymore. And with Mickey being a hairdresser, they had limited income, so they weren't blowing their hard-earned money on cover charges or alcohol. Not when they were saving up for an adoption and a better place.

This place really would suck without Mickey and Benji around, but it wouldn't be my first pick to raise a baby either.

She really needed to get a new apartment as well because, when they finally moved out, she would be alone.

Some of those late-night walks might make her a little more nervous.

Lexie offered her a room a number of times. She hated that Jen lived in this apartment building. But as much as she adored Lexie, the chick had a one-bedroom loft and lived a completely different lifestyle. They were best as besties, not roomies.

Her other friends offered as well but they all had their own dramas and lives. Relying on them felt too...intrusive. Jen grew up feeling like a burden, she didn't want to be that way now as an adult.

She shook her head. She didn't have to decide right now at least. It wasn't like she had the money to move anyway—not with her dad's latest gambling action. So, she'd make it work. Like always.

It just might take a minute.

God, she was so tired of just making things work. For once, she wanted to have it all figured out.

In another life, I guess.

Chapter Twelve

September 8, Wednesday
John

John gave two brusque knocks on the hospital room door and waited for an answer. He heard a grouchy 'come in' and pushed the door open.

Lenny's long frame made the bed seem small. He sported button-down flannel pajamas and a homemade quilt, that no doubt his wife brought from home.

He had small reading glasses perched on his patrician nose and a book resting on his lap. He smiled as John approached.

"Johnny, my boy, good to see you."

John clasped him on the shoulder and gave him a little shake. "You scared us old-timer."

Lenny smiled. "Well, it's good for your heart to get a little workout now and then. They don't work you boys hard enough at practice." Lenny reached up and patted John's hand.

Lenny's sharp gaze trailed down John's body and zeroed in on the way John's shoulder was hanging. When Lenny opened his mouth to chastise him, John cut him off by saying, "I know, I know. I'm heading over to the stadium in a little bit to get worked on." His performance was seriously suffering; he needed work done. Stat.

In fact, in the few days since Jen's offer, he'd barely been able to think of anything else. And it wasn't the massage part that he couldn't get off his mind. His cock got rock hard every time he thought of her oiled-up hands on his body. He'd watched way too much massage porn in the last month—there was no way he'd be able to hide his arousal, so he'd been avoiding her.

But John's body hurt too much, and he was tired of fighting it, so he'd give it a shot. Maybe it would suck, or she'd have bad breath, and he wouldn't be tempted anymore.

Jen's breath was always so minty and delicious though.

Hell, it would be glorious.

Her warm, strong hands gliding all over him in hot, long, strokes...

John shifted his thoughts before he grew hard again.

He turned and pulled up a chair so he could sit at Lenny's bedside.

"How's the ticker doing?" John's eyes darted down to the dressing peeking out from underneath his shirt.

Lenny waved nonchalantly at his chest. "It's fine. I'm fine. It will take more than open-heart surgery to stop me—"

His wife, Dottie, thrust open the door while saying, "No, dear. It won't. At least for now." Her tone brooked no argument. Her arms were full of veggies, sandwiches, fruit cups, and a delicious-smelling soup.

John jumped up and took some items from her overburdened arms. "Let me." He set the items on the table in the corner of the room and turned to face her head-on. "Dottie."

Dottie rushed into his arms and gave him a big squeeze. John wrapped her tight and rested his chin on her much shorter head. He took a deep, heaving breath and when he opened his eyes, he met Lenny's over Dottie's head.

Lenny nodded with sad eyes, communicating that yeah, Dottie had taken this whole scare pretty hard.

Dottie pulled away and rubbed her hands down the front of her blouse and slacks straightening the nonexistent wrinkles. She cleared her throat softly and turned around to Lenny. "I spoke with the doctors, and they said you were being difficult and not eating. Therefore, I'm here with goodies to solve that." She stared her husband down and gestured to the items on the table. "So, you're going to eat until I tell you to stop." She looked towards John. "Mr. Costner knows heart surgery will indeed stop you for a bit. You will be coming home and not visiting the stadium for the foreseeable future." She wrinkled her nose delicately and raised it a smidgen. "That place isn't good for your stress levels right now." She shifted her feet in a way that dared Lenny to contradict her.

Only an idiot would. Dot was a catch.

She was also a firecracker.

Similar to another determined beauty that John knew.

Lenny put out his weakest smile and agreed, "Yes, dear," before pulling his glasses off his nose and placing them on the side table.

Dottie's shoulders lowered. She must have been expecting more of a fight from him. She turned to the table to get some food ready.

"How's the team then, my boy?" Lenny asked him once he had a steaming bowl of clam chowder in front of him.

Was that even on the approved foods list after surgery? John knew better than to ask.

Lenny acted like it had been months rather than a handful of days since last being at the stadium with everyone.

Lenny scooped up a big dollop and blew on it slightly to cool it down.

The smell wafted towards John. God. How long had it been since John had a bowl himself? He made a mental note to grab some on his way home tonight.

"It's been a mixed bag. Everyone was worried about you but got back on task the next day." Lenny cut him a look with his spoon paused halfway to his mouth. A small drip plopped back into his paper bowl. "It took me a little longer," John conceded. He stole a celery stick from the tray when Dottie turned her back to them. Lenny and John shared a smile before John continued. "Gonna miss you as my wingman at charity events and airplane rides though while you recover." He gave Lenny a rough pat. "This week's been good though. The guys have been performing well. But I realized the other day, I don't think I've ever seen this many injuries in the opening half of the season." John snagged a couple of mini carrots and crunched away, smiling when Dottie tried smacking his hand away from the food. He thought back on the week. "It almost feels like we have more injuries than we have in the past several seasons *combined*. Have you noticed that?" he trailed off, combing through his mental archives of past seasons.

Lenny's gaze sharpened as he sat straighter.

Those were *his* boys John was talking about. Lenny's kids.

Lenny reached for his notepad next to the bed and pulled the pen out of the spiral. "What type of injuries and who?"

John shrugged. "Pulled hamstrings, sprained or broken fingers, couple of bruised ribs, torn bicep, one ruptured Achilles, a few quad injuries. Those sorts of things." As John gave him a breakdown, Lenny started scribbling and mumbling to himself, pen flying across the page. Lenny added more notes and dialogue as they went through the list, filling in the gaps John missed.

Dottie tried to interrupt Lenny's musings to get him to continue eating but he waved her away, focused solely on the list in his hands. Dot shot John a chastising look. John winced at his misstep of distracting Lenny from eating and shot her an apologetic look.

When Lenny finally stopped writing, he picked up the paper and held it a foot away from his eyes, pulling it in and out, trying to find the right distance so he could read it. His wife sighed as if she carried the weight of the world on her shoulders being married to Lenny. She walked over to the table and handed him the glasses that he had just taken off. Without looking, he took them from her. He muttered a quiet, "thanks, dear," and put them back on. He scribbled a few more lines, and then looked up at John.

"I'm assuming that Gabe Garcia is one of them."

John blinked.

Yes, he was.

"And I'm also assuming that Michael, Liam, and Tyler are also among the injured."

John's chin dipped and he raised his eyebrows.

How did Lenny know? Those men only got hurt this week.

Lenny nodded to himself, and then back down to his pad of paper. He scribbled a couple more notes and looked up at John. He then darted a look at his wife and said, "Excuse my French, dear."

He looked back at John, his bald head glinting in the hospital lights.

"Butch needs to get his head out of his ass."

John's head jerked.

"What?"

"Head. Out. Of. His. Ass." Lenny enunciated. "Do you notice that a lot of these boys are rookie players?"

John nodded. Not knowing where Lenny was going with this.

"These men have not adapted to the difference between professional football and college football. Yes, they're similar, but there *is* a difference once you're in the big leagues. And you and Butch are driving them too hard. These kids look up to you. Your expectations for their performance, and your opinions, matter. Tell them that they need to prioritize their health, or they'll ruin themselves and not have careers at all."

"Excuse me?" John blustered, his chocolate chip cookie that he just grabbed, now forgotten in his hand.

"You heard me, boy. You and Butch are running the boys too hard. The only ones brave enough to push back against him, or you, are the veterans who aren't afraid of you and a couple of rookies. I haven't decided if they're too dumb or too ballsy to be afraid." Lenny looked down at the paper. "Or in Ryan's case, too smart."

John's eyebrows drew together.

What did he mean by that?

Lenny looked back up. "Cut the crap. Your new coordinator is running the boys ragged. They need their recovery. Jen's good. But they need the time to see her. She's studied a lot of different techniques and has a background that gives her a unique perspective.

More so than the other two fellas in the department. They're good at their jobs, but Jen has a different touch."

"It's her touch that I'm worried about," John mumbled to his cookie.

What was he, a child?

Lenny laughed. "Just go see her already and get some work done. I trust her to take care of you. And I trust you to not do something stupid to your career or hers."

Truth time. Maybe Lenny could offer some advice.

Hell, here he was, almost forty and asking for girl advice.

"I don't know, Len. It's tough to be around her. There's this weird awareness there and having a massage by her seems too...intimate. Even with other guys in the room and being dressed." He rolled his lips and looked back at Lenny's sympathetic expression. "It's just...tense. I don't need distractions this year. Not if we're going to bring home a ring."

Lenny looked disappointed. "You've been hanging out with Butch a little too much if work is really all you can think about." A hint of a sneer crossed his face. "It's not all about the fucking ring." Lenny shook his head. "Use your head, boy. There's so much more to life." Lenny cut John a look. "Which you'd know if you ever made room for anything else."

John's head gave a jerk.

What the hell did Lenny want him to do? Sleep with her or not?

John tried harder to focus his thoughts, maybe he was missing Lenny's point? He had been having small moments of confusion lately—it wouldn't be that surprising to realize he missed the point.

Maybe he was getting old.

The beginnings of a headache formed as he tried to figure out what the hell Lenny wanted him to do.

All the while, Lenny practiced his wise sage look while eating quietly, giving John space to work through the riddle he left him with. Lenny spooned up another heaping dollop of clam chowder and brought it to his lips. Some white dribble landed on his chin and cast a bright contrast to his black and grey peppered beard.

John rolled his eyes before biting a chunk out of his cookie.

The guy was on a lot of pain meds, his wires clearly crossed, because none of what he said made sense. In one breath, he said to keep it professional with Jen, then three seconds later implied that John was too focused on his career and should stop to smell the coconut and lime-scented roses.

God, she smelled good.

John looked out the windows at the city and thought about his life. Football brought him to Springfield. He grew up on a small farm in Kentucky. His dad worked for a horse rehabilitation program there. Saving as many defunct racehorses as possible so they wouldn't all go to slaughter. His mom was the receptionist at the local high school. John didn't have much growing up, but they gave him everything they could manage. When he started needing more and more resources to play football, things started getting tight. They most likely never wanted to have a conversation about money with a hormonal teenager. But he promised them that if they found him the money, it wouldn't be for nothing.

He would make it all the way...for them. For their sacrifices.

He remembered it clearly: their life changing argument when he was a teenager.

"Son, we just don't have the money to send you to that camp. I'm sorry." His father's voice sounded so inflexible in his memories. Sports were not worth the sacrifice. How many players went pro? Not many.

John had looked at his mom, knowing she would cave first. "Mom, please. I'm good at this. Plus, all my friends are going." Her eyes had only narrowed.

Wrong tactic.

Abort.

He had switched back to his earlier strategy. "Coach said I might be able to play college ball when I'm older. I know I'm small now, but Dad was small when he was my age too. Coach said I have a mind for the game. If I can go to this camp, I can learn from some of the best professional athletes out there. You've seen me play, I do way better than all the other guys out there. I can do this. Did I tell you that there will be college scouts and coaches there? I can get in front of people I normally wouldn't see during the regular season. Plus, if I impress them and get on their radar, maybe I can get some college scholarships when I graduate." He gave them his biggest eyes from across the beaten and scratched dinner table that was big enough to seat four. There were only ever three of them though. His mom had a miscarriage a few years after John was born and to his knowledge, they never tried again.

"Buddy, we want you to go. We just can't afford it." His dad's pink cheeks gave him a twinge of guilt for pushing this, but he knew he could earn them their money back. And then some.

He knew it.

He felt the wet gather at the bottom of his eyes, and he grit his teeth to prevent more from gathering.

His mom pursed her lips, her knuckles bright white with how hard she was squeezing her hands.

"John, I have no doubt you could do well for yourself. It's not your talent that is in question." His dad softened his voice. "But football is a short-term goal. The chances of continuing to play after college are slim. And playing for an extended period after that is even slimmer. Heck, most quarterbacks are put on the shelf by the time they hit forty. Their bodies beat up from the grind. We don't want that for you. We want you to have a stable job. A job where you can settle in for the long haul. A job that, when you're forty, you're not getting the boot because your body has failed you. It's just a game." His dad's deep-set eyes were inflexible and unforgiving as he explained his rationale.

However, his mom's heart flashed in her eyes as she begged John to understand.

But John didn't. He kept at them. Ripping at their heartstrings with every plea. Every beg. Every negotiation attempt. When the conversation came to a heated close, John stormed out of the house, saddled up his mare, and rode the rest of the afternoon away, trying to rid himself of all his emotions.

By the time John got home that night, his mom had supper going and his dad was watching a game on the television. They called him down for dinner and, as they sat there, John felt shame as he looked into his mother's red-rimmed eyes. She forced falsely cheerful small talk while she spooned mashed potatoes and gravy onto her plate.

John wanted to apologize but just couldn't form the words. His temper had gotten the better of him. Again. And he hurt his mom. Again. That happened more and more often lately.

The next day, he picked her a bouquet of wildflowers as he walked home from school.

Only he didn't hand them to her like he thought he would.

He arrived home to his parents sitting at the kitchen table, talking in low voices to each other. They sat him down and broke the news that they worked something out and he could go to the camp.

John tossed the flowers across the kitchen as he leaped over the table to hug them.

He learned later that they contacted the retirement company to liquidate his mom's retirement and went to the bank to take out a loan, using their home as collateral.

They did everything in their power to help him achieve his dream. If that meant having no retirement, then so be it.

John made sure his first year's salary paid off all their debt and set them up for a wonderful retirement. His dad grumbled and bitched throughout all of it because he was a cantankerous and moody SOB that didn't like his bills paid for with money that came from "playing a game."

John also started a foundation in his hometown to provide opportunities for low-income kids to attend camps of their choosing. The director of the program was a high-school teammate that never left their hometown, and the guy did remarkable things for the program.

John would never forget the sacrifice, and risk, that his parents made for him. And not just because his father would never let him forget it.

The trust and faith they displayed were character-shaping.

To this day, he still appreciated what they risked trying to help him be happy with no guarantee he would play in college or beyond. If he failed, so much more than his athletic career would've been on the line. Yet, they did it anyway.

And professional football could indeed be a terrible and unpredictable mistress.

He'd gotten lucky so far. Still, he'd be fortunate to not have any career-ending hits. He needed to finish two more seasons. Then maybe he could try to have a personal life. But he learned the hard way, years ago, that a professional football life and a personal life didn't mix. Oil and water. The time spent on one was time away from the other. One thing always suffered. His team, his coaches, and his *fans* didn't deserve that distraction.

By the bed, Dottie chastised Lenny for trying to sneak another cookie out of the bag and John was wrenched from his reflection.

He owed a lot of his success to Lenny, and not just for the bodywork. Lenny became his stand-in dad those first few years when his own was too many miles away to smack John upside the head whenever John made foolish decisions.

He stole another carrot stick from Lenny's plate and conceded reluctantly. "I'll talk with the guys—make sure we're all on the same page about expectations. Including Butch. And as for Jen...we'll see."

Lenny looked towards his wife, and they shared an unreadable look that had John stiffening, but Lenny went back to his food before John could dig in further. Whatever the look was, it set him on edge.

CHAPTER THIRTEEN

September 10, Saturday
John

Two days later, John headed to the stadium on a free day to put in some hours. He exercised, connected with his teammates, and planned to study some film after a quick massage.

When he entered the massage therapy room, he saw Jen leaning over her sparkly pink phone typing out a freaking thesis, her ridiculously big golden hoop earrings were damn near resting on her shoulders.

Her nails looked different from the other day. Today, they were a deep maroon and navy blue that matched the team colors.

Adorable.

Everything about her was over-the-top.

He couldn't stop his small smile. She couldn't be further in personality from his reserved nature. Why he felt so drawn to her was anyone's guess. He wouldn't have to wait much longer to find out though. Lenny and management were sure to be filling her position shortly, especially now that Lenny was on the shelf. After she was off the clock...their fun could begin. He just had to practice patience.

Usually that was easy for him.

You didn't become a future Hall of Fame quarterback by rushing your plays.

John walked over to one of the other therapists and muttered. "Hey, when do you think you're going to have your next opening?"

He heard a thunk as Jen slammed her phone on the desk next to her.

The therapist looked sheepish and shrugged, looking back at the board and then at the clock above it. "I don't know. Maybe around 6:30?"

That was a few hours away.

John nodded and then repeated the question to the other therapist. "What about you?"

The therapist checked the board and clock, and then looked at John with an apology already written on his face. "Yeah, I'll probably be closer to seven. I have a lot of guys with injuries on my list tonight."

John scowled and the therapist took a small step back.

Jesus, what a wuss. It wasn't like John was going to punch the guy for not giving him priority treatment.

Whatever, no loss there. The guy massaged like a wimp.

Maybe he could find a massage clinic that took walk-ins on the DL?

He heard heavy footsteps coming towards him and let out a deep breath trying to think of a way out of his current situation but coming up empty. There was no way Miss Medina wasn't going to push the issue and tempt fate. He would have thought she'd be trying equally hard to avoid him until her time with the team ended. Clearly, the woman had a prideful streak...or was a closet masochist.

He luckily missed her a couple of days ago when he got back from visiting Lenny. He was surprised by the mix of relief and disappointment that flooded his system at the time.

"John," her smooth, melodic voice said. "Can I help you?"

In many ways...but not in a room full of teammates and co-workers.

John took a breath, held it, and let it go as he turned around to face her. Her arms crossed over her chest, and she stuck out her jaw in a way that screamed, 'Let me do my job.'

"Nope, all set," he said as he inspected her perfectly scrunched nose.

She worked her jaw for a second and then used her hands to encompass the room. "As you can see, these two guys are busy with full lists this afternoon, but you know what? My list is looking remarkably light. If you're here for a massage, I do believe I have some time to fit you in." She took her dainty index finger and rested it under her plump lower lip.

He wanted to bite it.

Shit.

"Nope. All set."

She visibly ground her teeth together. His little firecracker lighting up to fight. He felt his gut clench—he liked her fired up entirely too much.

He absently wondered if that wasn't part of why he refused to let her rub him. He could see how frustrated and tight she got; he could almost taste the tension they were eventually going to be able to work off in the most delicious way.

He tightened further at the thought of how soon that would be.

"Dude." Jen's head cocked as she gave him a beleaguered look.

"Jen," he said in return, partially hoping she'd get just how terrible of an idea this was and partially hoping she'd push the issue and keep building this tension between them.

The feeling growing in his chest felt similar to the season they went 17-0. The tension and electricity leading up to the playoffs and Super Bowl…it felt like that with Jen. Foreplay to their future date. Or dates…

She stomped her foot and waved towards the table. "Will you just get on the damn table? You can even keep your freaking shirt on if you're so shy."

The fire burned in her eyes, and he felt his blood start to sing in response.

God, he wanted to fuck her.

Instead, he scraped a hand over his face and took a heaving breath to let out a thread of the building tension. The breath shifted his shoulder resulting in an electric pinch in his neck and arm. Somehow it even activated a pinch point in his upper back as well.

Fuck that hurt.

He let out a hiss and looked around. Well, if he kept his shirt on and there were other people in the room, they could probably behave.

Probably.

"Fine," he said in a grumpy growl he hoped conveyed just how much he disagreed with her assumption they would be fine with her hands all over him. But damn, he really needed that trigger point worked on ASAP.

He slowly walked to the table and hopped up, careful not to show any sign of the limp he was hoping would go away soon. The look in her eye as she watched him made him think maybe she knew about it anyways.

Jen walked up behind him and started using her fingers to push at his flesh over his shirt.

It was assessing and fast, her fingers pushing and dancing down his back and arms.

That wasn't so bad. He could do this.

He answered her quiet questions as efficiently as possible, choosing to keep his mind focused on his breathing and anything other than her warm hands and soft, minty breath.

As she moved around to stand in front of him though, he lost count of where he was in his breathing. He watched her intense focus as her hands worked on a tender spot on his right shoulder and trap. Her long lashes fluttered, and she had a slight frown on her perpetually happy face.

It didn't suit her. Her lips shouldn't ever frown; they were laugh-out-loud lips. Lips for smiling, joking, and laughing. Lips for kissing and...

John felt his brows lower, and his eyes get heavy as he stared at the juicy lips in question.

The longer he stared, the more he realized Jen's cheeks developed a gorgeous flush to them. John felt his chest swell at the thought that maybe she wasn't quite as indifferent and professional as she was trying to make it seem.

His Cinderella was suffering from their avoidance dance as much as he was.

John let out a tight breath. He shouldn't have been relieved that she was struggling as well...but he was.

Jen's pretty eyes floated up to lock with his and they widened slightly when she saw him already watching her. Her blush deepened and she hurriedly looked back to his shoulder and arm as her hands worked on the muscle there.

She shifted slightly and somehow her unique smell drifted up to him. John shut his eyes and inhaled deeply.

Coconut and lime.

Glorious.

Jen moved again and this time his forearm brushed her breast. His brain short-circuited. John felt the familiar stirring in his dick and nearly groaned.

Fuck.

He opened his eyes, ready to tell her that he was done, but paused. Jen's eyes darted up to his and she rolled her lips as she looked at him, her hands still rubbing him and finding every single tender spot in his arm muscles.

As their eyes locked, he felt his heart skip before starting a hard, hammering beat. He wanted to shift his arm just to get another graze of her breast.

Speaking of which...his eyes looked down and saw the peak of a nipple through her shirt.

Ah hell.

John tore his eyes away and looked across the room toward his teammates. He tried to clear his mind while he watched them stretch and chat on the mats in the back of the room. No luck.

The small, quiet noises from Jen didn't help. John clenched his teeth and tried very hard not to focus on the tightening in his sweatpants.

A bead of sweat blossomed on his forehead.

Shit.

He braced himself to call it quits and leave the room...but he couldn't make himself do it.

His body wouldn't respond. It refused to move even an inch from his spot sitting on the table and under her hands.

Fuck.

Her hands wandered lower down to his forearm that rested on his thigh.

Right next to his junk.

Double fuck.

Grandma. Grandpa. Mom. Dad. Butch. Sweaty locker rooms.

Nothing worked.

He couldn't help it as his eyes drifted to her long neck and saw that her slight flush continued down. John swallowed hard.

As he felt more sweat start to form, he grasped for the first thing that came to mind to distract him. "I've been meaning to ask. What's up with you joining in on the bashing session to William Galloway at the gala? I came back at one point and you, and another woman were standing there with William and his daughter talking about how I was all washed up. What's with that? Thought you said you liked watching me play?" he teased, but the incident was a burr that hit him regularly in the middle of the night. He didn't know why he cared so much, he shouldn't. Yet, he couldn't stop the desire to know why she joined in. A fight about his age and performance would get rid of his erection.

Probably.

Maybe.

Her hands stilled for a moment before continuing their dangerous, yet magnificent, journey on his arm.

"I've known William forever. Lexie is one of my best friends." Jen paused. "Actually, she was my date for the Gala." He figured. "I didn't say anything bad...I don't think. I can't remember exactly what I said, but I know I wouldn't have done that. You're one of my favorite players. There's no way I would have said anything to drag your name through the mud." Her head tilted to the side as she tried to remember. At last, it dawned on her, and realization showed through those soulful tawny eyes. "I remember now, I didn't say anything bad at all. Lex made some comments about someone being hurt and I chimed in and said you played injured at the end of last year too." Jen's nose wrinkled as she looked at him. "Which is not earth-shattering. It's not like people didn't know." A defiant look grew on her face, but her fingers still worked their magic, now moving closer to his wrist.

Put like that...

Maybe she really didn't say anything all that bad.

John silently stared at Jen, trying to drum up the energy to be mad at her and argue with her. He needed a better angle to distract himself from wanting to bend her over the massage table, to hell with anyone else in the room. They'd get the hint and leave quick enough.

"Jen. The only people that should be talking to William about his players are the coaches, management, and the GM. It's no secret he's not a football guy. Unsolicited opinions from people who aren't experts in the game give him bad data. True, I had a couple of hard hits last year, but it didn't affect my play and I'm completely recovered now. Your comment put my Spartan tenure in jeopardy." There. That should start a big enough fight that he wouldn't need to order everyone out and beg her to continue her work on him but while he was naked...and erect.

Jen's fingers paused. John looked to her eyes, and he shifted in embarrassment. Her eyes were locked on his athletic shorts, where she could clearly see the edge of his erection. Her breathing got deeper and more audible as she stared, and John had to fight to not grow any bigger under her hungry, and *so* not professional look.

Her head gave a jerk, and she intently went back to massaging his wrist and hand. Her own fingers threaded through his, pulling and stretching.

How the fuck could someone massaging and stretching his fingers be sexy?

His imagination had her doing this with another part of his body.

She licked her lips and rallied, very clearly also attempting to break their spell. "Sorry, champ, but I disagree. William runs a multi-billion-dollar energy company and a multi-million-dollar sports team. He knows who the subject matter experts are and wouldn't let me cloud his judgment. My comments probably went in one ear and out the other. Plus, it wasn't even me who was critiquing you," Jen countered before adding as an afterthought, "and you're lying to yourself if you don't think your play was affected."

Say what now?

"How do you explain his last-minute interference with my contract restructuring then? And you have a lot to learn about football if you think it impacted my performance on the field." Not a single person besides Lenny knew about his injuries last year, and he planned on keeping it that way, even if she was sexy as sin and had a brain to match.

Jen looked up at him with disbelief. "A couple of things to unpack there... First, I don't know what happened during your contract negotiations but there's no way what I said to William in passing at a black-tie affair was the driving factor there. Maybe you should have your head checked for an injury because that's ridiculous and, frankly, giving me entirely too much credit. He's a ruthless Monopoly player, a terrible Taboo partner, and a second dad to me. I'm still a kid to him, and always will be. There's no way he took any of that talk about your injuries to heart. But it was that time of year, so it's not like he'd have to look far to find someone to hiss in his ear about your health. You took a ton of hard hits last year."

John started to interrupt but Jen talked over him, taking a few steps to the side of him so she could stretch his arm at a different angle while she poked, prodded, and massaged.

Shit. She was amazing.

"And second. I love you. You know...as a player," she hastened to add. "But you physically could not do your job at the end of last season. Especially when it mattered most."

Say what?

Well, now his erection was gone.

"Excuse me? We made it to the championship last season, Jen," John said. "Please, go on, tell me more about how I couldn't physically lead the team on a deep playoff run because I was so hurt."

Jen scoffed and a small smile grew on her lips even as her eyes stayed focused on his shoulder area. "Easy, a first-round bye, defense carried the whole team in round two against Tennessee, three hundred fifty rushing yards in the conference championship, before falling short in the Super Bowl."

John countered, blood pressure rising to her challenge and loving every second of it. "The first bye was *because* I could physically do my job during the regular season. The second two games were the results of great preparation and game planning from the whole team. We only lost the Super Bowl by six and I threw for two touchdowns—hardly a poor performance. I handed the ball off so much in those two games because that was the game plan, not because I couldn't throw it."

She moved so she was standing behind him and worked on something in the connecting tissue between his neck and shoulder and he almost groaned in ecstasy. "In my opinion, you're one of the greats, John. That's the reason you were able to take the team as far as you did while injured, but your neck wasn't right after the blindside hit you took in Buffalo in December. You didn't have full range of motion rotating your neck to the left side after that. Interesting, because *I* never saw anything listed on the injury reports after that game." Her tone ended on an accusatory note.

Fuck.

Hiding injuries wasn't exactly league sanctioned and extremely frowned upon. Hell, even some of his coaches didn't know.

To this day, he still didn't have a full range of motion looking in that direction, and the only person who knew that was Lenny.

Jen soldiered on. "Two key plays in the postseason last year told the whole story. In the second quarter of the divisional round, you threw a pick six on a pass intended for Liam up the seam. The corner that intercepted the ball was just out of your field of vision and you didn't rotate your head enough to see him licking his chops, waiting to jump that route. No harm no foul as special teams returned the ensuing kickoff for a TD and the defense didn't give up any more points that game."

John, rooted to his seat, had still not regained the ability to speak. A pregnant pause ensued as she waited for him to argue. When he remained silent, she continued in her quiet and mesmerizing voice.

Damn, his woman knew her shit. Was it possible that he wanted to fuck her even more now?

Wait. His woman?

"The second play was in the fourth quarter of the Super Bowl; third and fifteen on the San Francisco forty-five. Kenny, your favorite target, was supposed to run a seam route but broke to the left instead of right when he read a busted coverage up the sideline. He knew when you hit him it would mean a touchdown and another ring for the Spartans. You couldn't rotate your neck enough to see him veer off course into those greener pastures though. The pocket started collapsing and you settled on a check down to the running back." She paused while trying to remember. "I think Michael Dillion was in on that play, which got us six yards. Spartans ended up punting, hoping to use their timeouts and the two-minute warning to get the ball back in your hands, but the San Fran backfield couldn't be stopped, and after two first-downs, the game was over. I get it if some people missed it when your lack of neck mobility bit you in the ass against Tennessee, but I can't be the only one who noticed that missed TD throw to Kenny against San Fran. The media blew it up as a feud between you two rather than an injury so that worked in your favor, but don't blame me for William's alleged concerns over your health and physical well-being."

John's basic motor functions returned, and he decided to go with incredulous. "The experience in the middle of the gridiron, walls collapsing, fans screaming at the top of their lungs, adrenaline coursing through your veins...it's a fucking rush." Sort of like listening to her talk shop to him. "With that sensory overload, sometimes you miss things. You can Monday-morning-quarterback all you want but at the end of the day, an all-pro corner picked my pocket, and I threw to Michael because, during my reads, Kenny was not where he was supposed to be."

There. That sounded convincing and not at all defensive...right?

"Whatever you say, boss," Jen countered with a dorky salute. She placed her hands back on his shoulder which already felt a million times better "Have you talked to a therapist about this identity crisis and contract drama yet?" She paused before tacking on a saucy, "You should also be sure you address this age complex of yours, it can't be healthy." She shifted so she was now standing slightly behind him.

John barked out a laugh before he could help it and wished he could see the returning smile on Jen's face. He could imagine how wide and blinding it was. How it would make her eyes pinch and sparkle, and she'd get the barest hint of a dimple in one of her cheeks.

John sensed movement in his periphery and when he looked over, he saw Ryan Cole sitting in the corner. The young quarterback hopeful had a heating pad wrapped around his neck and shoulder, one hand elevated on the desk with a bag of ice resting on it, and a laptop in front of him. But his eyes weren't on the computer.

Instead, his bright blue eyes were squinting as he watched John and Jen banter and bicker like an old married couple.

John didn't break eye contact with the rookie, and his look basically dared the kid to say something.

Ryan just watched them, contemplation on his face.

When John frowned, Ryan's slightly knowing look grew until it became a mischievous grin.

Fucking kid.

As John opened his mouth to say something to him, the door to the massage rooms blew open and his chance to tell him to fuck off disappeared.

CHAPTER FOURTEEN

September 10, Saturday
Jen

"Jen!" Abby, the girl from HR, huffed into the room. "Can I talk to you in private for a sec?"

Jen's heart stuttered but she nodded, wiped her hands, and followed Abby out into the hall.

Saved by the bell because Jen was about twelve point two seconds away from crawling in John's lap and begging him to find the nearest empty office.

The man's hard muscles were intoxicating, his smell divine, and his goddamn brain aligned with her own so perfectly that it was borderline creepy.

He clearly got uncomfortable when she called him on his injury and as soon as he started to pick a fight, she saw his exact thought process. His feelings clear in his eyes.

She marveled that defensive players found him so hard to read because she had his number. She could read the man like a book.

The joy Jen got from sparring with him and impressing him with her sports knowledge clearly reflected in his own face and as amazing as it was to behold, it only made behaving herself even harder.

They were ying and yang and the man was fucking perfect.

Once in the hall, Abby dove into her purse and pulled out a large manilla envelope.

"Lupita wanted to give this to you, but she had to rush out to pick up her kid from school." Abby leaned in. "I guess he vomited everywhere." Abby, experiencing her own word vomit, continued explaining what happened at the school. In detail. She caught herself with a small shudder and stopped her graphic recap of the phone call.

"Anyway, Lupita spoke with Lenny yesterday and he outlined his expectations for the department during his recovery. Based on your performance, he requested that you act as the department manager in his stead. He knows it will cause some waves with you being relatively new here, but he ironed everything out with Lupita and management, and they have a new compensation package and offer letter for you. They also outlined all your new responsibilities and the things you will need to take over." She looked down at the packet. "I also think there is a letter from Lenny in there, as well as a document outlining what the expectations are once, and if, he comes back." Abby then handed Jen a second packet. "Lupita also wanted me to drop off the list of charity activities Lenny signed up for. Lupita had me change all of his signups over to you. So look it over tonight and let me know if you have any questions, but it should be self-explanatory."

The awkward young woman remained completely oblivious to the look on Jen's face. As she wrapped up her fast speech, Abby gave a little hop as she waved goodbye and dashed out the door, leaving Jen staring at the envelope like it held a bomb or anthrax...or her continued chastity belt.

Oh god. Did this just turn into a long-term commitment?

She couldn't leave the team mid-season with the massage manager out recovering from open heart surgery. If she thought William was stressed before, that would be nothing compared to how he felt now that his friend was recovering from a near-death experience.

Jen lowered her eyes to the package in her hand.

Dear god.

She wanted to vomit.

Just rubbing John over his freaking shirt had her wanting to strip out of her no-nonsense work clothes and beg him to take her. The entire time she couldn't keep her eyes to herself. Her fingers itched to rub even more of him...naked.

And aroused.

Jen groaned and slapped the envelope against her face.

Hell.

How could she be the manager here and continue to work on John and still maintain her sanity and morals? This job was the least she could do to repay William and now here she was, questioning ways to get out of it.

Shit. Now she really had to see this through.

No way did she want to be like her father.

But...maybe Micky and Benji were right. Maybe if she and John got it out of their system, things would be easier for the rest of the season.

She raised her eyebrows as she thought it out. The idea had promise.

Jen felt her stomach churn as she reviewed the details in the empty hall. The additional requirements for the interim manager role were steep but it did come with a decent pay raise. With this raise she could save up, so she wouldn't need to take out another loan anytime soon. Or maybe she'd be able to get a better apartment.

Jen took a deep breath to steady herself.

She flipped through a couple more pages. As interim manager, she would be expected to travel with the team to away games. Typically, only Lenny traveled with the team. The rest of the massage team stayed at the home stadium during those trips.

Now, she would be with the team everywhere they went.

Made sense.

Jen also needed to participate in charity events, which surprised her. She didn't picture Lenny as a charity-goer. When she attended events with Lexie, she certainly never saw Lenny. But Springfield and the surrounding communities were sprawling, so maybe it wasn't surprising that they never ran into each other. Then again, maybe they had, and she just didn't know it. Regardless, she would be expected to participate in all the charitable events he had already signed up for.

That didn't seem terrible. She had plenty of experience in that circuit from bopping around with Lexie, so she'd know what to do and how to act.

The door to the massage room opened with a groan and John sauntered out, his head turning to find her. He projected one hundred percent confidence. Like he wasn't rocking an extraordinary erection just minutes before. It was quite impressive. The confidence, not the erection.

Well, actually…the erection too.

They were lucky no one else saw. They might not be so lucky next time.

"Hey, got a second?"

"Now's not a great time. I need to get going." She waved the giant envelope in front of him as if in explanation and moved to step around him.

He reached out and put his hand on her arm. "Just one minute."

Fireworks exploded at his touch.

Her eyes dropped to where he was touching her, and he jerked his hand away.

Tingles started spreading through her hand and forearm.

"I really need to get going. I have a date in a few minutes, and I don't want to be late." She wanted to push him. To see how he would react to her tease.

Unhappy was the answer.

"Excuse me?" His eyes got dark and his eyebrows shot down. Even his fingers tightened and rolled into fists.

"Just kidding," she said softly. Jen leaned forward, placing her hand on his chest for a heartbeat to calm his glower. "Just a joke. A bad one. What's up?"

Nice to know the guy didn't want her going out with others. Then again, did he expect her to be celibate the whole time she was an employee of the team? Sure, she didn't have her eye on anyone currently. Not when her nights were filled with dreams of John with his piercing eyes and slow grins. Each smile he gave her felt earned. Like she conquered a mountaintop. It left her with a heavy feeling of success that didn't seem to go away, no matter how many times she won a smile from his serious lips.

He continued to frown at her, clearly at a loss for what to say.

"I, uh, don't have any right to have an opinion...obviously."

"Obviously," she said in agreement.

He gave her a tired look and she beamed up at him.

His eyes dropped down to her lips and she watched them get heavy with arousal.

Yeah, this was impossible.

Before he could say anything else, she said, "This is a promotion. Apparently, Lenny wants me to take over as manager and stay here long term."

His eyes lost their lust haze and reality set in. He raised an incredulous expression to hers.

"I can't fucking take any more of this. I lied to Lenny before. I didn't know I was lying. But I was. *This,*" he waved between them, "is a problem."

"Absolutely. I agree."

"So, what are we going to do?"

"I have some ideas."

John looked down the hall while thinking and absently scratched his beard. "I don't want you to think I think you're not good at your job. Because that was the best ten minutes of a massage that I've ever had. Period"

"But..."

He then cocked his neck and twisted it violently. Jen heard a sickening pop.

"But," he stressed, "it's probably not a good idea for you to work on me going forward."

The silence was heavy as they stared at each other.

Jen squirmed and waved the envelope with a grimace. "I can't turn this down. William doesn't deserve that stress." She gave him a pained smile.

His broad chest tested the limits of his shirt as he inhaled.

"Well," he sighed. "Shit."

Good God, this man sighed a lot.

"Yeah," she echoed. "Shit."

"The way I see it, we have a couple of options," John said. He shifted his weight and let his eyes roam her face. His body stiffened and she braced.

"I can hire an outside massage therapist."

She gasped in outrage. "*So* not what I was going to say. Can you even imagine how that would make me look?"

He had the grace to look abashed as he thought it out. "Ok, so what do you propose?" John looked down the still-vacant hallway, his dark eyes trailing along the thick carpet and noise-canceling wall panels. His eyes paused at the bend in the hallway that led back to the main offices before coming back to her.

"I don't really know. I have some good and not-so-good ideas. Right now, I'm leaning towards arranging our massages when tons of other people are around."

He raised an eyebrow, and she fluttered her hands in acknowledgment of her weak idea that clearly didn't stop the tension from building moments before.

"I'm trying here. It's not like this is easy." She rubbed hard at her cheeks before looking up at him. "I don't know," she said with a sigh. "If I take this job, it means a lot of things." Now it was her turn to look down the hall and imagine she was somewhere else.

Preferably a beach. Naked. Maybe with John.

John scratched at his beard before dropping his hand and saying quietly to her. "Ok. Ok. Here's what we'll do." John took in a deep breath and blew it out softly. Jen caught the soft scent of mint gum. "We're going to be adults and behave. I need work done, as you so eloquently pointed out, and you'll be the only full-time therapist to do so, so we have no other choice. We need to behave. We'll make sure we're doing massages with others in the room. And I'm staying fully clothed." He paused. "Maybe you wear a parka, hat, and sunglasses? And rub some tobacco on you so you don't smell as good?"

She laughed as he intended, and she looked up into his soft and wistful smile.

God, the guy was magnificent.

"Or...we can fuck now and get it out of our system."

Oh my god. She did *not* just say that.

She dashed a hand up to cover her mouth but it was too late.

John was staring at her in shock and frankly, she couldn't blame him.

"I, uh, don't suppose you could forget I said that?"

"Do you want me to forget you said that?" His voice was a scrumptious growl that had her toes curling with the promise in his tone.

"No? Yes? I don't know!" she said in a squeak.

"Jesus, fuck." He rubbed at his face and looked up at the ceiling. He took in a deep inhale, held it, and then blew it out before looking back at her. "You know, it's not a terrible idea. If we work out this tension on the side, the anticipation won't keep building, and we can get on with our responsibilities."

She had William and her dad and occasionally Lexie to look out for and try to take care of.

John had his career and the team. John knew what it meant to have responsibilities.

Shoot.

Jen looked at the floor as she rubbed at a spot with the toe of her shoe. "I don't know. I'm not entirely convinced that's a good idea. I shouldn't have said anything." She rubbed at her face. "I'm just strung tight and clearly not thinking clearly. Getting…intimate would be a bad idea. Probably. People would totally find out. Word would get back to William and it would break his heart. Not to mention what my future clients would think of me." Jen closed her eyes and sighed.

"Hey." John's almost-southern twang came out soft and silky. He peered down at her with a soft expression. "Don't worry. It's fine. We'll behave. We're adults. We got this."

She let her eyes roam his face, drinking him in. "Okay," she said quietly, not quite believing they could hold out much longer but willing to try. Falling into this addiction to John would make her too much like her dad to stomach.

John stared back at her, his eyes dancing over her face. "Okay," he echoed softly.

"Do you think this will work?"

He continued to stare at her, his normally hard face soft. He took in her earnest and worried expression, his eyes trailing down the line of her neck to her chest, hips, and feet. He gave her a wry grin, his eyes still soft. "Not a chance, but we can sure as hell try our damnedest before giving in if that's what you want."

Prickles danced on Jen's skin and immediately the hair on her arms raised with the tingles. Even her breasts felt heavier at his hungry but pained look.

He was so willing to try to behave when he clearly knew he could convince her otherwise with a single look or kiss.

Jen's heart thumped hard once. Twice.

Holy moly, he really was a stud of a human. Looking at him almost hurt.

Jen gazed up at him and absently wet her dry lips and the look on his face grew almost tortured.

She knew the feeling well. How did he think it would feel if she walked around shirtless all the time?

She'd laugh if she could.

What a tangled web they had gotten themselves into.

A player came out of the massage room, letting the door bang behind him. John and Jen jumped apart. She hadn't even realized they were leaning in toward each other.

John coughed lightly into his fist and then gazed at her. "So, we're doing this."

Crap.

Jen straightened her back and solidified her resolve, pulling on every ounce of willpower to do so.

"Absolutely. I need to do this."

He leveled a look at her that had butterflies erupting in her lower stomach.

Too late to back out now.

"As you wish," he murmured, his dark eyes skeptical and disbelieving. He gave a quick look toward the massage room door and nodded at it. "I'll let you get back to it. You can take the time to make a list of all the things you hate about me so the next time I need a massage you can rage rub me."

"I might not come up with much," she said with a tease and then winced.

Behave, Jennifer!

John just smiled big at her, his eyes crinkling and lines around his mouth cutting deep.

"Well, I already know that I've got nothing. So, it's up to you, Medina." With that, John turned and walked away, his long strides causing a soft pattern of thuds in the hall long after he turned the corner and was out of sight.

Crap.

CHAPTER FIFTEEN

September 14, Tuesday
Jen

Jen opened the door to an angry thumping.

"Jen. I've been trying to get ahold of you. Why haven't you been answering your phone?"

She looked up into her dad's flushed face. All she felt was exhaustion. She leaned against the door, not opening it any wider than necessary.

"What's up?" If she could make it to her bed, she knew she'd be out in less than three minutes. She just needed to get there. Her silk sheets were calling for her.

First, the raucous party going on in her building. Then she passed some time with Mickey and Benji while she waited for the hallway to quiet down. Mickey saw her on the broadcast of the game this weekend, massaging Danny Parker on the sideline during the game, and wanted to know everything about him. Danny was a wide receiver having a lot of hamstring and quad problems this year. Jen and Danny formed a good rapport, so obviously, Mickey wanted to know *everything* there was to know about Mr. McScruffy, as Mickey called him.

Fortunately, there had been no time to work on John. One of them was always busy, exhausted, or otherwise engaged. Their avoidance foreplay dance was plain painful.

A secret fling never hurt anyone. No one ever even needed to know. It's not like John was going to broadcast it.

After Benji escorted her back to her apartment, she flew through a shower while brushing her teeth at the same time so she could get to her bed as fast as possible.

Yet here she stood dealing with her snake of a father.

"You haven't been answering your phone."

"I've been busy."

"Yeah, I saw you on TV last night." He tried looking through the crack in her door. "Can I come in?" He waited and then looked at her in excitement. "Or is someone already back there?"

She rolled her eyes. "No, you cannot come in, it's late. What do you want?"

He snapped his teeth together with an audible click and scrutinized her.

"Here." He held out an envelope, waving it in her face.

She frowned at him as she took it. "What's this?" she asked as she opened the envelope. Inside was a roster of the Spartans' team and various notes next to each player—disclosed injuries, his theorized injuries, and whether they'd perform this upcoming week during their next game. Her eyes flew up to his.

What the fuck?

"What's this?" she snapped.

"Just some thoughts I jotted down while watching the game at the track last night. I wanted to run it by you before I posted any bets."

She stared.

"Who would have better insight than their masseuse?" She long ago had stopped correcting his terminology. "And it's not like it hurts anything. Just a little something on the side to get me through the latest hiccup at work." He let that hang there.

Hell. What now?

"What happened at work?" She didn't even want to ask but her tired brain betrayed her.

He waved her question away. "A misunderstanding. But I need the money and I didn't want to ask you for it again. Plus, my GA sponsor told me baby steps are the first steps. I need to stop asking friends and family for money and instead start repaying my personal debts."

He was going to Gamblers Anonymous meetings finally.

She wanted to scream with joy.

Jen's heart felt lighter. He had never talked about GA before. He always acted so insulted whenever she suggested it.

Easy, Jen. Play it cool. Don't scare him off.

She rolled her lips between her teeth and counted to five before shrugging. "That's pretty cool that you have someone to talk to about this." There, that sounded casual and collected. "I haven't done much research on them but I think it sounds awesome."

Weird,\ he'd still be betting though.

"Yeah, they've been a tremendous help. They've really opened my eyes to how I treated you and your mother."

Wow. Accepting ownership and responsibility for his actions, as well as bringing up Jen's mom?

Maybe he really was trying this time.

She leaned into the doorframe and smiled up at her dad, not being as strict about keeping the door mostly shut. "That's awesome, Dad. I'm so glad you feel like it's been worthwhile."

He nodded quickly. "Oh, absolutely." He paused. "So, can I come in? I have some things I want to go over with you." He waved the paper she had handed back to him.

She winced. "Dad, as much as I'd love to help. I don't have any information that the injury report doesn't already have. Plus, even if I did, I think I'd get in big trouble for sharing. Like...lawsuit-sized trouble." There had definitely been some confidentiality and NDA forms she signed that first day.

Her father's face tightened, and she stiffened in response. She wasn't up to fighting tonight. It felt like a fight keeping her eyes open.

He blinked and his face blanked. "Okay, kiddo. We can touch base later. I can see you're fried. Your eyes and nose are doing that little scrunchy thing you did when you were a kid."

Really? Her face used to do that? Her heart warmed at the hint of nostalgia in his voice.

She gave him a grateful smile and cocked her head. "Thanks, Dad. I'm beat. We just got back and I need my bed. I'm not even thinking straight anymore."

After they said their goodbyes, she dragged herself to her bedroom, still thinking about him going to GA and trying to change. Jen collapsed into bed with a soft smile. Maybe everything was going to work out after all.

For once.

Chapter Sixteen

September 15, Wednesday
Jen

Jen sighed, took a sip of her protein shake, and stared down at the near-empty stadium below.

It was technically fall, but Mother Nature decided to keep it summer for a little while longer. She took advantage of the nice weather while she could. The stadium woke up with the sun. Players wandered out from the locker rooms while staff set up tents and water stations. A few started jogging, doing their own thing on this rare day off. Across the stadium, she saw a couple of people enter the stands and start their own workouts, running up and down the steps.

As she sipped at her now near empty drink, she felt a large form plop down beside her on the steps.

"Hey there, gorgeous," Ryan Cole said, drenched in sweat with his dirty blonde hair spiked perfectly. She knew it wasn't from styling; beauty came naturally to him. He achieved hair commercial looks from running his hand through the sweaty strands. His chest, tanned from the sun, sported a small tattoo on one of his pecs. He was leaner than most quarterbacks, including one sexy quarterback in particular, and Ryan rocked the defined abs. With Ryan's more slender form, when he took a hit...he took a *hit*. He never complained though, not seriously at least. He'd come limping into the massage room, begging for her magic hands, and then have her do nothing but rub his shoulder quickly before rushing out the door. Sometimes she could convince him to sit still long enough to do some glute work, but the guy didn't like to be stationary for long. Fifteen minutes here. Fifteen minutes there. Some days he came in just to chat or sit on his computer in the back corner. She never got romantic vibes from him, but they built quite a friendship during their little fifteen-minute meetings.

It didn't make sense that he'd want to spend so much time with her, but she didn't mind. In fact, she enjoyed their time together.

"Hi, King Cole." She nudged his sweaty shoulder with her own while continuing to watch the people hustling around on the field.

"How are you liking the new gig?"

Jen squinted as she looked up into the hot sun. She accepted the promotion and really, not much had changed. She traveled with the team for away games, but not much else was different so far.

With the massive number of injuries the team already had that season, her time with the Spartans never got dull.

The anticipation between John and her was torturous. They tried to avoid each other in a way that wasn't obvious, but she was starting to think that people noticed.

Jen looked over to Ryan. "It's fine." She shrugged and looked back at the stadium.

He sat there for a moment, saying nothing.

"You know, I wanted to be a doctor."

She looked back over to him in surprise.

His shoulders seemed tense. "Mom couldn't afford the schooling and the loans would have been...impossible. I never would have been able to manage work, schooling, and football. I got my scholarship, did my four years, got out, and got drafted. My sisters won't have to pay a dime." He twiddled his fingers together as he looked out at the people milling around as well. "Maybe one of them will be a doctor for me."

They sat in silence for a moment.

"So, I guess what I'm trying to say is, I know what it feels like to not live for yourself and to live your life trying to make others happy."

Jen just looked at him, emotion making it hard to swallow, tears swimming in her eyes.

"But you and I," he nudged her shoulder again, "we like practicality. We like the feeling of being secure. We spent our lives not having that security. So, when we have a chance to take care of the people we love and repay some kind of debt, we do it. But sometimes," he put his fingers beneath her chin and looked in her eyes, "there are risks worth taking." He paused and coughed lightly into his fist. "Anyway, you're not alone. We sacrificial lambs have to stick together. If you leave, who else will talk to me about something other than football?"

She scanned his face, for the first time seeing the loneliness etched there. So clear in that very moment. She stood up and held out a hand.

"All right, big guy. Enough of this sad talk. Workout partner?"

He grabbed her hand and let her try to pull him up. When she couldn't budge him, he took mercy on her and pulled himself up to a stand.

And with their new shared understanding, they continued their jog up and down the countless steps of the stadium. Each lost in their own thoughts and decisions.

Was John worth the risk?

Maybe one day she'd figure it out.

CHAPTER SEVENTEEN

September 17, Friday
Jen

Jen finished up on the defensive end she was working on and patted his shoulder before she grabbed a towel to wipe off her hands.

Kobe stood up and rotated his beautiful, Samoan shoulder in wide arcs, testing out how it felt, and then turned to give her a bear hug. The man was a giant. At over six foot four inches, he towered over her. Plus, the sheer number of muscles he had bulked him out even more. His body as a whole, right down to his detailed tat sleeves, truly looked like a work of art. As he turned to grab his cut-off tee from a table next to her next, Jen admired the way his beautiful skin flexed and rippled with his movements.

In a purely professional way, of course.

She felt him before she saw him.

She looked over at the second massage table where John sat being worked on. His eyes were open and were not hiding his displeasure at catching her ogling his teammate. She gave a quick "psh" and flapped her hand in his direction, choosing not to engage in his jealousy. However, she couldn't stop her smile as she turned away and started washing her hands at the sink.

She picked up the packet that Abby had dropped off and read the top page. She waved a vague goodbye to Kobe and plopped down in her chair, picking back up where she left off when he strolled in.

As Lenny's replacement, she had to participate in the charity events that he originally signed up for. Tomorrow was an equine center event of some sort. Lenny was familiar with horses; Jen was not. At all.

She wanted to vomit just thinking about getting on something that had a mind of its own or could spook at a mouse running across the floor in front of it.

Eww, mice.

She wouldn't see mice at the barn, right?

Her skin crawled and she fought back a shudder.

Jen heard a deep hiss from John's table and looked up. The other massage therapist had John wincing with some odd technique he shouldn't even be doing..

His body was taking a beating—his linemen not really keeping him safe. Each time he took a hit, Jen could swear he took longer and longer to get up. But the only people brazen enough to bring it up were the media. Not a single teammate said a word. Not even the coaches. Jen was dying to ask if his body felt okay but she knew exactly how he'd take it.

"Hey, John. Are you doing okay?" she'd ask.

"Why? Because I'm old? You think I should be confined to an old folks' home too?" he'd fire back. Or something that basically boiled down to that sentiment. Drama King.

"No, get a grip. I wanted to check to see if you were okay because you aren't moving as quickly, and you've had a few interceptions. That's not like you."

"You've been listening to the media again. Blah, blah, blah."

It would get her nowhere. She had to get him alone, in person, and get her hands on him to really assess his body. Otherwise, he would be all distractions and affronts to derail the conversation.

But muscles? Muscles don't lie.

As Jen's eyes coasted over John's exposed back, she had to hide her own wince at the technique the other therapist was using. It wasn't her style, but none of the players complained, so some must like it. Her first week of the managerial role was not the time to step in and tell the guy how to do his job.

Yet...her hands itched to push the other therapist out of the way and take over.

The door blasted open and Ryan breezed into the room, all sunshine and sweat. He stepped in during the fourth quarter of the last game after John had thrown a few uncharacteristic interceptions. He did all right. Ryan was proud as a peacock that he could take a couple of snaps, but it did nothing to improve John's disposition.

He was furious about being benched. Still was, if his impressive glower was anything to go by.

Ryan looked back and forth between Jen and John and his blonde eyebrows shot high. "Hey cuties, how's it hanging?"

She could basically hear the enamel on John's teeth chipping away. Ryan knew exactly what buttons to push and did so frequently.

It was glorious.

Jen admired the kid for being so plucky. Unfortunately, she liked his predecessor even more.

CHAPTER EIGHTEEN

September 18, Saturday
John

"Hi there. My name is Julie and I own and run the Foals and Fillies Equine Center. We are a rehabilitation center for not only horses, but also for our human friends. We book out events and classes to people that might need a little bit of retreat and therapy time. It's beneficial for both the people and the horses and I could drone on and on about the benefits of the cross-therapy, but no one wants to hear that. Just visit our website." A chuckle rose from the crowd of volunteers.

The speaker was a blonde woman in her late twenties or early thirties. She was rocking a pair of cowboy boots, well-worn jeans, and a flannel top that already had horse slobber and hay on it. She had light scratches on her arm from the hay bales she tossed around this morning when John showed up, and she had a small dirt smear on her right cheek.

Julie's two dimples deepened as she continued to give the agenda for the day and thanked the Galloway Charitable Organization for sponsoring a series of events this year.

John waited for her speech to end and the crowd to mostly disperse before walking up to the board and looking for his name.

He found it. Right next to Jen's.

Where was the little temptress?

John looked around, conscious of the various pointed whispers around him. He found that if he kept his hat low enough, had sunglasses on, and didn't look directly at anyone, he was normally able to fly under the radar. He also sported some thick scruff that wasn't his usual clean-shaven look, so that might buy him some anonymity. Most of the volunteers today were office staff from the various Springfield sports teams. On this particular weekend, only a few of the actual players signed up. A weekend date sandwiched between two tough division games meant most players wanted to focus on recovery and prep. Months ago, Lenny convinced John that the break in intensity would be good for him.

He knew all about John's childhood and his love of horses.

He caught sight of Jen and gave a jolt. She wore a tight Five Finger Death Punch T-shirt, much tighter than her usual work polos, with tiny fraying jean shorts. He saw her running in the stadium in shorts, but never up close.

Those legs.

All day with those fucking legs on display.

He shook himself and walked over, girding himself with every step.

"Good morning, sunshine," she sauced up at him.

He gazed down at her, trying not to let his eyes wander.

And failing.

He refused to engage in anything besides getting through this day together in the barest cordial fashion possible, otherwise, he might try to have her sneak up to the hay loft with him. And with the various fans here, a well-timed picture could say a thousand words. He didn't need a picture of him checking out Jen blasted on the local sports news network.

She shot him a megawatt smile and donned her shades. "Feeling at home?"

He couldn't stop his own returning grin. "As much as you aren't, I'm sure."

"You remember that?" Shock showed on her face, mixed with a look of intense pleasure.

At the gala, when they started talking about his life back home, she had mentioned her fear of horses. At the time, he teased her about getting her up on one someday, and now look where they were.

Thank you, universe.

A thumping bass interrupted him from his visual perusal of Jen's all too lickable body. He turned his head toward the parking lot to see Ryan Cole zip into one of the spaces in an old-school Mustang that defined the word vintage. That car had seen some miles.

Rookies and their first purchases with their new league salaries. Predictable. Stupid and predictable.

He looked back to Jen to see him smiling over to Ryan.

"Ryan, over here. You're in our group."

"Jesus." John rubbed his temple preemptively. He could already tell this was going to be another headache day. Paired up with Ms. Sex-on-Legs *and* Mr. Migraine.

He knew he signed up for a special kind of torture when he decided to not bail on the event and subject himself to hours with Jen, but a part of him was itching for it. It was like his brain mentally rubbed its hands together in excitement at their possible sparring.

But now? Now, he had to deal with snuffing out their sexual tension on top of trying not to strangle his replacement.

Who had an irritating tendency to flirt with Jen.

The bastard touched her all the time.

Bear hugs, high-fives, hair ruffles. The pair were always fucking *touching*.

John wanted to pummel the little shit. And when he got done with that, he wanted to fuck Jen so hard she forgot the little pissant's name.

Jen looked up at him and broke him out of his mental pity party. A look of concern crossed her face and she stepped closer. "You all right?"

John nodded once before twisting his head sharply to crack his neck. It helped. A little.

Jen didn't lose the look of concern but at least her eyes were on him now and not the pretty boy jogging up to them.

As Ryan arrived, a couple of buses poured into the giant parking lot, kicking up dust that wafted over the entrance area to the barn. Staff in bright pink shirts brought out saddled horses and tied them to hitching posts. Other staff mingled about handing out name tags with group numbers on them.

Julie loped over to them as Ryan let Jen out of a hug with a noogie to the top of her head. Jen swatted at his hand, while laughing and dropping a low jab to his midsection. The kid let out an 'oomph' and jumped away while pushing her head down and away. Julie held out a tanned and calloused hand, focusing on the adult in the group. Him.

"Hi there, I'm Julie. Thank you so much for coming today, we all really appreciate it." She shook hands with each of them with a no-nonsense grip and a full smile. "As my three resident celebrities, I figured I'd keep you all together today. I know it would be more impactful for the guests if we split you up, but keeping your attendance today semi-quiet will help ensure it's not a media frenzy. The patients don't need that, and neither do the horses. So, I hope you don't mind."

John grunted when he felt a sharp jab in his ribs.

At Jen's chastising look, John nodded at Julie to reassure her of her assumption.

"That's totally fine. And to be clear, I'm no celebrity. I just work for them." Jen waved at the men.

"Works *with* us. Not *for* us," Golden Boy Kid Wonder chimed in, tossing his arm around Jen's shoulders. She didn't even bat an eye.

John fought the urge to punch the kid in his perfect nose.

Julie led them to a couple of horses where she gave them quick instructions and the outline for the day. She handed out helmets to each of them. John hesitated before pulling his on. Jen found endless humor in that for some reason. His scowl at her did nothing but make her laugh harder. Her booming laugh made his gut clench and he fought against doing something that would make it happen again.

Eyes everywhere, he reminded himself for the millionth time already.

As they mounted up and waited for their guest to be brought over, Ryan called out, "Hey there, champ. Did you take my advice on your headache last night?"

Shit.

Jen's head whipped over to him and gave him a questioning look.

John just grunted.

Jen's horse started to get a little antsy as they waited. It didn't help that she kept pulling on the reins and shifting in the saddle.

She looked totally out of place on a horse.

And completely adorable.

What would she look like on one of the ponies from back home? She'd be beating him in races within a week once she got over her fear.

He blinked in shock at the thought and quickly steered it in a different direction. He should not be thinking about her at his home, riding his horses. She was his co-worker.

But now that he thought it, he couldn't help the pang of longing that tore through him. He missed being in the saddle. He should make more of an effort to mount up. Maybe buy a horse or two of his own. It's not like he couldn't afford it.

But...time.

Priorities.

He needed to stay focused. Buying a horse and being a good owner would add yet another responsibility to his already long list. He needed to *focus*.

As Jen's horse continued to wander, Ryan tried to grab her reins and as a result confused his own horse. Jen's horse had enough of her rookie bullshit and started off towards the barn. John hid his smile as he steered his mount over and grabbed her horse's reins. He parked their horses next to each other as he watched Julie chase down Golden Boy and his own nomadic horse.

Jesus. This was going to be a shit show. Yet, he couldn't stop the smile from cracking through.

"So. Do you miss it?" Jen asked next while next to him, leaning forward in the saddle. Her shirt teasing him with delicious cleavage that had him wishing she was wearing a sweatshirt, maybe even a turtleneck. A turtleneck would really help him out. The horse shifted again at her movement and lack of balance.

To distract himself, he patted his own mare's neck solidly and gave her withers a quick scratch. The horse's upper lip started moving on the bit as she showed her appreciation for the rub. John peeked over to Jen to see her shifting again. Completely a fish out of water. He bit his lip to hide another smile.

"Stop moving. You're confusing her," John said.

"*You're* moving," Jen accused, her nose scrunched up.

Her fucking nose, so damn cute. He chuckled. "I know what I'm doing. You," he shot her a look, "do not."

"They must have left Lenny's answers on the signup form. Apparently, Lenny is a cowboy and can handle the wild ones."

John choked out another laugh. Even if she had Lenny's intended mount, her horse was near-retirement and just wanted to get to the barn and eat. Hardly a horse that needed an experienced rider, but still, Lenny would have asserted his authority in a way that the horse would have respected and listened to.

Jen? Jen was merely a passenger to this feisty little mare.

He smiled at her and watched in fascination as her eyes lit up. His stomach felt too warm, so he ripped his eyes away and watched Julie escort Ryan and his wayward horse back to their group. Some groups had already gone off, but as Julie would lead them, they were waiting for her before going and collecting their charges for the morning.

John heard Jen grunt in frustration and sensed her shift her weight again. Which, obviously, caused her horse to fidget. Her hands darted to the pommel, and she gave him a look. Again, John couldn't quite stop his grin. Out of the corner of his eye, he saw Jen shoot him a petulant scowl.

Adorable.

After being waylaid multiple times, Julie and Ryan finally made their way back to the group with Ryan's reins wrapped around her saddle horn. She cut a skeptical look at Jen sitting on her horse and darted a look at John. He shook his head. "She'll be fine. I got her."

Julie nodded and started off to collect the waiting charges. As she led them, she turned around in the saddle and spoke to them. "We have a couple of sessions today that will be multi-patient. The kid this morning is a huge Spartans fan and wants to be a quarterback when he grows up and the other person is an author and cancer survivor. They found each other during one of the support groups at the hospital and stayed in touch. It's a cute friendship. He's twelve or so, and she's in her late twenties. They both live in the area and come together to go riding whenever they can." She lowered her voice. "Which is less and less these days."

Within a minute, they met their first two charges of the day.

"Everyone, this is Jameson. Jameson is a professional cowboy and tends to be a bit of a speed demon. Even when he goads you, do not race him until we get out into the cornfields." She cut them all a mock-severe look. It basically screamed for them to indulge him.

"And this is Emma. Emma has been coming here for several years now. Not only for her own sessions, but she also volunteers. But when Jameson comes, she's always a guest and not a volunteer. Don't be mean to her or she'll write you into a book and kill you." Julie's deep dimples popped back into appearance.

Emma gave a rough chuckle and raised her hand. "Guilty."

They all laughed and set out towards the fields.

Jameson gravitated towards Ryan as they set off. Clearly an experienced horseman, he brought his horse alongside Ryan and didn't waste any more thought on navigating the large animal. All his attention focused on Ryan and how Ryan became a Spartan. They could hear his million questions as he fired them quickly at the rookie quarterback. Jameson's deep eyes were bright as he soaked up every word Ryan gave him. He looked frail and vulnerable on his smaller, half-dead horse, but he spoke with confidence and excitement.

The cancer hadn't taken that out of him.

Ryan said something that had both Jameson and Emma comparing biceps, and the group laughed.

John was on the other side of Jen and Julie, so he couldn't really hear what was happening, but that was fine. Jameson or Emma would come over and talk to him when, and if, they wanted.

John still had control of Jen's horse and she was holding onto the pommel for dear life. Her head turned to the right as she tried to listen to everyone. He looked down when he saw movement and let his eyes drift leisurely down her toned leg while no one was watching. God, she was fit. As he got to her foot, his stomach gave a small jump as he saw her sneakered foot shoved all the way in the stirrup.

Good God.

"Hey."

Jen looked over at him, sweat dotting her face.

"Toes in the stirrups. Not the whole foot."

"What?" A look of confusion danced across her pretty face.

"Get used to it," Ryan shouted from a few horses over. Clearly, the distance didn't bother his young ears. "Cap doesn't like to speak in full sentences. Wastes his precious few brain cells. You just need to infer what he means from what he's saying. If you catch my drift." Ryan went back to talking with the two guests and Julie.

Prick.

Jen looked down at her foot and frowned. She tried pulling at her foot but couldn't shake it out of the stirrup. While shaking her leg, she managed to get her foot free, but also kicked the side of the horse and the mare lurched forward. The sudden movement had Jen sliding on the saddle, her body drifting towards her left side, which had lost its foot in the stirrup. Julie cast her a quick look before looking to the right and back at the other three.

John leaned to his right, grabbed her calf, marveling at the soft skin there, and pushed her toes into the stirrup. He centered himself on his horse, thankful for the tight girth that made his saddle not slip around. He flexed his fingers on the reins to forget the feeling of her warm leg in his hand. Riding with an erection would be a new experience and not the good kind.

"It feels weird," Jen whined as she scrunched her lips and nose. She shoved her foot further in the stirrup so it would feel more secure.

"Don't." He didn't wait for her to listen to him and remove it herself. He couldn't resist reaching down and pulling back on her muscular calf until her foot was in the right spot again.

"But I feel uneven." She gave him big eyes, but there was a mischief there that had him wondering if she was liking his touch as much as he did and was maybe doing a little of this on purpose.

If so, this was a dangerous line they were walking.

But he'd take it.

He brought their horses to a stop and waved Julie ahead when she turned around to check on them. He dismounted, walked around the horses, and grabbed Jen's right leg gently in his hands. He got a whiff of coconut and lime when he eased her foot out of the stirrup. "Toes. Not the whole foot. If your foot got caught and the horse took off, you could get dragged." He looked up at her. "*Don't* get dragged."

She nodded militantly and gave him a little salute, despite the faint fear on her face.

Imp. Tough as nails, but still an imp.

He felt too warm, and his mouth felt dry as he stared up at her, but at the same time, his body felt fluid and light. How was that even possible?

John made his way around the horses and remounted. They set off after the group ahead of them. Laughter danced in the breeze as

Ryan wiggled wildly on his horse. Julie, as well as the other two, were eating out of the palm of his hand.

As long as Ryan wasn't hand-feeding Jen.

"Do you still ride a lot?" Jen asked.

"Not as much as I used to. Work doesn't leave much time for riding during the season."

"Oh." She stared straight ahead, focusing on the area in front of her horse with such concentration, he was surprised she could make conversation. "I've heard it can be therapeutic. Physically, emotionally, mentally, and cognitively. Hippotherapy is really gaining momentum in the wellness space." She rambled on, clearly trying to not think about being on a horse. Her ridiculous hoop earrings were swinging with the lazy sway of the horse's walk, and it kept pulling his attention to her long neck. Her neck smelled and tasted so good the night of the gala. He remembered placing a soft kiss there before getting up and he could almost still feel the warmth and tingles on his lips.

He blew a small bubble with his mint gum and frowned slightly. "Are you okay?"

Jen chuckled without feeling but didn't remove her attention from the ground.

"You won't fall," he said, trying to wipe the look of concern from her face.

She rolled her lips together and quickly looked down at her foot before darting her eyes back to the ground in front of her. "Is my foot ok? Is it in too far?" An edge of panic crept into her voice.

John stilled at the real fear in her voice and looked over at her. Sure enough, her usually golden skin had taken on a pale look, and she was sporting sweat on her forehead. He stopped the horses and waited until he had her attention.

"Jen. I have you. I won't let you fall."

"Yeah, but as you said, if my foot goes in too far and I fall, I could get my foot stuck and get dragged."

Shit.

"Jen, look at me." He waited until he had her eyes. "I *have* you. Absolutely nothing bad will happen. I promise."

A heartbeat. Two.

Finally, she nodded and swallowed hard.

He gave her a returning nod and clucked his horse into a walk again. He gave a gentle tug on the reins of Jen's horse and the mare followed along amiably.

John looked to Jen and still saw the pinched look on her face.

"Jen," he called and waited for her to turn to him. "I *got* you."

She gave him such an endearing and trusting look that his heart turned over. Jen was usually such a feisty one. To see her so...unsettled, brought out his inner caveman.

Damnit, he was in trouble.

After a few minutes of walking lazily behind the rest of their group, John saw her moving her leg again. He peeked down to his right and sure enough, her leg was pumping back and forth as she tried to pry her sneaker out of the stirrup again.

He looked down at her over the top of his sunglasses and she gave him a crooked wince, pink blooming on her cheeks. He reached down and gently moved her leg back again, assaulted with another wave of coconut and lime before he sat back up.

Maybe this would distract her. Or terrify her. Guess they'd see.

"Feel like trotting?"

"Wait, what?"

Her shriek turned into a deep laugh as they lurched into a soft trot. His additional cluck prompted a faster pace. Her horse followed along easily, clearly used to being attached to a lead. They caught up to their group as they rounded a corner in the hay field and faced a large path that extended as far as they could see. Jameson bounced in his seat while looking at Julie.

Julie laughed and waved ahead of them. "As you wish!"

Jameson looked at Emma and Ryan, his expression asking for a race.

Both shrugged apologetically and looked over to where Jen and John rode up alongside them. John untied Jen and tossed the reins to Julie.

Time to see what his horse could do.

John winked and smiled big at the kid before asking, "You ready, cowboy?"

Jameson's eyes lit up and he stared in awe at the legend brought to life. He nodded and John took off. The hoofbeats pounding in his ears, John couldn't stop the joy that spread through him. It had been too long since he had been in the saddle. He needed to fix that. Maybe he could get Jen out here again, just the two of them. Maybe she'd feel the freedom once she got over her fear of horses.

He heard a faint pounding behind him, and he turned to see the kid catching up, bent low over his saddle. The rest of the crew trotted lazily behind them, Jen's eyes big but happy as she held on tightly to the saddle pommel. John looked back to Jameson and smiled at the kid's focus. No way he'd let cancer beat him without a fight. He winked again at the kid and urged his horse faster. Jameson pulled up even with him and gifted him with a mega-watt smile that could blind the sun. They both faced forward and off they went.

· · · • · • · · ·

They rode back into the barnyard for the millionth time that day. The sun setting, and the sky cast in a red hue that would make a photographer drool. They rode all day long, switching horses at lunchtime to give their mounts a break. Buses came and went, bringing new patients and their families to the equine center. They finished with their last visit for the day and riders milled around, chit chatting and wiping down their horses.

John dismounted at a nearby hitching post and grabbed Jen's reins as her horse continued towards the barn on autopilot. He brought it around and tied the old gelding up next to his own. When they switched horses at noon, Julie adjusted Jen's horse to one who would be a bit lazier. She spent the afternoon on a tired, experienced gelding that simply just wanted to go with the herd and didn't really care how Jen moved on his back. The same thing with Ryan's horse—though, somehow, he still managed to get it to wander off and misbehave. Julie laughed good-naturedly as she chased them down, inciting more laughter from the little girl with them at the time. Julie dragged Ryan's horse back to the group as the little girl squealed with laughter at Ryan's red-faced ranting. John thought he saw a hint of humor in the young man's eyes as he raved, but then his own mount tried to take a small chomp out of Jen's caramel hair. It wasn't in her usually tight bun today, but instead, in a ponytail sitting high on her head with thin curls framing her face.

He wanted to brush his fingers across her face and push those curls behind her ears.

Great, now he found himself obsessing over her hair, so full and nuanced. The browns, the blondes, the caramels. How had he never noticed before? How would she look beneath him with her curls fanned out on his pillow?

John held her horse steady and Jen eased into a dismount. She swung her leg around gingerly and jolted into the ground. John reached out on instinct to steady her when she wobbled. His fingers touched the skin of her lower back, and he felt a zing. She bent down and exhaled, touching her nose to her knees, her ass in the air.

Goddammit.

He pulled back his hand as if he was electrocuted. He looked up and over the dispersing crowd before anyone could snap a picture.

It wouldn't be the first time he got caught doing something less than PG by the media.

"Why did the team promote this event?" exclaimed Ryan. "Good Lord Almighty. I can't feel my toes. Or my hands. Or my back. Jen, quick, rub me." He jogged over to stand next to her and pulled her flexing right hand up to his back.

John heard a muffled, "Rub your own back. I can't feel mine." Her head stayed down by her knees, her other arm dangling into the dirt.

Staff wandered over and relieved them of the horses as they stood around stretching and admiring the sunset.

"Oh. My. God," Jen said as she adjusted to stand upright. She placed her hands on her hips and arched her back, pushing her chest up into the air. John's eyes snapped away. It was like she was fucking *asking* for them to get splattered on a tabloid. "My lordy. That is *not* easy on your back or abs."

"There aren't many days that I'm spending the entire day in the saddle anymore. Even I'll probably feel this tomorrow," Julie agreed as she approached. "Thanks again for coming today, guys. The guests really loved it and I hope you enjoyed it, even with the body pains coming your way." She smiled kindly.

"Wait, *coming* our way?" Jen looked aghast. "This isn't the worst of it?"

John chimed in on a short laugh. "You might be sore now. But tomorrow will be worse." He smiled at the look of horror that crossed her face. His smile prompted a lip curl from her, which only made him smile bigger.

His heart thumped hard in his chest.

"Umm, if it's not too bold to ask... Can I get a picture with each of you? I'm a huge fan," Julie said.

Both John and Ryan posed for photos with Julie in front of the big Equine Center sign out front with Jen playing photographer.

As the men started to walk away, John heard Julie pull Jen to the side and say in a mock whisper, "Want to exchange numbers and come back when the delicate jocks aren't around?"

"Are you making plans without me, pretty lady?" Ryan grumbled out from up ahead, his nose buried in his phone.

She smiled gamely at his back, undeterred, and more than capable of giving and receiving a little ribbing between friends. She shot a look over to John and asked conspiratorially about Ryan, "Is he always so sensitive?"

Ryan snorted and kept walking.

John gave her his most serious expression. "Beautiful, dumb, and sensitive. It's his curse."

"A true burden," Ryan called back. Ears of a bloodhound, that one.

John caught himself smiling and locked eyes with Jen. She was watching him hungrily again. Her gaze darted away, and she tucked her wayward pieces of hair behind her ears. Her fingers brushed against an earring and caused it to swing slowly.

Julie interrupted his mental wanderings by handing her phone to Jen to share contact information. John increased his pace to give them some space and found himself level with Golden Boy as he stood by his car, his phone pressed to his ear, an out-of-place frown on his face.

"What's wrong?" John didn't want to ask. It was his job as a captain on the team to make sure nothing too bad was going on in his guys' lives. He felt compelled to do the right thing, no matter how much the kid irritated him.

Ryan didn't respond at first. He just continued to press the phone to his ear. He lowered it in slow jerky movements, not making eye contact with John. "Nothing. All good," he chirped out. Though John thought it felt a little forced.

Ryan swung into his car and didn't bother with choosing a song before he pulled out of his spot. Clearly, he was in a rush to leave. As he drove by the girls, he tipped an imaginary hat to the ladies and sped out of the parking lot.

John opened his mouth to say a quick goodbye when he noticed Jen limping over to her car after waving goodbye to Julie. He looked down at her legs and cringed. He didn't even think about what the saddles were doing to her bare legs all day. The different buckles and flaps on the saddles can pinch bare skin something fierce. He chastised himself looking at her red and blistered legs. Why hadn't she said something at any point? He was willing to bet that Julie had an extra pair of chaps somewhere that she could have dug out and lent to her.

He jogged over to her when she stopped in front of an old beater. Jesus.

This car needed some work.

He'd have to talk to Lenny about the salary for his people at some point. She should very much be able to afford something a little more reliable than this bucket of rust.

"You okay?" he asked as he got to her.

Her face was red and pinched in pain. She straightened upon facing him, rubbing her hands together. He looked down and realized that gripping the reins and pommel for that many hours without being used to that would be equally painful.

"You know this already but take an Epsom salt bath, and ice your hands. Take ibuprofen tonight to keep the pain at bay and the swelling down. Don't plan on doing anything too active tomorrow." He peeked down at her legs, *for research*, and looked back up. "And it wouldn't hurt to put some ointment on those once you get them clean. Barns are dirty places."

Her cheeks flamed. "Yeah...thanks. I'll be okay."

"You could have said something." He crossed his arms as he chastised her for not taking better care of herself. Her eyes dipped down to them before flying back up to his. He would have thought it impossible, but her face got even redder.

Checking him out again, Ms. Medina? The woman was always eyeing him like a slab of meat.

What he wouldn't give for her to eat him.

"And quit? You guys weren't quitting. I sure wasn't going to."

"We're professional athletes. You...are not."

She narrowed her eyes at him. "No, I may not be a professional athlete. But I'm not a wimp either."

"Who said you were a wimp?"

"You know what I mean. I'm fine. I've experienced worse. Trust me."

What did she mean by that? Did this have anything to do with that shady father of hers? She mentioned him a couple of times to John and he already didn't like the guy. Classic narcissist and toxic manipulator. Unfortunately, Jen didn't seem to see him that way.

As most kids don't.

Jen had an uncomfortable look on her face, clearly regretting what she said. She looked towards the car longingly and he took mercy.

He patted the hood of her car. "Okay then. I'll see you later?"

"Uh, yeah. See you tomorrow maybe," she mumbled almost inaudibly. As he started to walk away, he heard her say his name softly. "Uh, John?"

Fuck, it sounded pretty when she said it.

He turned to look at her, raising an eyebrow while he waited.

She looked down at her toes then back up at him. "At some point, we really should make the time to go on that date."

Fuck.

They locked eyes for a minute, letting the silence hang heavy between them.

"Heal up, cowgirl. We have a long season left. Longer if we go to the Super Bowl. For once in my life, I'm almost hoping we don't even make playoffs," he said softly back to her, not even believing that he said those damning words aloud.

Knock on wood.

John then turned and walked to his SUV, trying extremely hard to remind himself they could explore each other all they wanted soon enough.

Patience was a virtue.

Even though the public nicknamed him Saint, John never felt particularly virtuous.

However, the more he got to know her and listen to her talk about Lexie and William, the more he understood her. Her responsibilities and debt to them were clearly self-imposed. They meant the world to her, and she to them. He wouldn't be the reason that those relationships imploded. Not when she didn't have many others to rely on. He'd have his time with her eventually, but they wouldn't do it in a way that distracted him from his job, or in a way that risked her relationship with her family. Timing. It was all about timing.

And patience.

Fuck.

Maybe he was Saint John.

CHAPTER NINETEEN

September 18, Saturday
John

John sprawled on the couch, switching back and forth between applying heat and ice on his aching body and Facetiming his mom. He always felt sore now that Lenny wasn't working.

Combine that with riding all day?

Oof.

It hadn't been that long since he last rode. How could he hurt this bad?

Another charley horse hit his calf muscle. As he lurched down to try to straighten his foot and rub it out, his lower back spasmed.

"Oh! This Jen girl sounds wonderful," his mother gushed on the laptop screen in front of him.

She was.

John pulled his attention back to the call.

"No, Mom. This *Jen girl* is my co-worker." His mom would start a rumor mill phone tree if she even got a hint that John was interested in Jen. He might as well give an exposé to the paper himself.

"Oh, nonsense, you should ask her on a date. She sounds like a dear. Same with that sweet rancher, what was her name?"

"Julie."

"Oh, yes. Lots of J names. Good taste in naming, I say."

His dad chuckled out a rough grunt but otherwise sat mute next to his wife, letting her do all the talking. As was their routine.

"Oh my, and that Ryan Cole. I watched some of his college games before the Spartans drafted him, and my oh my, what a talented athlete. He doesn't really have the typical body type for a quarterback, and he plays a different sort of football. But it will be a good change for the program once you retire and settle down. Speaking of. Have you been on any dates lately?"

Subtle as a brick through a window.

"Mom."

"Mary," John's dad chimed in.

"What?" she asked innocently, like she did every time.

"No dating during the season. Especially not co-workers. And even if I did, I'm not talking to you about it."

"Are you gay?"

He spit his water everywhere.

He didn't know whether to be grateful his mom didn't know about his rather adventurous past or to be grateful that his mom, a strongly religious southern woman, seemed okay with the idea of him being gay.

"I told you he wasn't gay, Mary."

"Well, you never know. All those girls might have been his mustache rides."

John choked again.

"Beards, Mary."

She waved her hand. "Whatever. I just wanted to ask in case he was having a tough time addressing it with us."

"Nope, not gay, Mom. But good to know you're open to alternative lifestyles."

"When are you going to settle down and give me grandbabies? I'm not going to live forever, you know. And just look at your father. He's going to die of a heart attack before you're forty if he doesn't start cutting back on the butter and bacon."

"Woman," his father warned. She wasn't wrong. His dad lived a hard life. From childhood to now, the man worked his ass off. He came from a long family line of anger and discontent. How he ever landed his mother was still a mystery. The woman was sweet as pie but could still give you a cavity if you weren't paying attention. His father changed after John left for college. He could never quite place it—the change that happened. But he could never quite shake the feeling of being judged and found lacking. Well, that would change after another Super Bowl ring.

His mother continued needling him. She was not to be stopped. Per usual. He could feel the familiar headache creeping in.

Thus, why he only called once every week or two. She was a one-woman show and didn't know the meaning of the word enough. God help him if she ever met Jen. They'd take over the world.

Jesus, what a thought.

Yet, he couldn't stop his smile.

"No dating during the season, Mom. I'll let you know if I knock up any hookers in the meantime."

She stared at him, a petulant look on her face. "Well, at least then I'd have a grandbaby."

Stone-cold killer, that one. He couldn't make this stuff up if he tried.

"Welp, look at the time, got to go and nuke this lavender wrap for another go. I'll call you guys later."

They said their goodbyes and John sat back in the chair, sinking deep into the cushions. He never thought about having kids. He was always so focused on the team, but the kids at the equine event earlier were cute and fun. Something about seeing Jen interact with them had him questioning what he'd be like as a dad. He'd be a fantastic one, John knew that. His parents taught him well. But at the risk of sounding like his mom, when would he have the time and at what cost?

CHAPTER TWENTY

September 19, Sunday
Jen

After driving home from the equine center, Jen tossed and turned all night. Unable to think of anything else but calling John and asking him to distract her from her bodily discomfort. Maybe he could give her a massage.

Finally, Jen gave up trying to sleep and went into the stadium super early the next morning to see if she could get a quick session of her own with one of the other therapists. She was able to squeak a quick ten minutes out of her weak-handed coworker before she gave up and rolled off the table. God, he sucked at his job. How had Lenny tolerated him for so long? Was good, trustworthy help that hard to find?

Well, if her role in the organization was anything to go by...yes.

Jen had small bandages covering the sores on her legs where the saddles rubbed and pinched, and it caused her to move like a ninety-year-old grandmother. And of course, John and Julie didn't lie. Today felt worse.

To think she considered herself an athlete and in decent shape.

Ha! What a joke that was.

With every player she rubbed for the rest of the day, her stiff fingers screamed.

She iced them while mentally regretting her decision to work until John came in. When he saw her, a soft wince marred his handsome face. He then looked around for another therapist to save her from having to rub him.

Whether it was from sympathy for her hands, or reluctance to have her touch him, Jen didn't know.

When John saw that Weak Hands was the only other massage therapist in the room, his entire body deflated.

He visibly waffled as he stared at her. His eyes fixated on the ice on her hands and when they locked eyes, the indecision in them was clear. Jen found herself unable to say anything to convince him.

Jen watched with a mixture of disappointment and relief as his shoulders sagged further when he came to his decision. Saint John apparently refused to let her work through her pain, even if his body desperately needed it.

His full lips twisted to the side in an apologetic grimace, and he shook his head briefly before turning and leaving the massage room. As soon as the door shut behind him, she felt like she could breathe again, but at the same time, she also felt...lost.

That strange feeling left her buzzing and thinking about John for hours after.

A part of her hoped he'd throw caution to the wind and come back. How she itched to put her hands on him. Not necessarily in the way her job asked of her, but still. Jen ached for that thrill that lit her skin whenever she ran into him. Their verbal sparring felt electric and exhilarating, and for the first time in her life, she wondered if she could take the chance and risk her career for a shot with a guy like him. No, scratch that. Not a guy like him, just...him.

John.

Only John had ever made her question her strict moral compass. She never felt this way about anyone.

With how often she caught herself smiling after their scrapping and teasing, she wondered if maybe he would be worth the risk. If he'd be worth it all. Hell, two weeks ago they bantered and teased for an hour straight while Jen worked on Ryan. After John left, Jen's lingering heart flutters caused her to feel jittery and restless. In fact, she was so amped that even Lexie commented on her attitude that evening at their dinner date with William. Talk about embarrassing.

Clearly, John liked her too. The only question, how much, and would it be worth the risk? They'd find out soon, but maybe not soon enough.

Chapter Twenty-One

September 22, Wednesday
Jen

"Oh lordy, that scene was hot." Lexie fanned herself with her diner napkin. She had fluorescent pink, purple, and blue streaks in her black hair this month. "To celebrate Bisexuality Day this month," she explained at their confused expressions.

"You're not kidding. My emotions were having a crisis. I didn't know whether I wanted to have sex or cry," Chloe chimed in, slouched down in her signature comfy, yet baggy clothes.

"It's the hormones." Rose nodded in solidarity as she rubbed her rounded belly, happiness and exhaustion on her freckled face. Being pregnant with twins could do that to you.

Chloe was living through her postpartum period and was emotionally all over the place lately. Luckily, the mood swings were all variations of happiness: random giggle fits one minute, a content yet tired mini nap the next. Chloe's house of cards had toppled this fall when it was revealed that she was intending to act as a surrogate for Rose and to give her the babies she was carrying. Things only got crazier after that, but it all worked out in the end. Chloe was getting her happy ending.

Rose was experiencing a little more...volatile emotions.

"Do you think writers take from their own experiences when they write?" Jen asked.

"Sometimes, sure," Megan said while munching on a fry. "But think about it. It can't all be from experience. Otherwise, that makes me way more terrified of writers like Stephen King. Some of it must come from imagination and research." She paused. "I hope."

"God," Julie chimed in, "I really hope for the author's sake that some parts were based on experience." She sighed. "Every woman should get that kind of passion at some point in their life."

All the women joined in on a group moment of reflection. The book was freaking hot.

Jen invited Julie to join their hodgepodge book club and the equestrian fit right in. They picked up a couple of other people in the last few months, but it was a smaller group today.

Jen picked at a corner of the placemat which doubled as a kids' coloring sheet. As the book club crew continued to gush over the recent read, Jen read a printed trivia question while continuing her internal debate about having sex with John. The smell of diner food and the low buzz of conversation flooded her senses, souring her fantasy of John taking her on a massage table at work.

"My darling!"

All the girls' heads jerked towards the diner entrance as Ryan burst through the diner's front door. The man did nothing in half-measures.

Ryan came over to their corner table and squeezed into the booth next to Jen. He shrugged off his jacket and dropped it on the floor next to him. Ryan slung an arm around her shoulders and gave her a peck on the cheek.

"My queen, my life, my love. I've been looking everywhere for you." He looked at the ladies around him. "Ladies," he purred. "Looking fabulous as always." He elbowed Jen and demanded, "Why am I never invited to these?"

"Because you can't read."

"Lies!" he gasped in outrage. Ryan leaned toward the other ladies. "Excuse her, she's just grouchy. I can absolutely read and I would love to join your club. Thank you for asking. What are we reading this time?"

The women all chuckled and gave their greetings, all of them very used to Ryan and his theatrics at this point.

Jen nabbed her paperback off the table in front of him and put it on the chair on her opposite side. Far away from Ryan's nosy eyes.

"What are you doing here?" Jen asked.

He fluttered his lashes at her and said, "Nice seeing you too, sunshine."

His easy smiles didn't give her the butterflies like John's did. John's normally austere demeanor made each smile feel hard-earned. Like she won it in battle.

Ryan's smiles were just that. Easy. Even ridiculously handsome, they definitely only shared a sibling vibe. His flirting came off as absurd and playful rather than seductive. At least from her point of view. Julie viewed his charm differently and glowed whenever he pointed his pretty blues at her.

Jen simply found him ridiculous.

Ryan leaned over her to say something to Rose. Before Jen could react, he shot up and snatched the book from its resting place on the chair beside her.

"Well, well." Ryan shot her a contemplative look. "Kitty has claws." Jen ripped the book from his grasp and shoved it in her purse on her other side, hiding the half-naked man and woman on the cover. "This is interesting." He looked at her with a raised eyebrow.

"Shut up," she muttered, dragging her water across the table for a sip. She refused to make eye contact.

"What's interesting?" Lexie said from across the table, her electric ice-blue eyes narrowed on Ryan's deep blue ones.

"I knew you ladies had a book club. But I didn't know it was naughty." His voice was pure sex and Jen sunk further down into her seat. Her cheeks felt hot. Ryan cocked his head as he looked at Lexie. "I bet you picked this."

"Think what you want," Lexie said. "But why is it interesting that a healthy, adult woman would be entertained by a novel that had some spice to it?"

"I'm not insulting the book choice, princess. Just surprised straight-laced Jen over here would be into it. Heck, I was starting to get asexual vibes with all the attention she doesn't give us boys when we're half-dressed in front of her." He turned to face her directly. "Now I see that you're more into men who wear kilts." Jen blushed even harder as he put on a terrible Scottish accent. "Or maybe it has to be a certain man in particular." He let that hang there and eyed Jen with a glint in his eye.

Lexie watched him from across the table, her earlier humor gone. "Don't tease her."

Ryan looked up. "Jen's tough, she can take it. It doesn't bother her." He looked down at Jen and then stopped as he really looked at her. "Oh, it does." His eyebrows shot up. "My bad, darlin'." He gave her shoulders a tight squeeze, leaving his arm slung over her.

His body stilled for a moment as he looked at something outside the windows over her head. He got this look on his face that spelled terrible things for her, she knew it.

"What?" she asked, afraid of the answer.

She really didn't want to know but felt like she needed to for self-preservation.

"Just...helping a sister out and getting the ball rolling," he said. "I've always wondered, does reading these sorts of books get a woman's engine revving?" He looked over the ladies as a couple of them nodded more vigorously than others. "If they're done right, I mean?" More nods. "You guys ever read about Mr. Darcy and what's-her-name?"

"Obviously. *Pride and Prejudice* is a classic," Jen answered, and Lexie rolled her eyes.

Like he even had to ask.

"That's what I thought," he said as he looked down at her lips.

"What—"

He kissed her!

The buffoon leaned in and started smooching her right there in the diner.

What. The. Fuck.

To be fair, he kept his mouth closed and made it more of a pressing of lips rather than a kiss. Jen thought she detected the soft hint of bubble gum.

What was the doofus getting at by this stupid move? She tried to pull back but he simply followed her, his face smooshed right up against hers.

They had never even shared even an inkling of attraction towards each other.

She ripped further away, nearly toppling over, and scowled at him, wiping at her smudged lip gloss.

He simply leaned back and raised a thumb to wipe at the corner of his mouth while looking toward the front door. A smug expression on his face.

"You're welcome."

Huh?

Jen felt a chill dance down her back and she looked up. By the door was John, wearing the glower to end all glowers. With him, was his agent, Richie Mayne.

Fucking meddlesome Ryan.

She elbowed him hard and he oof'ed out a breath but otherwise hummed happily at his stupid, and reckless, matchmaking scheme.

He knew what was at stake.

"Richie," Ryan called out, not budging from his seat next to her.

Richie and John made their way over, and John's dark eyes zeroed in on the way Ryan's arm draped oh so casually near her breast.

She hastily shrugged off Ryan's arm and took a quick sip of her water. Again, she avoided eye contact.

"By all means, don't let us interrupt." John's tone was biting.

Well, maybe he'd get a taste of how she felt whenever his adoring half-dressed fans hung all over him.

She shook herself. She had no claim over him or anything. She needed to get her head examined, stat.

He cast a dark look over Jen and Ryan. However, his harsh expression softened as he greeted the other women. All the women ran in Spartan circles one way or another. He wandered around the chairs and benches to give Rose, Megan, and Chloe quick pecks on their cheeks. He gave Julie a solid handshake and a nod. By now, the Springfield circle of connections brought them all into each other's paths at one point or another, so no introductions were necessary.

John went over to Lexie and muttered, "Lex, good to see you."

She jumped up on tiptoe to give him a kiss on the cheek.

Which gave the entire diner a shot at her diamond-accented G-string that pulled up high on her hip and peeked out from under her low-rise jeans.

She felt Ryan freeze solid next to her.

Interesting.

Over the years, good ol' Lex failed to mention she was on such great terms with the sexy quarterback until after Jen cried to her about missing her chance with him. Lexie's response? "I've known him forever. He was my dad's first pick as a team owner. He's like my uncle or something. Why would I talk to you about my uncle? Just...ew."

As Richie and John made small talk with the ladies, Jen did her best to disappear into her seat. It didn't help that Ryan kept smacking his lips and rubbing the corner with his thumb.

Just what she needed.

John thinking that she was hooking up with Ryan.

"Jen," John said in a low greeting.

She jolted, whipped her head up, and saw John staring down at her expectantly.

"What? Still lost in the kiss?" John's lip curled.

Did she see a hint of hurt in his eyes?

"No. I—"

"She's probably still daydreaming about their erotica this month." Ryan helpfully chimed in. He reached around her, dug into her purse, and plopped her book on the table. "She loved the roguish brute who was a bit of a taciturn fellow. Bit of a forbidden romance, you could say." He cocked an eyebrow. "Interesting, is it not?" he asked, his face all innocence. The guy could get an Oscar.

Jen used her heel to drive a solid kick into his shin.

The bastard didn't even wince.

"I have to get going anyway. Jen, I'm heading back to the stadium for some afternoon video. Are you heading in?" Ryan stood up and donned his jacket.

"Yup, I'll be there when we're done here."

John looked between them, his eyes working something out.

"Ladies, it was my absolute pleasure, as always. And I look forward to next time." He swooped down and snatched Jen's book from the table. "For research." He shot them a wink and then turned to nod at John and Richie. He made his way through the diner and paused at the door. He shot a wave to Butch and Mitchell who were on the other side of the restaurant, grabbing a meal. "Coach." Ryan's head bobbed. Then he sauntered out of the diner.

Victor stomped over from around John and Richie.

"Pick a new book next month," he grumbled.

"Why's that?" Megan asked.

"You're making my other customers uncomfortable."

Lexie batted her eyes at him. "Uncomfortable or aroused?" she purred sassily.

Victor cut her a look that had men playing dead during the war. Lexie just waited, her perfect eyebrows raised, shameless mischief in every line of her body.

"Aroused," they heard a grouchy old timer wheeze out from the bar a few feet away. The old woman cackled into her eggs and bacon while jotting down another word in her crossword puzzle, not looking up once.

Guess they were louder than they thought.

Jen looked back to the men to find John watching her with a curious expression on his face. She felt her cheeks flame up again and she reached for her water. She made eye contact with Megan across the table. Megan just looked at her, her own eyes darting between Jen and John, clearly working something out.

Fine. Jen would focus on the table. The table wasn't looking at her.

Anything to not look at John's probing and anticipatory gaze.

She had a feeling Ryan had thrown down a challenge flag and John hadn't lasted as a starting quarterback for fifteen years without being able to handle the pressure.

John was absolutely ready for the game to start if his hungry expression was anything to go by.

After the men grabbed their food and left, the girls all swung their heads to Jen. As they all opened their mouths to interrogate her, Jen jumped up, made quick goodbyes, and rushed out the door. She had no idea what just happened, but something had shifted. Ryan might have ruined all of the careful avoidance she and John had been trying to navigate.

The scary part?

She didn't feel all that upset about it.

CHAPTER TWENTY-TWO

September 24, Friday
John

Their Thursday night game left John sore, frustrated, and angry. His attitude improved with a night's reflection and rest, but his body screamed for either a recovery massage or a soak in the whirlpool tub, so he dragged himself into the stadium on Friday afternoon.

He swung by the massage room and met a sea of faces, all exhausted and pained, resting on various surfaces and counting down the seconds until their turn. A couple of the athletic trainers were in there as well. They sat on the mats and stretched some of the players as they waited.

From the beginning, the Spartan model centered on a holistic wellness approach to health and fitness. Since the first season, there were massage therapists on staff to aid in recovery and healing.

The game yesterday had been more violent than usual; everyone got beat up.

John personally wanted to drown himself in a bottle of whiskey and pretend the game never happened, but that would solve nothing. He couldn't make excuses. His body hurt and his performance suffered. He needed to put a little bit of trust in Jen and see if she could work out some of the demons that the other massage therapists couldn't seem to touch.

He couldn't wait any longer and would risk the consequences.

The time has come to make a move. Get her out of his system. He didn't need any distractions right now, but thankfully Jen didn't seem high maintenance. She had a vested interest in keeping their fling discrete and maybe it would work off enough tension that he could get rubbed by her without wanting to strip her naked and lick every inch of her toned, golden little body.

Immediately, John's eyes zeroed in on her fine ass cupped in her khakis. This particular pair was one of his favorites. It had gemstones on the back pockets, and it hugged her thick ass and thighs like a second skin. John could almost imagine what she would feel like if he put a hand on each cheek and pulled her close. The thought of each soft cheek filling his hands already had him stiffening. That wasn't a great omen of how he'd be able to handle her rubbing him tonight.

Jen intensely focused on working a knot out of Liam Polowski's quad. The tight end had been lit up several times during the game. Because he was so large, the defensive players sometimes tried to hit him low to trip him up. The man had more hardware in him than a freaking robot.

Jen hit a spot and Liam let out a groan that had some of the waiting men ribbing him good-naturedly. However, a couple of the guys looked miserable as they waited for their chance to climb up on the tables. John couldn't blame them. The one guy therapist wasn't so bad, but the other had weak hands and damn-near wet himself if they tried to talk to him directly. The players on his list looked like they were heading to a date with a guillotine.

John took a breath and held it as he surveyed the room. He watched Liam's eyes close in pleasure as Jen worked.

John braced himself.

"Hey, Jen."

Her head jolted up in surprise, clearly not thinking John would talk to her.

"How late are you here tonight?"

The room got quiet.

Jen put her hands on her fit waist as she arched her back in a small stretch. She left a small oil smear on her polo where her hands rested. She touched her hair before lowering her hand and dashing a look over to the whiteboard. "Until everyone leaves, I guess." She shrugged, wincing at the movement. She leaned her neck to the side, where he heard a small pop echo across the room.

"I still have to hit the sauna for a bit, but will you have time to work on my shoulder after I'm done? I can leave my cell number next to my name. I'll wait until you're done with everyone else. Just give me a call when you're starting on your last player?"

Alarm bells were going off in his head.

Wait until everyone was gone? And *then* have her massage him?

Jesus Christ.

Nothing would stop them from letting things get too far if no one was around.

The alarms clanged louder.

He chose to ignore them.

The room seemed to hold its breath.

She blinked up at him, surprise in her amber eyes. She looked around the room and cleared her throat. "Uh, yeah, of course. No problem." She coughed into her elbow again and looked everywhere but at him.

He shuffled to the whiteboard, careful not to let any limp show in his step. He signed his name and number on the board at the bottom of her column and exited without meeting anyone's eyes.

As he shut the door behind him, he heard the room remain in absolute silence.

He sighed.

They were definitely not as surreptitious as they thought.

He hung out around the stadium doing various tasks for the rest of the evening. He spent some time in the sauna, sucked down a recovery shake while watching game film, paced the ever-empty halls, and then found himself wandering back down to the massage rooms.

He made himself busy for several hours. Yet, he never received a call or text. Vicki used to do that frequently as well. She'd be radio silent for hours, sometimes days at a time, but when she texted, she expected him to jump and ask how high. Vicki had to be the center of his universe, or so she believed. She needed to come first above all else, even football.

No wonder they didn't last.

John fumed that Jen forgot him. He never expected that of her. Sure, their connection centered around sexual awareness and desire, but he thought they cared about each other as well. That they meshed well intellectually, as well as entertained each other. Her with her peppy spirit, and he as a tired and quiet grump. And yet, here she was, forgetting he existed.

He ground his teeth together.

This sucked.

Maybe Weak Hands hadn't left yet.

As he pushed through the massage room door, John came up short when he found Jen working on Danny Parker, the other two therapists nowhere to be found. Ryan Cole sat in the corner, typing on his computer, icing his shoulder and knee.

They all looked up when he came in.

"Sorry, boss. Just trying to get Jen to work out this pull in my lower back," Danny explained, clearly feeling guilty for adding time to John's wait.

"No problem." John waved him off and wandered over to find a seat.

Ryan looked up and raised his brows. His blue eyes darted up at the clock and back to John, a clearly suppressed smile dancing around the corners of his mouth. Ryan snapped his laptop closed and hopped up. He arched his long torso and gave a dramatic groan. "Well, I'm out of here."

Jen shot him a look of surprise.

What the hell?

"Nah, nah, don't miss me when I'm gone. My heart can't handle the guilt." Ryan walked over to Jen, gave her a quick peck on the cheek, slapped Danny on the shoulder, and walked out without even so much as a hello or goodbye to his captain.

John watched his young replacement amble from the room, wishing he still had that energy. He surprised himself with the bitterness that hit him as he remembered Ryan and Jen's kiss. John had never been the jealous type. Yet, even after figuring out why Ryan did it, John still couldn't wash away the prickle of irritation at the kid. Jen's lips shouldn't be anywhere near that guy. They were John's. In a way. Or at least, promised to him. Not permanently obviously. But...there was a promise there...right?

Would it be worth the wrath of Lenny if he ever found out that John broke his promise to keep his hands to himself? She wouldn't be a distraction anymore if he could get her out of his system.

John silently watched Jen knead Danny's muscles, her face wrinkling as she worked on a particularly tight spot and thought yeah...it would be worth it.

Her brains, her wit, her drive, her humor...and that body.

Jesus.

He found himself staring at her chest and quickly pulled out his phone while he waited for Jen to wrap up with Danny. He caught up on some emails but found himself losing focus whenever Jen walked by. Each pass carried a small breeze of her signature coconut and lime smell. He never thought he was much of a beach person, but the smell made him want to go to the islands and drink frozen cocktails. With Jen.

Maybe a topless beach.

Or a nude beach.

He started imagining how her shapely body would look sprawled out...

Fuck!

He made himself refocus on his phone.

"Alrighty, Ms. Medina. I'm all good for now." Danny donned his shirt and jacket and slipped on his boots. "Don't know how you make a lower back injury feel better by working my butt and hip, but somehow you do. Thanks again, Jen." Danny gave John a low wave before exiting the room and leaving the two of them in awkward silence.

They stared at each other for a beat before Jen cleared her throat and wandered over to the sink.

"Let me wash down the table and my hands, and then you can hop on up," she said without turning around.

Her normal fiery demeanor gone, she looked exhausted. Her eyes didn't have their normal shine and all her signature makeup had faded away. In fact, even her hair was springing out from her moniker bun.

"You all right?" John peered at her, not moving from his chair.

She waved him away. "Yeah, totally fine. Just a long couple of days."

"If you're too tired—"

"God, no!" Jen looked embarrassed at the outburst but soldiered on. "I'm not passing up my chance to rub you. Not when you finally are letting me work on you." She blushed and cut herself off, wiping down the table with intensity. "And don't think that I don't know you're hiding a limp." She cast a quick look down at his legs and looked back to the table. "What, uh, what do you want to start with?"

John took off his shirt and tossed it on the chair. "Let's go with upper body and see where that takes us."

That came out funny and he hesitated for a second before approaching the table.

He felt a weird charge in the air and saw her staring at his torso. Her eyes locked on his chest. Her throat moved as she swallowed, eyes not blinking. She gave a start and turned to grab some oil.

Fuck. This was a terrible idea.

Yet, he couldn't stop himself as he walked to the table.

She turned back around with pink spread wide across her cheeks. Jen ran through a list of questions about allergies, sensitivities, prior reactions, and more.

"Okay, I want to diffuse some essential oils if you're good with that. I think I have a blend you'll like."

He nodded before hopping up to sit on the table, being careful of his left leg.

Jen walked over to the oil diffuser in the corner and started adding drops to it.

"Quick question," she called out. "What do you want as a base? Sandalwood or Coconut? I want to try something a little unusual."

"Coconut."

The speed of his answer must have surprised her. Her eyebrows rose before she turned back and added a couple more drops into her potion.

She came back to him, followed by a faint scent that reminded him of warm days and hot sand. The diffuser burbled happily in the corner, casting a cool mist up in the air.

"Um, I'll have you lay face down in the cradle." Jen gestured to the head of the table.

He shifted his body but couldn't help the small grunt that escaped when a sore muscle protested. John heard her rubbing her hands together above him as he got comfortable. The first touch of her warm hands on his back caused him to jerk.

"Sorry," she murmured.

"It's fine," John returned, his voice muffled.

Everywhere her fingers stroked they left a fire burning in him. Already he could feel his body tightening in response to how much he wanted her.

She spread the oil in long, warm strokes. He found his eyes closing at her firm and confident pressure.

"Firmer or lighter?"

"Firmer."

He felt his body start to ache as he thought of her doing this to him while he was naked on his back.

He felt the pressure increase. She worked up under his scapula, down his back, up to his shoulder, down into his lower armpit, and up to his neck. Everywhere she touched turned to liquid. He wouldn't have believed it possible, but the arousal faded a bit as pure bliss took its place. He still wanted to throw her on the table and treat her to a happy ending, but it took a backseat to the pleasure of having her touch him and how she healed his every ache. Her fingers found the tender points, her palms worked out the tight spots, and she worked out the tight knots in his neck. She lifted his arm and let out a slight exhale at the weight. Jen tucked his arm onto her hip and continued to work on his shoulder blade. The new angle uncovered a whole new wealth of aches and pains. By the time she finished with both sides of his back, he wasn't entirely certain he hadn't dozed off.

"I want to keep working on you. I haven't even gotten to your glutes and hamstrings but, John, I really need to ask if it's okay if I go home and go to bed. I'm absolutely toast," Jen asked, her voice sounding rough and scratchy.

He felt tingles up his back when she said his name.

It felt soft and foreign coming from her lips.

Seductive even with the exhaustion coating her words.

He pushed himself up to seated and took a closer look at her appearance.

"Are you okay to drive home? How long have you been here today?" He checked the clock. "Jesus. It's ten o'clock. You worked on my back for two hours."

She yawned behind her hand. "Yeah, you needed a lot of work. I recommend drinking lots of water tonight before bed. And maybe going to see Lenny's wife for some acupuncture and acupressure. I think it would do your body some good." She finished on another huge yawn.

He hopped off the table, wincing when his knee took some weight.

She eyed him with concern. "Nope—forget I said anything, I can work on that leg tonight. I can't in good conscience send you home without removing some of that tension. I shouldn't have asked to stop." She took a couple of tired hops and swung her arms around. She tossed her neck side to side like a boxer. She had just started rubbing her cheeks vigorously when she couldn't stop another yawn that had her eyes watering.

"Don't worry about it. I'm fine until tomorrow." He pulled on his shirt and checked his phone. "I'll walk you out to your clunker. Grab your stuff. Let's go."

"Hey!" She perked up in false afront. "Don't speak ill of Roberta. She's been through a lot."

He smiled down at her and felt a tingle of relief that she still had enough energy to show some of her signature sass.

"I'm sorry I called Roberta a clunker," he placated in a teasing voice.

Jen sniffed as she tipped her nose in the air. "Be sure not to do so again."

"As my lady wishes." John bowed.

"But for real, no worries about walking me out. I have to clean and lock up in here. You don't need to hang out."

"Are you kidding? I'm walking you out to your car. It's a Friday night, it's dark out, and no one else is around. Be smart." John knew all too well the craziness that could happen on the stadium campus after hours. The security did a decent job of keeping things lit and safe, but you never knew.

The massage door opened, and Butch popped his head in. "Jenny." He came up short as he saw John. "And...John. You're both still here." His eyes darted between them. "Everything okay?"

He really should have put on his shirt by now, but he was enjoying the deer in the headlights look that Jen got every time she checked out his body. Playing with fire. He knew it but didn't want to fight it anymore. However, now that Butch was also there, it just felt awkward, so John reluctantly put it back on.

"Yup, just walking Jen out to her car when she's done," John said while pulling the shirt over his head.

"Oh, ok. Jen, I pulled something the other day, will you be in tomorrow morning?"

God, everyone always needed something from her. They needed to give her a fucking break and let her get some sleep.

"She's taking a late morning at home. But she'll be in around noon." Both heads swiveled to him. Jen's eyes were huge while Butch's narrowed in confusion.

Where the hell did that come from?

"Um, yeah, I'll be in tomorrow around noon," she said slowly, almost like a question, shooting a look at John before looking back to Butch. "I can add you to my list when I get in."

"Sounds good." Butch's eyes darted between them one more time. "Well, ahh, I'll see you both tomorrow." He made a quick exit, and John and Jen followed soon after.

As they made their way through the halls and out to the parking lot, John kept getting whiffs of the coconut oil she used. It was at odds with the fall air blowing through the parking lot.

"This is me," she added after their long, silent walk, waving weakly at her beater of a car.

"I know."

John stood by her driver's side door as she nodded her thanks for the escort out. She squeezed into her car and gave a little wave after her door shut. He was about to walk away when he heard her engine turn...not quite over.

Damn.

He wandered back to her.

Again and again, she turned the key only to have the engine sputter out on her.

"Is it the battery?" he called through her shut window.

He knew nothing about cars.

She just sat there. Staring straight ahead.

He knocked on the window with his knuckles and got no response.

"Jen…"

She came back from wherever she was and looked at him.

Shit.

He could see tears filling her eyes and the stubborn line of her jaw starting to tremble.

Fuck.

"All right there, tiger. Get out of there and I'll drive you home. We'll get someone to deal with this later."

He pulled open her door and waited for her to unfurl from the car. He put his hand on her lower back and guided her to his SUV. Her jaw started shaking as they walked, and he didn't know if it was the cold or the tears.

He got her up and into the SUV, walked around to his side, and loaded himself up. John cranked up the heat and let it sit for a minute, surfing through the stations, and giving her a chance to decide whether she wanted to have a breakdown or not.

She was sucking in some deep breaths next to him, so he wasn't quite convinced she could successfully hold it back.

A car drove past them in the parking lot, its headlights illuminating their faces in the windshield. It looked like Mitchell or Butch, but John couldn't tell for sure with the tinted windows. He waved anyway before turning to face Jen.

"You okay?"

Jen's chin thrust out and her eyes filled to the brim. At his question, she blinked hard, and a solitary tear slid down the cheek closest to him. He watched it trail down her smooth cheek until it plopped off her chin and onto her black jacket. He looked back up to her face and saw her squeezing her eyes tight.

"I'm just tired. Would you give me a ride home, please?" Each word was tight and controlled.

"Of course," he murmured.

"Enter the address in here?" He held out his phone.

Jen took it, and their fingers grazed each other, leaving John uncomfortably aroused given her clear distress. Her throat worked up and down as she suppressed her emotions and entered her address. She handed it back without looking at him and faced the passenger window.

They rode in silence as he followed the directions on his phone. Apparently, she lived within a ten-minute drive of the Spartan's campus. When he felt the boom of bass and saw people stumbling about, he thought he must have made a wrong turn. He and his real estate agent had been over this way recently to look at a building he wanted to buy and renovate, and this was certainly not the vibe during the daytime hours.

The building had potential but had clearly endured some years without much care. It looked like there used to be commercial spaces on the ground floor but now graffiti covered plywood covered many of the windows. John could see the entrance for the residential spaces and how poorly lit it was.

"You live here?" He eyed the people warily.

A small sigh. "Unfortunately." Her soft voice was a whisper in the quiet car.

He surveyed the people milling about, most of them contemplating his vehicle in a very suspicious manner.

"I'm going to walk you up."

"No. Someone will vandalize your car."

"I don't give a fuck. Better my car than you."

"I can't wait to see you pull up to the stadium in your tagged car."

Ahh, he hadn't seen her sass in a little bit. He forgot how adorable it was. Like a kitten who thought she was a tiger.

He'd love to see if her kitten or tiger came out in bed. What he wouldn't do to make her purr. Even if, anatomically speaking, tigers couldn't technically purr. In his fantasy, they could.

"It's not like I couldn't get it fixed. You? You wouldn't be fixed so easily if someone decided to make an unwise decision and hurt you."

He'd fucking kill the motherfucker.

Her face took on an oddly vulnerable look at his words. Like he slapped her. John's chest squeezed at the emotion there. Had anyone *ever* given a shit about her?

Jen unclicked her seatbelt with an intensity that had him stiffening. "I can manage. I always do." She dug savagely around the inside of her purse, pulled out a can of pepper spray, and positioned her keys between her knuckles. "I'll be fine, John. Promise. I always am." She was now avoiding eye contact.

Alarm hit him.

Was this a regular thing for her?

Jen started energetically rubbing at her eyes, slapping her checks, and adjusting her purse to be inside her jacket and John felt ice race down his back.

This was very much her life.

The *risk* she was in, *every day...*

His gut clenched at the unfamiliar fear. "Hell, no. Stay in the car," he growled at her.

John found a spot to park and shot off a quick text to his PA.

"Stay in the car." He repeated as grabbed a ball cap and put it on, ignoring the people starting to mill around.

He pushed his door open and slammed it before anyone could look inside. Not that there was anything in there, but it didn't hurt to be careful.

John shoved through bodies as he stalked over to Jen's side and stared down some idiot that didn't get out of his way quick enough. He guided her from the vehicle, noticing she had donned a hat as well. John looked down to grab her hand, but she hadn't removed the keys from her knuckles. He took them from her hand and placed them in her other hand. John leaned in and whispered in her ear, "If you need those, then we've got bigger problems. I got you." He took her hand again, pulled her close, and pushed through the crowd, making sure no one bumped into her. John shouldered through a couple of groups too inebriated to pick up on his vibe and move out of his way. He led with his body, acting as her blocker. John looked back to his SUV before they pushed inside and saw people surrounding it, peeking in.

Oh well, he'd have to deal with that next.

The hallways and stairwells were equally crowded and filled with loud music and pungent air. He would have thought the frigid air would make people find another place to party, but judging by Jen's reaction, this happened frequently.

When the catcalls started, John could feel the tension in his neck ratchet up. She squeezed his hand, whether to comfort herself or him, he didn't know, but he squeezed back.

She led him up to the third floor and down the hall. A couple guys still called out to them and followed not so far behind. Jen hesitated in front of a door but continued on. She shoved her hand into her jacket pocket and kicked at the door. She mumbled softly, "Please be here."

Huh?

Louder, she said, "Open up, munchkin. I brought home dessert, and my God, is he a looker."

John cast her a look, but she didn't look away from the door. Instead, her body was stiff and seemed hyper-focused on the men that drifted nearer as they waited in the hall.

The door opened and the meanest motherfucker John had ever seen stood there.

And he'd seen his share.

The man pulled out a wicked-looking switchblade and stepped out into the hall, looking towards Jen's admirers. Then a crazy-ass man with bright rainbow hair stepped out as well, this one holding a small black handgun.

"Someone come looking for a party?" he asked, eyes wide and not blinking. He cocked his head and smiled insanely at the admirers. He brought the gun to his lips and very slowly licked the tip, eyes wild and dead as he stared them down.

When they disbursed, John felt the urge to go with them and drag Jen behind him.

Who the hell were these psychos?

"Come in, snookums," the big man said and ushered them into the apartment.

"Thanks for that." Jen pulled her hand free, flexing it. She leaned up to give each man a quick kiss on the cheek and headed towards the kitchen. She went to a cupboard, grabbed two glasses, and filled them with water. She plopped some ice chunks in them before bringing them over to John. "And thank you. I didn't expect—"

"Are you fucking kidding me?"

Her head snapped back.

"You were seriously going to drive home solo and walk through that alone tonight?"

As Jen stared at him, the rainbow man slid in between them.

"Hi, handsome. Name's Mickey but you can call me whatever you want. Even yours." He winked. "Look away, Boo Boo. He's on my list."

The big man just grunted. "Mine too, but you don't see me cuddling up."

John's eyes shot to Jen's, but she was still looking shell-shocked at his outburst.

"Are you kidding me?" he asked again over the rainbow man's head. "In no world was that even close to being safe. How often do you do that?"

She shifted her weight, and he felt a rock land in his gut.

Often.

Every. Fucking. Night.

Shit.

He sighed and grabbed the bridge of his nose. When he noticed a small twitch in Jen's cheek, he met her eyes and gave her a look that had her small smile broadening.

Jesus, maybe he did sigh a lot.

"Umm, hello?" The rainbow man waved obnoxiously in front of John's face.

John looked down at the man, his patience wearing thin.

It must have shown on his face because the big man grabbed the rainbow man by the shoulders and moved him to the side.

"Let's give them a moment, sweetie," the big man advised.

Smart move.

Rainbow man harrumphed and tossed his gun on the couch with such disregard John looked at him in alarm.

"It's a prop," he said over his shoulder as he sashayed towards, what John presumed, was his bedroom, his hips swinging wildly.

John looked back at Jen. She looked pale, so tired judging from her eyes, but the adrenaline had woken her up. Her eyes dialed in on him and she looked ready to fight despite clearly finding him entertaining.

Good. She'd need her wits about her if she wanted to convince him not to call his friends on the force and condemn this whole damn place.

"Start talking, darlin'."

She wasted no time. "It's not usually this bad. It's later than I usually get home. I'm usually in my apartment by the time things get too crazy."

He thought back on all the nights he saw her working late.

"That's not true!" the rainbow man shouted from the other room.

John narrowed his eyes on her.

Jen wrang her hands together. "Well, it used to be mostly true. Until I took over the interim manager job. Now I'm working later into the night. Sometimes when I arrive and it's a little...wild...I'll call Benji or Mickey to walk me up."

"Also lies!"

Her head shot towards the bedroom, and she scowled at the cracked door. When she looked back to John, he raised an eyebrow at her and crossed his arms.

Jen looked around for inspiration. "Well, it's complicated."

"Give it a try, I'll see if I can keep up."

She frowned at him before looking away again. "Well, I lived here in college."

"Lexie and William let you live here?" The scowl on his face indicated exactly how he felt about that. He thought he knew her surrogate family better. They wouldn't allow her to live in such a dangerous place.

Her jaw ticked and her hip jotted out.

There's my girl.

Woah, where did that thought come from?

"Let's get something clear here, mister. William and Lexie do not *allow* me to do anything. I'm more than capable of making my own decisions. Plus, they aren't my real family, just good friends."

Bullshit, William loved her as much as his own daughter, and Lexie treated her like a sister. That was as real as it got.

"They also don't visit; she always insists on going there," a voice called out from the bedroom.

They both looked towards the bedroom for a second before turning back to each other.

"Ok, so they also don't really know about the conditions here at night." She rushed to add, "*Some* nights, not *all* nights."

He cocked his head to the side. He gave her his best 'scare the rookie straight' face. She started talking faster.

"See, I lived here in college and used to have roommates. But they moved away, and I...didn't. I'm still here. I saved to move out and go to a better place, but some things happened with my dad and here I am." She gave a weak chuckle as he made a face. "So yeah, money is a bit tight. Until I have more saved up, I can't swing a safer apartment. Next on my savings hierarchy was reopening my studio but now with my car...it's looking more and more like I have to put life on pause for a bit." She trailed off, losing some of the steam that was rallying her. "Fucking Roberta." She pinched her lips together and looked away.

John heard a soft, "What happened to Roberta?" and an indistinct returned hiss of a whisper.

As much as he wanted to fold her close and invite her to live with him, he knew that wasn't his place. But not doing so felt...wrong. She shouldn't be here. And she shouldn't be suffering through life like this, especially alone.

"I don't know what you want me to say. I'm doing the best I can." Jen stomped her foot.

Well, that stomp was adorable.

John gave her a soft smile.

The woman was getting by on faith and fumes. She needed a break.

He gave her an out by looking around the apartment. It was...interesting and definitely flamboyant.

"You come here often?"

"Yes. I live two doors down."

"People follow you up the stairs a lot?"

She started to shake her head until she stopped herself. She cast a guilty glance at the bedroom door and decided not to lie. "Sometimes."

"Your landlord doesn't care?"

"My landlord is friends with them."

"You live in a fucking opium den."

She scoffed and then looked like she immediately regretted it when she saw the anger on his face.

She went back to playing submissive.

Like she had a submissive bone in her body.

The woman was a fighter and downright obstinate to the core.

"Do the cops get called?"

"All the time."

"Does it help?"

"Sometimes. I usually head home when the coast is clear." She waved towards the bedroom. "With Benji as my escort."

"Benji is..."

"The bigger one."

He nodded.

"I'm telling William and Lexie."

She blinked. "Excuse me?"

"They should know what you're dealing with. They're rich. They can help with any financial troubles you have. Also, I'll escort you home from now on. No debate," he said when she opened her mouth.

She closed it with an audible snap and her attitude barely restrained if her expression was anything to go by.

"You'll thank me later."

"Doubtful."

Blue and white lights flashed over the apartment walls as cruisers pulled up out front of the apartment building. John strolled over to the window and looked down. He frowned when he saw a police officer get out of the cruiser and shake hands with a couple of the partygoers. He made a mental note and turned around.

"Okay, Jen. Let's get you back to your apartment."

She was watching him warily, her earlier attitude gone. John instantly went on alert.

"What's wrong?"

"Nothing. It's just," she stumbled for words, "embarrassing having you see this."

He felt his forehead wrinkle as he approached her. "Jen. It's a place to live. You're doing what you can. There is absolutely nothing to be embarrassed about."

He looked closer at her. She looked exhausted. Still her normal pretty, well, stunning honestly, just more worn out. And now that he thought about it, she arrived at the stadium before him, and Roberta was in the parking lot when he left. And he'd been seeing her at more and more socials and volunteer events.

"Are you okay? Really?" He took a chance, alarms blaring in his head, and brushed his fingers down her cheek to her chin.

She leaned into his hand for the barest of heartbeats before jerking her head away.

That damn moral compass again.

"Don't go getting touchy with me now, Cap. I'm tired enough that I don't trust myself to say no. The guilt and anxiety that would hit me the morning after would be insane. My psyche wouldn't know what to do with it and my therapist would have a field day trying to process it all. Let's head back to my place if the halls are clear." She whipped her head back to him. "Oh my God. I didn't mean that you'd also come back to my place. Not like that. I just meant you'd walk me back to my place and then promptly leave." Her entire face turned brilliantly red. "I mean, you wouldn't need to leave. You could come in for water or something." Her eyes got big. "That's not a come-on. I just meant I didn't want to just use you." Jen now added flailing hands to the flaming car accident of an explanation. "For walking me back. And then just kick you out. You know, rudely. So, you could walk me back, and come in, or not, for a drink. And then leave. Promptly. No funny business." She started twisting her hands while fidgeting on her feet. Jen rubbed at her face. "I'm tired. I'm sorry. I'm done now." She peeked up at him and asked, "Do people die from jumping out windows three stories up?"

What a weird question.

Then John saw her eyes dart over to the windows across the apartment.

They stared at each other for half a heartbeat. Then John threw back his head and roared in laughter.

Perfect Ms. Medina was actually a hot mess. Who would have guessed?

He laughed until he had to reach up and wipe a small tear from the corner of his eyes. His chest and stomach ached from laughing so hard and his cheeks hurt from smiling so much. He heaved a breath trying to reclaim some semblance of control but froze when he took in the expression on her face.

God, he wanted to fuck her.

Nope, redirect thoughts immediately.

Grandma, Grandpa, Mom, Dad, shoveling stalls, two-a-days, Mitchell, Butch, Ryan fucking Cole.

He stepped forward, reached for her elbow, and guided her to the door.

"Bye folks," he called towards the bedroom door, now more open than before.

"Bye, honey! Call me!" He heard shushing and masculine giggles in the back before opening the front door and checking the hall.

When he saw it was clear, he guided her out and said, "After you."

He was frustratingly aware of how fragile she seemed at the moment.

Vicki seemed delicate too. But she certainly never had a dream to forge her own path, willing to eat endless shit in the process of pursuing it.

Jen was eating endless shit, for everyone else. Relying on herself and her faith in her abilities to make it on her own.

The pressure of those responsibilities, combined with the grief over the belief that she forever lost her chance at her dream?

No wonder she looked exhausted and beaten.

John fought the urge to invite her to live with him. She'd be safe. And she'd be able to save up cash quicker.

She brought them to her door and inserted her key. Before she turned it, she looked up at him. Her mouth opened and snapped shut. Jen whipped back around and unlocked the door. She pushed it open and shifted in the doorframe, staring at her exposed apartment but not entering, but also, not turning to face him.

John took mercy on her.

He put a hand on her lower back and urged her in, one hundred percent ready to turn around and leave. Until he saw some artwork on her living room wall. He nudged her and let himself in, looking at the frames.

"These are fantastic. Did you do them?"

The colors were bright and chaotic. Each frame a unique size that showcased various sites around Springfield. He saw Versailles' rooftop terrace depicted in neon paints and thought how much the restaurant manager would love to have that in their entrance.

His eyes drifted over Baystate Stadium, done in similar hues and John had to swallow the emotion rising in his throat. It hadn't changed that much over the years, but he remembered that outpost building. And the small snack shack the management installed to help the tailgaters replace anything that they had forgotten, lost, broke, or eaten. The snack shack had grown a lot bigger in recent years.

God.

Was it really that small back then?

He felt Jen move up to his side, facing the pictures, a small smile playing around her mouth.

"Nope. Not mine. My friend painted those. Super talented, as you can see." She wet her lips and continued speaking. "I wish I had half of her skill." She sighed and kicked absently at the throw rug by her feet. Jen turned to face him, grabbing her right elbow with her left hand. "I like what I'm doing now with the Spartans.

But I miss having something for myself, that I grew, that I created. Sometimes, I want to run away and start fresh, you know? Go where I know nobody and have no expectations or responsibilities and just start anew." She turned her head to look back at the paintings. "But I love this city and I love its people. It's not huge, but it's such a hub to New England. Like a bridge between Connecticut and New Hampshire. I love that. Small town vibe in a city atmosphere. So even though sometimes it feels suffocating trying to make all these people happy...I know I could never actually leave. I don't know how to describe it. Do you know what I'm trying to say?" She was staring unseeing at the wall, her eyes distant and unfocused.

"I think that a lot of your stressors are self-imposed. I don't think for one second that William would hold it against you if you said you didn't want to stay with the team. I also don't think Lexie would hold it against you. And from what you've said of your father...it's probably a good thing I don't know the guy because I'd probably have some choice words about his decision-making ability and the positions he puts you in. Then again, I would have cut him off a long time ago." He shrugged at her shocked expression. "Heck, the way I see it, you have more in common with William than your actual dad. You both like reading, a quiet space to think, being outside, and love this city." John looked meaningfully at the artwork. "Maybe the next step isn't just getting through your time with the Spartans and reopening your studio. Doesn't sound like that will solve your problems. Maybe instead, you should be thinking about how the current people around you see you, and choosing how you will let it affect you. Because you make it sound like you owe William this time because you owe him this great debt, but Jen, I don't think he sees it that way. I've known him for fifteen years. There's no way he would welcome you into his family the way he has if he didn't already consider you family. And if he didn't disown Lexie after her time in Italy a couple of years ago, or at least take money out of her trust fund, then there's no way he was holding any sort of debt between you two when he helped you out when you needed it."

Jen stared at him open-mouthed and eyes wide. Like she couldn't believe that he was saying those things.

Like she had never even considered it from that angle before.

Christ. Her father really did a number on her.

"People don't always expect repayment for a nice gesture, Jen," John said softly while looking into her eyes. He leaned forward just a bit and raised his eyebrows at her while he waited for her confirmation that she knew that. And he waited some more. Wow. "You know that right? Some people just want their friends and family to be happy and to succeed and if they have the means or ability to make that happen, they'll try to do so."

She still stared at him but now her golden eyes were swimming with unshed tears. Jen rolled her lips together, gave a soft cough into her elbow and looked away, blinking furiously. She took a deep breath, and John couldn't stop himself. His eyes darted down to Jen's chest before he wrestled them back to the wall. But the thought wouldn't leave him.

That ass. Those breasts. Those lips.

Ah, hell. What was wrong with him? Clearly, the woman was upset and here he was checking her out.

John shifted his weight uncomfortably. Did he hug her? Leave her to her emotions and realizations? Sit with her awhile?

"Thanks for walking me back and making sure I was okay." Her voice was thready, and she visibly started to lose hold on her emotions.

"That's what friends do. I, uh... Jen, are you sure you're okay?" She now sniffed daintily and swiped an angry hand at her eyes, catching a tear that escaped.

"Is that what we are? Friends?" She skipped answering his question and asked her own million-dollar question.

"I think so." John took a step closer. He didn't want to overstep and touch her when she didn't want that, but he also didn't want to have said things that hurt her and then abandon her to deal with that solo either.

Jen solved his dilemma for him.

"I'm fine. I just need space. Too many people today, too much talking. My body hurts, my head hurts, my apartment building sucks, and I feel very conflicted about realizing that I made William out to be the bad guy in this scenario of mine."

John opened his mouth to protest but she got there first.

"You know what I mean."

He did, so he shut his mouth and took a step back.

"I just...need some space. So, thank you for walking me home and giving me some good things to think about."

He walked to the door and hovered, not quite sure how to end it. The day had taken a weird turn and he didn't know how to handle this.

Jen followed him to the door, now much more in control of her emotions. Her face was clearer and calmer, and she didn't look like she was heading for a breakdown anymore. Instead, she leaned in and tentatively pulled him in a hug, crossing a line they had very strictly not allowed themselves to cross.

Even so, he pulled her tight and dipped his face into her neck, sucking in deep, memorizing her smell. He could hear her intake of breath as she took him in as well. On a wild hair, he slowly nuzzled his nose against her neck, not able to help himself. Her hips flexed into his and he pushed back slightly, now dancing his lips across her neck. She tilted her head to allow a little easier access and he smiled against her skin. His hands danced across her back while hers went up to the back of his neck.

A small pulse of her hips into his had him giving her the barest of open-mouthed bites on her neck and relishing in the goosebumps that danced across his skin and her slight moan.

Fuck, this had taken another surprising turn.

Her hands pulled him close and his gut tightened in response, only to bottom out when she pushed him away. Her gorgeous cheeks turning a brilliant red.

Jen was having trouble meeting his eyes as she pushed him the last step out of her doorway. "Uh, thanks for tonight. It was...good. I, uh...I'll see you tomorrow."

He opened his mouth, to say something, anything, but paused when he caught sight of her confused, tired, yet slightly aroused and conflicted face. Jen stared at him for a heavy moment before shutting the door solidly in his face.

Well, then.

He sucked in a breath, still imagining her hot, little body pressed tight against his own.

Fuck, she felt good.

The perfect size.

He put his hand on her door and waited until he heard it lock.

"Goodnight to you too, darling," he whispered.

Good thing she had the strength to stop because he sure as hell didn't. And next time...they might not be so lucky.

CHAPTER TWENTY-THREE

September 25, Saturday
John

John slept a total of four hours that night. He kept thinking of that awful hellhole that Jen lived in and the fact that her surrogate family could do something about it. Hell, half her friends in book club were fucking millionaires. If they wouldn't do something about it, John sure as hell would.

Even though Jen worked on his upper body for two hours last night, it still revolted that morning when he rolled out of bed. The tossing and turning all night didn't help, the violent game on Thursday still wreaking havoc on his body. His mostly rookie offensive line had a tough time protecting him and he got absolutely pummeled. In the fourth quarter, they were losing by so much and he was taking so many hits, Butch and Mitchell pulled him and put in Ryan. He did well, despite the less-than-ideal circumstances.

John did some early morning yoga to stretch out his body and headed into the stadium. He drank a ton of water last night after dropping off Jen and he was still sucking it back to help his body recover, both from the game and the massage.

John was eager to have Jen work on his body some more. If what she did last night on his upper body was anything to go by, then she'd be able to work out that lower back twinge, his glute soreness, and the tightness in his left hamstring and quad.

God, when did he get so old?

And, please God, let him get a ring this year so he could be guaranteed one more year and then fucking retire.

He cringed at his own thoughts.

He made his way down the vacant hall and towards the massage rooms. It didn't matter the time of day, the halls in this wing of the stadium were always empty. The carpeted floors buffeted any noise, so it stayed quiet.

A little spooky actually.

It was only eleven, so he wasn't expecting Jen to be in yet, but it wouldn't hurt to get his name on the board while he hit the sauna and practiced his breathing exercises.

The sound of a male voice floated through the massage room door, followed by Jen's deep laughter.

What the hell?

He pushed through and walked in on Ryan and Jen side by side on the mats, legs braced and arms up in a fighting stance. Jen was throwing out a series of punches and Ryan was trying to mimic her tight, controlled movements.

For a natural athlete, the kid looked terrible trying to copy her precise fighting moves.

John caught himself smiling at how uncoordinated the Heisman winner looked. If only the media could see the guy now, they'd never say he had more athleticism than John again.

He let the door shut quietly behind him and softly padded over to watch the duo work.

Jen instructed Ryan on the proper balance and technique in a no-nonsense tone that John himself used on the rookies. The similarities made his smile grow even deeper as he silently watched them play.

A series of quick jabs, ducks, and knee thrusts had Jen moving with brutal efficiency and sharp, controlled breaths.

Wow.

She was a fucking masterpiece.

Ryan hesitated before copying the progression with slow, awkward movements. As he lost his balance, he threw out a leg to catch himself and ended up facing John as his body twisted around.

Immediately, Ryan's young face turned bright red, but he rallied and puffed out his chest in invitation for John's forthcoming cutting comments.

However, after watching their comradery and platonic teasing, John could finally safely believe that Ryan wasn't after his girl.

Not that she was *his* girl. Yet.

He didn't want to be the reason for a rift between her and William, even if he didn't think it would cause one. But he also didn't want to be the reason Jen felt any more guilt than she already did.

He also didn't want to be her dirty little secret.

Shock rippled through him at the thought.

Did he...did he want to try for something more with her?

His heart rate picked up, in panic or excitement, he didn't know.

"All right, already. Out with it," Ryan said.

Hell, he wasn't that much of a grump.

Plus, after seeing how little support Jen had in her life, having a guy like Ryan in her corner seemed like a good thing. She deserved that friendship—who was he to be jealous of that?

John shook his head and approached the pair. At his refusal to tease Ryan, Jen's face lit with joy and...life. Her smile grew in wattage and again he felt the flutters in his belly at her clear happiness and optimism. All because he didn't give her new friend a hard time.

God, he could please her that easily?

And fuck, she was gorgeous. Especially when she smiled at him like that.

"Don't mind me," John said, not even trying to hide his humor.

Ryan retreated to grab his phone and small backpack. He was all grace and fluidity in his movements, not looking at all like a man who just bumbled a series of Krav Maga moves a few moments prior.

John gave him a bemused look.

Ryan just stared back, his mouth agape, clearly shocked at John's not-antagonistic attitude.

John hadn't been *that* hard on the guy...right?

John looked back to Jen. Her smile turned soft and John's heart flopped. Maybe he was that hard on the kid.

"Don't worry, man. I won't tell the guys that your natural athleticism doesn't extend to martial arts."

Ryan still stared, afraid to move and break their spell, their temporary bubble of peace.

Shit. John really was a dick.

John went up and slapped Ryan on the shoulder, rocking the younger man a little.

It seemed to shake Ryan out of his trance, and he awkwardly held up his stuff in front of him. "Uh, thanks. Just trying to learn something new while I waited for Butch's henchmen to leave his office. I have to talk to him about something and don't want those guys around."

John cocked his head in surprise.

What were Butch's buddies doing in his office on a Sunday?

Ryan turned to Jen. "Thanks for humoring me, my queen. As always, your service was beyond complaint." He bowed with a flourish and swept out of the room, his previous embarrassment hidden or forgotten.

John watched him go with an unfamiliar perspective.

A small cough. "Thanks for being nice to him. Some of the guys on the team can be dicks. I think he's getting worn down."

He looked back at Jen as she grabbed a towel and headed back to the mats, spraying, and wiping them down. She deposited the dirty towels in the hamper. "Hop up on the table, let's see what demons I can find."

The door opened as she washed her hands for a second time.

Butch pushed in and stopped short when he saw both John and Jen already in there.

Apparently, he and Ryan missed each other in the hall.

"John. You're here again. Thought you didn't usually have Jen work on you?" Butch eyed the two of them with a question in his eyes.

Well, there goes the theory that they were successfully being covert in hiding their attraction to each other.

"What's up?"

Butch waited for a beat, staring at them blankly in thought. Then he snapped out of it and shot her a wink, the change of facial expressions surprising John at how quickly it happened.

"Just needed a quick rub. I'll swing by later."

Butch shot John another confused look and backed out of the room, letting the door click shut.

John stared at the door for an extra beat before turning around to Jen. "Okay, how do you want me?"

"Let's start face down. I want to work on your glutes and legs. If time allows, I'll also have you flip over, and I'll chip away at the front of your legs as well."

"So..." He tried his best to appear confident. He was no blushing schoolboy, damnit. "Pants on or off?"

Jen looked up at him and her eyes went wide. Her heavy lashes fluttered before she wet her lips and stuttered out a weak, "Off."

She turned to the oil counter. "Would you like a peppermint or juniper base today?"

John shucked his pants and shirt and stood awkwardly in his boxer briefs.

"Um, do you have the coconut one from last night?"

"Of course. That's my favorite too." She turned back to the table and started mixing her oils.

When Jen turned back around, she gave a visual jolt. Her eyes trailed his body and snagged for a minute on his underwear before continuing down. John watched her cheeks bloom into a vibrant blush as she shot her eyes back to his.

Well, hello.

"You can lay face down on the table." Jen sounded like she was choking.

He'd give her something to choke on.

The thought came unbidden, and he almost laughed out loud at how immature that sounded in his head.

Jesus.

He needed to get control of himself.

John lowered himself onto the table, conscious about putting too much weight on his sore right leg.

Jen approached the table and placed her hands on his back. She only briefly rubbed his back, careful not to do too much because she worked it so thoroughly the night before. She continued to rub his glutes through a thin sheet. Even though the sheet and his boxes separated them, John was all too aware of every touch. Her every movement controlled and even. Every finger push, palm pressure, or forearm application on the exact spot with the exact intensity that his muscles craved. It didn't feel like a sports massage. It felt like a spa treatment on some island somewhere. Soft music played in the background. The smell of coconuts and the table warmer below him tempted him to doze off. He fought it, but barely.

She finished with his legs and for the first time in weeks, his hamstring wasn't screaming.

"You can turn over," Jen murmured above him.

As he rotated underneath the thin white sheet and rolled onto his back, she adjusted the headrest, and he slid down on the table. His feet were almost hanging off the bottom of the table.

And he wasn't even the tallest on the team.

Lenny needed to order a larger size table next time.

Jen pulled his right leg out from under the sheet and did another pump of oil into her hands from a nifty belt that held the oil dispenser. As she started to rub the oil into his thigh, John realized how close her hands were getting to his junk.

They barely skimmed the bottom of his boxer briefs but still. John's mind fixated on the contact.

He peeked at her from his prone spot on the table, opening his eyes just the smallest sliver.

Jen's eyes followed her hands up his thigh...but continued to his crotch. Even covered by the sheet, she looked.

When she noticed John's eyes on her, she blushed and went back to staring at his kneecap. Very decidedly *not* making eye contact.

Jen pushed on a tender spot, and he couldn't stop his groan.

"Yeah," she muttered. "You've got some stuff in there."

The more Jen worked up and down his leg, the more his awareness of everything about her heightened.

She stayed so focused and intense, and besides that one moment of ogling, she remained the consummate professional. He kept opening his eyes to watch her face as she worked.

Getting a bonus each time of some cleavage poking out from her deep V-neck shirt.

Things started to get a little more uncomfortable when she caught him staring at her breasts. Jen blushed again but when her eyes shot down to look at his mouth and she licked her lips, John felt a stirring in a place that was oh so close to her hands. When she looked back up to his eyes and then trailed her eyes down his exposed chest, stomach, and back to his thigh, John nearly moaned.

Especially when Jen's eyes paused on his dick.

Jesus.

Her fingers worked their magic up his leg and the higher they got, the more tense he got.

He tried thinking of football. The upcoming game. His career. Retirement. Taking out the garbage. Anything.

But as her dainty, painted fingertips skimmed the bottom of his briefs, again and again, the slight stirring he had before turned into a smolder. He twisted his neck to the side to give it a crack to see if that released some of his growing tension.

Football locker rooms. Sweaty, smelly locker rooms.

When he opened his eyes again, he saw Jen focusing on an outer area of his quad, slightly bent over as she angled herself for more pressure. The angle gave him a direct shot down her shirt, to her ample cleavage while it also put her face closer to his crotch.

John shifted.

She looked up at him, concern on her features. "Does that hurt?" Her hands paused.

"Uh...no...just, could we go to the other leg? I don't know who's planning on coming in today, I think most people are with their families for the holiday weekend, but I don't want to get kicked off the table before having a chance to have that one worked on."

She looked a little perplexed but agreed. "Sure."

Jen did a couple of wrap-up movements, pulled the sheet back over his leg and walked around his head to get to the other side.

A wave of coconut and lime hit him.

John closed his eyes and breathed in deeply.

Jesus.

He felt like a fucking addict.

He couldn't get enough.

Jen started working on his other leg which wasn't as tender. Rather than basking in the muscle tension release, John could only focus on her hands and how they were inching closer and closer to his inner thigh. He started picturing her tanned fingers, all glossy from the oil, digging into his skin, kneading, and pushing. Her darker complexion in brilliant contrast to his paler skin.

And...there's the start of a boner.

He coughed softly into his elbow and moved his other leg to try to bunch up some of the sheet.

John focused on his box breathing and forced his eyes closed to avoid any more cleavage shots.

After a while, Jen asked, "Are your pecs doing okay? I didn't get a chance last night to work on them. But they connect in with the back and shoulder, and I know that the other therapists aren't as firm in their touch as Lenny. I can work on them if you'd like. I don't have anyone else on the schedule."

John wanted to escape for a cold shower. But instead, he found himself grunting out, "Yeah, okay."

Jen tucked his leg back under the sheet and moved her way up his body. She picked up his wrist and forearm, tucked it into her hip, and started on his hands and fingers.

Heaven.

Her small hands threaded her oily fingers through his and his mind started imagining what else her small hands could wrap around.

He shut that thought down too.

As she started on his pecs, John peeped up from cracked eyelids and saw her eyes glued to his chest. The picture of professionalism.

However, when her eyes moved up to meet his, another faint blush tinged her cheeks. His eyes dropped to her mouth, and he became ridiculously aware of how dry his own lips were. John used every ounce of willpower not to moisten his own lips. He was all too aware of how that would come across.

But it was torture. Like an itch he knew he couldn't scratch.

God, his lips felt so dry.

Jen's hands moved up his arms and to his chest. He made eye contact with her again and her hands stalled. She rolled her lips between her teeth and stared at him with her honey eyes. He scanned her face, taking in her delicate features. The perfectly shaped brows, the beautiful glow to her skin, her pert nose, and the stubborn line of her chin. Even her big round eyes, which he found so full and wanting, now also looked confused and torn.

Yeah, babe. I'm torn too.

Her eyes drank in his features as her fingers rested on his chest, nestled into his sparse chest hair. Jen sucked in a shaky breath and John's eyes darted down to that damn V in her shirt.

And saw her nipples poking through her thin tee. And apparently even thinner bra.

Jesus.

Even though he knew he should, he couldn't look away.

Jen was either cold...or aroused.

And it wasn't cold in the room given the nature of the work the therapists had to do. Warm muscles meant healing muscles.

The longer he looked at her nipples, the more visible they became.

Fuck.

John licked his lips on instinct.

Her fingers dug in softly to his chest.

And damn if that didn't bring his cock back to life.

John watched in awe as her chest started rising and falling. Faster and faster. She shifted the way she stood slightly and pressed her legs together. John looked back up at her face and saw how her pupils dilated.

Without thinking, he bent his arm at the elbow and brought it up to her arm. He ran the outside of his thumb along her forearm. Her thumb rested ever so still on his nipple. As John stroked her soft forearm, Jen's thumb twitched ever so slightly on his nipple, and it shot fire through him.

There was now officially a tent under the sheets.

John stroked her forearm again and broke eye contact to look down at her breasts. Jen moaned softly and seemed to impulsively push harder on his nipple. The position of her hands had her slightly pinching it between the sides of her fingers.

More firebolts shot to his crotch. His hips rose on the table.

Her head turned at the movement and she stared at his erection pushing up from under the sheet. She licked her lips again. Not in a salacious way. But in a way that belied just how aroused she felt. Her soft pants echoed in the room.

Jen's fingers shifted and boldly held his nipple in her fingertips. She pinched with a lot more intent this time. Not moving her eyes from the tented sheet. She exhaled hard when she saw John's hips lift at the pinch. Jen's own hips shifted again.

Fuck.

John ate up every feature. The arousal there. The want.

Was she as turned on as he was?

With the way she was pushing her thighs together, she must be.

What would she taste like?

Jen turned her hand and used her nails to scrape along his chest. The lightest touch. When she scraped over his nipple with a sharp nail, his hips jerked hard.

Her eyes raced back to his crotch.

She took her other hand, which so far had been stationary on his chest, and added it to the light touch across his chest. Little rubs and then scrapes. Teasing his nipples. Teasing him.

He had never been a nipple man. But fuck if he wasn't now.

As she worked him, John stared up into her cleavage. He had a close-up view of how hard and tight her nipples were.

Did she ever do this to herself?

He reached up with his other hand and started making small paths on her opposite arm. The one reaching across his chest to work him.

Their labored breathing filled the room.

Jen's eyes were dilated to the max and her lips were puffy from chewing on them. She continued to rub, scrape, and pinch while staring into his eyes. Her body moved subconsciously with each of his hip thrusts.

John stared into her eyes and wondered if he had ever been more turned on.

He hadn't been the starting quarterback for so many years without taking a chance now and then.

Slowly, giving her time to stop him, John slid his finger up her arm and under her armpit, coming out in front of her chest. Jen watched his finger move and her mouth opened with a soft pop. Her minty breath came fast at him. Ever so slowly, he trailed his fingers across her chest. Just before he got to her nipple, he paused, staring and wishing it was his mouth instead of his finger.

Jen shifted, turning her torso just enough to push her nipple into his resting fingers. He made slow, barely-there circles on it. As he got the feel of her, he became a little firmer. He noticed absently that her fingers were mimicking his own finger movements. John lifted his head to make eye contact with her. As she stared into his eyes, panting, arousal clear on her face, he gave her a pinch. Her eyes rolled, and her hips pushed into the table. She pinched his own nipples twice as hard.

Message received.

He twirled once. Twice. Then he pinched hard.

She moaned.

He did it again.

Both of their hips started thrusting in earnest as they worked each other. They alternated between making eye contact and staring at where they wanted to really be. Her small moans became a little higher in pitch when he added his second hand.

Just as John was about to shift and pull her onto the table with him so they could finish together, the door to the massage room pushed open without fanfare.

Jen and John exploded away from each other. She rushed to the sink and John sat up immediately, pulling the towel into his lap and he twisted to give his back to the door.

"Yeah, yeah, I'll catch you Monday," the intruder said to someone in the hall as he stood in the cracked door, his back to the room.

John tried to control his rapid breathing and mentally berated himself.

Jesus H. Christ.

They were at fucking work.

"Hey, Jen, I was hoping you were here today. I saw Roberta out in the staff parking lot, and I had to grab some paperwork anyway so I figured I'd see if you could work on my ankle and arch again. It's still killing me from Thursday." Kenny McCarthy, one of the tight ends on the team jerked to a stop when he saw them. "John. You're here. Are you coming or going?" He looked at John's glossy torso. "Going. Good. I'm dying for a quick rub."

You and me both, man.

John cleared his throat, and lurched off the table, being careful to keep his body angled away. He grabbed his clothes and pulled them on stiffly. "Yeah." He coughed again. "Yeah, she's all yours. Thanks for the rub, Jen." He kept his gaze pinned on the floor in front of him as he dressed in sharp movements. When he finally finished, he tautly moved to the door. "Body feels much better. See you guys Monday."

He gave an aimless wave and left the room, pulling the door shut with a firm click. He stood there for a minute, gulping air, praying for his erection to disappear, and castigating himself for what happened.

What in the world were they thinking?

Sure, they planned on hooking up eventually, but he didn't think either of them were planning on actually doing that at work.

Someone nearly walked in on them.

They would have been in a world of shit. Her more than him, really.

Jesus, he needed to get his head on straight.

John set off down the empty hall. When he turned the corner at the end, he ran into Butch heading towards the massage room.

"No dice, man. Missed her again. McCarthy's in there now," John said.

Butch checked his watch and whistled low. "Damn, Costner. Are you just getting out now? What did she do? Give you a happy ending?"

Butch chuckled after his flippant comment, but it hit a little too close to home.

"Grow up, Butch," John gritted out. He ground his teeth and marched away, despite Butch's weak protests behind him.

He skipped the sauna and headed directly to his car. He needed out of there. Stat.

He also maybe needed to find a new massage therapist as well before he fucked the current one so hard they forgot about their damn moral compasses and decided to spend the entire month in bed doing nothing but exploring every inch of each other.

To hell with responsibilities and convictions.

CHAPTER TWENTY-FOUR

September 25, Saturday
Jen

What the hell were they thinking?

Jen called herself every name she could possibly think of as she worked on Kenny's lower leg and foot.

"Um, Jen? A little softer please?"

"Oh, God. Sorry, Kenny." She refocused and stopped taking out her anxiety on his poor body.

Oh God, oh God, oh God.

What had she done?

One. It was at her work.

Two. It was a gross cliché that could ruin her reputation.

A sexy cliché she'd be fantasizing about a lot of lately...

Three. Anyone could have walked in.

Kenny did. What if he hadn't paused in the doorway and looked into the room as he walked into it?

She could have lost her job. Her reputation. Her entire livelihood. William's trust.

Stupid. Stupid. Stupid!

"Uh, Jen..."

"Sorry," she squeaked, lightening the pressure again.

"You okay?"

"Yeah, fine. Fine. All good," she mumbled without looking directly at him.

"Do I need to kick his ass for you?"

As if he could.

John and Kenny were similar in size, Kenny a little trimmer than John, but John had a solid stature only age could provide. He had this...intensity and—

God, Jen. Get it together.

She shook her head at Kenny and looked back down to his foot and continued working on his arch.

Jen's thoughts were racing and she had no idea what to do.

Doing that with John was a terrible idea on so many levels. Yeah, they were planning on going there eventually. And truthfully, there was a chance it would happen during the season, but God, she never considered it would actually be here...in the stadium.

She shook her head. Maybe she was like her father. Always pushing the envelope and ruining a good thing.

She stared at Kenny's foot and worked out the small bundle of muscle tension in his arch that caused him to limp everywhere.

"You sure you're okay?"

His soft voice broke her inner rebuke. Which was good because the self-criticism was getting scathing.

"I'm fine. Just a lot on my mind."

"Okay. Just know you can always give Chlo a call if you need to take your mind off something." He and Chloe were the absolute cutest together. Jen loved how their story worked out, even if it did have its moments of heartbreak.

"Will do," she said.

Jen looked up into his grey-blue eyes and gave him a small smile. He had the tiniest hint of a brown spot in his left eye that was super interesting, and he had scruff like how John had grown his out. John's ears stuck out slightly from his head in an adorable way, and his nose was wide as if it had been broken many times. John had a salt and pepper coloring to his otherwise dark beard and his resting face always looked grave and serious. It took a lot to make him smile. Even more to make him laugh. When she earned those from him, she felt victorious. Light and triumphant.

Despite Kenny's superhuman good looks, she still found herself preferring John's slightly rougher look.

She needed to stop thinking about John's looks.

Stop thinking about him. Period.

She violated so many personal and business ethics.

Jen was going to be sick. She felt a lump form in the back of her throat.

Jen swallowed it down and tried to focus on her breathing.

Be in the now.

Jen finished working on Kenny and, after he left, she paced around the massage room. She tidied up the already orderly balls, bands, yoga blocks, and rollers. She wiped down the already clean surfaces. She sorted through paperwork that didn't need sorting. When no one else came in for any work, she figured she earned the rest of the day off. She loaded up her stuff, called a taxi, and headed out to wait. As she was waiting, she made the most of her time and looked up local auto repair and tow shops. Management probably wouldn't love Jen leaving the car there until she decided she could part with the cash to repair it, but what could she do? Nothing.

For the thousandth time, she wished Mickey and Benji had a car. Then again, they had left this morning to head up to New Hampshire for the weekend, so she wouldn't have been able to use them or their car anyway. And Lexie was...Lexie. Jen didn't want to bother her when a taxi would be fine.

She tried not to notice the all too familiar hooded figures hanging out by the back fence of the parking lot. They hung out there a lot. Just smoking and talking as they watched the stadium and exchanged thick envelopes with various visitors. Once or twice, she thought she heard her dad's voice carry on the air. She'd always pray it was her imagination.

Why security allowed their loitering, she had no clue. And she certainly wasn't going to poke that bear.

The one and only time she met a loan shark and his enforcers ended with her dad crying with a black eye and Jen nursing a very broken arm. Jen promptly signed herself up for self-defense classes after that. She was the only one who would look out for her; if her own father wouldn't do it, then clearly no one would. Because unfortunately the horrible experience didn't stop him from visiting the tracks or casinos. And for the millionth time, she realized she could only rely on herself and that there would always be a debt to pay. Hers or someone else's.

The taxi brought her home via the longest route possible and Jen winced at the meter. She trudged through the dirty halls up to her apartment.

She stepped inside, leaned against the door, and sighed.

If anyone had walked in today...

Jen rubbed at her face.

She walked to the small bathroom and turned the shower on. When the bathroom filled with steam, Jen dropped a shower bomb in and stepped into the molten water. She tried to let the lavender smell calm her but all she still felt was jittery and nauseous.

Jen stayed in until the water turned cold and then dragged herself out. She wrapped up in a towel and plodded into the small kitchen. She heard a small scuffle at her front door and looked over. The light played at the bottom of her door, indicating someone stood on the other side.

Her dad? He's the only one that wouldn't have called first.

But the person stayed too silent. Her dad would be pounding on the door and yelling.

Chills broke out on her still-damp skin. Jen watched in horror as the doorknob turned quietly. Her eyes shot up to the deadbolt and chain on the door, relieved to see both engaged.

She hadn't flipped the lock on the doorknob itself. She always forgot that part.

She heard a small groan from the wood as the person on the other side of the door tried to push in noiselessly.

Jen could only stand there. Frozen. Hyperventilating but trying to be quiet about it. She stared, unable to take her eyes from the door.

Was it her dad? Why didn't he knock? Was it someone else? Lexie's call about the most recent robbery echoed in Jen's ears.

After several too-long seconds, the shadow under the door disappeared. But even after, she couldn't shake the terror.

Someone tried to get into her apartment.

While she was in there. And they *knew* she was in there. Why else would they have taken pains to be quiet about it?

Jen felt her jaw start to quiver, then her hands.

Before she knew it, her entire body was shaking as she stared at the door, still unable to move.

Jen clutched tighter at the small towel wrapped around her body and had endless horrific scenarios flit through her mind.

Mickey and Benji didn't have the room to take her in. All her friends had roommates, kids, and spouses, or their places weren't exactly large enough to take on an interim roommate. She didn't want to move out of the city to a cheaper place and commute to the stadium every day. Many people had long commutes, but Jen didn't trust her car to make that trip daily. If her car could even be fixed.

She lowered herself to the floor, her towel still wrapped around her in a death grip. She sat with her back to the cabinets and stared at the door, completely lost in thought. Jen pulled her knees up tight to her chest and rested her cheek on them. Without breaking eye contact with the bright strip of light shining from under the door, she let the tears overtake her.

CHAPTER TWENTY-FIVE

September 26, Sunday
Jen

The next day's temperature was unusually warm, but no one blinked an eye. That was New England for you; seventy-one day, ninety the next.

Jen thanked her lucky stars for the beautiful day because she had another charity event to attend that evening. She had gone to a couple events in the last few months but tried to reschedule them to the more low-key socials. However, tonight was the yearly Bachelor Auction for the local professional hockey team so there was no getting out of it even if she wanted to. Management required the Spartans staff to attend to show support, but even if they hadn't, Lexie would have demanded Jen's presence as her wingman.

As she got ready that night, Jen couldn't stop fretting about seeing John at the event.

She finished checking her fancy updo, gave one last spritz of hairspray and setting spray, and slid her dangling CZ masterpieces into her ears. She found them at a craft fair, and they were her favorite statement piece whenever she went to formal events. Jen pulled at her side hairs and rested them by her ears, the darker strands made the sparkle of the CZs pop and shine in stunning contrast.

She checked her small clutch one more time and peeked out the window. Lexie's driver waited for her at the curb. She shot a text down to Lexie and left the apartment, double-checking the lock before she walked away. Yesterday's unknown visitor was still fresh in her mind.

Lexie's excited jabbering about her latest travels and adventures filled the car as soon as the limo door snapped shut. Lexie didn't even pause as she poured Jen a delicate flute of champagne.

They arrived at the event hall and the car dropped them off out front. Lexie's driver opened the door for them before they stepped out.

"I could get used to that," Jen remarked to Lexie. Lexie's bright laugh echoed off the brick building in front of them.

Despite the pleasant weather, they still hustled inside. Both eschewed wearing jackets for the night, going with fashion above practicality.Also, Lexie refused to let Jen wear a beautiful dress and then ruin her aesthetic, so there wasn't much choice there. Jen went along with it only because Lexie had a driver that could pick them up and drop them off right in front of the building.

Laughter and music filled the room. The entire hall, save the stage, bustled with people, some with name tags and some without. There were beautifully decorated tables with fabulous wood-burned numbers. A registration table with the seating arrangements was in the front hall as well as a small coat check station. The smell of the dinner being prepared had Jen drooling. A small but sharply dressed band played off to the front of the room next to the stage. She could tell where the celebrities were based on the location of the thickest crowds.

Lexie and Jen made their way to the bar and ordered some martinis. The handsome bartender gave them a friendly wink as he served them while Lexie shot a saucy smile back.

Then they started to mingle.

As they made their way around, sharing short greetings and small talk with various acquaintances, Jen and Lexie wondered aloud how one city could have so many attractive people. At the fundraiser were actors, singers, and foreign royals as well as local hockey, football, and baseball stars.

As Jen shook hands with the various celebrities, she felt like a princess in one of their book club reads.

When Jen craned her head to look for a certain quarterback, Lexie teased her relentlessly about him. Jen hadn't spilled what happened between John and her the prior day during his massage and wasn't planning to. Lexie would inevitably open her mouth at the worst possible moment and spill the beans. Jen loved her to death, but Lexie wasn't accustomed to subterfuge. Jen had to keep that little secret between her, John, and the walls of the massage room.

A secret.

Jen shivered.

The thought of keeping it a secret only encouraged her to do it again. If they were able to keep it quiet...

Maybe it could work.

Maybe Mickey and Benji were right. Maybe sex *was* the way to go.

When their friend, Megan, joined the group, she and Lexie started naming which players they would vote on in the auction. Jen tuned them out and imagined what it would be like if John participated in the auction. What would it be like to vote for him? She'd have a good excuse to have alone time with him. No one would think twice.

To be able to tease, laugh, and touch in public without anyone batting an eye. Maybe something would develop that made it worth the risk to try officially dating. Maybe it would mature into something more. Heck, maybe he'd...

Jen jerked out of her reverie as Lexie's squealed.

"My God, that's a hunk of man-flesh," Lexie gushed while staring at the imposing figure of Tommy Kolbeck as he flirted shamelessly with a small group of elderly ladies. Tommy played for Springfield's NHL team.

Jen heard the old ladies issue scratchy laughs as they stroked him, their gnarled and wrinkly hands touching whatever body part they could. He looked over their white-haired heads and caught Lexie and

Megan admiring him. He grinned like a rake and made some excuse to walk away. Then prowled over to their trio.

"Ladies," his deep voice rumbled. Despite the loudness of the hall, his voice had a timbre to it that cut through the noise. He sounded delicious. "Can I be so bold to ask if you're going to be bidding on a date with yours truly tonight?" He patted his chest. "I can promise I would have much more fun with any of you than with one of the... mature ladies I had the pleasure of speaking with." A wince hit his features that had them all smiling into their drinks.

Just as Lexie was about to open her mouth, a coy smile dancing on her lips, their little group grew as three more imposing bodies walked up: Ryan Cole, Kobe Richardson, and John Costner.

Immediately, Jen felt his heat, smelled his woodsmoke and cedar cologne, and wanted to nuzzle into his pecs and beg him to find the nearest empty room.

"Tommy," John grunted at him. They shook hands and when John stepped back, he turned to greet Jen.

And stilled without saying a word.

It took absolutely everything in her not to react when John's eyes snagged on her impressive and exposed cleavage, and he visibly lost track of where he was. He raked his eyes down every inch of her and his face grew even darker. He dragged his eyes back up to hers and stayed silent as the world moved around them.

The man looked ready to toss her over his shoulder and tie her to a bed naked for a week.

She wouldn't even put up a fight.

He gave a slight jerk, coming to, and gave a tight nod to Jen. He then shot a quick glance at Tommy who was watching them with a curious expression on his face which made John angle his body in close to Jen's. Crowding her...but not. Protective without being openly possessive.

He was clearly saying something to the other men.

Jen bit her cheek to hide her smile. Lexie gave her a questioning look that she pretended not to see. She also *may* have leaned a little closer toward John to see if she could graze his arm, shoulder, or hip as they stood there.

Jen could feel his warmth in the small space between them and if she turned exactly right, her shoulder would brush his arm, his hand would brush her hip, and—

"I was just begging these lovely ladies to save me from a night of being pet by some pervy, but I'm sure wonderful, older ladies," Tommy said.

Kobe barked out a deep laugh causing the tattoos that went up his shoulder and onto his neck to peek out from under his suit collar. "Hey, you agreed to this, you dumbass."

Ryan chuckled as well. "It can't be that bad. What if you found The One?"

All the men turned to look at Ryan, mild disgust on their faces at the thought of settling down.

Megan's usually skeptical features turned soft. Not so much for Ryan but for the thought of having that companionship. Jen's heart hurt for her friend. Megan was doing so much, and she was totally fried. She needed TLC and a helping hand—more than what a friend could offer. She needed companionship, love even. Jen made a mental note to follow up with Megan later this week and see if she wanted Jen to bring dinner and hang out. Save her the trouble of needing to find a babysitter.

Lexie snorted at the talk of The One and resumed flirting with Tommy.

Jen felt John turn his head to her.

"Hey, can we talk?"

Jen scrambled to find a way to get out of it. But Lexie shifted just enough to cut her from their small circle.

Ryan gave her big eyes and jerked his head at John, clearly telling her to seize the day.

Mind your business, meddlesome pseudo-bro.

"Sure," she mumbled, following John as he turned to walk to a less crowded area. Her cheeks burned as she tried to avoid eye contact with anyone. It felt like everyone could see the attraction burning between the two of them.

John cleared his throat into his fist, the fingers tucked in tight. Fingers that had touched her... "So, things got a little out of hand."

Interesting choice of words, Champ.

She simply nodded.

"And it shouldn't have happened. I think both of us agree it can't happen again at work." He waited, looking at her.

When she realized he wanted some acknowledgment of confirmation, she rushed to nod. "Yes, yes, of course."

It was still an interesting clarification to make. Her mind still hung up on the "at work" part.

"A moment's insanity. That's it. Whatever we have shouldn't interfere with work or our responsibilities."

"Of course," Jen repeated, nodding more vigorously.

John's eyes moved over to her dangling earrings and then trailed almost tangibly down the sparking strand to her neck and shoulders. Jen took in a harsh breath as tingles started spreading through her.

"Those are the earrings you were wearing the night we met." His eyes drank her in.

Jen fidgeted and brought a hand up to touch them, though she knew exactly what earrings they were. It felt more natural to touch the object of his focus than to keep her hands awkwardly by her side. And better than using those hands to slide up and under his shirt to touch his hot skin, which is what she wanted to do.

"Uh, yeah. They're my favorite."

His eyes landed on her nails and his face grew dark and hungry. "The nails are new though."

Jen had painted them a stark black, except for her pointer fingers, where she had done small white designs.

He noticed?

"Uh, yeah. Time for a change," Jen said.

John's eyes slowly dragged from taking in her nails, her neck, her breasts, and back up to Jen's face. Jen felt too hot in her skin and wanted nothing more than to shuck the heavy dress, with John watching, and then do something that got her much hotter. John's eyes shot back to Jen's and the look of guilt on his face almost had her laughing. His own face was ravenous, and she had zero doubt that his thoughts went to the same place. John's dark eyes started shooting around the room as he tried to wrap up this conversation.

He clapped his hands in front of him. "So, yeah. Lapse of judgment. Won't happen again. I have to focus on football when I'm at the stadium if I want my career to continue on its current trajectory. And you obviously have your reasons why that would be a terrible idea."

"Of course."

"So, that's that. I, uh... hope you have a great night." His face was tight as he nodded.

She stared at his lips as he spoke and nodded absently. They waited for a breath, both staring at each other, drinking each other in despite his cautionary words. Tingles and fireworks exploded on her nerve endings. She could almost still feel the scrape of his fingers on her from the previous night. She didn't think she'd ever forget the tug of rough skin against the fabric of her shirt.

John jerked, rubbed at his temple with a wince, and then stalked away. Jen turned to watch him go and sucked in a deep breath. She caught a whiff of his cologne and found herself taking in another quick breath to smell it again before it disappeared.

Jen shook herself and made her way back to her group. John was nowhere to be found.

They all chatted some more and checked out the silent auction items. After a while, the MC came on and declared it was time for them to find their seats for dinner.

Jen, Lexie, and Megan said their goodbyes to Tommy, Kobe, and Ryan and made their way to their table. Jen subtly pulled up her strapless black dress before sitting down so she wouldn't spill out of the top of her dress. She glanced around looking for John. Jen adjusted the bust again as she sat and listened to Lexie and Megan plot who they were going to introduce themselves to next.

Lexie was eyeballing another player on the Springfield hockey team that wasn't participating in the auction, while Megan's eyes kept drifting suspiciously toward Danny Parker.

Jen nudged her and Megan looked over. "Want an introduction?"

Megan's normally confident attitude disappeared, and a brilliant blush fanned out over her cheeks.

Interesting.

Jen grinned big. "Is that a yes?"

Megan swallowed hard and waved her away. "No, of course not. He's a professional football player. He lives in a completely different world than me. I was just...admiring from afar. He's even more handsome in person, it's surreal."

"They're just like us," Jen said to her. "He's probably one of the nicest and happiest guys I've ever met. Are you sure you don't want an intro?"

Megan rolled her lips together and looked back towards Danny's table where he sat chatting with Ryan, Kobe, Liam Polowski, and a few others. "It's like being surrounded by gods. Just look at them all. Larger than life." Her voice took on a wistful tone. "Just...do you ever get...lonely? Sick of being empowered and independent all the time? I'm my own woman, I can do what I want when I want, and I'd never let a man change me. But the random dates and short-term relationships aren't really scratching the itch like they used to. Ya know? Sometimes it would be nice to have a shoulder to rest on before bed. Someone to share life with and decompress."

Jen took a shaky breath. Megan wasn't wrong.

It would mean the world.

Unfortunately, the guy that Jen's heart decided to flutter around didn't want to saddle up for that type of commitment.

And wasn't that right there the crux of the issue?

If she was going to take a chance on him and risk everything with those she loved, she wanted to know that John felt the same, that he would give their relationship the same weight that she would.

But that wasn't John. He very much wanted a fling and Jen knew her heart wouldn't want to stop there. If she was going to risk her career and friendships, she wanted to know that she did it for something more than a quick fuck or ten.

After sneaking a quick peek over to John's table, Jen leveled a serious look at Megan. "Yeah," she agreed softly. "That would be nice."

Megan nodded somewhat sadly and went back to her meal, no longer casting longing looks towards the wide receiver.

Despite the melancholy that hit Megan and Jen, Lexie still had enough life left to keep their table entertaining. Dinner tasted delicious, and their tablemates were a blast to sit with.

As the bidding was about to begin, Lexie realized she never grabbed her paddle.

"Jen, come with me, quick." Lexie pulled on Jen's arm as she hopped to standing. Jen let herself be dragged from the seat and over to the bidding table. She stopped dead when she saw John cuddled up close to a busty blonde, her hand resting possessively on his bicep. His head bent low and his hand rested lightly on her full hips as they spoke in the corner. Her dress fit like a second skin and her heels were so high Jen would immediately fall on her face if she tried to balance in them. The world didn't exist for the two of them.

Those were the type of people John was attracted to.

Gorgeous. Stacked. Seductive. Low-time commitments.

Jen might be pretty, smart, and funny. But she wasn't *seductive*. She wasn't gorgeous. She wasn't sex on wheels.

She was just...Jen.

Jen watched as the woman leaned up slightly, aiming her lips at John's.

"Jen?" Lexie whipped Jen around to look at her, her hands on her shoulders. Jen shot out her hands to steady herself. Lexie peered into her face. "Are you okay? What's up? You looked devastated. What happened?" Lexie inspected her as her mama bear instinct took over. Lexie, not usually the caretaker in their group of friends, became a fierce protector if she thought one of her girls was in danger. At Jen's ashen look, Lexie's expression darkened. Lexie turned and looked behind Jen, cocked her head, and simply said, "Oh."

Her face turned thunderous and then smoothed out.

"Don't stare," Jen choked out, struggling to breathe. She shouldn't be upset. They owed each other nothing.

Yet...

Her heart hurt.

Jen took a breath and told herself not to look, but she couldn't stop her head from turning for a quick peek, dread in her stomach.

Only to see John Costner staring straight at her with a determined look on his face.

The bombshell nowhere to be found.

Her stomach did a flip when John didn't break eye contact and started making his way toward her.

So, Jen did what any woman would do in her situation.

She froze.

Chapter Twenty-Six

September 26, Sunday
John

John stalked over to the two women staring at him. Lexie peered at him with angry eyes full of questions. Jen, however, looked like she was watching an impending train wreck.

He couldn't stop his eyes from trailing down her earrings again to her elegant neck and then to her fabulous cleavage. Her dress was strapless and had a cutout dip between her breasts. It took an act of God to keep her breasts from spilling out the top.

What *was* it about her?

Simply put...she was stunning in every possible way.

"Hey there, big man," Lexie said as he arrived.

"Kid." He nodded at Lexie but didn't move his eyes from Jen. Though, her face still said she was a little shell-shocked, for whatever reason.

"You okay?" John watched her closely.

She chewed at her plump pink lip but nodded.

"Who was that?" Lexie butted in.

Ahh. They saw him talking to an ex. Hence Jen's expression. He needed to clear that shit up.

He turned his attention to Lexie. "An ex."

"Didn't look like an ex," she bit back, her eyebrows raised in challenge.

Lexie might be a wild child, but clearly she felt protective of her friend. Again, he was relieved Jen had someone to look out for her if her father wouldn't.

"Don't know what it looked like. She had too much to drink. I told her it wasn't going to happen again. She didn't want to take no for an answer." He moved his eyes back to Jen. "I eventually got my point across."

He watched her delicate throat swallow. John's eyes followed the movement and got stuck there. He could almost hear her thoughts.

Lexie chimed in again. "I'm going out with Megan tonight. We're leaving right after the auction, so I won't be able to take Jen home. John, will you take her home for me? We're not going back to that end of town." She looked at Jen. "That's ok, right?"

Jen looked at her, mouth agape. "What?"

Seemed like he had the Spartans' heiress' approval at least. Good to know.

"Yeah, we're hitting up an after-party while Meg has a sitter for once. You said you didn't want to come out tonight because you'd been fighting a headache all day. But I don't want you taking a taxi home." Lexie looked back to John. "So? Can you take her home for me?"

"Lex—" Jen started.

"I got her."

Jen whipped back to John so fast he heard her neck crack. "What?"

He looked down at her. "I got you."

Jen's mouth moved silently as she looked up at him with bright, brilliant eyes.

"Great! Come find her when the auction is over." Lexie blew him a quick kiss and marched Jen away. Jen's steps looked wooden and stiff, but damn if her hips didn't still just naturally sway. John found his eyes watching her ass move and fought off some of his dirtier thoughts. He reluctantly pulled his attention back to his surroundings, trying to remind himself that he was in public, and photographers were everywhere. John saw Ryan grinning at him from across the room with a blonde eyebrow raised. Ryan lifted his tumbler in a toast and turned back to a conversation with Mitchell, Butch, and William.

That kid. He needed to mind his own fucking business.

Though...he wasn't wrong. Jen Medina was certainly toast-worthy.

• • • • • • • • • • •

The auction was wild and ridiculous.

John attended this event every year because William wanted his players to support the other local professional sports teams. Like the football team, Springfield proved to be a great city for the new hockey and baseball teams. Everyone said Massachusetts didn't have the population to support the influx of additional professional teams so close to Boston. Turns out, they were wrong. New England very much supported another Massachusetts-based team. It didn't matter the sport. The teams for football, hockey, and baseball all became staples in the Springfield community and brought a wave of income into the city.

Heiress Ashley Winters, and Lexie Galloway, an heiress of a different type, had gotten into multiple bidding wars during the auction. The first one over a veteran on the Springfield hockey team. They both lost out to a blonde fox in a pink dress. Then, they started competing over hockey star Tommy Kolbeck. That only stopped when Jen held down Lexie's paddle and refused to let Lexie hop up and make a bigger scene. Lexie, for all appearances, calmed her bidding ways after that, but when Jen escaped off to the bathroom a few bachelors later, Ashley and Lexie were back at it, competing over Ty Daniels, a new trade to the hockey team and media heartthrob.

John looked over at William's table to see William was still deep in conversation with Butch and Mitchell. John wondered if the man even realized how desperate his daughter was for attention. Ryan watched her intently though, and he didn't look happy.

As the auction wrapped up and Megan and Lexie stumbled off, dragging a giggling Ashley behind them, John sought out Jen.

"You ready?"

She nodded and gave goodbyes as they wound their way through the crowd.

John led Jen to his SUV, parked a little way down the street. As she kept pace beside him, he noticed she started to shiver. He shrugged out of his jacket and held it out, careful not to let his fingers touch hers. He wrapped it around her shoulders and as he did, he leaned in, his mouth so close to her ear and whispered, "You were the most beautiful woman in the room tonight."

She turned to look at him but words refused to leave her lips.

When they arrived at his truck, he opened her door, and gave her a hand up. As he leaned across to buckle her seatbelt she quietly said, "You have no idea what that means to me."

Fuck.

Has no one ever told this woman she's beautiful?

Don't think about last night.

Don't think about her hands.

Don't think about what they did.

He needed to change course quickly, so he punted.

"So, you never said," he asked into the silence as he drove away from the venue. "What made you want to be a therapist?"

She veered with him only hesitating for a second before saying, "I've always been intrigued by the human body and how all its systems interconnected, constantly compensating for one another. Plus, I love sports."

John looked over at her as he stopped for a red light.

Her small shoulders raised under the mountains of excess material of his jacket. "I worked for a bit at various New England colleges with their athletic programs but felt like something was missing."

Jen's face flashed green as the light turned. John turned back to the road and started driving again.

"After a couple of years of education and training, I became a Licensed Massage Therapist. I couldn't afford it, but I figured it would be worth it in the long run. I wanted to promote the prolonged healing that regular massages could provide while also offering physical therapy and pre-hab treatments that help athletes perform at their highest levels. My mom died around that time and that left a mark. And as you already know, my dad's a real winner." She cut him a look and stressed, "I was doing fine until I had to pay for my mom's funeral and a handful of big gambling debts. I thought, after the last one, he'd be good for a while." She shrugged. "But you never really know with him, even though I still hope he'll change."

John saw Jen wince and look out the window again, lost in her thoughts.

"It can be hard to change a lifetime habit," he said after a heartbeat of silence.

"Don't I know it." She trailed off and John waited for her to expand on that, but she remained silent. She sighed and sank deeper into the seat. "When Mom was around, she helped carry some of the burden of taking care of him. Now that it's just me? Family debt can be a real bitch."

Her hand reached up to rub small circles on her temples, so John let the conversation drop, but he was curious if her wince had something to do with her headache, the mention of her father, or the stress of going back to her somewhat dangerous apartment.

They made their way down the streets back to her apartment building and saw only a couple of people milling around outside, smoking cigarettes. No drunken party like the other night.

All the same, he got out of the car to walk her up.

Luckily, she seemed to expect it, so she didn't give him her normal, feisty attitude.

They walked in silence up to her floor, making eye contact sporadically, both getting lost in each other for heartbeats at a time.

By the time they got to her floor, he felt like his skin was on fire and his heart was going to burst from his chest.

Was this it? Was he finally going to go there with her?

When their fingers brushed softly in the stairwell, they both gave a jolt.

John was half ready to throw her up against the wall and kiss her senseless to see if it would quell the fire burning in him. He needed her out of his system; even her perfume made him nuts.

When she made eye contact and held it for an entire heartbeat, John decided to fuck keeping his distance.

As soon as they were inside her apartment, it was game on.

Her small gasp had him bracing.

That plan just got certifiably fucked.

Her apartment door was busted wide open.

Jen moved to enter but John grabbed his jacket that she was still wearing and hauled her back.

"Call the police," John commanded, handing her his phone. "Get over to your friends' place now."

"They aren't home," Jen hissed, her grip like iron on his wrist when he tried to leave her in the hall and enter her apartment. He needed to see if anyone was still in there. Jen's hold had her stumbling into his side as he entered the apartment. John vaguely registered Jen's soft voice talking to 911 dispatch on his phone.

Should they be entering the apartment or waiting outside?

Fuck it. If there was a chance he could catch this motherfucker...

John turned his wrist and caught hold of her hand. He gripped her fingers as they stepped through the apartment. Luckily, it was a small enough apartment that there weren't many places to hide.

But Jesus.

The place looked totally trashed.

"John?" Jen's voice wavered.

She squeezed his hand with enough force that he felt his bones groan. The longer he looked at the destruction, the harder he squeezed back. "I got you."

It was a promise.

One he never meant more.

Chapter Twenty-Seven

September 26, Sunday

Jen

The police showed up and took their statements. They closed off the apartment and Jen wished she grabbed some of her things before they ushered her out. They then received a berating from the officer out in the hall for not only contaminating the crime scene but also putting themselves in danger for entering an unknown situation.

John stood there impassively, clearly used to being chewed out, and clearly not caring. In fact, at one point he literally pulled out his phone and started shooting off texts to his people.

Whatever that meant.

So, the officer changed his tactic and started just to focus on her. The weaker of the two.

She was feeling a little emotional given the last few days and didn't know whether to cry or yell. John however, was done with the reprimand.

"We'll come into the station in the morning. When can we leave?" His posture and clipped words had the cop giving him the hairy eyeball, but it got the job done. After some more questions and paperwork, John loaded her up into his vehicle and they sat there.

"A hotel is fine. I don't want Lexie or any of the other girls to worry," Jen said, not taking her tired eyes from the police lights flashing outside her building.

"I'm taking you to my place."

She tore her eyes from the lights and turned to face him. The shadows under her eyes were deep and her hair was breaking free from her fancy updo. Thin pieces framed her face. Dark smudges outlined her eyes from where she rubbed at her mascara and eyeliner.

"You don't need to. I can take care of myself." Her face turned away from him. "I always do."

John winced but kept watching her, waiting for a meltdown.

"Hotel, please?"

He scowled at her and shifted into drive.

Jen's eyes narrowed on him. "This is not the way to the nearest hotel."

"I'm hardly going to let you stay in a hotel." John's face remained focused on the road.

"Excuse me. This is not a situation of what you *will* and *won't* allow me to do. I'm a grown-ass adult."

"Trust me, I'm aware. But I have a spare room, I'm already with you, and I'm not going to let you go to some hotel and spend the night alone after someone ransacked your home. I don't know what, if anything, is going to hit you in the middle of the night, but I want you right where I can get to you quickly if I need to."

Jen's shaking had started back up again, so maybe that wasn't the worst idea.

Without saying another word, John's strong, warm hand lowered onto her own and softly started rubbing small circles into her skin. Absently. Like he noticed the shaking and wanted to remind her that she wasn't alone.

He drove to a gate in front of an elite condo complex. Some mechanism in the gate recognized his truck and raised the gate for him. He drove to a numbered space in the parking garage.

John threw it in park and looked at Jen. "We're going upstairs, grabbing something quick to eat to counteract whatever shock you're feeling, and then heading to bed. Then, in the morning, we'll head into the station to see what's going on. And throughout this, you will be agreeable and won't mention a hotel again. Got me?"

"Like hell." She curled her lip at him.

"Jen, let me help you." His voice went soft, and the imploring note made her flinch.

She wasn't that difficult.

She leaned towards him and matched his subdued tone. "John, there's no way I can afford rent at a place like this."

His eyebrows shot together. "Who asked for rent?"

Jen rolled her eyes and gave him a look. "I can't just crash in your spare bedroom and not contribute. That's freeloading."

"No, that's friendship."

Jen paused.

"That's what friends fucking do, Jen. They help each other out. I don't need the cash and you're not taking the space away from someone who would be giving me cash. It's a spare fucking room. I'm a fucking millionaire. I don't need shit. So, take the fucking hand I'm offering and accept that you have people in your life who give a shit and don't expect payback for it."

"But—" She opened her mouth to argue.

"But nothing. Life is not all 'you scratch my back so I can scratch yours later.' That's not how relationships work."

Relationships?

He meant friendships, right?

She bit her lip and saw his eyes and nose flare in anticipation of needing to rant at her some more. Lucky for him, Jen felt the world trying to suffocate her and just wanted to get out of her dress and into bed.

"Fine."

But she'd be looking for alternate living arrangements in the meantime.

John gave a relieved sigh, exited the truck, and escorted her up to his place.

He guided Jen through his foyer, pointing out which direction led to what. John steered her towards the kitchen and propped her on a stool before pouring a couple of glasses of water and sitting next to her. He slid a banana over to her as they both stared blankly ahead, not speaking.

Jen took a small sip and winced at the cold. Her mind danced back to everything that had happened that night and wished for it all to be a dream.

"Did you hear one of the cops tonight talk about the possibility of there being a drug ring in one of the downstairs apartments?" he said as he cast her a worried sideways glance.

"Psh. Exaggeration." She waved her hand. "It's never been that bad." Even as she said it, she wondered if the rumor was true.

Were other women followed home by strange men on a nightly basis? She wasn't naïve, she didn't think it was normal per se. But the men had never done anything to her. Just comments. She could handle comments. They wouldn't actually do anything physical...would they?

Her subconscious brought up the keys between her fingers and the pepper spray. Maybe she always knew she was on borrowed time with her luck.

God, what was she supposed to do now?

John jerked as he remembered something. "Did I hear you say you don't have renter's insurance?"

She put her elbows on the table and placed her head in her hands. She groaned. Loudly. John's warm hand started rubbing up and down her back in long, slow strokes.

"No. My dad always said it was a scam when I was growing up."

John's features pinched and his nose wrinkled.

His opinion clear as day.

She threw her face back into her hands.

"Fuck!" she yelled as she pounded the table in front of her with her fists. "Fuck! Fuck! Fuck!"

John twisted his lips and looked back to his glass again.

Jen felt the emotions swirl and claw at her body. Her stomach felt nauseous and her chest burned. Even her eyes and throat ached.

Before she lost it in front of John and had a full-on panic attack, Jen pushed to a stand and demanded, "Where's my room?"

John stood and started down the hall, a slight limp to his step. Jen frowned as she watched him. After a couple of steps, the limp was gone, but she wondered if maybe he remembered to hide it rather than it working itself out.

"You can stay here." He popped open a door into a hotel-looking bedroom. Simple bedspread, neutral tones, and generic art scattered throughout. Through one of the doors at the back of the room, she saw a bathroom. Thank God, a private bath.

"Thank you." Jen moved into the room, ready to wash the day away.

Understanding her need to retreat, John nodded once and headed back down the hall.

After her shower, Jen realized her mistake. She only had her cocktail dress to wear. She hadn't been able to grab any clothes from her apartment. Wrapped in a towel, she set out to find John and ask if he had any extras hanging around from family members or girlfriends past.

Instead, she found a folded little pile on the ground in front of her bedroom door. She looked around briefly for him but when she didn't find him, she collected the offerings and retreated to her room.

They were clearly his clothes and much too big for her, but better than nothing. They smelled like him, his naturally woodsy smell, and she found herself taking deep breaths to get more of it. That only served to remind herself about all the lines she crossed during their massage yesterday. She felt her headache come back in full force.

Of course.

She took the extra pillow, pulled it over her face and yelled into it. Hoping the sound wouldn't travel.

And part of her not caring if it did.

•••••●•●••••

Jen stumbled out to the kitchen the next morning, still bleary-eyed and exhausted.

John looked the same as he gazed unseeing at the coffee pot.

"Want some?" he mumbled. His short, dark hair was messy and flat on one side.

"Please."

He just turned back to the coffee pot. She thought she saw his eyes trail quickly down her body before turning though.

"I had my PA run out and grab some clothes this morning. A bunch are in the bag over there. Keep what you want."

"You have a PA?"

He shot her a look that said, 'of course,' and turned back to the gurgling machine.

It was adorable.

She wandered over and gave the inside a peek. All expensive stuff.

"I can't afford these brands."

"Can we *not* do this again? We can save the oxygen. The planet will thank you." He gave her a tired look that clearly said he was fed up with her already.

She weighed the pros and cons of accepting the clothes.

She needed clothes, and he offered. But after the massage on Saturday, it felt like a line had been crossed. Now she lived at his house and he was buying her things? It felt...weird. She wasn't Julia Roberts.

"We'll head out to the station when you're ready. Then I'll call up our attorneys at the stadium and see if there's any way you can recover anything despite not having insurance."

Fear and anger were currently duking it out for top seed in her stomach. One second, she'd want to punch something, and the next, she wished she could curl up in John's lap and have him protect her from the world. The fear was twofold. Not only for herself but for the other tenants as well. The police called this morning with an update, the building was now part of an open investigation. Apparently, some maverick cop not on the payroll noticed something during their search of the building last night and now shit was really hitting the fan.

John wasn't that far off when he called her apartment an opium den.

The non-corrupt officer found a meth lab.

Isn't that fucking great?

Now, she and the other tenants were out on their asses while the special agents and officers combed the place and assessed it for danger and evidence.

She had some money in savings, but she also had a bunch of savings in cash in her now-trashed apartment. Not the most intelligent move, but her father always told her it was good to have cash available to use that she could get to quickly.

She needed to stop taking his advice.

She checked her hiding spot last night before she let the cops escort her out and it was gone. Out four grand in the blink of an eye.

So, now, she needed to reassess.

Her rent was her big monthly expense. Her car was paid off, but she didn't know much it would cost to fix, if it could even be fixed. She really didn't want to have to take a taxi or car service everywhere. Plus, that could really add up if she couldn't find a place close to the Spartan facilities.

And now she had to replace everything in her apartment.

Her entire savings would be depleted.

Fucking fuck.

Even though she knew she could ask Lexie, William, her friends, and even Ryan, for some help, she was reluctant. She didn't want to owe Lexie and William any more than she already did. Forget her dad. And her other friends had their own lives and dramas. John really was a perfect solution...when you didn't consider her growing feelings.

The temptation between them was already at its boiling point and now that they'd possibly be living together, it felt like the universe was demanding that they hook up already.

Fucking universe.

Jen chewed at her fingernails, pausing when she realized she was ruining the paint.

John noticed her fingernails.

He noticed everything.

She could never repay him for his kindness or for the millions of other things that he was sure to pay for between now and when she moved out again.

Then again, with all this uninterrupted access to his body, maybe she'd finally be able to work on him in a massage capacity that healed his body. No more skipping out on massages because of embarrassment at the stadium. She could rub him in privacy here at his home, and he'd finally get the work that his body needed.

That sounded believable...right?

Fuck it. Fuck it all.

She wanted John Costner and she was sick of letting responsibilities weigh her down. Responsibilities and duties had done shit for her so far.

It was time to enact Plan Patron Saint of Penetration.

CHAPTER TWENTY-EIGHT

October 1, Friday
Jen

"He said I should fucking retire," John said through his teeth.

"That's ridiculous. You're having a good season. Just ignore him."

"I can't ignore him. He runs the most popular New England sports podcast and people take his word as gospel. Now he's got even more people chirping about it."

"Since when do you care what people think? Just play the game you know and love and fuck the haters." Jen gave him big eyes and shrugged.

"It's not that simple," John grumbled adorably.

"If it makes you feel any better, you've had a couple of tough games, but I don't think you're ready for retirement. And you know I'd tell you the truth." She crossed her arms and gave him a look from across the massage room where she was cleaning up before they headed home for the night.

John ran his hands through his hair, still wet from the shower, and it stuck up at funny angles.

"Maybe, I should retire, hand over the reins to Ryan, and fade into obscurity." John pouted as he slouched into Jen's chair at her desk.

Jen rolled her eyes and swiped at the table in front of her again. Without looking up she asked, "Do you think he'd be ready to face Miami next week?" From the corner of her eye, she saw him shoot up.

"Absolutely not. Their safeties would eat him alive. He's not connecting well with a couple of the—" He cut himself off and gave her a droll look. "Point to you."

She blew him a kiss with a saucy wink and went back to scrubbing. She twisted her lips and wrinkled her nose as she moved to the next table. "The mechanic called today, said my car was toast. Something about an engine rebuild and fuel lines, whatever that means."

John raised his dark brows at her.

She squirmed, hating to ask but needing to all the same. "So, no car for a bit. Are you okay with still driving Miss Daisy?"

Just keep on racking up that debt, Jenny girl.

John gave her a soft smile with now only one eyebrow up. He placed his hands over his head and leaned back in her chair, stretching his back. His shirt slid up enough to expose a strip of his stomach. Yum.

"Was that so hard?"

Sexy jerk.

Jen gave him a silent snarl. "Fine. I'm sure one of the girls will give me a ride."

He smiled with a bemused expression on his handsome face.

"Ryan could give me a ride."

"Have you seen that kid drive?" He laughed. "It's not a problem. We work similar hours anyways. It's perfect for you."

His eyes drifted to her mouth, down along her neck, and then down to her cleavage. She felt like he was undressing her.

Slowly.

She crossed her arms as if that would help.

"John!"

"Hmm?" His eyes stayed focused on her cleavage.

"By the way, the clothing your PA picked out was entirely unprofessional. The guys have been gawking all day."

John brought his attention back to her face. "Hmm?"

Men!

She threw her towel in the hamper, washed her hands, and stomped over to her small bag on her desk. "Fine. I need your help. Happy? Now, take me back to your place and feed me. I'm hungry, but I'm not in the mood to cook. So, it's on you tonight. If you thought you'd be getting a chef for a roommate, think again."

John smiled serenely as she stomped past the desk and out of the room. He shut off the lights in the massage room for her and followed along, his long legs easily keeping up with her shorter ones.

God! Why did he have to be so level-headed all the time?

She ground her teeth together but marched on, definitely not thinking back to the way his sweatpants hung on his long legs and how they cupped all the right spots. Level-headed *and* sexy as sin. It was unfair.

As if reading her mind, his small grin turned smoky as he watched her throw a mini hissy fit.

Jen felt heat bloom in her cheeks.

Damn him.

"Why are you suddenly Mr. Zen? Remember the sports host that said you were old and washed up? Let's talk about him again."

The spicy grin morphed into a slow smile. "My, you're feisty tonight. Is this what I have to look forward to? The many personalities of Jennifer 'Sweet Cheeks' Medina?"

She glowered. "Who calls me Sweet Cheeks? I want names, John."

He tossed her a wink. "Team secret. Bros before hoes."

He opened the door of his SUV for her, walked around to his side, and poked around on his phone as they sat there in silence.

Minutes passed but he still didn't make a move to drive away.

When she couldn't take it anymore, she barked, "So, have millionaire athletes gotten the sole rights to teleportation? Because we're not moving, Champ."

He just grinned, still looking at his phone, and kept thumbing around.

She crossed her arms, twisted her lips to the side, and tapped her foot audibly as she waited for his highness to get a move on.

As she practiced her most impressive scowl, she stared at his long fingers and remembered what they had done to her. Sure, it was through a layer of clothes, but Jesus. The man's touch was electric.

Okay, new topic.

She was combing her brain for anything that could replace the memory of the tingles that had rippled through her when a Five Finger Death Punch song came on. Jen whipped her head over to John. He simply set his phone down and started to drive away.

They rode in silence. Jen sent a couple of messages to Lexie, promising her that she didn't need to fly back from whatever yacht she found herself on that week because of the break in at her apartment.

Jen did a double take as John didn't drive straight to his condo but instead to a little Indian joint she didn't think many people knew about. She eyed him as he expertly parked in the loading zone, hopped out, and said a quick, "Be right back."

The man didn't talk much, but apparently that didn't mean he wasn't paying attention.

As he got back in the car, her mouth started watering. The smell filled the inside of the SUV and her stomach growled. It had been at least six hours since lunch.

"If I eat in your car, will you kill me?"

He looked over before looking back to the road. "They'd never even find your body."

"I'll be careful," she wheedled.

"Not even a trace."

"What? You know a guy?"

He paused for an uncomfortable length. "Actually, I do." He darted a quick look at her. "But you never heard me say that," he said quickly. "But for this job, I wouldn't need to track him down. For you eating in my car? I'd do it myself." He gave a sneer and spoke in a sinister voice at the end, all crackly and low.

She smiled and stuck her head in the bag and spoke lovingly to the food waiting for her. "I'll be with you soon, my pretty. Hang in there."

He laughed but otherwise remained silent.

When they got back to his condo, they unpacked the feast on his kitchen island.

"Yikes, did you order one of each item on the menu?"

John smiled as he grabbed drinks for them.

"Do you eat there a lot?" Jen continued to ask as she spooned heaps onto her plate.

"Never, actually."

She paused and looked over at him.

John shrugged and kept spooning out his own, much larger portions. "I heard you and Danny talking about it one day. When you wouldn't stop whining about everything, I figured this was the quickest way to cheer you up."

She stuck out her tongue at him.

He winked and her heart stuttered.

She started grabbing more items from the boxes while peeking at him from under her lashes. He went about his business, completely unfazed and unrattled. Meanwhile, her heart rate was racing.

As Jen sat down to eat, he paused, hovering at the chair next to her, looking at the place settings.

"What?" Jen looked down at the utensils, napkins, and matching glasses of milk. What was wrong?

"You're always taking my chairs. It's cute. It's like your *thing*."

She jerked. "What? No, I don't. And this wasn't even your chair. They're the same chair!"

John hummed and mumbled something about the 'lady protesting too much'.

Jen smacked in the arm. "It wasn't your chair."

"This time," he grumbled.

Dork.

She playfully tapped his biceps once more, struggling to contain her laughter.

How did she go from having a shit day to teasing about chairs?

John's grin widened as he selected a blues album, filling the room with its sultry melodies.

She hesitated. Blues? Was he setting them up for something?

Did she want him to be?

She eyed him over forkfuls of delicious food.

He eyed her back, much less suspiciously.

"So. You want to have sex?"

The entire mouthful went down the wrong pipe. As she felt her throat constrict and the pain radiate out, she coughed trying to clear everything. Her eyes started watering and her nose was running by the time she could breathe normally again. She blew her nose as delicately as she could into the tissue John handed her and then looked up.

His grin was impish.

What a way to kill the silence and throw her off guard. Troll.

"So that's a no?"

She scowled.

His grin morphed into an outright smile.

He shrugged. "My mistake. I must have read the situation wrong the other day. It must have been some other masseuse that got aroused while rubbing me."

He wanted to go there? Fine. Challenge accepted.

She brought a finger up imperially. "First of all, we prefer the term massage therapist. Masseuse is outdated. And secondly, I wouldn't have gotten aroused if you hadn't touched me like you did."

He just cocked an eyebrow. "Lady, you were ready long before I touched you. You were ready months ago."

Danger, danger.

"Sure. But that was then. Before we were coworkers. Lenny ended that. No fraternizing with the players."

John looked around comically. "Lenny's not here now."

He sure as fuck wasn't.

"I was rubbing you. Doing my job. Completely professionally, I might add. And you had to go and...and...and pitch a tent."

John's smile was slow and very entertained.

"No, no, none of that. I was doing my job. Period. Have you ever gotten an erection with Lenny?"

That seemed to shake him out of whatever sexual fantasy he had fallen into.

He seemed insulted. "God, no."

"Then really, the whole situation was your fault."

His eyes narrowed and he scoffed. "Hardly. I responded to you and your fucking stellar breasts. Which, I might add, were looking right at me the whole time in that sexy fucking shirt." He echoed her words back at him while his eyes drifted down to stare at the aforementioned breasts. His face got that hungry look again.

More alarm bells.

"Sexy shirt?" she squealed out. "It was a v-neck tee! Hardly anything to write home about." She paused. "And we need to talk about the clothes your assistant picked out for me."

He smiled big around a mouthful of food.

She swatted at him. "I knew it. You told him to dress me like a starved sex-kitten. Admit it."

He laughed. "Would you believe me if I actually didn't give him those orders and he chose to do that all on his own?"

"Not a chance."

"Didn't think so." He grinned at his feet before looking back up at her. He waved back to their plates and asked, "Shall we?"

She squinted at him as she tried to work out whether he was going to keep teasing her.

He held up his hands and made a small x over his heart. The childlike gesture done by a man that exuded masculinity like it was second nature had her fighting a smile as she continued eating.

"So, no sex." At her sharp look, he smiled and forked in another bite. "What *do* you want to do with our time together?"

She faced forward at the island and rolled her eyes at the cabinets across the way. She took a healthy slug of water while thinking of something to say.

"How's your family?" she asked.

Family seemed like a safe topic. Can't think about sexing each other up while discussing family.

She didn't want their first time together to be right after a long workday with a belly full of Indian food.

John's eyebrows pitched in and he scowled. "Riveting topic, Medina. I expected more from you. That's on par with asking me about the weather. I think we know each other a little better than that by now."

Jen shrugged. "Just warming up to the good stuff. We'll work our way up to childhood trauma and greatest fears in a minute."

He grinned again and took a sip of his own water before answering.

"They're fine. Mom is an overbearing mother hen, despite my age and their distance from me. Dad is a weary soul who finds her brand of crazy endearing." He paused and eyed her skeptically. "Must run in the family." He shrugged. "Otherwise, same old, same old."

"I'll take that as a compliment." Jen sniffed and forked in another heaping bite.

"Yours?"

She mimicked his shrug and smiled at him. "Dad's...Dad. He's been suspiciously silent lately. I try not to talk about him much or else the universe brings him to my door."

"Ah, my bad. I asked about him the night we met." John gave her a wry smile, his eyes dancing.

"Hence, why I had to run out of there and miss our date."

"Error on my part. Won't do it again." His face wrinkled in entertainment.

"Now that I think about it...it's really all *your* fault we never had our date. You had to go asking about my family. Total asshole move, teasing fate like that."

Her teasing caused the right side of his mouth to tip up and he ducked his head as he spooned another bite in.

They continued to eat in between bouts of teasing and banter. Jen idly drew doodles with her finger on the counter. The hard granite was smooth under her fingers, and it reminded her of the smooth skin on John's back. How it felt firm yet soft under her hands. She whipped her eyes up guiltily and caught him watching her. She couldn't stop the heat that bloomed across her cheeks as she shoveled in another bite.

John absently scratched at his beard and Jen could hear the faint scratch of his nails on his coarse hair.

"So, I was thinking, if we're going to be living together, there are a couple of things we need to discuss." Jen tried to read his face from the corner of her eye and continued talking to her plate. "Like massages and our...possible hookup."

He stilled. Well, she certainly had his attention now.

"I was thinking...well, I know I said it before and then immediately took it back, but I'd be interested in working out some tension with you in various ways if you were amenable." She let that hang there and refused to break eye contact with the food on her fork.

"I didn't know you liked the food there that much. If I had, I never would have made you wait to eat until we got home."

Jen froze, her heart beating hard, and then looked up at John with a horrified expression on her face. He gave her a comical smile and rolled his eyes. "You're not a chicken. You're direct. I like that about you. Watching you talk about sex while looking at food, though intriguing, isn't what I want right now. You're Jen. You fear nothing. Even awkward conversations. So lay it on me. What are your terms?"

Damn, he was good.

She rolled her eyes but agreed. She needed to step up. Okay, fine. Jen put down her fork and swiveled to face him. "I want to have sex with you." John blinked but didn't show any other reaction, letting her finish her thought. "I'm living with you and that has the potential to be awkward, but I like you, I think you're great, and I think we'd have a great time. Honestly, I could use a fun time right now. And even though my concerns about William still feel valid, I...I trust you." John's face softened the barest amount. "I don't think you're going to broadcast this everywhere and I think you and I can handle whatever *this* is with civility and professionalism." She winced. "Professionalism makes me sound like a hooker for hire, but I think you understand. We can be adults about this. And when it ends...it ends. Easy peasy."

John's expression tightened the barest amount.

Why?

"John?"

His expression smoothed out and he nodded before taking a sip of water. "Yeah, I agree. To all of it. One clarification though. Don't know if it needs to be said but while we're *together*, I want it to be exclusive."

Jen choked on her drink and had to wipe at her eyes, stunned to find John looking one hundred percent serious. Jen sobered her expression, so he knew she took him seriously. "Of course," she said softly, reaching out quickly to rest her hand on his. "Goes without saying. And just to be clear, I had my physical last month, I'm all clean,."

He nodded and threw his own medical clearance out there. "Same."

A heavy pause fell between them.

"Not tonight," Jen rushed to say.

He chuckled and went back to eating. "Even though it's a given, it must be spontaneous. Got it."

"Oh, you think you have women all figured out, do you?" She got ready to clean up her plate. Then she paused.

He was a master manipulator.

Jen stopped and gave him a look that said she knew exactly what he was doing. He simply gazed innocently back. Like he didn't successfully derail her train of thought to save her from any embarrassment.

God, she loved him.

She jerked and rushed to the sink.

Nope.

Definitely not.

Her hands started shaking and she frantically washed off her plate and she could hear her heartbeat in her ears.

Jesus Christ.

She didn't fucking love him.

She was just...appreciative of how well he seemed to know her after their relatively brief time together.

Jesus. What was wrong with her?

She tugged at the collar of her shirt and used her forearm to swipe at her forehead, convinced sweat must be pooling there. Her stomach rioted and she couldn't stop her foot from bouncing as she loaded up the dishwasher.

John rinsed and handed her his own plates pausing when he saw her expression.

She did her best to ignore it and hide her inner turmoil.

But the ringing in her ears was thunderous and distracting.

She squeezed her eyes tight to get some semblance of control.

"Jen? You okay?" John's eyebrows drew together, and his head tilted as he examined her. He leaned towards her and down, trying to see her face, and his forehead had little lines running across it.

She rallied and waved him off. "Yeah, no, spontaneous would be great, thank you. It feels too transactional otherwise." She gave him a half-hearted attempt at a smile. He wasn't the only one that could play the distraction game. "Once again, I'm reminded of how much I owe you for letting me stay here and taking care of me."

His face was soft and not altogether convinced that was the reason for her silence, but he let her use it anyways.

Once again, proving how well he knew her.

"I know someone who wouldn't have blinked an eye at taking the room and would not have viewed it as a favor at all." He paused. "I'm glad you didn't, but you really need to stop mentally tallying your debts."

Jen blinked and her skin prickled.

Was he talking about Vile Vicki?

She joked earlier about opening up about their traumas. Is that what he was doing?

She stayed still so as not to distract him.

"She didn't have the same...heart as you. The same drive. The same willingness to give to others before herself. She wanted to be the center of the universe. And she didn't care what lies she had to tell, or whom she had to sleep with, to get that wish."

Jen winced.

Definitely Vile Vicki.

"I heard she was back in Springfield," Jen added softly.

"So it seems. I blocked her number years ago." He looked out the window at the city lights for the briefest moment.

"Are you okay?"

His head snapped up and he gave her a funny look. His eyebrows pulled down into his normal scowl.

"Yeah? Why wouldn't I be?"

Jen grimaced and waved. "Vicki?"

He paused a moment before letting out a couple snorts of laughter.

"God, yes. I dodged a bullet with her. Thank God I learned who she really was before the wedding. I don't give her much thought at all anymore. Especially now that I find my thoughts consumed by a feisty little number who seems to have been placed on this earth simply to torment me and give me a perpetual case of blue balls."

Jen guffawed and was horrified at the spit that flew out at her sudden laugh. As she frantically grabbed a napkin to wipe at her face and wrist, she relaxed when she found him watching her in appreciation rather than disgust.

John grinned and she beamed cheekily back at him. Jen felt winded as she stood there, staring at him. John's breathing seemed to have picked up as well.

Jen shivered and tingles went up and down her spine.

She stared at him and wondered what life could have been if they hooked up that night after the gala. This was the type of man who would move the whole earth if you hurt someone he loved.

If it didn't interfere with football.

In another life, they might have a chance to have something long-term. But now? Jen forced herself to remember that she was firmly in the short-term fling category.

He gestured back to the table and Jen breathed a sigh of relief. "So, about those childhood traumas…"

They smiled at each other and dug into dessert in companionable conversation. Jen was careful to avoid all talk of Vicki, John's contract, and anything to do with John's aches and pains.

As they ate and laughed side by side, she couldn't help but appreciate how his low laugh made her feel warm all over, how long and strong his hands and forearms were, or even how the light dusting of hair on his forearms looked so attractive. She found herself marveling at the slight salt and pepper coloring of his otherwise dark beard, and she wondered if he always kept it this length or if he changed it up depending on how the team was doing. As an athlete, she could appreciate the magic of superstitions. She just couldn't bring herself to ask. Instead, they spoke of their childhoods, their hobbies, and the drama of the men on the team. She even wheedled out some more information on his past relationship with Vile Vicki.

When Jen asked about his plans for the future, John expertly distracted her and moved her back to safer waters. She realized that anything age-related was off the table. Even though he was only a handful of years older than she was, he was still at the end of his career. And here she was, not even working towards her dream.

One day.

Eventually.

As she got ready for bed that night, she couldn't help but feel bubbly and light. She was jittery and couldn't calm her mind. The night felt like a date.

Their first date.

But they weren't dating. They were going to be a fling. An affair.

But God, she loved how he listened intently when she spoke. When his phone went off when she was talking about her dad, he didn't even hesitate. He silenced it immediately, without even looking at the screen. Then he urged her to continue speaking.

That simple act of respect made her belly warm.

There was one moment when their fingers touched that had her heart in her throat. Her nerves were all over the place with him, even after knowing him for this long. She kept rubbing her fingers where his hand had touched.

She needed to get a hold of herself, or she'd come off as totally crazy.

What if it wasn't a fling? What if it turned into something more?

Her head hurt with the what ifs.

John was the type of man that took, and gave, exactly what he wanted. He was not a man that wanted long-term. He didn't want to trust and get burned again. He wanted to hold onto his escaping youth and his waning career for as long as he could. He would be risking a lot less than her by announcing a relationship. In a contest between work and a woman, a woman would always come second.

And she'd seen that movie already. Her mother was a perfect example. She loved her mom and missed her dearly, but Jen decided early on that wasn't the life for her. She'd settled for nothing less than being the center of the world. She stilled when she remembered what John said about Vicki. Maybe they were more alike than Jen thought.

She fell asleep in his comfy guest bed, wondering what tomorrow would bring and if it would be a day with something spontaneous.

Also, she feared that spontaneous time with John might end up being yet another thing that tried to break her.

And it might be the thing that finally did it successfully.

CHAPTER TWENTY-NINE

October 3, Sunday
Jen

"Okay, Saint. I've given you a week to come to me with your massage needs and it hasn't happened, so I'm taking initiative. We're stuck in this flying metal tube with teammates all around us. If we can't manage ourselves here, then we have bigger issues. Stop with the massage stalemate and help me help you." Jen kept her voice low so as not to disturb any of the sleeping players, but it also meant that she could get a little closer than propriety suggested so John could hear her. Man, he smelled good.

John looked up from his book on architecture and gave her a weighted look over his reading glasses.

Fucking fuck, he was sexy as hell.

"And what do you plan on rubbing on this red-eye flight back from the west coast? My feelings?"

Jen rolled her eyes. "No, you grump. Your arm, your shoulder, neck, hand, anything I can reach."

John looked around the dark cabin and gave her a dry look. "What if I moan too loud and wake the others up?" His facial expression matched his teasing words.

"Stop trying to get out of this." Jen chuckled and swatted at his arm. "I mean it."

"And here I was thinking you were coming over here to accuse me of taking your chair again. Chair thief."

She barked out a laugh at his revisionist history and shot a hand up to cover her mouth.

Damn, that was loud.

John chuckled low and deep and it vibrated through her.

Even when it wasn't intentional, damn, she loved making him laugh.

With a tired shake of his head, John flipped off his overhead light, the only one on in the sleepy plane, and placed his book neatly in the airline pocket in front of him. Thank God, their private jet was so roomy because these dudes were huge, and no way would they have enough space in a normal coach cabin.

"Okay, Ms. Medina. How do you want me?"

Naked and inside me would be ideal.

Jen smiled at his willingness to try. It wasn't exactly an open invitation but at least he was cooperating. She'd get his shoulder fixed in no time. The game earlier that day only reinforced her belief that something was going on with him. His body wasn't working right, and he looked off. It could be shoulder pain from last year, or maybe his hip and leg again. Either way, she'd do her best.

"Lose the jacket, Saint. We have work to do." She pulled out a bottle of oil and slicked it on her hands, rubbing them together eagerly.

He chuckled softly as he removed his suit jacket and tossed it on the seat on Jen's other side. He then wadded the giant throw blanket on his lap.

"Just in case I end up going camping." He winked at her.

Jen felt the urge to squeeze her thighs together but powered through. She was a professional, damnit!

"Shirt too."

"Jesus' tits, it's cold in here. Do I have to?"

Jen gave him a haughty look. "Don't be a baby."

He removed his shirt, all the while grumbling soft nothings to himself that wouldn't carry throughout the plane.

When Jen's hands were properly warm, she dove in. Her thumbs worked gently into his shoulders, kneading deeply, stretching his muscles, loosening them like they needed. When she reached the back of his neck, he let out a long exhale and groaned. He was tense.

"Holy mother...damn," he finally mumbled.

His brows furrowed as she continued to work the knots away. She let him relax his head back on his chair and rubbed his nape before moving his body, digging deep.

"Jen?"

She turned to see he was watching her intently now, watching every move she made.

"Hmm?"

"That feels...amazing."

"Good. That's what I'm going for." Jen smiled at his peaceful expression. "Now, I'm going to do some work on your chest."

His eyebrows shot high. "You sure that's wise given what happened last time?"

Her cheeks flushed and Jen couldn't help but giggle. "Well, we're about to find out."

John shook his head but otherwise didn't stop her.

As John's muscles began to loosen, Jen noticed again how incredibly fit he was. For being thirty-eight and having fifteen years of grind, he didn't look like a war-torn veteran. Even though his injuries seemed to plague him, he never stopped training and his dedication paid off. His body was a masterpiece.

His muscular abs and tight, thick arms glistened in the moonlight streaming through the windows.

"Damn, you're built."

He shifted slightly so she could reach a different area.

"It looks good on you," Jen whispered. She moved back over toward his left shoulder and massaged her fingertips along his neck and jawline. "How's your shoulder?"

John shrugged. "Still hurts but not as much."

"What did you do?"

He snorted. "Hell if I know. But it feels better now, don't worry."

Jen smiled. "If it doesn't hurt tomorrow, I'll know you were lying."

Jen kept up her routine, her fingers sliding across his skin like hot steel. She followed the contours of his body, letting her hands trail over his arms, chest, and side until she finally reached his lower stomach.

"Gods, woman. You are going to kill me."

Did his hips flex up into her hands a little bit there?

Yum.

"We have to switch seats so I can get the same access to your other side as well."

John groaned and shifted again, this time using his hand to adjust himself in his pants. "I can't handle another bout of that."

Jen smiled. "Baby."

"We'll see who the baby is."

Jen's teeth grabbed onto her lower lip.

John's face darkened instantly. "Behave, you harlot."

"Make me," she said before she could stop herself and they both stilled.

The look in his eyes spelled trouble. "Maybe I will." His low murmur shot straight to her core, and she found herself pushing her legs together at the promise in that quiet whisper.

She pulled at him to switch seats so she had better access to his other side. After minimal grumbling and groaning, she finally successfully traded places with him. Jen fought to keep in her laughter at his silent theatrics. "Was that so hard?"

He gave her a pointed look and looked down at his very prominent erection, but other than that, he stayed silent.

Jen added some more oil to her hands and started work on his other side, quieting her mind and letting his body speak to her. The tension in his shoulders flowed from his body and she felt his muscles relax. His peace in those moments transferred to her and before she knew it, she was ready to curl up and doze like the rest of the team on the flight.

"That's enough for now. Rest up. You can work on me more later if you want. Now that I don't have to worry about you taking advantage of me," John whispered in her ear, his minty breath tickling the hairs fanning her ears. The skin on her neck prickled at the sensation.

As if he sensed her sudden arousal, he went one step further and ran his nose along her ear. At her shiver, he used his teeth to latch on and give the slightest pull on her earlobe. The sensation shot straight through her, and she squeezed her thighs together.

"John, behave, remember?" She kept her voice quiet, repeating his words back to him.

He cocked his head like he couldn't hear her. "What?"

Maybe he was getting old if he couldn't hear her. Jen bit back a smile at the thought.

She leaned closer to him and inhaled, ready to chastise him again, when he leaned forward quickly and wrapped a warm hand around the back of her neck. He pulled her so they were forehead to forehead, their position hidden by the high seat backs in front of them. Jen's breath hitched.

Anyone could walk by.

Her heart beat faster at the thought.

"What were you saying?" he said, his voice barely audible while his lips almost rubbed against hers.

"Nothing, ignore me. No behaving," she breathed out, fully on board with whatever he wanted to do in that moment.

"Good. Now lay back."

"What?"

He gave her a soft push that had her leaning back in the window seat, curled up in the darkness. A second later, the puffy throw blanket landed down around both of them.

That was sweet.

Jen turned to smile at him, but her breath caught in her throat when she saw his hungry look. The darkness made it hard to make out his features completely, but she'd have to be blind not to know that some form of spontaneity was coming.

"My turn," he growled low and deep.

Then things got...spontaneous.

John had apparently stolen the oil bottle at one point and used a bit because when his hands found hers under the blanket, they were slick and warm. He threaded his fingers through hers with care and delicacy, his movements slow and deliberate. John's hands worked her own, massaging her palms and fingers, giving her a wonderful sensation of finally being the caretaken rather than the caretaker. He migrated up her arm and to her forearm and then bicep. The sleeve of Jen's shirt kept getting in his way as he made long strokes up his arm, but it didn't seem to bother him.

Boldly, Jen watched him as he watched her, their eyes locked on each other in the dark. John's hands moved from the arm closest to him and traveled across her belly to her other arm. He lifted up the hem on her shirt so his fingers could rub the skin there as they moved to her other arm. Jen's breath hitched again at the rough, possessive feel of his fingers on her lower belly. His body inched closer as he leaned over her to rub the opposite arm, his own breathing heavy.

This was on par with them getting frisky in the massage room. A terrible idea. A wild idea. A reckless idea.

And brilliantly sexy.

After John gave her opposite arm the same detailed attention, his left arm came back to rest on her belly, making possessive circles on her skin.

"Okay?" His voice was barely audible.

Jen nodded, so eager to see what would happen next. Damn the consequences. If he could take the risk, she could take the risk.

John's hand made an interesting little trip up and under her bra, wasting no time in the process. The way he cupped her bare skin in her own had her arching her back into his hand and biting back a whimper at his hot touch. John moved his head a little closer to her and whispered, "Still okay?"

"God, yes." Jen basically moaned back, her chest moving in small jerky movements in time to his caresses and delicate pinches.

"Good."

And just like that, his wonderful, magical, fantastic hand was gone from her breast, leaving her panting and wet.

Before she could even complain, his hand dipped below the waistband of her pants. Jen froze again and locked eyes with him.

"Still okay?"

God, the man had a complex with asking for permission. She ground her teeth. "*Yes*, John. I'll tell you if I'm ever not."

A calculating expression came over his face and he pulled back the slightest amount. "Are you getting feisty with me, Ms. Medina?"

"No," she protested, arching her hips to try to get his hand back.

He gave her a chiding look that, despite the moment, had her grinning slightly.

How was he so...everything?

He adjusted the cover with his free hand, making sure they were both fully covered, and then settled back in his chair, facing her.

"Open your legs." He breathed the command and instantly Jen separated her legs. No way was she going to fight this.

Her senses were alive and screaming at the new sensations flooding her body. Her eyes widened as he dove right down and in.

He parted her folds and immediately started playing. Eventually, he swirled his moist finger around her clit and the change in pressure caused her hips to buck, desperate for more. He shook his head, warning her to hold still and not ruin the moment.

"Shh."

But she couldn't hold still. She bucked harder, wanting more. When he didn't oblige, she grabbed the back of his hand and shoved him in deeper.

He twisted his fingers inside of her and Jen let out a small whimper.

"Shh," he murmured again in her ear, but she was already halfway gone. Her hips thrusting and riding his hand.

He was building her up slowly but surely. He teased her clit, circling and pressing gently.

She focused on the short breaths in and out of his lungs and the feeling he was creating in her core.

The fact that anyone could walk by and see them, or hear them, only upped the excitement.

His other hand slid under the blanket and cupped her breast, his thumb rubbing back and forth across her nipple.

Her hips moved in rough jerky movements, desperate for release. Jen's breath lost all sense of rhythm as she stared into John's eyes and begged him to take her there.

He was looking at her in a way she'd never seen and her whole body shivered in response.

John growled his approval and began rubbing in earnest, his fingers hitting her just right. Jen started to rock harder against his fingers and he tilted his head, watching her with a dark, predatory look in his eyes. It wasn't until she saw him lean in, his fingers still buried inside of her, that she realized he meant to kiss her.

At first, she resisted, knowing that would be visible to any passerby. But...

His fingers went deeper and she needed to come.

So, fuck it.

She leaned forward and opened her mouth and let him attack, her tongue meeting his. Their lips crushed together, kissing hard and messy as if they were trying to devour each other, her hips still grinding against his talented, long fingers.

Jen managed to wrap a hand around his neck and hold onto him, to anchor herself against him. Her other hand traveled boldly to his crotch where she started to stroke him over his pants.

He let out a small grunt at the contact and she inhaled. Eating the sound and wanting more. Eagerly, she undid his button and zipper and dove that hand below the waistband of his pants so they could have skin to skin contact.

After she found him, she wrapped her hand around him, squeezing and stroking.

"Fuck, baby."

With heavy eyes, Jen stared up at him, stroking him in time with his own finger in her. His half-lidded eyes devouring her.

"Fuck, I want you riding me."

"Yes," she breathed, arching her back.

God, she was so, so close.

His own hips thrusting now.

"Think you can be quiet if you climb on top of me?"

Fuck.

"God, no," she breathed, reaching even higher. Desperate to have his lips on her.

"If I get down on my knees right now and eat you under this blanket, will you be able to be quiet, baby?"

Jen's thrusting paused as she squeezed her knees together around his hand.

John's eyes closed for a beat, and when he opened them, he looked pained. "Fine, baby. You don't get my cock or my mouth if you can't be quiet. Time for you to remove that hand before things get messy. Tonight's all about you."

Jen wasn't even sure she was still breathing as she pulled her hand away. For once, she took orders without complaint.. Her complete focus was on her building orgasm. She needed to come. To fly. She needed that intense pleasure that would stall her breath and make her mindless. She needed it from *him*. From John.

He lowered his mouth to hers again and kissed her as if he didn't give a damn about anything else in the world. "Okay, baby," he whispered onto her lips. "Come."

Light flashed behind her eyes as she came harder than she ever had before.

And then he proved that he was only playing before.

Now? Now, he meant business.

By the time the sun rose on their flight, John brought her to orgasm three more times, and Jen had never been so eager for them to get home so she could return the favor.

CHAPTER THIRTY

October 4, Monday
John

Jen received a last-minute brunch date text from Lexie and William Monday morning after their flight landed and couldn't say no, so John had to wait to get his hands on her again.

He used to think of himself as a patient man, but not anymore.

This was the longest game of foreplay he had ever had, and he was over it.

When she texted him later that day saying she had to meet up with her dad for a quick visit, John felt his tension skyrocket.

Everything she did for his body the night before, was completely erased by one little text. Her dad was a dirtbag. From what she told him the night of the gala, combined with multiple passing conversations over the last two months, John got the picture. The guy bled toxicity. A degenerate gambler who didn't care who paid the price of his addiction, a Grade-A narcissist, and a manipulator to boot. He had Jen convinced that she owed him allegiance despite the fucker literally getting her arm snapped when she was a fucking teenager because he couldn't control his fucking debt-to-equity ratio with his loan sharks.

Fucking fucker.

Combine that with him repeatedly and continuously putting Jen in jeopardy time and time again?

John wanted to fucking kill him.

By six that night, when John still Thadn't heard from Jen, he felt about ready to explode from his skin. Every noise from the hall, every elevator ding, every beep on his phone, left him anxious and stressed.

Where the fuck was she and was she okay?

He paced the entryway for the millionth time and checked his phone for a missed text in case he accidentally switched it to silent.

He hadn't. Volume was still at the max.

Fucking hell.

He ground his teeth and checked the time.

In twelve seconds, he was calling the cops.

Make that five. Twelve was too long.

Fortunately for her delicious ass, she chose that moment to breeze through their front door.

"Where the hell have you been?" he ground out, flexing his hands, trying hard not to punch something.

His heart stuttered when he saw tears in her amber eyes.

Concern and dread pooled like acid in his stomach as he approached her.

"What happened?"

Without missing a beat, Jen walked straight into his chest, hugging him tight. As soon as her face contacted his chest, she broke down sobbing. John held her tight, feeling her wracking sobs tear through him as if they were his own.

Had he ever felt this type of worry?

"It's okay," he whispered. "It's okay."

It probably wasn't, but that didn't have the same comforting factor.

As Jen's tears slowed over the course of several minutes, a surge of protectiveness washed over him. He knew he couldn't change Jen's past or her family, but he could be there for her in the present. And though it wasn't strictly legal, he had ways to take care of her dirtbag of a father as well if it needed to go there for her safety.

"He needed money. A lot of it." Jen sniffed wetly and wiped her face with the sleeve of her shirt. "I gave him what I could, but I got cleaned out pretty good during the robbery. I kept a lot of cash in my apartment." She hiccupped and sniffed again before peering up into his face. "Do you think he'll be okay? At what point do sharks start taking body parts these days?"

He would have bet his life savings that he could have gone his entire life without ever needing to hear her ask him that question. Yet here he was.

He just shook his head and tried to look sympathetic despite the fury roiling in his gut.

Jen looked out towards the window and swiped at her eyes again. "Guess GA didn't stick." Her voice sounded so soft and heartbroken.

Fuck.

"He's a grown adult, Jen. He makes his own choices. Have you ever considered cutting him off? Just saying no?"

Jen looked at him in horror. "You don't just let your family get beaten up by loan sharks if you have the means to help them, John. Are you telling me if your dad needed a kidney, you'd say no?"

A kidney? Is that what she thought this compared to?

"A kidney for my dad to live is a lot different than enabling your dad's addiction." She reared back like he slapped her, but he kept his arms clasped behind her back, refusing to let her retreat. "You don't owe him anything, Jen," he said firmly. "You don't owe him your loyalty or your safety or your money. You owe that to yourself."

Jen's face crumbled as she looked up at him. "I know," she said. "But what if the time I say no is the time he gets seriously hurt."

"Then he needs better betting skills, or he needs to quit. Maybe that would be his wake-up call."

"It's an addiction, John. He can't help it."

John sighed, feeling the weight of the situation on his shoulders. He knew it wouldn't be easy for Jen to break away from her father, but he also knew he couldn't stand by and watch her get hurt.

"How can you still care after everything he's done to cause you pain? The no-shows, the money requests, the literal breaking of your bones?" John asked, unable to keep his frustration at bay.

Jen looked up at him, her eyes filled with sadness. "I can't just cut him out of my life, John," she said. "He's my father."

"So what? He donated sperm to create you, but he doesn't act like a *father*," John countered. "He acts like a parasite, feeding off of you and everyone else around him. How can you let him do that to you?"

Jen shook her head, tears starting to pool again. "It's not that simple, John. You don't understand."

"I understand that he's hurting you," John said, his voice rising. "And I can't stand by and watch that happen."

Jen's face contorted with emotion. "But this is my life, my family. You can't just come in and tell me what to do."

"I'm not telling you what to do," John said, his voice hoarse. "I'm trying to protect you. Help you. Help you protect yourself. Can't you see that?" John clenched his fists and finally had to separate from her before he started yelling. That would only make things worse. "Tell me why you keep going back to him, even though he hurts you every time."

"Because he's my father," Jen said,

John let out a frustrated sigh. "But he's not acting like a father, Jen. He's acting like a criminal and putting you in danger. What about when you have a family? Kids? Are you still going to let this shit fly? Let him and his poison infect your kids and put them in danger?"

Woah, where did that come from?

John stilled and took a deep breath, trying to get himself, and his thoughts, under control.

"Kids?" Jen croaked out, mirrored shock on her own face at the direction the conversation had taken.

John waved his hand. "It was an example. When do you draw the line? Who has to get hurt before you make a choice that is healthy? You deserve better than this. You deserve to be safe, happy, and loved. And if your father can't give you that, then he doesn't deserve to be in your life."

Jen shook her head, her face contorted with pain, and she pinched her lips together to stop additional tears from falling. He could see her fighting for control.

John's heart hurt. His head hurt. His fucking hands hurt from clenching and unclenching so much.

He knew he couldn't fix everything, but he wanted to try. "Listen to me. You deserve more. You deserve everything. Let me help you."

Jen looked up at him, her face tired and lost. "And have you fix another thing for me?"

John took a deep breath, trying to keep his frustration at bay. "I'm not trying to fix everything for you, Jen," he said. "I want to support you. To be there for you. And if that means helping you physically, emotionally, and mentally to get away from your father, then I'm willing to do that." John took Jen's hand, squeezing it gently. "I know it's not simple or easy," he said, "but that doesn't mean we can't try."

Jen looked up at him, her eyes filled with grief and confusion. "I know," she said. "And I thank you for that. But I'm just not ready to give up on him yet. My dad is still in there...somewhere."

John took a deep breath, feeling a sense of defeat wash over him. He knew he couldn't force Jen to do anything she didn't want to do, but he also couldn't stand by and watch her get hurt again.

"Okay," he said finally. "You need to promise me something, Jen."

"What?" Jen asked, looking up at him.

"That you'll put your safety first," John said firmly. "That you won't put yourself in danger again for anyone. Not even your father."

Jen nodded. "I promise," she said. "I'll try my best."

John took Jen in his arms, and put his face in her hair, holding her tightly. "Those two aren't the same thing. You know I know that, right?"

But despite his reassurances, John couldn't shake off the anger that burned inside him. He hated Jen's father for what he had done to her, for the pain he had caused her, and for the fear he had instilled in her.

Jen buried her face in John's chest, matching her own deep breaths to his. Even now, in the heat of this drama, her fingers rubbed small circles on his lower back, like she couldn't stand not touching him or trying to heal him in some way.

A sense of helplessness washed over him. He knew he couldn't fix everything, but he wanted to try. He wanted to be there for Jen and help her get over this monumental hurdle. No one should have to deal with something this heavy and depressing alone.

Part of him hoped it would never come down to asking her to choose between him and her father. He had a sinking feeling, no matter how much she liked him, her father had his hooks in too deep, and for the first time in a long time, he'd lose.

CHAPTER THIRTY-ONE

October 5, Tuesday
John

The next night they were finishing dinner and catching up on their day.

John was teasing Jen about their latest book club read. A sexy little number about a small-town vet getting it on with a client.

"Are they all romances?" He laughed as they dumped the leftovers in the compost.

"They didn't used to be. Now, if they don't have a romance thread, we don't read 'em." Her sultry chuckle shot straight to his balls, and he had to fight an erection.

A simple laugh shouldn't have that effect on him. Damn her and her sexy ways.

Even as she wandered through his kitchen, washing off dishes and plates, hands covered in suds, he watched her...enraptured. She looked so at home. Like she belonged.

Whether she was wearing yoga pants and a large tee, a skimpy number while working out, or a business suit, she always looked so perfect.

"You should have seen the book we read a couple of weeks ago." Jen fanned herself and shot him a look over her shoulder. "Now, that was a fucking spicy book. It even made Megan and Lexie blush, and they're unflappable."

"So are you, would be my guess."

A delicate pink bloomed on her copper cheeks and John smiled at the way she could still get embarrassed after the two indecent sexual adventures they shared. His little voyeur.

He loved it.

He spent his whole career trying to behave and not draw any attention to himself. It was like he was a kid again when he was with her. He was looking forward to many more moments of indecency and spontaneity with her.

They worked in tandem, cleaning the kitchen with an ease of a couple that had been together for decades rather than roommates for a few weeks.

When she wandered off, John settled on the couch to pick up where he left off in his architecture and construction book from the plane ride home. Just remembering their little tryst had him stiffening in his pants. Reading about the newest techniques in green home production did nothing to distract him from remembering her hands on him.

When Jen came back into the living room, lit some candles, and turned on some soft music, he braced himself.

Ah, hell.

Yoga night.

He already had to live through one of these last week. Jen had come out wearing a bright pink crop top that showcased her toned midriff, captivating John with the hint of flexed abs during her complex poses. On her exposed midriff was a delicate and beautiful tattoo, which boasted her last name in cursive script. It traveled up the side of her ribcage and disappeared under her top. John wanted to trace the decorative swirls with his fingers...or tongue. Jen's matching leggings had clung to her like a second skin, further increasing his torture. It was the longest evening of his life. Hell, two masturbation sessions in the shower after it was over, and he still fell asleep hard as a rock. He had barely survived. He didn't feel fear often, but the thought of what she was going to put him through tonight...

John's fingers convulsed around the book when Jen came back from her room with a yoga mat.

Jesus!

He sat up straight.

She was wearing his jersey.

It was no token jersey for a casual fan. It was ratty and basically see-through from being worn and washed so often. Through the jersey, he could clearly see a plum-colored sports bra that zipped in the front and squeezed her full breasts up to the max. To top the outfit off, was the smallest pair of black yoga shorts he had ever seen.

And he had seen his share.

Did they even count as shorts when they were that small?

She rolled out the mat and proceeded to go through her stretches and poses.

His book sat in his lap. Completely forgotten.

John couldn't pull his eyes away.

Jesus.

He took a sip of water and scratched at his jaw, not breaking eye contact with the way her breasts pushed against his tight jersey. She shifted poses turned away, giving him a nice view of her ass and back. As John once again saw his number emblazoned there on her back, he fought the urge to go to her and fit his body to hers. He wanted her to feel what she was doing to him. John could imagine how her thick and muscular ass would feel pressed up tight to his erection. It would cup him and he would slowly-

Jen turned and saw him staring.

Busted.

"Will you stop? You're distracting."

"You think?"

She beamed at him, all her white teeth flashing, before she shook her head and went back to her poses.

After ten minutes, she wasn't the only one sweaty or breathing heavily.

He should leave and go into his room. Read in there.

Better yet, *she* should leave. This was his house. She should be doing this in her room.

John shifted. He felt voyeuristic, but she seemed to preen under his attention, so he figured she'd bark at him to get lost if she really minded. She certainly didn't seem to mind bitching at him for things far less awkward than that.

Instead, his fiery massage therapist transformed into a little minx right in front of his eyes.

A thought hit him, and his heart stuttered and then pounded harder. Two weeks ago, when she had her first yoga night at his place after moving in, he had heard her get off in her bedroom. When he finally processed that he was hearing the dull buzz of a vibrator and her soft moans and grunts, he became instantly erect. He waited, like a psycho in front of her door, unable to move until he damn-near felt her climax vibrate through the floor.

Did she do yoga when she was feeling *tense*?

Well, good thing he could help with that.

He watched as she moved and bent, stretched and twisted. Her slow and measured breathing moving her chest and diaphragm in and out. Up and down. John found himself mimicking her breaths. The slow, controlled movements echoed in his own chest.

A faint whisp of coconut and lime hit his nose as she pushed up into a downward dog that gave him a fantastic side angle of her fit form.

He felt heat rise in his throat when he saw her eyes slide over to him and maintain eye contact. She darted her gaze down to his lap, where he wasn't exactly able to hide his erection anymore and licked her lips slightly.

Yup, okay. He was done.

John stood up and adjusted himself, not breaking eye contact from his interloper of a roommate.

Fine. Two could play this game.

He reached down and grabbed the hem of his shirt. Not breaking eye contact until the shirt blocked his view, John pulled it up and over his head. Jen's eyes got big as she watched him roll it in a ball and toss it on the couch behind him.

"If you're not in there in two minutes, I'm starting without you." He turned around and sauntered to his bathroom. He left the doors open behind him and turned on the water in his waterfall shower.

Just as he stepped in and doused himself under the warm water, he felt her enter the bathroom, shucking her own clothes.

She slid open the heavy glass door of the shower and stepped under the warm spray. Jen stood there in front of him, statue still. Her gaze traveled over the rough edges of his battle-won body.

He let his gaze rake over her. Examining every curve. Every hollow. Every mound. From her elegant neck to generous breasts, to her slight ab muscles, to her well-defined legs.

She was a sight. The water cascaded over her every curve. Damn lucky streams.

The longer John drank her in, the stiffer he became. He could hear the thud of his heart in his ears. Could feel it rattling in his chest. His fingers were damn near pulsing with it.

He saw Jen's matching flutter in a small vein in her neck.

As their eyes met again, his heart paused. He took a deep breath and held it, hoping she'd make the next move. A guy could only take so much.

Just as he was about to pass out, she reached a delicate hand forward and rested it on his chest. She took a step forward, her eyes trained on where her hand rested. She took a shuttering inhale before she looked up at him, pure trust, and arousal in her eyes.

"John," she whispered, her voice barely audible over the falling water.

He pounced.

John grabbed her by the hips and pulled her close. Just before their mouths hit, he paused. Their lips were millimeters apart. As they breathed the same air, both huffing as if they finished a marathon, his eyes sought hers out.

"You sure?" he growled.

God, he'd hate to finish alone but he'd gotten quite good at that the last few months.

"Yes," she whispered again, her eyes lasered in on his mouth.

Finally.

Well, ask and she shall receive.

He lowered his eyes to her mouth, barely seeing it over their touching noses. The waterfall stream falling on her back and ass, bouncing from her skin, and splattering on his fingertips.

John stood stock still as he felt her breathing, an infinitesimal distance between them. Her journey took years, each breath an exquisite sort of torture. Her eyes drifted up to his and, just as their lips had the barest touch, her dreamlike eyes fluttered closed.

John's own eyes followed suit as he felt the faintest pressure applied. The faintest movement of her lips had him opening his and he had to fight the urge to not ravage her right then and there.

The tip of her tongue poked his lips and he opened, wanting more. But she retreated. Desperate for another taste, he leaned forward and chased her kiss only to feel her lips turn up in a small smile against his own.

His little tease. She knew exactly what she was doing.

John flexed his hands, digging into the muscle at the top of her hips and butt. She moaned onto his lips. Her breath a sharp whisper on his tongue. He gave a small caress with his tongue as she dallied. And this time, when she chased his lips for more, she took the last step between them that had their bodies pushed together tightly.

Game on.

Her hands shot up his body, one hand burrowed in his short hair and one hand scrambled up to his cheek, her fingers digging into his short beard. She moaned as her fingers clenched, pushing her hips against his own.

John shifted a hand down to the bottom of her ass, squeezed, and pulled up, pushing her deeper into his erection. The contact had

Jen gusting out an exhale of pleasure. His mouth captured it. Their mouths battled for dominance. Giving and taking. Challenging and acquiescing.

Their hands roamed. Their bodies thrust.

Just when he was about to change it up, Jen beat him to the punch and bit his lip. She licked the spot as a peace offering but then continued her journey, nuzzling his neck and his chest as her fingers danced on his wet flesh.

When Jen got to his right nipple, she looked up and the expression in her gaze had his hips thrusting automatically. A tiny thrust that he couldn't stop any more than he could stop his heart from beating.

She wet her already wet lips and leaned in, not breaking eye contact. He watched in fascination as her tiny pink tongue darted out to capture a droplet from his nipple peak. She did it again, this time with the flat of her tongue, using a little more force. When she saw his pleasure, she darted in and grabbed his nipple between her teeth in a gentle pinch. She licked the area in teasing apology and continued over to the next. Her hands traveling indolently over his abs and back.

When John felt her shift her legs restlessly and start to direct her movements towards a much larger target to put in her mouth, he grabbed her by the hand and pulled her up.

"Turnabout is fair play, darling." He winked as her eyes got wide. He shifted her and pushed her against the tile wall. The chilly tiles had her gasping and arching away.

Perfect.

He bent his head and breathed on her dark nipples being careful to not actually make any contact.

She shifted anxiously, trying to push them into his mouth. Desperate for the teasing to end.

John winked at her, causing her eyes to roll back in her head, and making her arch her back even more.

God, he felt like he was on fire.

His breathing was too harsh, too frantic.

It's not like he was a virgin for Christ's sake.

But with Jen, it felt different. New. Important.

John trailed his hands over her shoulders, arms, and sides. When he got to her breasts, he cupped their heavy weight in his hands. He teased and played. John watched Jen's already heated gaze become molten as she wiggled against the wall.

"Someone's a little impatient," John muttered as he watched her pant. Her eyes were downcast, fascinated with watching his fingers dance in large circles around her nipples. Her stuttering breaths showed how desperate she was.

"Mmm," she agreed distractedly.

Rather than stopping his spiral around her nipple, he zeroed in and barely touched the peak. He groaned as he watched her body shudder at the contact. She let out a breath that had him smelling and tasting the mint of her toothpaste.

He tickled the tips with the barest strokes and taps. Her hips start pulsing to a rhythm only she could hear.

When he started adding a little bit of pinching to his play, her hip pulses became faster and more forceful, her moans like music to his ears.

He looked up at her. "I want these in my mouth."

"What are you waiting for?" she gasped out. But before he had a chance to move, a hand darted into his hair and pulled him towards her breast. He opened eagerly. More than ready.

He licked and tasted. Sucked and bit. Teased and pinched. His fingers played on her other breast.

Her soft moans became something else. Something...more animalistic. Rougher.

Could she—?

Well, now he had to try.

He doubled his efforts. Really going at her now. He built up the tease. When she really started quivering against the wall, he clamped down just on the smallest tip of her nipple with his teeth and fingertips. He let the faintest scratch of his nail scrape along her nipple and off she went.

Like a firecracker.

He licked and sucked gently as Jen came down, quaking slightly in his arms. His beard wasn't usually this long, so he scraped it slightly across her nipples and she moaned. Her fingers flexed in his hair again. He pressed some soft kisses to her breast as he moved to stand upright again.

John captured her lips in his own. Savage and fierce, but she matched his fire. Her vigor renewed at the contact of his erection on her belly. She rubbed slightly against him, and he returned the favor. Both gave a slight moan at the contact.

Jen's delicate hand reached between them and stroked him. She ran her thumb over his tip. She pulled her hand back, and without breaking eye contact, popped that thumb in her mouth and sucked.

"We doing this here or on the bed? You have two seconds."

"Hm?" Her lust-filled eyes met his, but no comprehension was there. She just rubbed her heat against his thigh again. Even with the jets pounding them, he could feel her wet pussy gliding along the thigh he had thrust between her legs.

"Okay, excellent choice." He decided for her.

He shut off the water, slid open the door, and picked her up.

She gave a soft 'whoop' as he carried her out and tossed her on the bed. He got above her and picked up where they left off. Even though they were soaking the sheets with the water from their bodies, neither cared. He inserted his leg back between hers and ground against her, relishing in her noises.

No roar of the crowd or buzz of competition could compare to this rush.

When he was situated at the bottom of the bed in between her legs, he looked up.

Her chest was heaving and her nipples looked desperate for more attention. He reached up and plucked one softly at first, then roughly when he saw her face darken in ecstasy.

"More," she grunted out, her hips thrusting slightly in front of his face.

He could smell her now too.

Divine.

John licked his lips and dove in. He treated her to the same wonderous teasing swirls and almost touches. He built up the anticipation and brought her down. Built it up. Let it down. By the time he was ready for playtime to end, she was a quivering mess of nerves beneath him.

When she couldn't take it anymore, she shot up, yanked at him to get him where she wanted him, and pushed him onto his back.

Fuck yes.

She mounted his face and put her hand back in his hair.

As soon as she pushed down, he pushed up, attacking her with intent. He added fingers and one hand reached up and plucked at her nipple.

"Harder," she panted, rocking violently.

Fuck, yes.

He used his hand at her nipple to pinch it and pull down, acting as a nipple clamp. She responded gloriously. Pushing herself harder into his face, Jen's body vibrated above him.

The moans intensified.

"More."

His woman liked it rough. Fuck yes. So did he.

He obliged and she came instantly.

She screamed as she rode it out, her body shaking and convulsing. Trying to get away from all contact with him.

He didn't let her. He twisted her back down onto her back and sprinkled her with little kisses. He lapped and stroked. The gentlest and most delicate touches his calloused hands and greedy mouth could muster. Each stroke brought a new wave of shakes to her body. All the while, he absently stroked himself willing away his own impending orgasm.

God, what else would she be into? He couldn't wait to find out.

He leaned forward and danced his lips back up her hot, wet body. Her hands dove into his hair as he moved up.

He licked and kissed her soft skin, offering scattered love nips on her breasts, her neck, and her lips.

She was back to writhing underneath him by the time he was completely over her again.

"Got to grab a condom, babe." John shifted to grab one from the dresser but she held on tighter not allowing him the space to move. She thrust up. Her eyes heavy and hungry.

"I'm clean and on the pill." Her hips flexed into his and he automatically pushed back. She opened her thighs and—

Fuck.

There he was. Sliding in between her wet lips. Not entering her but getting damn close.

She moved again and he pushed back.

Sliding together.

His eyes were watching the way her breasts jiggled with every small thrust. He thrust a little harder to watch them move a little more.

Hell.

He wanted back at them.

He pulsed again, rubbing himself against her but still not entering.

Jesus. Fuck.

He was going to come on her just doing this.

He couldn't seem to stop. He kept rocking against her, not entering, and she kept shifting her hips trying to bring him in. He could feel her opening, hot and wet, as he pushed against her. All it would take was one slightly more aggressive pump and he'd be in. One catch of her opening and with the force of them rocking together, he'd be hilt deep and fucking her so hard she'd taste his cum in her throat.

Fuck.

Her slick opening radiated heat. And if he wasn't mistaken, she was pulsing her hips in a way that would have him slipping in if he didn't keep counter-acting that.

"John, please," she whispered in his ear. Her hips rocking hard along him. She moved so her clit caught on the tip of his shaft, coating themselves in each other.

"I've never," he grunted out. All focus on how hot she felt. "Are you sure?"

Her hands grabbed his cheeks, and the tender action caused him to look up from her gorgeous breasts into equally gorgeous eyes. "I think we've played enough now, Saint." Her eyes darted down, eyeing every inch of his exposed body. "Are we going to do this or are you going to play 'just the tip' until you give up and say fuck it?"

He paused. Her words finally registered.

He reared back, tilted his hips a millimeter, and thrust in.

God, her sounds were better than any roaring crowd.

He felt like a king. A champion.

He gloried in the sound of her moans.

And would, several more times that night.

And again, several more times the next morning.

And the morning after that.

They had a lot of time to make up for.

CHAPTER THIRTY-TWO

October 17, Sunday
John

Jen was still living with John later that month and they settled into a peaceful and sexy routine. Contrary to what they believed, now that they knew how the other felt and tasted, they were even more hard-up for each other at work. They still *tried* to maintain professionalism at the stadium but when no one was around, they had a tendency to get...*spontaneous*.

It was glorious.

John looked forward to the moments where she would rant and ramble; seemingly unaware of the true chaos of putting words to her internal thoughts. She had moments of word vomit every day and it didn't matter what it was about. He found that, even if he agreed, he'd find himself disagreeing out loud to get a dose of her feisty heat. Her spirit was addicting. The way that she couldn't seem to stop the words coming out of her mouth. Or the way she used her hands and bounced around when she got excited.

And Jesus. When she thrust out a hip while giving him attitude? Her dainty little neck cocking to the side like a fucking snake ready to strike? Pure fire. Pure challenge. Pure spice.

He didn't know how to react in those moments. He spent day after day fighting erection after erection. But even though his mind struggled with what to do with her, his damn body seemed to know exactly what it wanted. All he had to do was hear her full belly laugh or even get a whiff of a coconut with lime, and up he went.

It was torture.

It was also bliss.

His teammates seemed to notice the change in dynamic between the two but none of them said anything. Their bickering was still very much present in the massage room, or on the side of the field during practice when she was rubbing out a charley horse. He found himself smiling a bit more. Being a bit more willing to laugh with the guys.

It didn't hurt that his body felt a lot less sore as well.

"I can't do a deep tissue every day," she had scolded him one night at their condo.

"Why not?"

Being a roommate to a massage therapist should have perks.

"You need to give your body time to heal. I can do a light massage, but I can't do any kind of deeper sports massage on the same area. You need time for your kidneys to process the fascia breakdown."

What the hell did that even mean?

She rambled on a little bit more, but he lost track of her words as she started pacing and lecturing him on the ins and outs of massage therapy and muscle treatments. Every time she'd walk away, his eyes fell on her ass and strong thighs, enshrined in tight black yoga pants. Every time she'd stomp back towards him, still oblivious to his perusal, he'd watch the way her chest moved. Or her mouth. Or her hands.

Heck, even her hair had a fall to it that was sexy.

When she got back to his place, she always released it from the confines of its vicious bun. She then threw it into a haphazard ponytail that sat high on her head that allowed tendrils to float down around her face. It looked perfectly styled, but it intrigued him more than it should to know it wasn't.

All of that didn't even touch on how intelligent and witty she was. The woman was sharp as a tack. One night when they were discussing her old business, John asked to see her business plan. She timidly brought it up on her computer and paced the living room while he read. He may have been drafted before graduating college, but he took time during the off seasons to catch up via summer school. He had eventually graduated with a degree in Entrepreneurship and Business Management. It took him a few years given that he was only able to take classes during the summer, but he was determined to graduate. He needed to show the Spartan administration, and the world, that he was a safe bet. A sure thing. A guy who knew his worth and would demand nothing less than equal respect and consideration both on and off the field. He would honor his responsibilities above all else. It took him a couple of extra years to graduate once he started playing pro ball, but a degree was a degree. He earned every decimal of his 4.0 GPA.

When John finished reading through the business plan, he sat there, stunned. He knew she was smart. He knew she was dedicated. But that business plan was magnificent. It was a picture-perfect case study on what every business plan and organizational document should be. If William hadn't guilted her away, her clinic would have bloomed and won contract work with the area professional sports teams. They discussed, for hours, the ins and outs of her approach and why she chose some offerings and not others. He was intrigued by how her mind worked and how she prioritized the offerings in the various phases of the company's roll-out.

She had it all planned out.

Then she let her fucking guilt ruin it all.

There was no way William would have put her in his position if he knew how much work she put into her startup rollout phase.

Maybe he hadn't...maybe William thought she was struggling and doing her a favor... Shit.

Regardless, John's heart ached for her.

Once Jen got the break she needed, she'd have the best damn clinic in all of Massachusetts. If not all of New England.

He was half tempted to call his business manager and have her put together an angel investor offer for Jen to get it going again. And to import a massage therapist or two that would impress Lenny who could take over for Jen. However, if he knew Jen, and he liked to think he did, there was no way she was taking that offer. She was determined to do it all on her own.

Though he itched to prove to her that she didn't *have* to.

Their time together was easy and comfortable despite the sexual tension that wanted to choke them. It felt like they had been roommates for years rather than nearly a month. They anticipated the other's responses and reactions, meal preferences, music choices, and more. Hell, they even started working out together, passing the time with yoga or jogging.

As Jen and John walked into the stadium on Thursday, the guards didn't even blink as she entered through the player's entrance side by side with John. She was ranting about his 'gas-guzzler', and he had to smile. She had no idea what a rarity it was to use that entrance and not be redirected to a different entrance. Even as an employee that worked with the players, that entrance was specifically for the players on game day so they could remain focused and not distracted on their way to the locker room.

Little Miss Oblivious didn't have a clue.

She pulled up and blinked dazedly when they stopped in front of the locker room door, just now realizing where they were.

He smiled down at her adorable expression. He then nodded toward the door where they could hear music thumping beyond. "Can I go in now?"

Rather than blushing as he expected her to, she instead pulled out the sass. "Perdón, Mr. Costner. I didn't know I was being such a kidnapper. By all means, *please*, don't let me keep you any longer." She scrunched her face at him before continuing her rant she had started in the car ride into the stadium, clearly not ready to let him go quite yet. "But the damage done to the environment from emissions from vehicles like yours is worth everyone's time." She huffed again, scolding him with her eyes.

Ha! Like her clunker was any better for the environment. Which reminded him, he needed to check in with his PA on whether he paid for the repairs yet or not. Jen would rip him a new one, but she'd learn that not everything needed to be paid back. He'd never met a harder worker.

He smiled down at her, more than ready to get the game over and done with so they could go home, and he could see what additional sass she could dish out at him. "Yes, dear. We'll talk about my emissions later. Can I go into the locker room so I can do my job now?"

She blinked and her eyes got huge. John felt his own heart give a jolt when he realized what he said. He opened his mouth to say something, closed it, and tried one more time, but nothing came out. They stared at each other in silence, the music faint behind them. Finally, he just pursed his lips, gave her a curt nod, and retreated into the locker room, letting the smell of cleaning products and years of sweaty men assault his nose as he made his way to his booth.

Jesus.

Why the fuck would he say that?

It felt right at the time.

But she was not his 'dear.' She was a fling, despite her live-in roommate status and that she was in his bed, wrapped around him like a vine all night long.

She was temporary, his career was the priority...so why didn't it feel that way?

CHAPTER THIRTY-THREE

October 29, Friday
Jen

"So how are things going at work?" Chloe asked as she piled her plate high, breastfeeding twins was hard work and she was hungry all the time.

"Things are great. Dottie even called the other day and said Lenny is doing fantastic with his recovery, so he might even be able to make it back for short visits at the end of the season if he behaves himself. Not that she told him she's going to allow that." Jen chuckled as she stacked her plate high with turkey, prime rib, and green beans. Having daily *sexcapades* with John was exhausting, so like Chloe, Jen was also hungry all the time, but for a different reason. "The team is really gelling, and it looks like they're ready for a strong rest of the season.

"How's the team handling the injuries?" Megan asked, her analytical mind no doubt tallying her next Fantasy Football trade.

Jen shrugged. "Totally fine. John's throwing fire. Kenny, Liam, Kyle, and Danny are getting mad receptions, and Michael Dillon has been doing amazing at RB, so it hasn't seemed to affect morale at all."

"You probably can't give me any insider tips." Megan laughed and went back to her food before even looking at Jen for an answer.

Jen smiled, knowing her request was just a tease, but her heart still squeezed. Megan was joking...but her dad from not that long ago, was not.

God. If she had told John that her father needed money *on top* of intel on the players, John would have lost his *fucking* mind.

"What does your boyfriend say about him?" Lexie asked with an attitude laced in her voice.

Jen choked. Her throat burned and her eyes started watering as she worked to clear the food from her windpipe. "What?" she gasped out once she could breathe again.

"Your boyfriend, Mr. Boring Golden Child, what does he say about Dillon?" Lexie semi-repeated, looking at her with a funny look that either said she was concerned for her physical health after choking, or for her mental health at her overreaction to her question.

Lexie was being kept firmly in the dark about all things related to John Costner. Same with William. The same with everyone. John and Jen agreed to keep their relationship a state secret. Only the Pentagon knew what happened between them behind closed doors...or dark planes. Or buses. Lexie knew they were roommates but was still under the impression Jen was postponing their inevitable hookup until she was off the clock, so to speak. Therefore, her best friend had no idea that Jen was breaching all her ethics and sleeping with her co-worker.

Megan interrupted Jen's guilty conscience. "Speaking of: he's had a good couple of snaps, but he's no Saint. What's his deal? That was a terrible freaking play last weekend." Megan hijacked Lexie's line of questioning with her own.

Jen's racing heart slowed.

Ryan. They were talking about Ryan.

"Ryan doesn't talk to me about the other players. And I think Ryan played fine. The defense saw the throw coming." Jen defended her pseudo-brother. She grabbed for her giant glass of water and started downing it, hoping to wash away the remaining dryness in her throat from the cough fest.

Crap, crap, crap.

The foolishness of dallying around with John and what she was risking by doing so was inexplicable, yet she couldn't stop.

She felt like her father on a winning streak. Being with him felt so good.

She was being stupid and selfish to risk it all for a fling in the sheets...or shower...or his SUV...or their favorite empty back office at the stadium.

She was risking her job, her reputation, her future, William's trust in her...

All for some orgasms.

So many orgasms.

Really, *really* great orgasms.

When she tried to call it off with him, he got this predatory look in his eye and smiled with delight. Her heart raced and she could feel her fingers twitch, eager to dig into his thick head of gorgeous brown hair. He knew all the right ways to get her going and just watching that wicked smile cross his face had her panting.

They did it in the foyer of his condo against his front door..

So, yeah. They were still going at it like teenagers. All hormones and no sense. All she had to do now was smell his cologne and she started to get aroused.

Damn him.

He was too sexy for his own good.

She tried talking to him one night as they laid on his bed, both still winded and panting.

"You know we have to stop this."

"Of course." He breathed out, staring at the ceiling.

"Like, maybe this was our last time?" she ventured.

"Did that feel like the last time?" he asked, rolling on his side to make eye contact.

She felt his eyes trail along her exposed breasts. She sucked in a breath as her nipples peaked. The man wasn't even touching her, but his eye contact felt tangible. The guy was a god.

"Focus. We can't keep doing this. It's a gross breach of ethics, in every way. We did it. We got each other out of our systems. We had a taste. Now it's time to back burner this puppy so we can be professional and focus on our responsibilities."

His eyes stayed on her chest, his eyebrows pulling down.

"John. Yoo hoo. Up here. We need to be adults."

Then again, adults used condoms. Thank God she was on the pill because she'd absolutely be pregnant by now. With triplets probably.

"I definitely think I gave more attention to your right breast."

Jen blinked. "What?"

"Yeah, I definitely didn't give your left breast the same amount of attention this last time. She's mad at me." He started wiggling down the bed. "Don't worry, baby. I got you."

Before Jen knew it, his lips were closed around her, and she forgot all she was trying to say.

She tried a couple more times in the next weeks to break it off, but something always stopped them from having that conversation. And to be honest, she was happy. He made her feel wanted and needed. Irresistible. Attractive. Intelligent.

Jen enjoyed their sparring and how it extended to their bedroom dynamics. Both were competitors. Both were passionate, though John was quieter about it. They meshed perfectly. And even though their illicit relationship was causing a bundle of nerves to live ever-present in her stomach, the romance was making her heart fly. She wasn't anywhere close to being able to start her own business again, her apartment complex was questionable, and though her car hadn't needed as much work as the mechanic originally thought, it was still expensive to repair. However, when she was with John...she felt *good*. Happy. She was always taking care of everyone else. With John, she didn't have to do that. In fact, he was usually trying to take care of her. In more than the sexual sense.

There was such an addicting power in that dynamic with him. So yes, she was risking everything for a rendezvous with the veteran quarterback, but for the first time, in what felt like her entire life, she felt valued and cherished.

The drug investigation in her building was resolved, and the building was under new ownership from some sort of cloak-and-dagger deal. Jen hadn't seen her old landlord or any of the riffraff in weeks. It was a relief, but it also felt... weird. Like something was waiting. Biding its time. She tried to express the heaviness in the air to John, but he waved her away and assured her that a friend on the force was keeping an eye on things.

Yet, even with the all-clear to go back to her apartment, through an unspoken agreement, it was always his bed or hers. Didn't matter where they slept, as long as they did it together. Usually, it was at John's because it was so much nicer, but Jen liked sharing her space with him as well. Just as long as it wasn't too frequent. His place was much nicer, after all.

"Are we all going to the Halloween party at Versailles?" Chloe asked. "Well, besides Rose."

Rose shrugged unapologetically, her near-auburn hair fashioned back in a complicated twist that looked gorgeous and put together. She had finally achieved peace in her life and, even though she was tired as all hell, she wore it with happiness and serenity. She patted her swollen belly with a glow that emanated pure joy.

The Halloween party at Versailles was supposed to be an amazing night. 'Pure class, no trash,' as Lexie put it. The slutty afterparties were for elsewhere. Jen didn't need the slutty party. A cute dress, Lexie as her plus one, and a secret coatroom nookie date or two planned with John and it was destined to be a night to remember.

As Jen listened to her friends talk about what they were wearing to the event, her mind drifted back to her conversation with John about the party.

John asked her what she was going to be wearing as he sprawled naked on her tiny bed, avidly watching her pull out outfit after outfit from her now-meager closet and inspect them for damages. He had frowned with every dress she showed him. When she pulled out a smart pantsuit that she thought looked rather flattering with her hourglass figure, he outright scowled and reached for his phone.

He typed and tossed it back on the nightstand where it rolled off and onto the floor.

Jen's eyes narrowed on him.

"What do you think you're doing?"

He grinned unrepentantly. "I ordered you some dresses. My PA will have some for you to choose from." Before she could reply, he added, "He'll also bring the receipts so you can reimburse him." John never paid for her. Not after that first week when he supplemented her wardrobe. Not that he didn't try. But after she passionately stated her reasonings for not wanting to take handouts, he always gave her the choice. He would pay, and if she paid him back, great. But he always made it clear, he didn't want to be paid back.

Tough luck, buddy. A Medina always repaid their debts.

When Jen had seen the dresses that his PA picked up, she nearly fainted. They were...scandalous. They screamed 'sex.' She modeled them for Lexie, who hooted and hollered in her over-the-top fashion, so she wasn't a reliable source. Then Jen called up Benji and Mickey, who cat-called her so loud, Jen was sure the police were going to be called.

Mickey was similar to Lexie – dramatic. But Benji? Benji was reserved and level-headed, as long as no one fucked with those he loved. Therefore, having Benji's approval of the dress was all she needed.

That one would work beautifully.

It had a delicate chain clasp that went around her neck, with a *plunging* gap in the front of the dress. The opening dropped almost to her belly button. The side boob game was *on point.* The delicate chain that held the folds over her breasts wrapped sexily around her throat in an enticing and teasing way. The dress barely covered her ass, and even then, still had a slit up to the hip, rendering underwear an impossible wardrobe choice. It was a dress made for indecency. It was a dress made for sex. And it was a dress John's PA picked out, but John hadn't seen. There was no way she was missing out on showing up at that party in that dress and watching him lose his mind.

A part of her balked at the idea of wearing it around co-workers...but then again...one of them was John.

And a small part of her wondered when he was going to get her out of his system. If she was Cinderella for only a short while...she might as well enjoy it while it lasted.

· · · ● · ● · ● · · ·

John's eyes when he saw her in the dress? He was worth the risk, no matter how long they lasted.

Her heart sang.

He was worth it all.

He was worth *everything*.

Chapter Thirty-Four

November 4, Thursday
John

John settled deep into his recliner facing the windows of his condo listening to his mom chatter in his ear...or trying to anyway. The exhaustion from nonstop events over the last few days was taking its toll. He could barely keep his eyes open. The build-up to, and the days after holidays, even small ones like Halloween were always exhausting for the Spartans. Interviews, charity events, photos, appearances, and more got piled on top of their work schedules of practice, rest, film review and analysis. That didn't even include their own family or friend obligations and commitments and going back and forth between his house and Jen's. They spent almost every night together at one house or the other. He didn't want her to go back after the investigation cleared her to go back, but she insisted. Of course.

The Springfield city lights danced in his view, and he couldn't help the twinge of nostalgia as he looked up at the sky. He loved this city. It was his. Luckily, he lived in a fantastic part of it. Swanky restaurants, little crime, cleanly kept. But he didn't live in an area that ever got dark. True dark. Like back in the country.

Damn, he missed seeing the stars.

He took a sip of his water as he waited for his mom to take a breath.

"So, I told the girls, 'My son's a big football star, ladies, he's not going to come home for a bachelor auction. No matter how successful the hockey one turned out.'"

John rubbed his face with his free hand and wished, not for the first time, that his hometown didn't get internet.

"Yeah, there's no way I'm doing a bachelor auction."

He heard his mom sniff prissily. "That's what I told them. But then I got to thinking, did you know your old flame moved back to town?"

"My old flame?" He felt his eyebrows draw down as he combed the archives. He wasn't *that* old but for the life of him, he couldn't guess who she was talking about. His memory really was slipping a bit lately. Just last week, he forgot a play while on the field. It caused him, and his receiver, to get lit the fuck up. He covered it up well enough, but he could still hear ringing in his ears.

"Beth Ann, dear," his mother supplied, giving him a curious look. John groaned.

"I wouldn't exactly call my homecoming date from twenty years ago an old flame. We went out only a couple of times."

Mothers.

"Well, she's back in town, and she had a little one in tow, and my goodness, he's the cutest little thing, and I think you two would hit it off marvelously. And I heard the other day that she has tickets to a late-season Spartans game, so I gave her your number and told her to call you."

John imagined what it would be like if Jen came home to his condo to try to break up with him again, like she did every once in a while, and saw another woman in his kitchen. He couldn't help the small smile that flitted across his face. His hellcat would unleash fire on poor Beth Ann. Beth Ann's southern heart wouldn't know how to handle his firecracker.

"Nah, Mom. That's not a great idea." He paused, weighing his words. "There's kind of someone I'm seeing."

He ripped the phone away from his ear as his mother shrieked wildly for his father. John could hear his father rush into the room, his thunderous footsteps booming even through the phone.

"What's wrong? What is it?"

"Johnny's got a girl!"

John rolled his eyes. Ah hell.

"Whose Johnny?" His dad's voice came through the receiver, much calmer this time.

"*Our* Johnny."

"Our Johnny's got a girl?" his dad repeated.

"Yes!" his mother squealed.

There was a slight pause before John heard his dad say gently, "Now, honey, I don't think getting girls was ever a problem for Johnny."

John smiled again as he flopped his head back against the chair, sinking into the deep cushions.

"No, of course it wasn't. He's handsome as the devil. But he certainly never told us about any of them."

"He told me about them," his dad returned.

"Well fine," his mother's voice snapped back. "He never told *me* about them."

"And?" his father asked.

John waited, eager to get off the phone and run to pick up Jen from her late night at the stadium. He drove her home after work, it was routine. He paid her mechanic directly to fix her car and keep it discreet. Sure, it would have cost about the same to buy her a new car for what it cost to replace her engine, but Roberta held a special spot in Jen's heart. Not to mention, it wasn't likely Jen would have accepted a new car from him. His lady had too much pride and too much of a chip on her shoulder about looking out for herself. As it was, she wasn't *quite* buying that a junior mechanic misdiagnosed her car.

Yet, even with her car being fixed, they still preferred to ride together. Sometimes he stayed at her place, sometimes they stayed at his. It varied. But what didn't change were the nerves that popped up every time he thought of her alone in that apartment. He purchased the building under his real estate management company and had people working on making it a safer place to live. Though, the longer he spent with Jen, either via work or play, the more he didn't want her to live there.

She belonged at his place.

With him.

Jen had no idea he was her new management. If she did, he'd never hear the end of her grumbling about overreaching, egotistical wealthy men who thought they could control the universe.

John didn't think he could control the universe, but he did think, no he knew, he had the means to make it safer for her. The woman was too damn concerned about taking care of everyone else that she frequently forgot to watch out for herself.

"And," his mom stressed, "he told me about this one!"

At his dad's shocked silence, John questioned his decision to share. He felt nervous. Like he did before a big game. Tiny little butterflies swarmed his gut as he waited for someone to say something.

When silence became too much, he leaned forward so he was sitting more upright. You shouldn't ever deal with an opponent on your backfoot.

"It's not a big deal. It's casual. So casual, it's not even really a thing. But she wouldn't be pleased if Beth Ann called me up when she was here." He paused, waiting for his parents to break their silence.

Still crickets.

"So maybe tell Beth Ann to lose that number, okay?"

"Oh my goodness, I bet it's that wonderful girl from the equine center. The one that's been working as the new team massage therapist. I've been seeing her on the sidelines during the games. Quite the looker, that one." His mom's voice pitched high and fast. "And don't worry, dear, a touch with horses can be taught. Your father could get her riding bareback in no time." She rushed to reassure his rock-steady nerves.

John rolled his eyes at his mother's excitement and fought back a grin. When he didn't immediately deny it, his mother burst into more happy squeals. When he realized he rolled his eyes, it converted his reserved grin into an outright smile, thinking of how Jen always mocked him for his rogue eye habit.

She said everything about him screamed professional and polite, but his signature eye roll, as she called it, belied a rebel soul that teased at his maverick side.

John's response to her eye roll analysis was, of course, an eye roll finished with a sigh. She laughed so hard she cried. John felt his cheeks tug up higher at the memory.

His mom then gave a small shriek that wasn't one of excitement and clearly dropped the phone, saying something about the kitchen.

"Careful, son. You've been there for a long time, but people always look out for themselves, and she might be looking at you for what you can give her, not for what she can give you." His dad's slow voice came through the line.

"What?"

"I'm just saying, I know you've seen your share of users. Just make sure you aren't the one being used again."

John's head gave a jerk. "It's not like that."

"Well, okay, if you say so. Just be careful."

"It isn't like that," he said with more force this time. Jen asked him for essentially nothing.

Sometimes when he saw her, his heart skipped. He literally felt winded and lightheaded. He didn't think he'd ever seen a more beautiful sight. It took all of his strength to not stake his claim on her in front of everyone. He wanted to tell the world she was his. He was a fucking Springfield legend, damnit, and he had to pretend to be just some friend of hers in front of their friends and co-workers. It was maddening. He hadn't hid a relationship since he was fourteen and dating an eighteen-year-old in high school. Nonetheless, he understood her fear and trepidation at revealing their relationship.

It was torture pretending to be nothing but co-workers. A finger drag here, a leg touch there. A small lean in for a smell of her elegant neck. A quick touch of the delicate skin on her face.

He wanted to give her everything.

But the woman didn't want *anything* from him. She was adamant about doing things for herself. He even offered to loan her money to start up her business. She politely but firmly shut him down.

But he could do one thing for her. He could keep her safe in that hellhole she called an apartment.

The woman needed a break. She needed to do something that made her happy. Despite how happy he felt she was with him; he could feel the guilt and worry wearing on her. Hell, just the other night, he caught her trolling Facebook, looking for pictures of her dad at the casino just to be sure he was still alive. So even though she was happy, she wasn't *happy*. Not yet.

John continued to push in the hopes that he'd wear her down.

John pulled his attention back to his dad.

"She's not around for my money, Pops."

"Maybe not your money. Maybe your connections? Maybe to get knocked up and get child support? Who knows? Just watch yourself. A woman that is willing to sleep with her clients and co-workers doesn't really sound like a woman who has a strict moral code, if you know what I'm saying."

John's stomach dropped and his temperature started to rise. "She's not like that."

And who the hell was spouting stories about Jen to his dad?

"I'm sure she's not. I *hope* she's not. Just watch yourself. You might not be the only power player she set her sights on. Women don't like to be in second place. You'll see. She'll be asking you to change or to put your career on the back burner in no time. She might even have a point. It's not like you're a spring chicken anymore. All that pain and risk for only a season or two more? Hell, you're probably looking at your last season with the Spartans anyway after how Ryan handled the last few snaps. The boy did well."

John heard nothing but roaring in his ears.

"Say what?" He tried not to growl.

"Like I told you when you were a kid. Football is a game. Not many can last until they're forty and actually do something with that time. A ring is more than many have. Be happy with that and sail into the sunset, kiddo. Find a different hobby, one that isn't as hard on your body."

John gritted his teeth and summoned every iota of willpower not to snap at his dad. A fire raged in him at the insinuation that John had done nothing with his life. Hell, this season had a chance to be another shot at glory. Fortunately, the game scores had been wide enough for some of the wins this season that Ryan was able to get some snaps, but he was a far cry from John's skill and experience.

Fuck him.

"Yeah, it's too bad I've done nothing with my life and wasted all this time on a fucking game. Definitely a disappointment and a waste of time. Then again, playing this *game* has afforded me the opportunity to make millions of dollars that have not only gone to various charities, but right back home into the community I grew up in. Yeah, definitely sucks that I've wasted all this time when I could have been doing something useful like hemorrhaging money saving a few retired horses over the years. I'm sure the kids with cancer would agree that money supporting their families during the hospital stays should have been better used rehabilitating an old Thoroughbred or Standardbred." John took a deep breath. "Sorry to be such a disappointment to you, Pops. Wish I could say that I wish life turned out differently but I'm pretty fucking happy and proud of what I've done. Sorry you can't be. So yeah, I think I'll keep my current *hobby* and let fate decide when I'll be done. But again, thanks for all the endless vibes of support for my career choice. And notice I said career, not hobby. Because this game is not a fucking hobby. It's a full-time job and then some. I would have thought you of all people would have seen that but guess not. And I'm done waiting for you to show any sign of approval for this. I'm a grown man, don't know what I was waiting for anyways."

Silence.

His dad then coughed softly. "I, uh, Johnny, I...."

John grunted and quickly said he needed to go, more than over that conversation. Once he ended the call, he sat back and closed his eyes. He counted, trying to remind himself that his dad loved him and was just doing his part as a father to prepare him for disappointment. His dad had lived a hard life. Not to mention, he came from a different generation. He needed to remember that so he didn't call his father back up and continue to berate him for all of the unintended baggage he had saddled John with.

Fuck.

John was thirty-eight. He shouldn't be feeling like a needy teenager with daddy issues. He was more than successful, he didn't need anyone's approval.

Yet...

It felt like something was sitting on his chest, suffocating him. Bubbling and boiling, trying to overflow.

Fucking hell.

He needed to call his dad back and apologize for exploding. It had been a long time since John had a temper tantrum of that size.

To give himself time to calm down, he tried to change his takeaway from the conversation. His dad was also trying to warn him about anyone that he thought might be manipulating John. That was nice enough, and proof of his father's love, but again, a negative outlook to have.

Like his coaches always said, pessimism was contagious.

No matter how hard he tried, he couldn't shake his father's words. Not only about women not wanting to be in second place, but about his career possibly closing with the Spartans. His entire adult life, hell, his entire *identity,* centered around his job. He didn't know what he'd do if he didn't have football to prepare for and a Super Bowl to work toward.

After brewing on his newfound negativity, John dragged himself out to pick up Jen at the stadium. For the first time since they started their fling, John brought Jen home that night, gave her a chaste kiss, and told her he wanted to go straight to bed. Her shocked expression registered vaguely but mostly all he saw was her concern replacing it. He could see the instant that her caretaker mode took over. He forced himself out of his funk long enough to drag her to bed with him and cuddle her close, not allowing her to tend to him as her instincts demanded. She just needed to be there and he was good. He didn't need or want to be yet another person that she worried about. He could take care of her well-being as long as it was on his terms, and it didn't distract from the goal.

A ring.

CHAPTER THIRTY-FIVE

November 5, Friday
Jen

Jen pushed open John's front door with a sigh only to stop short when all the lights were on in his entry and kitchen.

"Hello?" she called out.

Neither one of them was the type to leave lights on.

She made her footsteps soft as she rounded the corner and entered the kitchen. Jen stopped short.

"Dad?"

What the fuck was he doing here? Who the hell gave him a key?

"Jenny," he said, standing from his stool at the table and pushing the papers that were in front of him away from him. "Your home." He walked up to her and gave her a big hug squeezing her tight.

He smelled like cigarettes and cheap perfume. Jen wrinkled her nose and pulled away.

"What are you doing here? How did you get in?"

Good Lord. John would lose his ever-loving mind if he found out that her dad was in his condo, especially unaccompanied.

Her dad waved her off, a happy smile on his face. "The doorman let me up as soon as I showed him my ID. Just told them I was your dad and poof, up I came." He gave a light punch to her shoulder. "Being your dad is finally paying dividends."

The thought made her skin crawl.

"Dad, I put you on there for emergencies. You can't come up when I'm not here."

Her heart raced, and she had snakes coiling in her stomach.

This was completely out of line. Other parents didn't do this...right?

She looked quickly around the condo looking to see if anything was out of place.

A terrible thought hit her.

"You didn't bring anyone, did you?" She took a quick step away and started looking around corners, like his entourage was going to start coming out of bedrooms, carrying the family heirlooms.

"Jennifer," her dad's raspy voice scolded from behind her. "I wouldn't do that."

She held back her scoff, but just barely. She whipped around to face him. "What are you doing here, Dad?" she asked again.

He squinted at her and scratched his chin, his skin discolored under the beard. Were those bruises on his knuckles?

"I came to visit my daughter. Why is that so hard to believe?"

This time she didn't hold back her eye roll. "When have you ever visited me just because?"

John's earlier words rang in her head.

Her dad's wild smile slipped from his face, but he pasted it back on. "Don't be like that, Jenny. I used to come visit you all the time."

She felt her forehead wrinkle. All the time?

"When? When I was in utero?"

This time the smile stayed off his face.

"Watch your tone, young lady."

The acidic tone made her recoil. Snapping at her dad was an unknown plan of attack for her, and already she was feeling sick from it, but she had to make her point. More than just her feelings were on the line.

Jen saw papers spread out on the counter. Jen and John were both orderly people. Everything had a place, and messed up documents on the counter was not it.

"First you come to my house unannounced, and then, apparently, go through my stuff?" She waved at the papers. "Not to mention, I never gave you a goddamn key. So tell me, how'd you get in?"

She started tapping her foot to release the building tension. Her heart beat so hard it felt like she was having a heart attack.

Her dad stared at her hard for a second before shrugging nonchalantly. "Wasn't that hard of a pick."

"You can't pick my boyfriend's lock!"

He raised his right shoulder. "If he didn't want people breaking in, he should get better locks. And, you admit it, he is your boyfriend." His expression turned carefully blank.

"His building has security. He shouldn't need Fort Knox locks." Her tongue tripped on the funny combination of words, but she soldiered on. "Once again, Dad, you can't pick my boyfriend's locks and let yourself into his fucking house!"

"Language," he barked out.

Now he wanted to play Dad of the Year?

"You broke into the fucking house!" she shouted. She curled her hands into fists and framed them on either side of her face, not knowing what to do with them. She opened them and slowly grabbed at her face, completely at a loss on how to handle this.

He reared back and gave her an assessing look. "So, that's how it's going to be."

"How's what going to be?" she asked, feeling the slime from him oozing onto her own skin.

Jen thought of John and immediately felt dirty and grimy and guilty. *She* did this. She was responsible. She set her dad up for this opportunity.

John would never forgive this.

Panic bloomed.

"Now that you're hooked up with a big superstar you don't have time for your family anymore. Is that it? I heard you were with him, but I didn't actually believe it. I thought my own daughter would tell me if she was dating John 'The Saint' Costner."

She had done nothing wrong, yet her father made her feel like an errant child.

Was she being too hard on him? Was he really just coming to visit?

"What? No, that's not what this—"

"No, I get it. You forgot your roots. I understand. I probably would want to forget them too." He looked around the condo and whistled long and low. "I get it. I just never pegged you as a person to actually do it."

Jen ground her teeth. "I'm not forgetting my roots, Dad. You *broke* into his condo and I—"

"Cut the crap, kid. You put me on the approved visitors list. I asked to come up. They let me. That's on you for adding me to the list if you didn't actually want me here, and them for not calling you."

What?

No, it wasn't.

"It's on you to call me to tell me that you were here or that you were coming to visit. You don't just come into a home unannounced and wait around for God knows how long. That's not normal, Dad!"

"Couldn't call."

Why did the air feel so suffocating whenever he was around?

She sighed. "Where's your phone?"

He gave her an assessing look. "Don't know, I lost it."

Bullshit.

"Please tell me you understand how inappropriate this is." She waved her hands between them. Jen raised her eyebrows, begging him to understand.

A part of her wished that her father would cop to it and apologize. Another part was hoping he had some form of social misfire in his brain, so he honestly didn't realize what a misstep he made.

Her father's face lost the angry look and instead he asked softly, "Are you ashamed of me, Jenny?"

Jen pinched her lips and took a heaving breath, trying not to show any outward reaction to his open manipulation.

"Dad, you broke into my boyfriend's house."

"It's your house. I thought I was welcome at the home of my daughter."

"Dad—"

"You know what, forget it." He turned around and stomped toward his ratty coat hanging on the back of the kitchen stool. "I had some good news I wanted to share with you, but clearly you don't care." He dug into his back pocket and angrily ripped out a worn and ratty looking envelope. He ripped out some bills and slapped them down on the counter. "There's your fucking money. I'm paying you back. My debt is officially paid. If I taught you anything, it's that you always repay your debts. Hope you haven't forgotten that while you're shacking up with Mr. Millions."

Hurt stabbed through her.

She couldn't figure out what to say as she stared at the money on the counter. He'd never paid her back before.

Maybe he really was just turning over a new leaf and trying to reach out? Mend fences?

"Dad." Jen stepped forward to say something, anything, to repair the situation.

"Forget it, Jen."

He looked once around the room, a slow long look, before looking back at her. "Proud of you, honey. You've done well. Keep it up. Love you, kiddo." He stepped in quickly, placed a quick kiss to her forehead, and was out the door before she could unglue her feet from the floor.

As the door snicked shut behind him, Jen ran to it and threw it open, hoping she could catch him before he vanished.

When she opened the door, he was gone.

What did he really want? Why was he there? Was he okay?

She dragged her feet back to the kitchen and sat on the stool that her dad had been sitting on moments before.

She thought she could faintly smell him in the air. Though the smell didn't bring back necessarily joyous memories, it still belonged to her dad. He might not be the easiest man to love and he certainly had his flaws, but was she being too hard on him?

She looked down at the money on the counter and winced.

Maybe he was trying to turn his life around.

Her breaths were heavy and she felt a headache creep in.

As Jen pulled the discarded papers toward her to put them back into the pile, she saw that they were her notes on the various players she treated in the last week. It was a list of what injuries she worked on and who needed what treatments.

Her eyes absently scanned the page while her mind replayed every moment with her dad. She needed to update her player notes while the day was still fresh in her mind, but she couldn't get her mind to work.

She stilled when she saw John's name and a note about his neck and shoulder pain in the margins and how she thought he might be sitting out for the upcoming Sunday game.

When she brought it up with him, he lost his godforsaken mind and insisted his body felt fine. He went from being questionable to active on the roster. A thirty-eight-year-old hissy fit let the man get his way. Jen was still pissed that he wouldn't give his body time to recover. They were on a winning streak, would easily make the playoffs, and the game they were playing Sunday was predicted to be a blowout. A guaranteed win. She tried to suggest that he should sit it out and let his body recover but he wouldn't hear it.

Speaking of shit he didn't want to hear.

She groaned.

Did she have to tell John about the break in?

Could she twist it as if she was here with her dad the whole time? That she invited him for a visit?

That wasn't much better.

Could she get away with not telling John at all?

What if the doorman told him and she didn't? That would be worse.

Jen didn't want to lie to him—that wasn't fair.

But she also didn't want her father's presence to make waves and ruin a great relationship.

Again.

With a sigh, Jen leaned forward and rested her head on the sheets in front of her. The paper stuck to her forehead, and she didn't even bother adjusting it. She tried to copy John's box breathing technique to calm her racing heart and queasy stomach.

Jen tried to tell herself that John wasn't going to hold her accountable for her father's actions and wouldn't judge her for her father's poor choices.

Yet she couldn't shake the feeling that there was only so much that any given person could take, and forgive, and Jen's dad's baggage might be more than John wanted to handle while also trying to manage his career.

CHAPTER THIRTY-SIX

November 6, Saturday
John

"Ha! Suck it!" Jen laughed as she jumped up on John's couch and wiggled her body dramatically.

John rolled his eyes and leaned over to grab his beer. He tipped forward over his knees so her rocking movements wouldn't cause him to spill his drink on his relatively new couch. It had been a few days since his phone call with his parents and he pushed his father's warnings out of his mind. He didn't need that negativity in his life.

John's body pitched as Jen plopped back down on the cushion next to him.

Jen swiped at her own beer from the coffee table in front of them and turned to face him, absolutely gloating.

"Dude," she said while shaking her head, her eyes disappointed.

He rolled his eyes.

"How can you be *this* bad at Madden?" She laughed after she swallowed a sip of her beer. She set it down and twisted back to him. "You're literally playing as the Spartans, and you can't beat me?"

"The players on my team aren't performing," he grumbled, fighting to keep a smile from his face.

Her eyebrows climbed up into her hairline. "It's *this* season's roster!"

"Precisely," he pouted.

Jen grabbed at his forearm that held his gaming controller and howled with laughter.

John wanted to do the same but found himself more interested in watching her joy in the moment. The complete and utter abandon that invaded her. She always burdened herself with one thing or another. But here, in this moment, she looked lighthearted and happy. Even though Jen reminded him constantly about their need to be discreet, he felt confident he could convince her to come out about being in a relationship soon.

"Hey, I wanted to talk to you about something."

Jen wiped at her eyes and tried to sober herself. "Sure, let's talk. Now that you know I can kick your ass in hockey, soccer, *and* football."

Truth. The woman had a knack for video games.

John rolled his eyes and she giggled and scurried closer to him. He opened his arms wide on instinct and she curled into him and looked up.

"What's up?"

It was time to come clean. The lying to her was fraying his nerves.

John smiled at her. "I wanted to let you know I called in a couple of favors."

A cute little v formed between her perfect dark brows, and he leaned forward to kiss it away.

"It's a good thing. Promise."

A solitary eyebrow lowered but she left the other raised high as she cocked her head up at him. She had the smallest frown pulling at her full, pink lips and he bent down quickly to kiss that away too.

When she smiled up at him, he continued. "Basically, I called up a few of my contacts last month and one of my real estate companies bought your building." He hesitated. "So, you're my tenant now, I guess."

Jen stilled in his arms.

He gave her a gentle squeeze. "I know how you get sometimes—"

Before he could finish, Jen sat up and laid kisses on every inch of skin she could reach. Perched on her knees, she assaulted him with wet smooches all over his face, neck, shoulders, arms, and hands. Everywhere. John laughed as she found a particularly sensitive spot.

"John," she murmured after she paused. She stared deep into his eyes and he felt it.

Little fireworks shot up and down his spine at the look on her face.

"That was *so* stupid. It's a crap building."

"Crap *then,* yes," he stressed. "It's getting better now. And it will be great when we're done with it. Great and safe. And..." He trailed off.

"And?"

John shook his head slightly. "I forget where I was going with that." Damn that was happening a lot this week.

"John. You don't need to add me to your list of people to take care of. I don't expect that from you."

"I know you don't expect it. That's why I like to do it. You don't ask me for anything. You accept me as I am and let me be me. Just like I'm doing my best to let you do you, despite your questionable relationship with your long-lost, suspiciously silent, father."

Jen winced.

As he was about to ask her about that look, she got closer and said quickly, "Thank you for making it safe for my friends and me, that was a very generous gift."

"An investment," he corrected.

She paused and stared up at him, her face taking on a somber and curious look, like she was seeing him for the first time.

"You're really something, John Costner." Her voice was a whisper. "I'm not sure what I did to catch your eye, but wow, am I lucky."

John returned her whisper. "Thank you for letting me be one of the few people that you'll let take care of you. I know what an honor that is."

Her eyes got suspiciously bright and shiny.

Nope. No crying on his watch.

John leaned in and snagged a fierce kiss. When her lips chased his as he pulled away, he gave her another and another.

Before they both knew it, they found themselves naked on the very couch John tried so hard not to get dirty.

So apparently buying her building was an acceptable way to keep her safe but walking her to her car at night was overkill.

Damn confusing woman.

He wouldn't have her any other way.

CHAPTER THIRTY-SEVEN

November 7, Sunday
Jen

Jen bounced into work Sunday morning. Finding out John was her new landlord, of a sort, was a bit weird. A small part of her was squeamish about paying him rent. But if John's ownership turned her building into a safer place for the families around her, then she shouldn't and wouldn't make John feel guilty about it. Other people were affected by his actions – for the better. She needed to trust him and not begrudge him this kindness, even if it was her connection to the building that spawned it.

It was scary to consider.

Trusting John.

Trusting him not only with these *debts*, these favors, but with her *heart*.

Trusting John with her heart.

It felt right.

Jen hummed along to her current ear worm and bounced next to Ryan as they made their way across the parking lot and into the stadium.

John had an early morning appointment with Spartan management to discuss his contract renewal options. Jen didn't like that they made this appointment on a game day before the season even ended, but John just shrugged and said Richie would handle it. He seemed a little off this morning, so she let it drop.

Without John being her normal chauffeur, Jen called Ryan and he agreed to bring her in. Ryan stayed silent for the entire car ride, sporting dark sunglasses and a slight bruise on his cheek. Jen tried to get the story out of him, but he said nothing, staying unusually closed-lipped about it.

"Will you be less...*happy*?" Ryan grumbled as they made their way across the parking lot.

"I'm not happy." But she couldn't stop the smile from spreading over her face.

"God. People in love annoy the crap out of me."

Jen felt her stomach give out and stopped in her tracks. "What?"

Ryan rolled his eyes and Jen wondered if he mimicked John's signature move on purpose. Her own eyes narrowed.

"God. You think no one knows? You two are both so obvious. Blech." He turned and kept moving towards the entrance.

Say what?

She stomped after him and tugged on his sleeve before he got more than a couple of paces ahead of her.

"Explain," she bit out, giving him her best big sister look. Her hands started shaking as she clutched his sleeve. The November chill wasn't bothering her at that moment. Something entirely different caused these jitters.

He gave her a careful look and saw her worry. "Well, maybe it's not *obvious* to everyone. But, I mean, come on. Anyone who knows the two of you and isn't completely self-absorbed should have noticed by now." He paused and looked at her questioningly. "Did you really think no one knew?"

Jen's breath came quicker.

"Hell, you guys can barely keep your eyes off each other. It's amazing more people don't know." He looked long at the stadium before looking back to her. "The media would lose their mind."

She felt her brow wrinkle as she stared at him. "Who do you think knows?"

Ryan pulled his arm away and rubbed it absently. His exhale caused a plume of grey fog to coast up and over his face. Jen was blasted with a wave of bubblegum as she waited for his answer. Her feet tapped a nervous staccato as he took his time.

"I don't know. I think Liam. Maybe Kyle Justice. Definitely Kenny."

Her eyes grew big as he listed the names. That was three more people than she felt comfortable knowing about them. All great guys. But the fewer people who knew about her and John and...whatever they were, the better.

"Oh my god," she said. The cars and trucks in the parking lot started to blur and fuzz.

She was going to be sick.

"Oh, and I think Butch and Richie have noticed something too."

"Anyone else?" Her voice started to get that slightly frantic quality that always made Lexie tease her about being possessed by a demon.

"Nah, that's probably it."

She stared at him in horror. Her eyes felt frozen open from the cold morning air, but she couldn't help it.

This was bad.

Her head turned toward the stadium and she felt her stomach twirl and twist.

She was totally going to be sick.

She scrambled in her pocket for her phone. Her fingers bumbled around until she pulled her hand out, ripped off her mitten, and shoved her hand back in. She shot a quick text to John.

I know you're in a meeting but can you step out for a few minutes so we can chat really quick?

She debated sending the next piece but went for it anyway.

People know we're dating. We need to get our story straight.

She bounced on her toes and stared at her phone, holding her breath. When no text message or call immediately came through, she started to sweat.

"Okay, okay, this is fine. This is fine." Her eyes stayed glued to her phone.

"Easy there. Let's get inside and you can lose your shit in there. It's colder than a witch's titty out here." Ryan grabbed her arm and escorted her inside, careful to lead her around cars and posts in the parking lot.

"Jenny! Jen! Over here."

Jen looked up dazedly, twisting her head this way and that, trying to locate her father's voice. He was standing by the fence where the questionable visitors always hung out.

Crap. Just what she needed right now.

Jen gave a look to Ryan and waved him inside. "I'll catch up with you later."

Ryan looked unconvinced but he nodded and headed inside.

Jen walked briskly toward her father, her bag slung over her shoulder, and her hair tied up in a tight ponytail. She could feel the excitement and tension among the fans on the other side of the fence. Even though the game wasn't supposed to be a close one, a game was a game and the fans were already amped.

"Hey, Dad," Jen said, trying to sound cheerful. "You managed to score some tickets? Great game to come and blow off some steam."

The way their last meeting ended left a sour taste in her mouth and she felt awkward and out of place as she stood there talking to him through a chain link fence. It gave her prison vibes.

Miguel's expression softened slightly. "You know how it is. They always play better when I'm here. Figured they could use me here if the Saint wasn't going to be playing," he said, his voice low.

Jen bristled, her stomach twisting with anxiety. "Dad...John's playing today." She let it hang there and felt a hot poker in her chest as her father blanched.

His fingers darted forward and curled through the chain links, grabbing it tight despite the chill. "What do you mean he's playing?"

Jen's heart gave an uneven patter in her chest at the terrified look on his face.

"John didn't want to take the weekend off. He decided to play. What's up? What's wrong?" Jen took a step closer, trying to keep her voice down now that people were looking toward them.

"You're fucking notes said he wasn't playing," her father hissed through the fence, his own amber eyes wide and unblinking.

Fuck.

"Dad—"

"And you're fucking notes said Ryan had something funny going on with his throwing hand."

Now, just one minute.

"And now you're telling me you fucking lied to me? You've fucked me."

"Dad, I didn't tell you anything."

"You did. You said that John wasn't going to play and that Ryan would be playing injured. I. Read. Your. Notes."

Jen shifted on her feet, uncomfortably aware of the other staff walking through the parking lot behind her. Her neck started burning and she got the overwhelming feeling that they were being watched. "Dad, those were not notes for you. Just thoughts to myself during this week's therapy visits. You *never* should have read them, and you *never* should have placed a bet on them."

Miguel's voice dropped a pitch and he began pleading. "I made a bet on this game, Jenny. A big one. I put five hundred grand down on John not playing, and Ryan Cole playing terrible. I bet that the Spartans would lose. You have to have them throw the game."

Jen's mouth fell open and tried to make sense of his words.

Five hundred grand?

Oh god.

"You did what?" she whispered, she started to shake and tasted bile in her throat. Jen rubbed hard at her chest.

"I had to," Miguel said, his voice low. "I owed some people money, and this was my only chance to get it back. My final bet. But you have to talk to your boyfriend. And I saw you a minute ago with Ryan

Cole. You're close to him. Just tell him I need his help. I need to make sure my bet's still good. My life, hell, maybe even *our* lives, depend on it."

Jen closed her eyes and held up a quivering hand between her and her father. She blindly took a step back and shook her head. Jen took in a shuddering breath and slowly opened her eyes. "This is not on me. I have nothing to do with this. Tell them to keep the fuck away from me."

"You know I don't have that kind of power, Jenny. You need to do this. Keep him from playing. Hell, maybe they'll even go after him."

John's words about her dad manipulating her, conning her, and putting her into danger played over and over in her ears.

Going after John to punish her dad? She would be responsible for that. She brought her dad's toxicity into his life.

What if John and she evolved into something real and they had kids? Would she want to open them up to this risk? To this poison?

Jen took another step back, shaking her head as she eyed her father through new lenses.

He kept pleading with her through the fence, but she couldn't hear it over the roar in her ears. She stumbled as she took another step back.

Tears started to fill her eyes as she continued to stumble her way backward. She watched her father turn blurry, his mouth still moving though now the only thing she could hear was her own ragged breaths. She rubbed at her chest absently and when a horn honked next to her, she finally realized she was backing out in front of cars in the parking lot. People were staring.

Jen turned and fled into the employee entrance of the stadium, on autopilot as she scanned her badge and went through security.

She wanted to feel numb, but instead, guilt and terror consumed her.

CHAPTER THIRTY-EIGHT

November 7, Sunday
John

John finished clipping his fingernails and popping a couple of ibuprofen when Butch found him. The meeting that morning had been fantastic, and it looked like management would discuss a contract extension of three years at the end of this season. The way he'd been playing proved that his body could take it.

Jen's frequent massage therapy attention had no doubt helped.

Though, her massages did nothing for his memory lapses and now-frequent headaches.

"Hey, John. Can we talk for a minute?" Butch asked.

John nodded and followed Butch into his office. He took a seat across from Butch, who leaned forward in his chair.

"I need to talk to you for a minute as a friend, not a coach. I've recently discovered that you and Jen are having a relationship." Butch waited for John's confirmation and then continued. "I'm worried about her loyalties. I think she might be using her position as our team's massage therapist to get inside information for her dad."

John scoffed. "No way in hell, man. Jen would never do something like that."

Butch sighed and rubbed at his forehead. "I saw her at a local bookie hangout with a big envelope of cash."

John's eyes narrowed. "Unfortunately, her dad has a bit of a gambling problem and she has too big of a heart to say no. But she's not the one placing the bets, Butch. She's paying off bookies to protect her dad."

Even if he didn't deserve it.

"I'm just telling you what I saw, John. I'm just concerned about your well-being. If her dad is a gambling addict, he could be putting pressure on her to get information."

John shook his head. "Jen would never do that to me."

Butch hesitated before continuing. "I also saw her with her dad this morning in the parking lot of the stadium. I overheard him chewing her out for giving him wrong information about you not playing today."

John's jaw dropped and his lungs seized. "What?"

Jen had pushed him to take the weekend off, said he wasn't acting right and that his body could use a break. She kept saying he was distracted and spacey on top of his body being a little worse for wear.

She couldn't have...

"I know. That's why I'm worried, John. Apparently, she also said something to him about Ryan's hand. And you know that's not public knowledge."

John tensed. It sure as shit wasn't public knowledge.

John stood up, his face felt hot and he clenched his hands. "Is that all you got?"

Butch held up his hands in a placating gesture. "I'm not trying to upset you, John. I want you to be careful. You're our star quarterback, and if someone is using you for their own gain, it could hurt our team in the long run. It's game day, so I need you to stay focused, but I just wanted to let you know in case she tries convincing you of anything before the game."

"Like not playing," John said, his voice rising.

"Or something."

John stormed out of Butch's office, more than ready to find Jen and figure out what the hell was going on. His mind raced with conflicting thoughts and emotions.

She would never betray him or the team that way.

But...she needed the funds.

And she did have a soft spot for her dad.

As he walked to the massage room, he searched his pockets for his phone. Damn, he must have left it in his gym bag.

John heard hurried footsteps echoing down the hall and looked up just in time to see the woman in question, turning the corner and hurtling down the hallway towards him, a look of guilt and dread on her face.

John's stomach tightened and ice washed down his spine.

Fuck.

CHAPTER THIRTY-NINE

November 7, Sunday
John

John stopped walking and let Jen meet him in the middle of the quiet hallway. Before she could say a word, John went on the offensive, hoping not to hear what he was starting to suspect was true.

"Jen, have you been giving information about the team to your dad?" John asked, his voice shaking with anger that he was trying extremely hard to suppress.

Innocent until proven guilty, right?

"What? No, of course not." Jen's expression however, remained wary. Her brows lowered in worry as she stepped close. "Are you okay? You look—"

"So, the big envelope of cash at one of the bookie hangouts was for your dad?" John said, trying to keep his voice steady.

Jen's face lost a bit of its color at the accusation and her head snapped in a painful-looking jerk. "Yes, it was for my dad. I don't bet on anything. What's going on?"

"And you have *never* fed him information on any of the players on the team so he could make a bet?"

She flinched, it was barely there, but he saw it. He knew her. Her face now had lost all its color and John's stomach tightened.

"Jesus, fuck." He cursed out, taking her in, horror making its way up his gut and into his chest. "Jesus Christ, Jen."

She stepped closer. "No, it's not like that, I promise. John, please," she said, reaching out for him. "I know it looks bad, but—"

"But what?" John interrupted. "Are you trying to tell me you're not involved in this?"

"No, I had no idea. I wanted to tell you. I was on my way to tell you. He was looking at my notes the other day and he took my notes to myself as gospel. He went and placed a bet and—"

"When?"

"What?" Her eyes looked frightened.

"*When* was he looking at your notes? And do you frequently share your notes with those not in the organization?"

Jen squirmed and then her whole body deflated. "When I came home...to your house...the other day, he was already there waiting for me. I wanted to tell you but I didn't know how."

"What the fuck?" John narrowed his eyes knowing he wasn't going to like the rest of this conversation one bit.

"He had...let himself in." Jen peeked up at him and stilled at the fury on his face.

"You gave your father a key to my home?"

Jen winced at the fury on his face.

"Not exactly."

"Spit it out," John barked.

Jen's head twitched and she continued to avoid eye contact. "He...sort of picked the locks and let himself in." She started talking faster. "I yelled at him. Told him it was entirely inappropriate and totally not acceptable. I even went downstairs and removed him from the approved visitor list." She trailed off, her face taking in the expression on his.

"That fucker was alone in my house, and you didn't think to tell me?"

"I was going to," she said in a small voice.

"Yeah, I *bet*."

She cringed and looked down at her feet.

"Jen." He waited for her to look up at him. "You told your dad I was *injured*?"

"No! He read that on a note in my notebook!"

She was making notes about him being injured? He had never played better! Fine, fuck her.

John slashed a hand through the air.

"I'm done. You're right. This has gone on long enough and now your dad is starting to interfere with our outside lives. You're right, we should have ended this a month ago."

Jen stood there, staring up at him with big eyes, her mouth slightly ajar.

"You'll want to be more careful about your fucking notes if you're keeping that fucker around. All the best to the both of you. I hope keeping him in your life brings you immense joy and doesn't get you killed. All the best."

At the horrified expression on her face, John turned and stomped away, proud of himself for not punching the walls with the war raging inside of him.

He had a game to win, he needed to focus, so why did it feel like he already lost?

CHAPTER FORTY

November 7, Sunday

Jen

Jen had always been fascinated by the world of professional football. The power, the intensity, and the sheer physicality of the game always drew her in.

Being the focus of that power, intensity, and energy was a different thing altogether.

She now understood why John was a feared quarterback on the gridiron.

That intensity, that anger, directed at her? She wanted to curl up into a ball and die.

As she walked the halls getting ready to head out onto the field for sideline setup, she paused at the corner of the hallway when she heard some unfamiliar voices say John's name.

"Did you see they're letting Costner start today?" one of them said. "He was all over the place this week. Couldn't remember a damn thing."

"Could hardly finish a sentence either. That hit last week fucked him right up."

"It was a fucking *hit*. The dude got destroyed. Probably should have gone immediately to concussion protocol but he played it off cool as a cucumber. No one noticed a thing."

"Half the team noticed, but they're all so fucking whipped by him that they're not going to say shit against The Saint."

Jen paused, her heart sinking. She knew John had memory problems, this week in particular, but she just thought he was distracted, not that something was actually wrong with him.

"Come on, guys," a third voice said. "You know that's not it. John's taken one too many hits to the head. He's got brain damage from all those concussions he's had over the years. You see how often he rubs at his head? The guy has nonstop fucking headaches."

He did. All the time he rubbed at his head. This week more than most.

Jen felt her stomach clench. She had heard about CTE, the degenerative brain disease that affected many professional football players. But she never thought John could be suffering from it.

"Add in his mood swings, the writing is on the wall. The coaches are going to get him fucking killed if they keep letting him play."

"Hell, it's like that movie with a concussion countdown. One left for Costner before he's..." He made an odd sound and Jen closed her eyes as she leaned against the wall, praying they were wrong. Yet, Jen couldn't shake the feeling of unease that settled in her chest. She knew football was a dangerous sport, but she never thought about the toll it took on the players' bodies and minds.

Now that she thought about it, she could see that something was off with John. He seemed distracted, distant, like he was struggling to keep up with the demands of everyday life. Her subconscious noticed, that's why she kept uncharacteristically nagging him about playing this week.

How in the world was she supposed to talk to him about this? After everything that happened, he'd probably never talk to her again.

Something was seriously wrong, and he needed to get checked before he played today.

In her mind's eye she saw the concussion countdown meter flip to one and her heart stopped in her chest.

God, she was going to be sick.

Surely he would see reason and get checked out before playing again, right?

Maybe...if they hadn't already had a fight about not playing and him thinking that she was in cahoots with her gambling addict father.

Shit.

She needed to find John. Stat.

CHAPTER FORTY-ONE

November 7, Sunday
John

John took a deep breath and prowled back and forth in one of the empty conference rooms. X's and O's peppered the whiteboards, obvious signs that he should be focusing on the upcoming game in a few short hours. But instead, all he could think about was Jen manipulating and lying to him.

She wasn't evil.

She probably never set out to hurt him or betray him like this.

But her fucking father.

He told her time and time again that the guy was bad news and she always pretended to listen to him. They'd had countless conversations curled up on his couch, in his bed, dancing on his building's fucking rooftop terrace about ways that she could phase him out in a safe and least hurtful way. Hell, he even offered to pay for a live-in addiction resource center for him and have him seek the treatment he needed.

Personally, John didn't believe you could fix jackass, but he offered it to Jen, nonetheless.

Not that she took him up on it.

Knowing that she chose her manipulative father over him, that she betrayed his trust like that...it made him sick.

How could one person be so angry, hurt, and confused all at the same time?

He stormed back and forth, unable to stop himself from tensing his already sore shoulder. The headache he'd been fighting all week, reared its ugly head again and pulsed behind his eyes, making it hard to see. Damn, that last hit. He technically should have gone through the concussion protocol on that one. But it was a close game and Ryan had a tough time reading the defense during their film analysis the week before. The kid would have folded, and the team would have lost. What kind of leader would that make him?

"John." Jen poked her head in the door. "Can I talk to you for a minute?"

How did she always manage to find him?

Goddamn his head hurt. He rubbed at his temple and squared up to face her.

Her eyes crinkled as she watched him rub at his head, a look of fear creeping onto her face.

Jesus, what now?

John adjusted his stance and braced himself for whatever shit came out of her mouth.

Jen hesitated for a moment, then plunged ahead. "I've been hearing some rumors, John," she said, taking a small step forward before jolting to a stop. "About you."

John hardened his expression. "And?"

Jen took a deep breath. "Some of the guys are saying that you've been having trouble remembering plays and that it's because of all the hits you've taken over the years and especially that hard one in the last game." She took another huge breath that had her team polo expanding. "They said you might be showing signs of CTE." She paused and stared up at him, her expression terrified. "You've been having headaches..."

"From stress."

"John," she said softly. Her eyes roamed his face.

"I've been checked out by the doctors and I'm fine. So you can take your rumors and shove them. And I want the names of the assholes who are making light of CTE and accusing teammates of having it."

That's just what he needed the media to pick up on—that John was sitting out of the game because he had headaches. His father would eat that shit right fucking up. Nothing like raising a pussy who couldn't handle a few knocks.

Jen shook her head, her golden hoops swinging. "I don't have names. I overhead them in the hall." She took another small step closer, her movement making no sound on the ultra-thick maroon carpet. "But they have a point, John. That hit last weekend was fierce. And you have been distracted and somewhat confused this week. You forgot what you were saying mid-sentence several times, and you always have a headache lately."

"Yeah, I have headaches, I'm constantly being questioned by the media, management, my family, and apparently my own fucking ex-girlfriend and teammates about whether I'm too old to keep playing."

"That's not what this is."

"Bullshit."

Jen winced and looked at her feet. "I'm sorry, John," she said softly. "I didn't mean to insinuate anything. I am worried, and I wanted to make sure that you were okay. I just...I think you should sit out today and get checked out by a doc."

John stilled.

Fuck.

Fuck him.

That's what this was.

An attempt to get him to sit out this game.

"How much?"

"What?" Her confused expression hurt to see, knowing that she could hide her emotions so well. She turned out to be one hell of an actress.

"How much do you guys have on the game?"

Her face shut down. "That's not what this is."

"Just tell me." His voice sounded tired. Defeated.

"I have nothing on the game. My dad has half a million dollars."

Jesus.

John whistled low.

"He's an idiot," Jen said.

"On that, we agree."

John glared at her for a moment, then sighed and shook his head. "I appreciate your concern, if it's legit. But we're not together anymore, and you're not a doctor, and you're not my therapist. You just rub my aching muscles. So keep your opinions to yourself and you might want to get your dad straightened out before he takes you down with him."

Jen's face took on a nasty look, her pretty nose scrunching. "Oh, don't worry. I've already been warned that this will blow back on me if I don't convince you otherwise. But that's not what this is about."

"So now you're trying to guilt me into not playing?"

She stamped her foot and stuck out a hip. He used to find that so attractive and now?

Now it was still attractive, and he hated the part of him that thought so.

"John, that's not true. I care about you. I'm not trying to sabotage your dream or anything like that. I want you to be safe and to simply talk with someone to make sure everything is okay with you. I'm worried about you." Her lovely lilting voice broke on the end and he steeled himself not to care. If she didn't want to choose him, he certainly wasn't going to choose her.

"It's not your job to worry about me, Jen. Not anymore. Not ever again. You worry about you, and everyone else that you worried about before we met. But take me off the list. I don't need your kind of baggage in my life. Not if I want to end my career on a high note, not covered in gambling scandals." John shook his head.

Jen's eyes got glossy. "I don't want to see you get hurt." Her voice was thin like she was struggling to breathe.

Join the club.

The knife sticking out of his back made him feel the same way.

John shook his head and walked out of the room. This was why he didn't date, especially during the season.

Relationships brought drama, and even the good ones, the great ones, the best ones, left you feeling helpless and alone.

But now? Now he had a game to win.

CHAPTER FORTY-TWO
November 7, Sunday
Jen

The hit made Jen want to vomit.

It was completely legal, but hard and loud.

Her pulse drummed loud in her ears, drowning out the now-quiet stadium as John still didn't move to get to his feet. Kenny squatted over him and then frantically waved to the sideline, screaming...something.

Jen couldn't hear over the roaring in her head.

She tried to swallow but something lodged in her throat. Something much too big.

John continued to lay motionless on the field, his body limp as the medical staff circled around him. The players circled; worry etched on their faces. The crowd was silent as the medical team rushed onto the field, their gear clanging as they made their way to the quarterback.

Jen watched from the sidelines, her heart pounding in her chest. She knew that John had been playing with a concussion, but she never expected him to take a hit like this and simply not get up. Was he breathing?

As the medical team surrounded John, Jen felt tears welling up in her eyes. They ended on such a horrible note. So much hurt and anger and betrayal.

She was completely honest when she spoke with him, she was concerned for his health. But her track record of choosing her father and enabling him, spoke louder than her words. Louder than her actions.

She should have told him she loved him.

As she watched the man she loved lying unconscious on the field, she wished she could do it over. Tell him about her father's break-in. Tell him about her fear of being a quitter who couldn't hack it when a family member had a problem. Tell him about loving him so much she could barely breathe when she thought about him.

And now...he might never know.

She rushed to the side of field, pushing her way past the crowd of reporters and cameramen. She saw his teammates gathered around him, their faces grim and worried. She heard one of them mutter something about being unresponsive.

Her heart constricted.

The medical team worked quickly and efficiently, stabilizing John's neck, and carefully lifting him onto a stretcher. Jen watched as they carried him off the field, his body still and lifeless. She chased after them, desperate to be with John, desperate to hear he was okay.

She got to the back room where they were working on him and heard his voice.

But...something wasn't right.

CHAPTER FORTY-THREE

November 7, Sunday
John

"I'm fine! Let me up."

"John. Son. You aren't fine," a somewhat familiar voice said above him.

John had been making his reads when he got blindsided with a hit to his left side. Fourth quarter, down by seven, and the team needed him.

So his head felt a little woozy. It always did after a big hit. He was fine. As long as he kept his eyes closed.

The ridiculousness of that thought didn't register.

"I'm fine!" John tried to push his way through the arms trying to restrain him and came up short. Something pressed against his chest. His mind focused on not throwing up.

Fuck, his head hurt.

"Yeah, John. You're fine. Just settle down a moment." Someone patted him on the foot.

Mumbled and indistinguishable conversation made its way to his ringing ears.

Fuck, were his ears bleeding? He raised a hand to feel but someone intercepted it and placed it back in his lap.

His nose was running too. He lifted a hand to swipe at it, but his hand was caught again.

He felt a strap that rested across his arms. How did they do that?

He tried opening his eyes.

Shit.

"Can someone turn the damn lights off? We don't need it brighter than the Fourth of July in here," he demanded.

The lights dimmed.

Why were the lights so bright?

Did they get new bulbs?

"Hey, John? We have to bring you to the hospital for a quick check, okay? No fighting us," a ridiculously loud voice thundered in his ears while John kept his eyes shut tight.

Jesus. Couldn't they see his ears were bleeding?

Where was he going?

"To the hospital," a voice said.

Did he ask that aloud?

"Hang in there, buddy. Okay? We'll have you home in no time."

Home. His home. With Jen.

"Nah. Can't go. Got to stay here to take Jen home." He tried sitting up but the straps across his chest held him down. He struggled to get out of them.

"Jen?" someone asked.

"The massage therapist?" another person asked.

John heard their questions but tried to focus on moving his hands to release the strap without needing to open his eyes.

Damn thing was impenetrable.

His runny nose was driving him nuts.

Fuck his head hurt.

Where was Jen? She would have a tissue to soak up his running nose. She was always prepared like that. A mother hen at thirty-two.

"I need Jen." John tried pushing through the straps. Hands pushed him back down and he seized in panic. He started pushing back. They were holding him down. If he didn't get up now, he'd never get up.

He needed to get up.

More hands pushed at him.

I *need to get up!*

"John?" Jen's out-of-breath voice came at him but when he tried to turn his head toward her voice, it wouldn't move. It was stuck in something. His vision blacked out and he felt bile rise again. He clenched his jaw tight so he wouldn't vomit everywhere.

Soft whispers echoed around the room.

What were they saying?

Coconut and lime made its way to him.

Home.

He stilled.

John felt cold hands on his cheeks and through his slitted eyes saw someone lean over.

"Hey there, Saint. You have to stop moving now. Can you hear me?"

"You smell good."

Her hands ran down his shoulders and into his hand. He could tell they were hers versus the others by how chilly they were. John squeezed them tight.

He was on a bed.

The bed was hard.

"Why is the bed hard?"

"Shh. Just a minute. Let's get this moved." Her soft voice calmed him.

Wait, was he supposed to be mad at her?

"What was tha'?"

"Okay, John, I'm going to let go of your hand now, okay? I'll check in on you later." Her voice sounded worried. Why was she worried?

"Jen?" He started fighting the straps again. He needed a tissue. "Jen!"

"I'm here, I'm here." John felt her hands in hers. He squeezed.

"Just take her with you guys. Go!" another voice barked out.

A slam echoed and the sound reverberated around his head.

"I need you to wipe my ears. They're bleeding," he mumbled. "I can't sleep if they're bleeding."

Jesus. He was tired.

Her panicked voice roused him. "Your ears are bleeding? Is...is that okay? Is that okay that his ears are bleeding?" Her normally smooth voice sounded broken and choppy. It was also shrill. It made John wince away.

"He's confused. His ears aren't bleeding," someone murmured to Jen.

"Shh," John said. "Who's that?"

"Shh," she repeated back. Now much quieter. "Shh." She rubbed soft swirls into his hands. That felt nice.

"Why is my bed hard?"

"Shh," she said again.

"Jen?"

"Yeah, John?"

"I can't see."

"Your eyes aren't open, John."

Oh. He thought they were.

"My head hurts."

Silence descended.

Chapter Forty-Four
November 7, Sunday
Jen

When they arrived at the hospital, the medical team rushed John into surgery. Jen, William, and several others sat in the waiting room. Jen hung her head in her hands and fought back her nausea.

She cursed herself for not being more forceful, for not doing more to convince John to sit out the game, and for not going to management or the coaches with her concerns. Maybe she could have prevented this.

She never could have dreamed it would come to this.

As the hours passed, Jen sat brokenly in the waiting room, watching as John's friends arrived. William had already sent a private helicopter to go get his parents and they were all waiting for them to arrive. John's teammates all came to wait, their faces etched with worry and fear.

William sat silently by her side, even more quiet than usual. Lexie fluttered about, bringing everyone drinks and snacks, trying to be optimistic, and generally harassing the staff for updates.

"Here. Drink this, you need to keep your strength up." Lexie handed Jen another coffee.

Before Jen could even wrap her second hand around the warm cup, Ryan walked up and plucked it from her fingers.

"She doesn't need coffee, Alexis. She needs caffeine like she needs a hole in the head. She needs to rest. *You* are not being restful." He then thrust a pillow, still in the plastic wrap from the store, into Jen's lap. "This pillow is restful. Leave her be and let her sleep for a bit." Ryan commanded through gritted teeth, still in his post-game clothes, and his blonde hair matted with dried sweat from the game.

Lexie grew eight inches with how big her next breath was, no doubt preparing to ream him a new one, when Mickey and Benji swooped over, linked elbows, and forcibly escorted her away.

Ryan placed the full coffee next to the four others on the nearby table and gave her a somber attempt at a smile. As he walked away, his presence was replaced with that of her girls.

"She means well," Megan whispered softly, taking Jen's hand in her own and patting it gently. She slid into the seat on the opposite side of William. "She doesn't deal well with hospitals and doctors."

Rose grimaced and leaned down quickly for a peck on Jen's cheek, and then went to sit with her husband a couple of seats down.

Chloe knelt before Jen, her big brown eyes wide and worried. "Can we do anything? Anything at all?"

Jen swallowed back the tears and looked down at her feet. She pushed back the lump in her throat and looked back up. "No," she croaked out.

Chloe winced and nodded solemnly. She stood and went to sit over by Rose, Brandon, and Kenny.

It wasn't the end of her visitations though, because shortly after, Victor arrived and placed ten huge paper bags filled with food on the center table of the waiting room.

"Food. Eat." He then looked at Jen and limped over with a bag still in his hand. "Wrap for you. Eat it. Don't make me tell you twice. I know you. Bet you haven't eaten shit. Eat it. And in the bag is a vanilla shake for John when he wakes up. I know how much he likes them." His blank expression had the briefest moment of grief before he caught it and cleared the look from his face.

But it was enough.

As soon as he walked out of the waiting room, Jen couldn't hold on anymore. She finally gave in to the terror that John might not ever wake up to enjoy that milkshake and sobbed into William's waiting arms.

CHAPTER FORTY-FIVE

November 7, Sunday
Jen

Finally, after what seemed like an eternity, the surgeon emerged from the operating room. Jen stood up and rushed to him, her heart pounding in her chest.

"How is he?" she asked, her voice shaking. She felt William and several others approach as well.

The surgeon looked at them, a grave expression etched on his face. "He's in a coma," he said. "With a severe brain injury. We won't know how much damage there is until he wakes up."

Jen felt a surge of emotion wash over her and her knees gave out. Only Ryan's fast reflexes kept her standing.

She had been prepared for bad news, but this was worse than she imagined.

"It'll be okay. He's alive. He's a fighter." Everyone around her kept echoing those words. Like they were trying to manifest it into reality.

"He's a survivor. He's tough. He'll beat this." More empty reassurances from her friends, no—her *family*.

But God! They needed to stop talking!

The elevator gave a cheery ding that felt so at odds to the atmosphere in the room. Jen, on autopilot, looked over to it, trying to get a grip on her emotions and block out the fear.

A frantic older couple burst through the still-opening doors, both looking disheveled and worried.

"My son. John Costner. Where is my son?" The woman's voice was high and scratchy, like she had spent the last sixty years smoking.

Or maybe an entire helicopter ride crying.

John's father was looking around, looking for anyone to come forward with an update.

Was she supposed to do it? She felt her stomach drop, which made her want to drop into insane giggles because the didn't think it was possible to feel even worse than she already did.

Jen smothered the desire to laugh, which really would have devolved into insane crying, so that was probably for the best.

Okay, shock was definitely settling in if she was feeling that unpredictable with her emotions.

Fuck, just the thought that she might have missed a recurring issue with John.... She stifled that train of thought immediately too. Self-blame would get her no where right now.

Jen walked a couple steps and grabbed a cold coffee from the table.

A doctor approached John's parents and saved her from being the one having to share the depressing news. John's mother gave a pained moan and leaned into her husband, while her husband's face took on a tortured look that Jen could feel down to her soul.

William approached them after the doctor left and shared some quiet words, he then brought them over to Jen.

Jen froze with her coffee halfway to her mouth at William's introduction.

"Mary. Bobby. This is Jen."

Why was William introducing them to her? Did he know about them?

An icy tingle shot down to her toes.

She shot him a wary look but quickly focused on John's parents.

"Hi, I've heard a lot about you. It's nice to finally meet you. Despite the circumstances." Jen swallowed hard and tried to keep a lid on the burning sensation crawling up her throat.

Mary looked at her through red rimmed eyes before pulling her in for a tight hug. "Same to you, honey. Same to you. You're even lovelier in person."

John talked about her? Jen's frozen heart gave a single thump in her chest.

"All right, Mary, that's enough. Give her a second to breathe." John's father gently pulled at his wife; his gruff words lost all bite to them with the tender way he turned her and the look on his face as he placed a soft kiss on his wife's trembling lips. He then turned his attention to Jen.

"So, you're the masseuse."

"Massage therapist." Mary corrected absently while dabbing at her eyes with a handkerchief.

Something about the man's small smile hinted that he did that on purpose to give his wife something to correct him about. Jen felt her heart warm towards the man John didn't usually wax poetic about.

"How do you feel about a hug? It'd be nice to have a hug from the woman who has my son's heart. It will almost feel like a piece of him is holding me back."

Jen couldn't stop the burn in her sinuses from making its way to her eyes. Tears spilled over and down her cheeks, coming fast. She was surprised she had any tears left. "A hug would be perfect," she whispered brokenly to the man who looked so much like his son.

For the millionth time, Jen found herself enclosed in the arms of a loving father figure who let her cry it out. Mary stepped close and joined in the hug.

"We're so glad he has you in his life. He finally seems settled. At peace."

Jen cried harder into Bobby's shoulder. "I never told him I loved him," she sobbed out.

They both stilled around her before Bobby said in a gruff voice, "My son is no dummy. He knows."

Over the next few days, Jen spent all her time at the hospital by John's side. She watched as the medical team worked to keep him stable and she made sure he was getting the best possible care.

She saw the effect John's injury had on his family and friends, how they were all struggling to come to terms with the possibility of losing him. She saw the toll it was taking on his teammates, how they were all trying to keep it together while the backbone of their team lay in a coma. His mother was an absolute mess—as any mother would be—and his father wasn't doing much better. Both were in and out of the hospital as they tried to wait with him, but teammates and other members of the Spartans organization rallied. Long-time friends, coaches, and teammates, all invited John's parents to family dinners, coffee catch ups, and more. Anything to keep their minds busy and their eyes off their son and the clock.

Jen's own friends tried to get her out, to go home, to think of something else. But she couldn't. She couldn't eat. She couldn't sleep. If she closed her eyes, she saw his still body as they carried him off the field. Jen needed to be with him. She needed to feel his warm skin to keep her thoughts grounded in the knowledge that he was alive.

She had never needed anything more.

CHAPTER FORTY-SIX

November 10, Wednesday
John

"Ultimately, Ryan did well. The offensive line, especially the running backs, really came through, and everything ended on a happy note. So, stop worrying about the results of the fucking game and just take a minute. Yeah?" Lenny chided him. "And no more asking for game film, it makes the nurses nervous."

John had been awake for only a couple of hours at this point and was already going stir-crazy. His body felt weak and itchy like he needed to *move*.

His head, on the other hand, felt like it didn't want him to move. At all. Ever.

As soon as he woke up, the nurses and doctors briefed him on his status. It was fairly confusing. Some sort of traumatic brain injury. He might have some memory loss. There might be other complications. Blah blah blah. Unknown, unknown, unknown.

Fortunately, he felt all right.

He could move his fingers and his toes.

He even remembered the play and the hit.

The thing he wished he *could* forget was Jen's face when he left her in the conference room after she shared her heartfelt and well-intentioned concern for his health.

Maybe her dad got at least some of his bet back? The Spartans didn't lose, but John certainly didn't play the whole game. Maybe it wasn't a total loss for him. Still, it didn't sit right that Jen helped her father make that bet. It didn't feel...right. It didn't seem like *her*, the woman he had grown to love.

And if she did make that bet...was that really a dealbreaker? If he genuinely loved her, wouldn't he take her, even with the shitty father? That wasn't her fault. Having too big of a heart was rarely a bad thing. Maybe over time, he could work with her to—

"I already spoke with William and Dottie and got the all-clear to come back on a limited basis so that will be great to see the guys again. I've missed my boys. William was all excited about it too. Something about misunderstanding Lexie when she told him Jen was unhappy. Guess the bleeding heart thought she was working herself ragged trying to make a go of her business but didn't know how to bow out without defaulting on the loan he gave her. Turns out he thought he was doing her a favor, and she thought she was doing him one." Lenny chuckled absently as he continued to look at the magazine in front of him. He continued prattling on his stream of consciousness, clearly trying to keep John entertained and not focused on the monumental life changes that were coming his way.

"I'm thinking about offering her a permanent job though. We could use her—

"No." John interrupted before Lenny could say anything more. "She loves her career. No more in house massage therapy work for her. She misses her true work, and it wouldn't be fair to her. She doesn't know how to say no. For a woman who thinks she always has to look out for herself, she does a poor job of it sometimes," John finished on a disgruntled mutter.

Lenny looked up from his magazine and gave him a droll look. "If you would let me finish... I'm thinking about offering her a permanent job within the Spartans as our in house Pre-Hab Specialist."

Oh.

John's silence had Lenny smiling victoriously. "That's what I thought."

Just then, John's dad poked his head into the room.

"Good. You have someone else here to babysit you now. I'm going to head out, tell the nurses to ban all visitors so you can rest, and I'll swing by in the morning."

Had Jen come to see him at all?

"Lenny..."

Lenny turned around at his name, his face openly waiting to answer John's question.

John waved him away. "Never mind."

Lenny frowned but gave a slow nod after a moment. "Your memory lapses will improve with time, John. There's hope for a full recovery."

John didn't have it in him to debate the point. His brain might make a full recovery, but his heart felt irreparable.

· • • • • • • • • · ·

"How you doing there, son?" Bobby walked to the chair Lenny just vacated but didn't sit. Instead he hovered next to it, putting his hands on the chair's back before pulling them off and then putting them in his pockets, just to pull them out and rest them on the chair again.

When was the last time John had seen his dad look this uncomfortable? He'd seen him briefly a few hours ago when he woke up, but he fell back asleep shortly after waking up. When he woke up again, both his parents were gone, and Lenny was there.

"I'm fine. Already sick of being in bed."

His dad nodded and then looked out the window, his lips firmly pressed together.

"I didn't ask earlier, how was the drive up?"

Bobby jerked and looked back at John in the bed. "We, uh, we flew."

John blinked.

His dad didn't *fly*.

Ever.

John had been playing in Massachusetts for almost two decades and not once had his father flown to see him. They always drove.

"It was...quicker." Bobby gave a small shrug, and he quickly transformed his haunted face into one of neutrality.

"Oh." John felt the hair on his arms raise at the memory. The barely audible heart rate monitor beeps increased in tempo. "That makes sense."

"John—"

"Dad—"

They both stopped and gave each other matching weak smiles. John waited for his dad to go first.

"Johnny, I never meant to...I never meant to imply..." His dad took a deep breath. "I'm proud of you. So damn proud. I...I'm sorry you felt like I wasn't. That I made you feel like I wasn't. You're the best thing I've ever done. And those things you've accomplished...they're nothing short of extraordinary. I...again, I'm sorry I've never told you. I didn't think I needed to." He finished on a whisper.

John's body had gotten still as his father spoke and when his dad's voice broke on that weak whisper, John's whole body was tighter than a bowstring.

"Dad—"

His father waved him away. "I should have told you. A near-death injury shouldn't have been the catalyst for this conversation." Bobby swallowed hard. "I love you. More than breathing, I love you. And whether you have fifteen Super Bowl rings or zero. No matter whether you were never drafted or had your number go down in NFL history, you're still my son. My everything. You don't have to prove anything to me or anyone. You are *always* more than enough."

Tears pooled in his father's eyes as he stared down at him, his expression broken and devastated.

John swallowed hard and blinked rapidly, trying to dispel his own tears that were building. The burning in his sinuses was a welcome distraction from the budding headache. John used his knuckles to rub quickly at one of his eyes and coughed once. Twice. He then looked at his dad and said gruffly, "I'm thirty-eight."

"I know."

"I shouldn't care this much."

His dad shrugged.

"Thank you." John rolled his lips together and looked away briefly before back to his dad.

"I love you too."

John's father, a vision of what John would look like in twenty-two years, raised his hands to his face and rubbed, also trying to prevent the tears from falling. He then rounded the chair and finally settled in by placing his elbows on his knees, and leaning towards John.

After a moment of silence between the two men, Bobby then chuckled into the silence.

John didn't have to wonder what caused it for long.

"So, your Jen's a firecracker, huh? I think your mother has already started planning your wedding."

John felt relief wash through his body.

Jen had been here.

Chapter Forty-Seven
November 10, Wednesday
John

A little while later, John wheeled down the hall, avoiding the area where the nurses seemed to congregate. He wasn't supposed to be using the wheelchair at the current moment but the five minutes they allowed him earlier was not enough. He felt restless. He could hear his heartbeat echoing in the sterile room, the beeping of machines, and the distant chatter of nurses and doctors filling the silence. It drove him nuts.

At Jen's lilting voice, he paused and slowly rolled himself to the corner of the hallway. He looked around the corner and saw Jen standing toe to toe with her father, her face red and devastated.

Hell, she must have lost ten pounds. His heart squeezed.

John strained his ears, trying to hear. He could feel the tension in the air, the anger and desperation emanating from Jen's father.

He was getting ready to go to them when her father spoke in a raspy desperate voice.

"You have to help me, Jen," her father said, his voice trembling. "I'm in deep this time. With a debt this big...they'll kill me if I don't pay up. I can never pay that back on my own. I'll be a poster child for them. The cautionary tale they use to remind their other betters. Don't let me die, Jenny."

"Is this really the place for this, Dad?" Jen said, her voice firm. "In the hospital, one hundred feet from where my man recovers in a hospital bed?"

Apparently, she hadn't heard he was awake yet.

"Jen, you don't understand."

"Oh, I think I understand."

John could hear the anger in Jen's voice, the frustration and hurt. He squeezed the wheels of the chair tight. There was a moment of silence, and John could almost hear the gears turning in Jen's father's head.

"You're my daughter," her father pleaded. "I know you have connections. You can get the money if you want to from William or Lexie. Hell, even your boyfriend. Just ask them for a small favor. That amount is nothing to them. It was your bad advice that led to this."

From the way Jen cocked her jaw out and her face tightened, her father just made the wrong move.

"One, you read my personal notes after breaking into my boyfriend's home. Are you sure you want to bring that up again? And two, it's not their responsibility, and it's not mine either. It's yours. It's always been yours." Her voice broke. "Dad, this is never going to stop. You're never going to quit. If I go to them once, I'll go to them twice. There will never be an end."

"There *will* be. I'll quit. I'll get help. I'll do whatever you want. Just tell me what you want."

Jen shook her head. "If I had a dollar—"

"I mean it this time. I'm so sorry, Jen," he said. "I know I messed up. I don't know what to do. I don't want to die, but I don't see a way out of this." It looked like he hadn't slept or showered in days.

Probably hadn't if he was avoiding his collectors.

"I don't want them to come after you or John. They know how much you mean to me. I'd hate to see you dragged into this. I could never forgive myself."

John was about two seconds from rolling out there and socking the guy in the face. Jen's face mirrored the fury roiling in John's gut.

"Bullshit," Jen bit out.

"What?"

"Bull-fucking-shit. You don't give a rat's ass about me. If you did, you would have made more of an effort years ago. Hell, after they fucking broke my arm when I was a *kid*, you would have made damn sure you kept your nose clean. But no, you kept dragging me right back into those circles for you."

"Jenny, I had no idea they were going to go to your place that night."

John felt the hair on his arms raise, something about this felt...familiar.

A heartbeat of silence and then...

"*What*?" Jen's shriek echoed down the halls. "That was because of *you*? You're the reason I lost everything?" Her shrill note had a couple of visitors stop and look over toward her. She didn't notice. "*You're* the reason I lost my home and almost everything in it? You?" She spit the words out and her arms flailed as she came to grips with this latest information. "Are you fucking kidding me?"

Her anger felt palpable but so did her sadness. She may have been yelling but tears streamed down her face.

Jesus Christ. John felt his chest get heavy and he sank in his chair. He could literally feel her hurt and sense of betrayal in his own chest. God. His woman couldn't catch a damn break.

"They took *everything*. Grandma's rings. My savings. Abuelo's watch. Everything, Dad." Her voice broke.

"Jenny." A vein throbbed in his neck and forehead as he continued to plead with her. A fevered look came over his face as he started to sweat, his voice starting to shake.

"You need to leave. Gone. Out of my life. I don't want to see you again. Maybe in ten years, when I've calmed down. But maybe, by then, John will have forgiven me. If by some miracle, I haven't lost him and if we have kids, there's no way in hell he's letting your shit into their lives. There's no way *I'm* letting that into their lives. So, move on, Dad." Jen turned and grabbed her purse from the floor. She rifled through it frantically, pulling out her wallet. She grabbed a handful of bills and quickly counted them. "Here's a hundred dollars. Take it and get out of the city. Find a new place to call home. Stay away from the casinos and bars and try not to draw attention to yourself. But do everyone a favor and leave."

"Jenny."

"I've bailed you out too many times already. That's on me. But right now, you have your own lesson to learn. You need to take responsibility for your actions. Pay your debts. Take the money. This isn't a debt to me. It's a gift. Take the money and the advice and fucking leave."

John's heart swelled with pride at Jen's words, at her understanding, at her compassion even with her heart clearly breaking. He knew that she was a strong woman but seeing her stand up to her father like that made him love her even more.

Her father opened his mouth to speak but Jen pushed the money into his chest. "Leave," she hissed. "And please forget I exist so I don't become another failed attempt at coercion. Do you know the most fatherly thing you could do for me?"

"What?" he said quietly.

"Forget I ever existed."

With that heartbreaking plea, Jen turned and raced down the hall.

CHAPTER FORTY-EIGHT

November 10, Wednesday
John

An hour later, Jen threw open John's hospital room door and rushed in, her face flushed and her eyes wide.

He looked up and stared at her, his heart thumping in his chest.

Oh God, what now?

"You're awake," she breathed out, drinking him in. "You're awake."

After seeing it with her own eyes, her body finally decided it needed a break. She collapsed on the floor right there where she stood, head on her knees, sobbing uncontrollably.

John had overdone it earlier in the wheelchair and didn't have the strength to go to her and he'd never felt more helpless as her sobs shook her entire body.

"Jen. Jen." He continued calling her name, trying to shift in bed to get closer to her but his muscles weren't working right, and his head was starting to pound a little harder. "Jen." Still nothing. "Jen, honey, I'm okay. I'm okay and I love you too," he repeated softly.

Slowly her tears quieted and she looked up.

Silently, he opened his arms.

In an instant, she was in them, cuddling close and sobbing out incoherent babbles. He caught a wet "I love you" in between her crying bouts and it just made him hold her tighter.

"Shh, shh, shh. It's okay. I got you."

And it was okay. Or...it would be. He'd make it so. No matter what, because he was a champion, and that's what champions did.

CHAPTER FORTY-NINE

Epilogue: April 2, Saturday
John

John's decision to retire wasn't easy, but it was the right one. He had many talks with the coaches, management, William, Lenny, and Jen about his options. Eventually, he sat down with Ryan and briefed him about the importance of taking care of himself and his health while still giving his all to the team.

Ryan had potential, but he was still young.

It only made sense to coach him and make him one of the greats.

So, even if John didn't get another ring as a player, eventually he knew he'd get one as a coach. With Ryan growing under his tutelage, how could he not?

Then again, that wasn't necessarily the ring he wanted more than anything anymore.

Plus, if John stayed on as a coach, he could keep an eye on Butch. Something about how everything played out felt strange to him. Coincidences were one thing. But after a handful in a row, it started to defy the odds of being pure happenstances. However, his doctors had said that some of his medications could induce paranoia. So maybe it was nothing. Or maybe, two plus two wasn't adding up to four.

Regardless, as soon as John left the hospital, he focused on getting healthy and mending his relationship with Jen. The rehab time taught him one main thing: Jen and his mother together in the same room meant anarchy. True insanity. Yet...it was also heaven. The women controlled his world and gloried in every second of it.

In fact, Jen had been asking for another visit with his mom, so as spring approached, John decided to take Jen to his parents' ranch. He wanted her to see where he grew up and the life he lived before he became a professional football player.

The nerves that filled him when she saw it for the first time made him feel like a rookie all over again.

On the first day of their visit, John took Jen on a horseback ride through the fields and hills surrounding the ranch. Naturally, Jen was nervous at first, but the old pony under her was unfazed. John's own mount was bulletproof and neither horse was going to be misbehaving on their trail ride. After thirty minutes of John's calm and steady presence and the slow, steady gate of their geldings, Jen started to finally relax and enjoy the experience.

As they rode, John talked about his childhood and shared stories about his family and friends. Jen listened intently, realizing how much she missed out on by not knowing him sooner.

He pointed out his favorite views, where he had his first kiss, where he broke someone's nose for the first time, and where his horse bucked him off and he had to walk home with a broken collarbone.

Through it all, with each passing heartbeat, Jen sank a little deeper into the saddle. His little pieces of privacy offered up to her on a silver platter, and she greedily soaked up every little morsel.

The scent of home and fresh air filled John's nostrils, and the sound of the horses' hooves hitting the dirt path echoed in his ears. The sun shone brightly, casting a warm glow on everything around him, and the breeze gently brushed against his skin.

As they rode, John felt a sense of peace wash over him. His body was mending, and though not completely healed, it was getting there. He finally found someone who loved him, not just the star quarterback. Jen's laughter filled the air at his stories, and every now and then, if the country wind blew exactly right, he could catch her warm coconut and lime smell.

As they rounded a bend in the path, John spotted the familiar clearing up ahead. He led Jen towards it, and they dismounted their horses. John took Jen's hand and walked with her toward a nearby tree where they sat down in the grass beneath it.

"What do you think about getting a couple of horses?" John asked, taking a deep breath. "We could also take a look at some houses that have barns as well."

Jen gave him a silly look. "If you think for one minute I'm going to clean a barn and expose myself daily to barn rats, you don't know me at all."

John rolled his eyes and tugged her in for a quick kiss. "I already have the numbers of some staff who could manage the mucking of stalls and daily chores. But if we had a place with horses, when we got home from work we could just…ride." He couldn't hide the wistful tone in his voice.

"You're not hurting being in the saddle at all?" Concern laced her tone.

He shook his head. "Julie's therapy sessions at the barn have done their job. My hands on the reins even feel somewhat steady today."

Jen's eyes dropped to his hands, and she immediately scooped them up and started massaging. She peeked up at him, her eyes glowing. "Are you asking me about looking at a house together?"

"I know you didn't want to date a player…but how do you feel about being married to a coach?"

Being the new pre-hab specialist for the Spartans was a full-time gig, there was no escaping him now. Hopefully, her recent heart-to-heart with William led her to a sense of peace about intercompany dating. The man wanted her to be happy; he didn't care how many HR violations were made to get there. A father's love was endless. But, if Jen didn't get that message, he guessed he could coach at the college level if he really needed to.

Tears filled Jen's eyes as she looked at him, and she reached out to take his hand. "Well, that's a whole different kettle of fish," she said, her voice raspy and filled with emotion.

John couldn't stop his laugh.

John pulled her into a tight embrace, burying his face in her hair. He couldn't imagine his life without her now. She brought such happiness and contentment to his very soul.

Jen stilled and looked up into his face, squinting in the bright sun.

"Are you happy? Truly? Are you honestly okay with coaching, not playing?" Her voice was small, and he pulled her in for a tight hug. They'd discussed this a million times, but here in the clearing, he wanted to give her a little more. A final piece.

"Of course I'm happy. My job was my job, and now my job has changed, evolved. It's a change, but to be honest, I ache a lot less now." He tried to give her a teasing grin but she wasn't letting go.

"But...how? How can you really be this okay with retirement when you *so* weren't okay with it just a couple of months ago?"

"Easy. I got you." As easy as could be, he slid a shiny diamond ring on her finger and pulled it to his lips for a kiss. "Don't panic. I won't ask you to pay me back for it. It's a gift...for me."

Jen swatted at him before leaning up and starting a bout of long, leisurely kisses in the quiet clearing. After they finished their fling in the grass and made their way back to their mounts, Jen kept holding her hand up to inspect the ring in the bright sun.

He got his girl.

Unable to keep it in any longer, John leaned down and whispered in her ear. "I have a secret for you, my little thief. You stole my heart, you stole my ring, I hope you'll steal my name. But one thing you never stole...was that chair."

At Jen's sputtering outrage and following rant, John couldn't stop his smile as he looked up into the blue, clear sky.

Bliss.

• • • ● • ● • ● • • •

A sexy professional football player. A single mom's quest for her son's biological father. As hidden truths unravel, will she risk not only her custody but also her blossoming romance?

Click now to read the next book in the series – https://mybook.to/SSuc- **Unsportsmanlike Conduct** – A Steamy, Single-Mom, Who's-Your-Daddy, Sports Romance

About Author - Ella Haines

Ella Haines is a lover of all things love. Raised to know that she could be anything in the world, she made the wild and crazy decision to become a neurotic accountant. Balancing trial balances and filing taxes didn't quite fill her bucket, so she started dabbling in short stories. Those short stories evolved into complex storylines with empowered women, their families and friends, and the hunky men who adore them.

Request For Review

If this book brought you a smile, please review it on your purchasing platform (and copy it to Goodreads if you're willing and able).

This helps to spread the word about the book. Social proof to other readers is important.

It also makes the next book come out faster ;-)

Discover More From Ella Haines

Springfield Spartans Standalone Romances:
Crystal Clear: A Steamy Springfield Stripper *Novella*
Offensive Holding: A Forbidden Friends-To-Lovers Stripper Romance *Novella*
Illegal Substitutions: A Friends-To-Lovers Steamy Sports Romance
Illegal Contact: A Steamy Sports Workplace Romance
Unsportsmanlike Conduct: A Steamy Single Mother Sports Romance
Intentional Grounding: A Steamy Opposites Attract Romance
False Start: A Steamy Second Chance Romance
Springfield Cyclones Standalone Hockey Romances:
Boarding: A Steamy Hockey Romance *Novelette*
Hooking: A Steamy Bachelor Auction Hockey Romance

Praise For Ella Haines

"It kept me hooked with the angst and sweet moments" - Nicole, book review

"All the feels from the frustration, anger, pain and hurt that came flowing out from the never ending angsty-ness truly hit hard many times throughout. Putting you through the ultimate wringer in what was a super emotionally charged ride." – Maddie, book blogger

"Is it friends to lovers? Women's lit? Humorous romance? A sports romance? In the end, it's a little bit of everything." – Cat, book review

"This is a well written emotional roller coaster, which is a friends / lover's sports romance, with angst, friendships, secrets, truths, drama, twists and turns, revelations, and love, which leads to an entertaining and compelling page turner. I look forward to reading more from this talented author whose work I highly recommend." - Wendy, book review

"I would definitely pick up another book or two by this author." – Reading In the Red Room, book blogger

Content/Trigger Warnings (may contain plot spoilers)

Warning:

This book will contain explicit language, threats of violence, and sexy times (which are sometimes *somewhat* public). It also has a gambling addict family member and a character experiencing serious medical brain injuries. If these are triggering for you – here is your warning to maybe avoid this book. Regardless, I promise there will be an HEA.

This book was a work of my imagination, but I did consult with professionals when writing. Any mistakes are my own and a big thank you to the massage therapists, medical professionals, editors, proofreaders, and others that helped me craft this story.

Social Media Information - Ella Haines

Did you enjoy this book?

If so, please visit **www.EllaHaines.com** and sign up for the newsletter to receive additional scenes, freebies, and updates on future releases.

Newsletter signup here:
http://ellahaines.com/newsletter-for-freebies/

Also, if you have an eagle eye and caught any typos that slipped through the rounds and rounds of edits, take a moment and think if you'd like to be an ARC or beta reader for any future releases! If so, drop me an email! I'd love to have you on the team.

If you find any typos, you can let me know here: EllaHaines.author@gmail.com